Blended

A REDEMPTION NOVEL

SASHA BRÜMMER

Blended
Copyright © 2016 Sasha-Lee Brümmer
Published by Sasha-Lee Brümmer
ISBN: 978-0-9863049-8-9

Editor: Lisa Aurello

Cover Designer:
Sommer Stein, Perfect Pear Creative

Interior Design & Formatting:
Christine Borgford, Perfectly Publishable

The following story contains mature themes, strong language, and sexual situations. It is intended for adult readers.

I dedicate this novel to all of those who suffer from an invisible illness. There is nothing worse than having to prove how sick you are to wondering eyes.

Remember, you are tough, you are courageous, and you will not go unnoticed. Have faith in yourself and surround yourself with those who love you, and don't let the illness define you. You are beautiful.

Acknowledgments

WRITING THIS STORY has been an adventure for me, and I've enjoyed every minute of it. It's one that I thought I would never be brave enough to do alone, but here it is. Thank you to everyone who supported me and helped me make decisions while writing this novel.

I'd like to thank my parents, Andrew and Vanessa, for constantly providing me with support in all that I do. You both have no idea how much it means to me knowing that you each support my dreams and goals. We've been through a lot as a family, but we wouldn't be where we are now without experiencing all of those negatives. I love you, Mom and Dad.

A special thank you to my brother, Tynan, who has become my best friend over the last twenty-one years. There are not many people that I can truly let my hair down with, and you are one of the few on that list. Thank you for always fighting for me, whether it be just for fun or more. I love you, bud.

To my best friend and co-author of The Date Series, Jess Epps, thank you for always being a supporting shoulder for me. Whether it be writing-related or personal, I greatly appreciate it.

Thank you to Courtney Stephens, your friendship and support in my personal life has been something that I didn't know that I needed. I love you to the moon and back.

A very special thank-you goes to Linda Russell, Melissa Saneholtz, and Sharon Renee Goodman for your belief in my words between these pages, and your unwavering support.

I want to thank each and every one of the following ladies for help in this journey: Jess Epps, Ashley Scales, Dani Naas,

Desirae Shie, Jillian Crouson-Toth, Amy Briggs, Holly Main, Erica McKinley, Linda Russell and Sophie Broughton. Thank you all so, so much for helping me when I needed it the most. This novel would not be finished if it weren't for each and every one of you. I adore our friendships as well as you.

The biggest thank-you to my editor, Lisa Aurello. I have learned so much from you since working on my debut novel. Thank you for always supporting me and my dreams even when I still have much to learn.

Lindsay Michelle Minnehan, I fell in love with the name that you gave your son. Thank you for being a doll and sharing Waylon with the world. Tonya Nagle, thank you for raising such a kind-hearted woman. You should be tremendously proud of Lindsay.

A very special thank-you goes to Pete Ladino for supplying me with the liquid courage that I needed to write *The End*.

Playlist

Alive—Sia

Bloom—The Paper Kites

Brooklyn Baby—Lana Del Rey

Closer—Nick Jonas ft. Tove Lo

Faded—Alan Walker

Fantasy—Alina Baraz and Galimatias

Final Warning—Skylar Grey

Fucked My Way Up to The Top—Lana Del Rey

I Found—Amber Run

I'll Show You—Justin Bieber

Island—The xx

Is There Somewhere—Halsey

Midnight River—Vaults

Never Be Like You—Flume ft. Kai

Never Forget You—Zara Larsson & MNEK

Pillowtalk—Zayn

Shells—Laurel

Two Weeks—FKA twigs

Wild Things—Alessia Cara

One

Hadley

LOVE IS SUPPOSED to be some overpowering sentiment that breaks down walls and intoxicates each part of the body. It's said to be an invisible and weightless compression on the heart, an organ whose sole obligation is to keep the blood surging through my veins, not to cry out for devotion and the presence of another. From what I've heard and read, love is supposed to somehow enlighten those who have been in the dark, providing them with strength when they are weak and mending their previously bruised and bound hearts.

It's all bullshit.

Love has denied me.

Love has neglected me.

I detest the notion of love and all of the sticky residual emotions that go along with it. There are more things in life than a heavy heart and an overbearing ache—there's fucking.

Fuck 'em and chuck 'em is what my mother drilled into my head for ten years before she passed away from a damaged heart. A selfish, fragmented heart, that is, since she decided that living without my father for those excruciatingly painful ten years was intolerable. She took her own life while I watched her bleed out in a filthy clawfoot bathtub, draining the life out of her body, one vein at a time, so she could finally be free of her longing for him.

Has my upbringing been unconventional and unreservedly

immoral? Yes, but it brought me to life in a way that I don't think would have been possible through any other channel.

Being forced into the foster care system the day after my mother's blood turned the bathwater I was seated in a dark crimson was foolish and unthinkable. It was unforgivable. *It wrecked me.* It has been eight years since I've been in the system.

I lived in the Colorado foster care system for eight years before I was able to free myself from the abusive assholes who stole every ounce of my virginity, innocence, and virtue before they wore it on their bloody latex-covered dicks.

I can still feel the pain ripping through my core as if it was the first time I was taken advantage of, which was a mere two weeks after being in my first foster home. The only way to numb that memory is to avoid letting those emotions weigh down heavily on my heart and let my libido do the aching instead. I hide in sex, lust, and any man who will make time for me. I keep my past to myself because, in reality, nobody actually gives a fuck.

Sex is supposed to be this overstimulation of intense swelling passion, an extension of that dirty L word—love. Sex to me has just been, well, sex—waves of corrupt orgasms and glistening cocks. Shove it in, pull it out, and repeat the process in hopes of some relief-filled orgasm that won't ever satisfy me long enough. I've been worn as a trophy on more men's dicks than I can count at this point in time, and I look forward to the next time someone new pushes into me. But each time a new dick presents itself to my pussy, the burning ache from sixteen years ago scorches my core, forcing me to feel what I wish I could erase. What stole my life entirely.

My coping mechanism has turned me into someone I watch from the outside, a desolate and repulsive skank who gets all of the sex that she wants. Each and every sexual act is unique, and I compare it to traveling in order to escape my reality. However, instead of island hopping, I've gone from man to man, and if I'm being completely honest, there have been a few women thrown in the mix as well, but everyone experiments at some point in their lives.

The familiarity of sex steadies me and provides me with the best affairs that an orgasm can buy. Pleasure has been the mindful and receptive reprieve that I've grown to accept through my years.

Sure, I've looked for what some seem to see in romantic relationships, where there seems to be a magnetic force holding two people together. Frankly, that thought makes me want to gag. Fortunately, though, all of the gagging that I've been doing is on a salivary cock.

There have been plenty of late nights that turn into early mornings, when I stare up at the ceiling from a bed that does not belong to me, watching a fan rotate in an attempt to comprehend what my life has turned into. Regardless of which way I look at life or how I twist certain events in my head, the outcome seems to remain the same: an easy skank who only has the physical connection to sex that makes me want to live.

As I turn my head to the side on a white overstuffed pillow, a programmed leer meets me, eradicating my thoughts for the moment as it fills Lawson's face. "You're still trying to figure out how this happened so fast, aren't you?"

I simply nod my head because saying the words makes it seem surreal. It makes it absurd. *What the fuck was I thinking?*

"Come here," he says as he pulls me to his side. His body frames mine effortlessly as he lifts my left hand to his lips, smirking to himself when he sees the engagement ring that he placed on my finger last night. It's barely a karat, but it is beautiful and it should not make me feel this worthless. It does, though, when I consider how loaded the asshole is. The only reason I said yes to him was because I was looking for consistency in my life, something more stable than the springs that hold up my mattress.

I swear it seems like it was weeks ago that I made the senseless decision to marry him.

I angle my head back up to the ceiling and blink in an attempt to quash the images of Lawson and Tegan Corely running through my head. Hours, *yes*, hours after I said yes to him, I found his head stuck between his housekeeper's thighs as he ravaged her until she came uncontrollably all over his face. As sickening as it was, it held a fiery passion that has ceased to exist in our *relationship*—a passion that I don't have a sliver of in my overused body. I decided not to make my presence known at the time because I was still completely thrown off of the tracks with his proposal. To say that what I witnessed was randy and heady would be a complete understatement, and that's why I'm still here—regrettably sober—in his bed, replaying the scene continuously in my head. How can I be annoyed at him or anyone else for showing that much hunger toward another woman? The answer is simple: I can't.

He's never even taken the time to go down on me—not once, not even an attempt, which irks the fuck out of me. Maybe the thought of his collagen-enhanced lips touching such an overworked part of a woman's body disgusts him—particularly my body since he knows just how much sex I partake in. How can he want to link himself to me legally when he just lies on top of me and pounds away until he loses himself in a stupor within my vaginal walls? If he's looking for that gold trophy to wear on his arm, he's found the wrong woman.

I manage to put some distance between us as I roll out of his arms and prop myself up on one elbow to look down at him. He seems to be content, just as I'm sure his dick is right now. I did not stay to watch the rest of the show earlier since it made me hornier than he had ever gotten me before. I decide to take my chances and see what he has to say in regard to his earlier fuck session, but before I'm able to, he reaches up and runs his tongue over my bottom lip before kissing me forcefully.

I place my hand on his chest and slightly push against his pecs to stop his advances. "I can still taste Tegan's orgasm on your lips, Lawson."

He pauses and stops breathing entirely before he drops his hand from the side of my face. "You know?"

"Mmm-hmm. Why do you look so . . . shocked?" I ask, honestly wondering why since I know that he sleeps around on me on a daily basis.

He moves to lie back on the bed while he runs his hand through his unruly chestnut hair. "You don't seem to be pissed about it in the slightest."

"I'm not, considering how intense it got between the two of you."

The corner of his lips perk up. "Which means, what? You wouldn't mind if she joined us? I can share my cock if you can share that pretty pink pussy of yours. I'm sure Tegan will enjoy a taste or two if you'll allow it. She's actually asked me a few times if you would let her go down on you."

I purse my lips while I think of what to say to him. This is nothing new. I mean, I've known him for the two years that I've been here, but I've only been sexually active with him for the last two weeks. In those two weeks alone I have seen him go down on and fuck more of his staff than he cares to know.

"I think I'll pass," I say vehemently. I'm not infuriated or even the slightest bit distraught, but I'd rather find a superior dick elsewhere. As I sit up, the white sheet falls from my bare breasts, and I slip the cheap-ass ring off of my left ring finger before sliding down his body to his hardened cock. He hisses through his teeth as I take him into my mouth and pop him back out. He tosses the sheet off of the bed to get a better view of me while I lock my eyes with his. Intentionally slowly, I place the ring on the top of his head, crowning him with my goodbye.

"I'll see you around, Mr. Stafford."

He jerks upright as if I've just bitten his cock. "Get the fuck out of here. I want you out of my casino within a week, you foul whore."

I shrug, outwardly unaffected by his harsh words as I pull on my white shift dress sans underwear and slip on my sandals. I grab my purse and make my way out of the residential penthouse suite of the Stafford's Casino and Resort.

The elevator door in the private lobby opens before I have a chance to hit the call button, revealing a sultry Tegan in its wake.

"Hey T. You might want to suck him off a little harder this time because he was still hard when I left."

She stares at me for a few seconds before she visibly wilts and our friendship fragments. "Hadley, don't be like that."

"Tegan, I genuinely do not care. He's all yours and I will be out of this glowing shithole in a week. I'll see you around."

I hit the button for the first floor once I've stepped past Tegan and into the elevator. As the doors begin to close, I hold up my *fuck-you* finger to the asshole that just rounded the corner to ravage Tegan instead of me. I won't be missing a thing, not even a whimper.

As I'm whisked down the thirty-two floors to the all-white marble lobby of Stafford's, I search through my purse for my phone, cursing myself if I left it in his bedroom. I hike my knee up and readjust my purse on my thigh to get a better look inside of it. The elevator comes to a sudden stop too soon and I lose my balance, which causes me to drop my bag on the immaculate white flooring while the doors slide open. All of the contents spew across the floor of the elevator, bringing it to life with more color than it will ever see again. I let out an annoyed exhalation as I bend down to pick up my baby pink thong which is ironically lying next to a twelve-pack of unopened condoms that I picked up earlier today after my shift.

A dark chuckle meets my ears and the sound vibrates straight through me. I snap my head up to find its owner, and I'm stunned when my eyes are drawn to the most expressive blue eyes that I've seen. I take in a deeper breath as I search his eyes, seeing a crystal clear sea, which is momentarily interrupted by a powerful blizzard when he pulls his slacks up on his knees as he bends down to pick up my thong with expert fingers.

"I'm going to assume that these belong to you."

I take in the sight of him again as his lips curl up in the corners, apparently knowing that he's affected me, but I suspect I'm doing just the same thing to him. He's wearing an Armani tuxedo, which is tailored to fit his body flawlessly. His dark hair is styled and seems to be recently cut to perfection in contrast to his jaw, which is shaded with stubble, a bit too long for it to be a day's worth of growth. I can imagine him at the end of a bed with his angular jaw skimming across my bare skin, nipping his way up to the apex of my thighs as my body burns from his stubble chafing against my skin.

He stands, bringing me back to the present moment and away from my wayward thoughts, still holding onto my thong before offering his other hand out to me. My eyes stray from his eyes to his hand and then back to the chilling blizzard that has taken up residence behind his eyes. I quirk a brow at him and begin to pick up the rest of my belongings from the floor, including my phone.

The elevator pings once, announcing that we've arrived at the lobby when the doors open, and I glance up at him again. His eyes are trained on me, watching my every move as I pull the hem of my shift dress down a notch.

His ocean-blue gaze sears me. He holds out his hand with my thong, offering it to me as if it's the most important thing in this confined space.

"Keep it," I say as I turn and step out of the elevator and into the lobby where a few of my co-workers murmur greetings to me. I make my way across the vast space to a rear elevator, which leads to the staff quarters. Entering the available one, I turn around as the doors are closing, only to lock eyes with him again while he brings the thin material up to his nose and inhales my scent.

My pussy would sing his name if I knew it.

It's seldom that I stay up through the night when I'm not being ravaged by an exceptionally handsome fuck; however, tonight I'm alone in my room, and I cannot close my eyes. Every time I shut them I see a stark blue sea within his eyes and the most gorgeously set jaw.

I toss the sheets off of my body, get out of bed, and reach for my phone to check the time. It's just past six in the morning and only two hours since I saw those sapphire eyes. I quickly come to the conclusion that I will not be getting a wink of sleep tonight. Instead, I make my way to the bathroom to freshen up as much as possible for one of my last days at Stafford's. I have no idea where to go from here, though. The casino has been my saving grace and home for the longest time. I've worked my way down the strip, and Stafford's was my last remaining option. When I left Denver, I ran as fast as I could toward the West Coast, away from everyone who was trying to destroy me, and instead ended up in Vegas and right into a family of money-hungry assholes.

This lifestyle has provided me with job security and plenty of men to ride into the early-morning sunlight. I've been working at Stafford's, the largest casino and resort on the Vegas strip, for the last two years as a blackjack dealer. It's where I met Lawson, as well as Tegan. She may work as a housekeeper during the day, but as soon as the sun goes down, Tegan's body is usually wrapped around a silver pole, thrusting her boney hips at strangers. Not that I'm much better.

When I get out of the shower, I dry off and apply lotion to my pale skin before styling my set of curls into its straight 'do.

An hour later my face is painted, I've finished two espressos, and I'm pulling out two oversized rolling suitcases from my closet to start packing up the last two years of my life. I need to figure out where to go from here, and this time, I think I'd like to get my own place for a while. I've lived most of my life since I was eighteen as a nomad of the world, traveling and moving as if it has become my profession. I've been able to save more money than I thought was possible these last two years at Stafford's, thanks to the generous men who seem to assume that sleeping with a dealer means paying me what they won at my table. Pricks, but who am I to turn down such a generous tip?

The day passes in a blur as I pack and do a little research on where I'd like to start over.

The alarm on my phone goes off, informing me that I have fifteen minutes before my shift starts at eight in the evening. I stretch out my stiff legs before sliding my tights down my thighs and pulling off my baggy sweater in exchange for my uniform of a black Victorian-style corset with white embellishments, sheer thigh-highs, and a black skirt that barely covers my ass—classy.

Lawson Stafford prefers for all of his dealers in the casino to be women, not that I mind because I wake up knowing that I'll be making more money than Tegan on her pole each day. I grab my phone and shove it down my barely contained cleavage before walking out of my room and down the never-ending hallway to the staff elevators, which will lead me straight to the casino level.

I check in with the manager on duty in his office before making my way to my designated table. Once I'm seated, I'm handed five fresh decks of playing cards. I open the first pack of cards and instead of the usual instructions card that lies on top of the final pack that I open, I find a small card folded in two.

Hadley,

You have two choices: you can either meet me in my suite after your shift or you can collect your last check and vacate my building.

Lawson.

I'm not surprised that he's given me an ultimatum . . . it wouldn't be the first time that I've had to move because some asshole doesn't know how to control his boner around me. I take the piece of gum I've been chewing out of my mouth and stick it onto the card before pressing it underneath my table.

Eat shit, Lawson.

Two

Wade

"GET ME THERE by midnight. Use whichever airport has the ability to house my jet for the evening."

"Yes, sir. I understand the urgency to get back. I will call you once it's done."

"No. Send an email to my pilot to inform him of the flight plan and then notify me as to what time I need to be on the tarmac."

I hang up and place my phone in my suit pocket before buttoning it. I do not have time to waste on this goddamn weekend away when my company apparently cannot function without its chief executive officer. These fuckers will soon come to understand exactly how much fun their Labor Day weekend can be once I'm breathing down their necks.

I adjust myself in my slacks as I stand and move to the king-sized bed in my suite, where a blonde-haired whore is lying on her side, naked. She hasn't been able to take her eyes off of me since I woke up, all the while watching me like I'm a goddamn prize. "Get out."

She doesn't say a word back to me or hesitate as she slips out of the bed, collects her belongings, and vanishes from my suite. The sight of her ass causes my balls to tighten and my cock to stir, but I ignore the urge to go after her. Sure, I got enough of her last night to keep me content, but I wasn't with the platinum blonde that gave me the damn hard-on twelve-plus hours ago. I pick up her pink thong from my nightstand and shove it in my suit pocket, grab my wallet, and walk out of the room to find another conquest in hopes of passing my time until later this evening. I allow myself a few weekends away from my city and business each year, in which I partake in as much sex and alcohol as my body will allow. Whether it is a paid whore, sex in numbers, or with some woman that I pick up, I make sure that my cock is content. Aside from these weekends, I have strict rules involving alcohol and women. I don't have the time for some money-hungry whore reaching into my pockets while I manage my international company and its ventures.

By the time I leave dinner from the resort's steakhouse, I have another tight-assed blonde on my arm. I lead her away from the restaurant and across the hotel to the casino floor with the knowledge that she will be my second today—the second blonde in twenty-four hours, and I do not as a rule do blondes. Correction, I didn't do blondes until the one from last night unselfishly let me keep her panties.

I join a craps table to pass the time while I wait impatiently for Jacobs to send me my flight details or for this woman to show me she wants my cock halfway down her throat. Instead of being forthright and just grabbing my dick as I can imagine the platinum blonde doing, she's hanging off of my shoulder like a goddamn child. A few games in and I've tripled the amount of money that I laid down when I first rolled the die. I'm handed the red die by a woman dressed in far too little as I take a sip of my Macallan 25, savoring the intense palate of coconut, vanilla, and wood smoke. The lingering hints of sherry, lemon, and spice keep me grounded for the moment. I was less than pleased when the waitress told me the oldest Macallan that Stafford's served was the 25-year, a true disappointment. I will need to have that corrected.

I'm about to roll the die when a weightless laughter fills my ears, causing me to gaze across the floor, searching for its source among the crowded casino. When I hear it again, my eyes lock on its owner: the platinum blonde of the pink thong. I down the remainder of my single malt before placing the glass down and the die in the hands of the tight-assed blonde that I'm no longer interested in. She looks at me with wide eyes, her features wrapped in confusion.

"It's nothing personal. Take what's on the table and go cash it out before you leave."

"But I can't . . ."

I step away from her and the table before she has the chance to speak another word as I make my way over to the next section of tables—blackjack.

There isn't a seat available at her table when I arrive. I stand back with my hands in my pockets as I watch the game proceed. She reaches in front of her to place a card and then another in front of some cocksucker that cannot take his eyes off of her tits as he makes a 'hit me' motion on the felt. I shift from one foot to the other as I watch her collect the chips across the table, stack them up and then place them in the correlating slots in front of her. These assholes keep losing to her, and I can't help but grin. She knows what she's doing, and she does it well.

It takes a few minutes for a suit to shake his head and stand before leaving the table empty-handed. I fall into step and take his seat at first base before anyone else gets a chance at it. Her eyes lift to mine as she adds the remainder of the cards from the previous game into the top of the continuous shuffle machine.

My presence does not get a reaction from her, which is oddly appealing. She knows how to lure a man in without a word from her lips; she's doing it to me right now.

I decide to take my chances of being removed from the premises, regardless of my status, by speaking to her. "What is your best advice for a blackjack player?"

The men around the table turn to glower at me. I glance down the line at each of them and silently dare them to challenge me when her voice breaks through my unspoken threat.

"My sole suggestion would be to return those stolen panties," she says without any hesitation.

I glance back at her and tilt my head to the side, taking in her attitude that I know I can get her dismissed for. "They're not stolen if they're freely offered by their owner."

"They're stolen if they weren't removed directly from said body."

My cock jumps at her response. I pause for a moment; her eyes haven't moved from mine as she deals two cards in front of each player.

"How about we make a transaction? One that involves you getting these pink panties back on for a moment and rectifying this situation." I pull her panties out from my suit-jacket pocket, presenting them to her. I notice the slightest blush glow underneath her pale skin, making me want more from her than this thin material.

"If those two men weren't walking toward me right this minute," she says, lifting her chin up as I shoot a glance over my shoulder, "then I would already be on your lap with your dick buried deep inside of me. I never claimed to be innocent in this exchange."

I turn back to her, attempting to keep the shock out of my eyes just as the men reach her, flanking her on either side before one of them places his hand at the small of her back to escort her out of the casino. She glances back over at me, eyeing her panties before looking me directly in the eyes. "Come on those, and while you do, think about my lips swallowing you."

The men are gaping at her while I stuff her panties back into my pocket and shift off of the seat as I watch the three of them move across the casino floor and then out of sight. I mentally review the options I have, which have all presented themselves in an intriguing way, but my phone vibrates, distracting me from my thoughts. I pull it out and read over the message from Jacobs: TAKE-OFF IS IN THIRTY MINUTES. I'M OUTSIDE WITH THE CAR.

I look up once more before turning in the other direction and striding off of the casino floor.

Three

Hadley

I WAS DELIVERED to the front of Stafford's where my suitcases were patiently waiting for me on the sidewalk. Lawson greeted me with a nauseating grin on his face as he handed me a white envelope, sealed shut, containing what I assumed was my last paycheck.

Deviant fucker. If I hadn't already been packed and planning on leaving, this might have rocked me, but I couldn't care less at this point.

It's been about four and a half hours since I was put out on the curb by his goons, and I have since made my escape. I rented a car during that time and drove myself across the Nevada state line and into Southern California where I've been taking in the sights ever since.

I could possibly pass as a Cali girl, but my skin might not contain the appropriate amount of melanin in it to fit in seamlessly. I'll get a hotel room for the night and try to figure out where my next adventure will begin. I've circled around LA a few times before I decide on something a little bit more risk-worthy. I pull the rented car into the rental return line at LAX, deciding to forgo the hotel and buy the next available plane ticket out of here—let the world decide where my next stop will be.

The rental agency attendant walks up to me, taking in my casino attire before asking for my name. I give it to him while his eyes shift back and forth from my cleavage to the touch screen device before he tells me that the total will be charged to my American Express card.

"Thank you," I say emotionlessly as I move to the back of the vehicle to get my suitcases out.

Thirty minutes later, I've managed to change into a comfortable pair of black leggings, nude Steve Madden booties, and my beloved black *She's Whiskey in a Teacup* tank. Once I've trashed my casino uniform, I head out. It takes me another hour to get to the front of the Southwest check-in line to purchase a ticket to my final destination.

"Do you have a reservation with us this evening?" the red-headed woman behind the check-in counter asks.

"I actually don't have one. I was hoping that you could book me onto the next available flight out."

She glances at me and then at my luggage before lowering her voice. "I can do that. It's none of my business, but are you all right, ma'am?"

"I'm great, thanks. I'm just surprising myself with a domestic vacation."

I'm sure that she assumes I'm running away from my life or an abusive relationship, but I'd rather not get into my life's details with a stranger.

"Oh, well, there is nothing wrong with treating ourselves every once in a while." She goes quiet for a minute or two before offering up any more information. "All right, the next flight that you will be able to catch after going through security is leaving in a little over an hour, and it will be going to Chicago Midway. Would you like for me to reserve your seat?"

"Please," I answer as I take out my license and credit card, handing them both to her before she tells me to put my first bag on the scale. Both of the bags are overweight, but I really don't give a fuck. I pay up and take my cards and boarding pass before making my way through the airport to stand in the hellish security lines.

Another hour later I've made my way through security and I've taken my seat on the plane, just as the flight attendant closes the doors and my journey to Chicago begins.

I step out of the jetway and shiver in the slightly cooler air of the North as it hits me through the thin material of my outfit. My phone vibrates in my hand with an incoming call from Lola Marc, a friend I've had since I was placed in my second foster home with her. We grew close rather quickly between the abuse and lack of parental guidance. I texted her while the plane taxied to the runway before taking off from LAX, telling her that I would be landing in her city at this god-awful time in the morning. She's a saint for coming to collect me at six a.m. while the sun still struggles to make an appearance.

"Hey Lo. I just stepped off of the plane, and I'm on my way down to baggage claim."

"Hads," she squeals, making me cringe away from my phone. "I'm beyond excited to see you. Do you have a place to stay yet? I honestly don't mind if you crash with me."

"That's really sweet of you to offer, but I don't want to be a burden."

"Stop being polite and be the bitch I know you to be. You're crashing with me whether you want to or not."

I laugh at her response. "I'll see you in a few minutes."

"Bye."

Lo has been the only person to understand the inner workings of my mind when it comes to sex because she was in the same place with me for a while before I left. I know that she's moved on since our past foster-care abuse, unlike myself.

Even though it's been eight years since I've seen her, I don't doubt that we'll pick right up where we left off. She's always been involved in my life, checking in with me at least once a month to find out where I was or what adventure I was on or whose dick I was riding at the time. She's the one person in my life who has been worth holding onto.

I turn the corner and search the sea of faces waiting for their loved ones, looking for her dark hair.

"Hads," she calls out to me, and I turn in the direction of her voice just as she slams her body against mine. I can't contain the giggle that escapes me, making me feel like a teenager again as I embrace my oldest friend.

"Holy crap, Lo . . . I can't . . . breathe."

"Sorry," she loosens her grip on me before holding me out at arm's length. "You look exhausted."

"Gee, thanks," I say as we walk to baggage claim together where my bags are already circling on the belt. She grabs one while I grab the other and we head out to her car while dragging them behind us.

"Please tell me that these will fit in your vehicle."

"I have an SUV, so they should. If not, though, I'm sure your toned ass won't mind walking."

I roll my eyes at her response as we get to her white Mercedes-Benz SUV.

"Holy shit. Who are you banging?"

She snickers as we lift my suitcases into the trunk. "I don't need to bang anyone if I can afford this baby on my own."

"Wow, Lo. I'm . . . proud of you."

"Thanks. You know, if you plan on staying here, I'm sure my place wouldn't mind hiring an extra hand."

"Well, I'm here, aren't I?" I beam at her as I buckle up. "But I'm sure that I can find my own job, and if not then I'll consider taking you up on your offer. What the hell are you doing nowadays, by the way?"

She backs out of her spot, and we pull out of the parking

deck and onto the highway before she offers up an answer. "Uhm, well, I've kind of opened up my own boutique which hosts a variety of my own designs. It's only taken off in the last year, though."

"Wait, what? Are you kidding me? Lo, that's incredible."

"I know, right?" she all but yelps at me.

"I don't know if I could live with you and work for you . . . and manage to remain friends. That might be pushing it."

"You may be right, but the living part won't be unruly because you will have your own room and neither will the friend part. Had-Lo for life, bitch."

"That damn nickname needs to go before it gets re-introduced to the wrong people," I say before we both burst out into laughter.

Being with Lo has always been simple and amusing. My thoughts of Lawson and his dick have evaporated as she pulls into a high-rise apartment building called Walton on the Park. We walk into the lobby and her doorman takes my suitcases from us while Lo signs me into the long-term guest registry. Once we're done signing in, the doorman shows us to an elevator, and we ride up to the twenty-third floor, walk down a hallway, and stop at double doors at the end. She opens the doors, and we're suddenly engulfed in the early-morning summer sunshine. The apartment is bathed in light as I walk to the middle of the foyer, taking in the bright and spacious place.

"Holy shit," I murmur under my breath.

"I know, right? I'm still trying to get used to it myself. I've been here for only four months, so this is all still rather new to me. This is probably one of my favorite parts of the city. We're right next to Washington Square Park, which is a great little escape. Come on, I'll show you to your room and let you get ready for the day before I assault you with questions and take you out to see the city."

I follow her through the apartment to a closed door that she swings open. I step through and smile to myself as I enter. "This is stunning, thank you, but you don't have to take off work to cart me around Chicago. You've already done too much."

"It's Sunday, Hads. My boutique is closed today, and regardless, I wouldn't miss my first day with my new roommate."

"Oh, well, if you insist."

"I do. Now get changed and I'll see your skinny ass shortly."

She closes the door behind her once the doorman places my suitcases in the room and I glance around, taking in my new space. I swear if I didn't know her better, I would think that this was the master bedroom. The walls are a pale gray color with a king-sized bed in the middle of the rear wall. The block drapes are gray and pale peach. The bedding matches her color scheme with pale grays, whites, and pale peach accents. I personally would have never paired the two colors together, but the room is warm and delicate at the same time. I pause to place my purse on the bench at the end of the bed. I can think of a few different positions I'll be able to get into with a man standing behind me right here.

I kill that thought for now and move to my suitcase in search of my makeup bag and hairbrush.

Throughout the morning, Lo has been showing me the most beautiful architecture that Chicago has to offer. I swear every building comes with a story in this city, and I've been held captive by it all. Who knew that architecture could be so enthralling?

We've just finished brunch at *Taverna 750*, where I've had a few too many bottomless mimosas when Lo asks me what I know she's been holding back since I landed. "Are you still doing it?"

I lift the champagne flute to my lips and throw back the rest of it before I set it down and glance up at her. "More than ever."

"Hads, I can hook you up with my therapist if you'd like. He's helped me over the last few years. I'm sure he'll be more than able to assist you through the same thing."

"Thank you, but I genuinely don't want help or a handout from anyone. I've made my bed, and I'm going to curl up in it until I no longer want to be there. I'm cozy and warm with being exactly where I am."

"You've been in that bed for nearly sixteen years."

"Well, I'm still alive, am I not? I'm nothing like my mother, and I refuse to bleed myself out just because I was taken advantage of as a young girl."

"I've never said that you were anything like your mother. I just figured that since you're here . . ." She stops herself before she continues to torture me. "Never mind."

I reach across the table and squeeze her hand. "Thank you. Honestly, I'm happy with my life right now. Sex has become a cure while everything else seems to be mundane."

"I know the feeling all too well. My offer still stands, though, and don't you dare forget about it."

I was Lo's support as she went through therapy. She'd call me after the end of each session that she attended; as the weeks drew on, it was easy to see her progress. Every time she asked me for my help, I did not hesitate. Oddly enough, I actually took a liking to helping someone who needed my invaluable support.

We stand up after the waiter brings back the bill, and we make our way back to her apartment building as I try not to drift off in the front seat.

"I think that I'm going to crash for a while," I tell her as we walk into her foyer, which I still haven't gotten over. It's modern, yet so simple with sharp lines and intricate details. This place is what any twenty-something-year-old dreams of living in.

"Sure thing. A Sunday nap sounds great right about now. Help yourself to anything around the place, okay?"

"Will do," I say as I walk into her guest room and close the door behind me. The neutral tones of the room seem to soothe me of my racing thoughts as I plop down on the bed and pull out my phone, eyeing a text message from Lawson: HADLEY, WHERE THE FUCK DID YOU GO? THAT THREAT WAS MEANT TO SCARE YOU ENOUGH TO COME BACK TO BED WITH ME, NOT TO RUN YOU OFF LIKE A FUCKING LOST PUPPY.

I contemplate my response, typing out a few variations of *fuck you* before I settle on one: MR. STAFFORD, I APPRECIATE THE GENEROSITY OF YOUR BED INVITE. HOWEVER, NOTHING ON THAT NAKED BODY OF YOURS INTERESTS ME IN THE SLIGHTEST.

Lies. Lawson's cock is striking; he just needs to learn how to use it properly. And by that, I mean he needs to learn how to pleasure a woman with it, rather than just get himself off.

YOU'LL BE BEGGING ME FOR IT BEFORE YOU KNOW IT. YOU CAN'T EXPERIENCE ANYTHING WITHOUT ME. YOU NEED ME, HADLEY.

Cocky bastard. I toss my phone to the other side of the bed before I roll over to face the large framed windows, taking in the azure-colored sky. The physical and mental exhaustion of the events of the last twenty-four hours has started to consume me one ounce at a time. Lo will just have to bear with me while I plaster on a fake smile. Fatigue takes over my body as I allow myself to sink deeper into the mattress, making me realize just how tired I am. Hell, my tired is tired.

I close my eyes, convincing myself that my life would go to shit if I weren't already ruined.

When I wake up, I'm veiled in darkness with the only glow of lights coming from below. I stretch out my body along the side of the bed, realizing that I did not move once while I slept.

There's a light rap on the door, and I gather that it's probably what woke me up.

"Hadley? I'm going down the hall to a friend's place for

dinner. He wanted to know if you would like to join us."

I sit up and smooth my hair down before wiping underneath my eyelids. "Sure, come on in," I call out to her.

The door opens silently, spilling the hallway light into the room. "Oh hey, I didn't think that you would still be asleep. I'm sorry."

"I wasn't," I say quietly as I swing my legs off the side of the bed. The feeling that washes over me has somehow found a crack in my emotions and has filled me with . . . what? Disappointment? I squash that thought just as fast as it entered my system and stand up, stretching my arms above my head. "Okay, maybe I was, but I'm starving. What's for dinner? Come?"

Lo drops her head to the side and gives me her best *what the fuck* look before rolling her eyes and crossing her arms over her chest—something she's always done since she was a teenager. She does it to protect her heart, and it seems to have worked, seeing that I'm the soulless, cold-hearted bitch while she's living a life of bliss.

"If you're going to come with, you need to swear to me that you won't ruin this for me. Owen and I have been talking since the day I moved in, and I think it might actually develop into something."

"Owen, huh? Fine. He's off-limits, but if any of your other neighbors show me their dicks, I'm not holding my tongue."

"You're such a whore."

"You love me."

"True, but don't push it." She laughs and crosses the room to one of my suitcases. "Wear something comfy and cute. I think his brother might be there."

"Oh? And what is said brother's dick size?"

"You're seriously asking me what the size of his penis is instead of his name? You're unbelievable, you know that?"

"Yup, I'm well aware."

She hands me my nude scoop-collar sleeveless, and see-through, asymmetrical blouse. "This would go great with those booties you had on this morning."

"Nice change of subject, Lo." I pull my shirt off by the hem and turn around to slip my feet back into my booties when she hands me the blouse. "Thanks."

"Wait, you're not going to wear a bra underneath that?"

"Nope, that way I can get naked faster." I smirk at her, and she shakes her head at me in admonishment.

"You're uncontrollable, and I may be able to see your nipples."

"That's nothing new."

She sighs and holds her hands up in surrender. "Fine, but I'm serious about Owen, Hads. He's off-limits and mine."

"You've got it," I say as I follow her out of the room and to her front door. This Owen guy lives a few doors down from her . . . well, us. We're standing outside of the door to apartment 1318 as it swings open and we're greeted by a rather fuckable piece of . . .

"Hey Owen, how are you?"

. . . and there goes that dick. I can see her attraction to him; his blonde hair is pulled up into a man bun, and his beard is neatly trimmed. I can't help but imagine what it would feel like scratching my inner thighs. He's built, tall, and lean all at once. He's a head turner.

"Hey, thanks for coming. You must be Hadley," he says, and he holds out his hand to me. I offer him mine, and we shake briefly.

"Sure am. It's nice to meet you, Owen."

His eyes stray from mine and down my body, pausing at my nipples before he looks back at Lola. "Holden will be joining us. I think the asshole is trying to play nice for once."

"That's sweet of him. Hads, Holden is Owen's roommate

and older brother."

A darker-haired stud walks around the corner, wiping his hands off as we walk into the living room. "You fuckers already talking about me?"

Owen shakes his head and gestures towards me. "Holden, this is Hadley. Hadley . . . Holden."

"Hey, thanks for inviting me to dinner. You definitely didn't need to, but thank you nonetheless."

"Nah, it's not a problem. We've got plenty to go around. Why don't you join me in the kitchen and we'll give these two some privacy," he offers as he gestures to Lo and Owen. Owen has his arms round Lo, and she is looking up at him over her shoulder, begging for him to lay his lips on her . . . anywhere. Shit, I can feel the sexual tension rolling off of them.

"Uhm, yeah, that sounds good."

I follow him into the kitchen, and he pulls out a beer from the refrigerator. "What do you drink?"

"Whiskey if you've got it, please."

"Sure thing. We've got a few different bottles. They're in the cabinet you're standing in front of. Help yourself to any of them," he states as he reaches for a rocks glass. I take the opportunity to drink him in. He's tall, possibly six-foot-one or -two. He's got on black pants, a plain white shirt and a beanie. The part of his hair that I'm able to see seems to be a dark blonde, almost brown in color. *Huh, he's actually pretty fucking gorgeous.*

I turn around and pull open the cabinet, revealing his bottles of whiskey. Most of them are inexpensive, but they taste classy. Elijah Craig will have to do for tonight. I hand him the bottle of my choice and lean back against the countertop.

"So what do you do, Hads? I can call you that, right? I've heard Lo mention you a few times."

"Hads is fine with me." He holds up a large sphere of ice with a questioning look on his face. "I'll take it straight up, thanks. And I just uprooted and moved here, so I guess that I don't really have an answer to that question yet."

He pours me two fingers before handing the glass off to me.

"Fair enough, but what are you interested in?"

I take a drink of the sublimely smooth whiskey, noting the creamy sweetness to the finish. "Whiskey, yoga, and sex."

"My kind of girl."

"Oh? Because of the whiskey?"

"Nah, I can't stand that shit. Owen and I keep that on hand for when our father comes around. I'm a craft beer drinker at heart. I meant the sex."

If there's one thing that I cannot drink, it's beer. He just became as hipster as his brother. The taste of caramel malts and the bitterness of hops is a huge turn-off for me. It doesn't matter how hard I try to stomach the liquid bread: I just cannot do it. I'm a whiskey girl down to my toes.

"Ah, well, there's nothing much better than sex."

"Are you offering?" He takes a swig from his bottle and eyes me, waiting to see how I'll react to his all-too-direct question.

"Nope, but I'll take you up on *your* offer. I need to be fucked, so make it good."

Lola and Owen walk into the kitchen before Holden gets a chance to respond. I turn to Lo and take in her flushed complexion: she's radiant. Oh, she has it bad.

"I see that you're getting acquainted with the other Parker brother, Hads. What are you guys talking about?"

"Sex," Holden and I say in unison.

"Well then, that escalated quickly," Owen comments as he pours Lola a rather large glass of pinot noir.

"I'd say so," Lo says as she takes her glass from Owen by the stem and sips on the translucent red liquid.

I look up from the glass tumbler in my hands as I bend over the kitchen island, giving Holden a little ass show. "It went from whiskey to sex, so it wasn't as straightforward as you might think it was," I joke.

Holden walks up next to me and places his hand on my lower back before I look back at him and smile, not stopping his advances, but instead welcoming them.

Owen chuckles. "I think my manwhore of a brother has found his match."

"I sure as fuck don't see the problem," Holden replies and squeezes my ass. I push back into his hand, wanting more of him already. I can tell that he'll, at the very least, know how to use his hands on me.

Owen clears his throat, apparently surprised by my forwardness. "Are you done fucking up dinner, Hold?"

"Sure am, considering the heating instructions are barely legible. Get the ladies to their seats and then you can help me move everything to the table."

The table? Oh, so we're going to be fancy assholes and use china and crystal. *Joy.* As if I didn't already feel completely out of place in this apartment building in the first place, I sure as shit do now. Am I used to seeing money thrown around? Sure thing. Am I used to being the one that the money gets spent on? Nope. Not for one second. My only money rests in my savings account, and it's gotten quite comfortable there. I should probably invest some of it or, at least, purchase a vehicle, seeing as it's easier to travel beyond the city with one.

I follow after Owen and Lo as they walk into the dining room and I take a seat across the table from Lo. As sure as fuck, we're going to be dining on expensive china and sparkling crystal wine glasses. Owen grabs a bottle of 2009 Gevrey-Chambertin pinot noir and decants it into an intricate looking decanter—it looks like arteries as the wine fills the glass structure. Is it too much to ask for people with this kind of money to act, I don't know, normal?

I sigh silently but hide my face with the mask that has been securely in place for the last sixteen years of my life.

Holden walks in carrying what appear to be two already-assembled plates of filet mignon, asparagus, mashed potatoes and sauce to accompany it. I find this rather interesting considering they are brothers. Shouldn't this be served more, I don't know, family style?

"Grubs ready," Holden says as he places a dish in front of Lo and me before striding back into the kitchen to grab the last two plates.

"Holden? You made this?" I ask skeptically.

"Nah, we had Maggie come in and prepare dinner tonight."

"Would you mind my asking who Maggie is?"

"She's been our personal chef for the last two years. She makes some mean mashed potatoes. You'll cry out for more, and that's a promise," he says as he settles down in the seat next to me.

Oh yes. Fancy-asses.

"We'll just have to see about that, won't we?"

Owen speaks before Holden has a chance to reply. "Hadley, would you like some wine?"

"Oh, no, I'm all set with whiskey. Thank you, though."

"Are you an avid whiskey drinker?"

"I am, and I have been for years. It's something that I've gotten to know intimately. I enjoy the taste of warmth, sweet, and smoke—it's like its own campfire. And I like the smooth burn that it provides. It straddles the line between pleasure and pain."

"It's the first time I've heard a woman speak so well of the stuff."

I laugh and take a bite of the filet before speaking again. "There's a lot to know about it, and it definitely is an acquired taste."

Owen smiles, and Lo watches us closely as if I'm going to

crawl under the table and give him head for conversing with me. Silly girl. I don't need to have a conversation with someone to sleep with him, but as tempting as it is, I would never hurt her.

"Since you like the stuff so much, has Lo taken you to the whiskey library? It's on the Magnificent Mile."

"A whiskey library?" My interest is piqued. I've heard of something like it before, but I've never been lucky enough to stumble across one.

"Oh yeah, isn't it rather new? I've never been, but I've heard great things about it from those who enjoy that foul stuff. No offense, Hads," Lo says.

"None taken. What's it called? I'd like to stop by and take a look for myself."

"If I remember correctly it's called Blended," Owen says with a smile as he sets his glass down on the tabletop.

"Huh . . . thank you, Owen."

"No problem. Let me know if you need any more suggestions of places to go in the city. I'm sure Hold wouldn't mind showing you around either."

"Nah, I wouldn't mind one bit, but I'll need your number for that," he says as if his ploy isn't obvious. Just in case his meaning is not clear, his eyes let me know that it's more than just a line that he's throwing out.

"Smooth," Owen adds to the awkward silence before the four of us laugh at how ridiculous Holden is—sexy as hell, but preposterous nonetheless.

We all settle into a comfortable conversation while the apex of my thighs aches for relief. I've been deprived for over twenty-four hours, and my libido won't allow me to forget it.

Four

Wade

I UNWIND IN a dark leather wingback chair in my office as I page through a file involving my latest venture here in Chicago. I've been impressed with my staff and its outcome thus far, given that it's one of the smaller venues that I own at the moment. It seems to be thriving.

I place the folder down on the coffee table in front of me before reaching for my tumbler of 1937 Glenfiddich; the hints of cedar, cinnamon, cloves, and toffee fill my mouth as I take a sip of the rare bottle. A total of sixty-one bottles were made, and I happen to own another four.

I breathe out and find comfort in this particular whiskey. The tradition, feel, and aesthetics in drinking whiskey have been enjoyable to me since I can remember. Each bottle in my collection comes with its own history, sharing its tales by taste and scent rather than words. If a drink could restore memories from the past, then whiskey would be the answer. I roll the tumbler between my fingers as the walnut liquid slides from side to side.

I take another sip as the flavors emerge across my palate, groaning as the warm sensation makes its way down my throat and through my body. Unable to sit for much longer, I get up and walk across the span of my office to the windows, glancing down at the people walking around on the sidewalk below. At this moment, I wonder what it would be like to be one of them—to consider myself *average*.

I've managed to keep my life to myself; I wouldn't call my-self an introvert, but I've been known to hole up with a bottle of whiskey from time to time. I turn away from the windows and those who occupy the sidewalk space below.

The majority of my time is spent dealing with Brass Global, working out, or drinking Scotch. I've limited myself to whom I interact with in Chicago, and I have a set of rules that I abide by to keep sane.

I was born in London, England, and moved to the United States with my mother when I was still an infant after the death of my father. She raised me as a single mother, striving to be the best she could be for me, and it's because of her that I refuse to lose sight of my goals for something or someone inconsequential.

An abrupt knock on my door interrupts my thoughts as well as the silence in the room. I glance at my watch and frown: it's eight in the evening. Who the hell would still be here?

"What?" I call out, annoyance laced in my voice.

The oversized solid wood door opens silently and my sec-retary, Adriana Hugh, walks in, her heels clicking softly against the black marble flooring. She's been with me since I launched my company, and I could not imagine replacing her. She's beauti-ful, but I haven't shown any interest in this all-American girl. She may be someone I would naturally go after, but my rules forbid me from doing so.

"I apologize for interrupting, Mr. Brass, but I just wanted to ask if you needed anything else before I leave? I've arranged the meeting in Australia for three weeks from today, which will give you the time you needed to review and make your final decision on the properties you were interested in acquiring there."

"Thank you, Adriana. Is there anyone else left on the floor?"

"No, sir. It is just the two of us."

I nod. "Very well. Have a good evening."

"You too, sir." She smiles timidly before placing a few phone messages on my desk and walking out of the room, shutting the door silently behind her.

I place my now-empty tumbler on my desk before picking up the messages she has written down for me. Two are from my mother, another is from a C-level employee, Gage Cooper, and the other is from Lawson Stafford. Adriana holds all of my personal phone calls during the day unless I ask her otherwise. She usually keeps my cell phone on her desk as well. I don't have time to play tag via text messages when I'm busy with crucial financial decisions involving the multiple companies comprising Brass Global. Of those companies under the BG umbrella, some mean more to me than others do, but those who work underneath me to make my empire thrive will never know the difference. Our subsidiaries are varied with some being in the business sector while others are in the hospitality industry.

Some of my biggest projects, however, revolve around a global charity called Mothers of Brass, an organization that is dear to my heart. Mothers of Brass runs safe houses in which women experiencing domestic violence find their refuge. Many of them suffer from physical as well as mental abuse, and many of them escape their abusive situations with their children in tow. This charity helps to put these women back on their feet in the time they need and require. In addition, it offers counseling and support groups at no charge.

It's an incredibly personal part of my business, but no one outside of Adriana and Brass Global's C-level positions are aware of that.

After reading each one of the messages, I decide that tonight is not the night to call them back. None of them will get anything worthwhile from me this evening.

Now that everyone has left the office, I remove my tie, undo the first few buttons on my white shirt, grab my jacket off of the back of my chair, and then leave my office, picking up my phone from Adriana's desk on my way out. I text Jacobs to inform him that he may take the rest of the evening off after he delivers my personal vehicle to my final destination.

This evening will be one drowned in the light and spicy, yet slightly bitter flavor of a 10-year aged rye whiskey. Once I arrive at my building's lobby, I walk out after greeting the third-shift security in all-black suits. Instead of taking the car with Jacobs, I walk the two blocks to my most beloved place in Chicago—Blended—where I'm greeted by name upon arrival. I'm shown back to a spot next to the oversized fireplace and ask a librarian for a neat WhistlePig straight rye whiskey. Blended has proven to be my saving grace in the last two months since it opened; it's provided me with a peace of mind every time I walk through the doors. It's home.

She's back a few minutes later with a tumbler designed by Rikke Hagen filled with two fingers of amber. I thank her before breathing in the aged liquor, taking a sip, and sinking a little farther into the seat. It's a Monday night and Labor Day weekend, so the crowd is light this evening, just how I prefer it.

I choose to stay invisible although everyone knows me, and if they don't yet then they shortly will because I'll soon be gracing the cover of one of the most popular magazines in the nation. I may not be looking forward to the undue attention, but I'm pleased with my accomplishments that have ultimately led me to getting the cover. Regardless of the recognition that this may bring, I'd prefer to remain unseen.

Five

Hadley

I'VE BEEN IN Chicago for just over a week since Labor Day, and I have yet to get laid. How pathetic am I? It's an early Sunday night, and I cannot stay in this apartment for one more minute, regardless of how beautiful it is. I need to get out of this building and find myself an easy lay or simply be someone's easy piece.

I doll myself up after a hot shower, spending more time on my hair and makeup than usual before I walk into the foyer and call out to Lo, who is huddled up on her couch with Owen. "I'm heading out for a few hours. Please don't wait up if I'm not back. I'll see you later."

"Have fun, Hads. Make sure that he wears a condom," she jokes.

"I'd never go without one. Bye!"

I leave the confines of what quickly seems to be becoming my very own anti-sex prison cell. Hell, even the straight men in prison get more dick than I have this last week—which is none.

I'm antsy as I walk out of her building and hail a cab, telling the driver to take me to Blended, the whiskey library that Owen told me about last week. I've been job searching like it's the one thing I need to breathe and I haven't taken time out to just explore Chicago's treasures on my own. The only thing that I've left the apartment for is yoga and whiskey. I've been to the park a couple of times in the morning—before there are too many people around—to practice yoga in the slightly humid summer air. I'm not yet acclimated to these northern summers. I'm used to the dry heat of the desert, but I'm adapting.

The cabbie pulls up to the address, and I hand him some cash before getting out and walking through the front door. The place has a low buzz of noise; it seems to be more of a place to relax and truly savor the whiskey than a place that hosts wild events and drunken loons. The lights are dimmed, and there's music playing over the speakers, but it's not loud enough for me to figure out what song is on. There are large pieces of comfortable furniture—sofas, wingback chairs, coffee tables, and seating nooks—around the open room. Wooden beams soar overhead as they stretch from one side of the room to the other. A massive fireplace sits in the center of the far wall, which is currently surrounded by people drinking; some are even smoking cigars. *How do they not get fined for that shit?*

I walk up to the bar and take in the two walls of shelves in front of me that are filled with hundreds of bottles of beautifully aged amber liquid. I glance to my left and see a petite woman sliding a wooden ladder across another set of shelves before climbing up it as if she was going to retrieve a book. Instead, she comes back down with a bottle of whiskey.

The petite bartender . . . uh . . . librarian snaps me from my thoughts before I've noticed that I'm next to be served. "Bourbon, rye, Tennessee, Canadian, Scotch, or Irish?" she asks, and I look at her wide-eyed.

"That's how you greet people here?" I ask, recalling her saying the same thing a little louder when I first walked in.

She cracks a smile, yet I feel as if she's mocking me. "It sure is. What will it be?"

"Macallan 10-Year. Straight up and neat."

She raises her brows at me, her smile seeming to be the slightest bit more genuine as she turns away from me. I'm sure she's used to pricks coming in here acting like they know a thing or two about whiskey. She comes back and places a gorgeous tumbler in front of me. "I'll hold onto your card," she says as I pull it out of my purse and hand it to her. "Take a seat wherever you want and you can either come up here to grab a drink or ask one of the librarians to bring you something."

"Great, thank you."

"Oh, if you actually like the place and if you'd like to make this a regular spot for yourself then come by and chat with me. We offer a private membership, which requires approval from the owner. It's like a library card—you get to try out the most expensive bottles a few times a year. We also hold socials for the members, and every once in a while someone gets to add the stamp of the Macallan 64-Year to his or her list. Let me know if you're interested and I'll grab you an application."

"That's great, thank you," I say before walking away to find a seat, surprised by the detail involved in this space. I take a seat in front of the all-brick fireplace that is burning real wooden logs instead of the conventional gas alternative, inhibiting the camp-fire smell that the Scottish single malts provide.

After a few minutes of glancing around the place, I swirl the amber liquor around the glass. I love the vibe that this place gives off. It doesn't feel ostentatious even though they own the most expensive whiskey in the world beside many others that I have seen gracing their shelves.

I feel welcomed here as if it's a place that I've visited hundreds of times before. I shift in the seat and get a bit more comfortable before pulling out my phone and calling up my Kindle application to read some sappy know-it-all romance novel that has barely been holding my interest. Okay, that's another lie, but I won't admit to my fixation of fictional characters to just anyone.

I don't notice the time passing until my second tumbler is

empty and I stand to stretch out my legs, which are stiff after sitting still for so long. I look up and out toward the large windows; the street lights are on outside and it's now completely dark with very few people walking past. I hadn't realized that I was so absorbed in this book. So much for finding someone to ride tonight.

"That must be an interesting novel," a deep, dark voice says as I sit back down to read again, hoping that one of the librarians will come by so I can order another Macallan.

I glance up with a small smile on my face before it falls once I lock eyes with the man sitting diagonally from me.

"Oh."

"Ah, so she does recognize me."

It's the man from Stafford's. The one who probably still has my thong hostage. I feel an odd vibe shift between us, so much so that I'm a bit uncomfortable with the way he's looking at me.

"I suppose I do. Did you grace my thong with your come yet?" I enjoy shocking men with my mouth—in more ways than one.

His lips rise up in one corner, "No, I have personal rules when it comes to women. It's a trophy of a non-sexual encounter that left me lightheaded."

"That's an interesting choice of words."

"Speaking of words," he says, nodding toward my phone, "what are you reading?"

I glance down at the sex scene unraveling on the page in front of me before locking my phone and setting it on my lap. "Does it matter?"

"Not entirely, but I've enjoyed the myriad of emotions crossing your face as you read it."

He's been watching me? I don't know whether to be creeped out or grateful.

"Is this the part where I call the cops on a stalking,

panty-hoarding asshole?"

He chuckles and takes a sip of his whiskey. "No, not one bit."

We're interrupted by a librarian, the petite one from earlier, asking if she can get him anything else this evening before she leaves. He shakes his head and thanks her before she walks over to me.

"I'm sorry, but it's two a.m. and we're closing. I'm going to have to ask you to leave. If you are still interested in the membership, then I can grab you an application on your way out."

"Thank you, I think I'd like to take a look at the membership details. An application would be great."

Two in the morning? *Holy crap.* That means that I've been sitting here for more hours than I care to count. I glance around the space, and we're the only three left.

"Isla," he says and the petite woman glances over at him.

"Yes?"

"Bring her another and clear her tab. Once you're done, feel free to leave. I'll be staying a while longer."

"Of course, Brass." I swear that she rolls her eyes before thanking me for coming in and walking back to the bar to fetch me another glass.

"How . . . ?"

He grins knowingly at me. "I own the place. You're welcome to stay and finish your book. I don't plan on leaving for a few more hours."

"Oh. That's incredibly generous of you, but I'd rather not be in your way." I go to stand, but he holds up a hand, halting my movements from across the coffee table.

"Stay."

One word.

One demand.

I relax against the leather again as Isla brings me a new

tumbler. "Thank you."

He nods at her dismissively, and she walks away from us and back to the bar where she grabs her sweater and purse before walking out the front door, locking it behind her.

"You didn't have to buy my drinks."

"Call it an even exchange for pink lace."

"I think this one glass of whiskey is more than twice the price of those panties."

He shrugs and lifts his right leg, placing his ankle on top of his left knee. "Tell me something about yourself."

"About myself? Uhm, my name's Hadley but . . . I'm not one to give out personal details to a stranger."

"Well, Hadley, it's a pleasure to finally call you something aside from 'platinum blonde.' You've had my balls in a knot since the elevator ride, so I wouldn't exactly call myself a stranger."

"I'm sure I have." I'm not subtle when it comes to sex or flirting or hell, telling someone that I want to be ravaged.

"Cocky. I like it. I'm Waylon Brass, but seeing as I'm rather familiar with your most intimate parts—their scent, at least— you can call me Wade."

"Well, it's nice to meet you, Wade."

"As it is you, Hadley. What are you drinking?"

"It's a Macallan 10-Year."

"Finish that off and I'll grab you something with a bit more history behind it," he says as he gets up and moves around the coffee table to stand in front of me. "Come."

I stand and place my hand in his offered one before he leads me to the darkened bar area where I watch him pour me a glass of Glenfarclas John Grant 60-Year-Old. His body moves underneath his suit as though every movement is thought out in advance—he's very sure of himself in a physical way. If he wants to fuck me right here on the bar top, I won't stop him for a second.

"What are you doing in Chicago? I thought you worked at

Stafford's?"

I take a sip before answering him. "Well, you sort of got me kicked out," I joke, but his face turns serious.

"I'll call Lawson and have that changed by tomorrow morning. I won't be the reason for your dismissal."

"You know Lawson?"

"I do. He works for me."

Holy shit.

"You know, I rather like Chicago. I think that I'll stay for a while."

"Ah, my library has won you over, hasn't it? It wouldn't be the first time."

If I'm being honest, it's a huge part of why I want to stay. I've never felt more comfortable in any one place before. "I wouldn't want to stroke your ego."

"My ego can handle it."

"Well, if you insist. I think it was the final deciding factor. There's just something about this place that holds me captive. I can see myself wasting hours in here . . . sort of like today."

"You should apply to be a member then. I'll have the fees waived for the application as well as the annual membership."

"There's no need for that," I say as I get up onto one of the barstools and pocket my card that the librarian left on the bar top.

"Maybe not, but I want you to be part of something that I own," he says as he moves between the chair adjacent to mine and me, and stands there, looking down at me. My blood heats at his proximity.

"What do you want out of it, Mr. Brass?"

"I'd like to take you on a date."

"A date? You mean that you just want another pair of my panties because you've already worn out the first."

"No," he says firmly, "I'd like to take you out and possibly enjoy a drink or two in neutral territory."

I pause and watch him for a while before I give him my answer. This is possibly the worst idea I have ever had, but something about the way he's looking at me makes me want to oblige. "All right, when and where?"

He pulls out his phone and glances at it for a few seconds before looking up into my eyes. "Tomorrow evening at eight. Leave the where up to me."

"I think—"

"No, don't think," he interrupts. "Give me your number and I'll text you the details." He slides his phone into my hand and after a moment of consideration, I give in and dial my number into his phone. I call myself and wait to hear my phone go off before I hang up and save my contact details under Whiskey and Rye instead of my first name.

He takes his phone back and pockets it without looking at the screen. He moves his hand to my knee, and my eyes shift from his face to where his hand is scorching my skin as if a frozen static has stung me. His long fingers trace the seam of my leggings, and I'm entranced with watching his hands move before I'm able to look away.

"Are we going to fuck now?" My voice is too soft and needy; it's not my own, and I'm sure that he notices because I swear I just felt his entire body stiffen even though he's inches away from me.

"Not yet. I have rules, remember?"

"Oh? You don't sleep with someone on the first date?"

"No. I don't date women in Chicago at all."

Confusion becomes me, and I raise my brow at him. "Then why are you taking me out?"

"I'm asking myself that exact same thing right now, and if we don't get out of here, then I'm going to regret taking advantage of you."

"I like being taken advantage of."

For some reason, my statement doesn't seem to surprise him, which in turn shocks me. "I don't doubt that. Did you drive here this evening?"

"I took a cab," I say coldly as I take the last swallow from my tumbler. For some reason, I'm pissed the hell off now. I don't understand why he won't just fuck me right here when it's obvious he wants it too. To hell with him and his moral standards. I need to be penetrated and fucked like a goddamn savage.

"I'll take you home. Grab your things."

Asshole. Who does he think he is? He sure as hell isn't in charge of me—or my actions either. It doesn't even look as if he's going to be in charge of my orgasms. What a shame. His rejection swims through my veins like poison, and I cannot figure out what it is about sex with me that doesn't intrigue him.

"I can find my own way back since you're refusing to put your hands on me. Thanks for the offer, though."

I stand and head back to the leather chair that I was in earlier to collect my things. When I turn around, he's directly behind me. He looks just as pissed as I feel at the moment. He grabs ahold of my hips and pulls me flush against his body. "I said that I would take you home."

I swallow hard, concentrating on the feel of his hands on my needy body. I selfishly press my body against his. I can feel his muscular physique underneath his suit and my body and mind give in to the feel of him.

"Okay," it's barely a whisper, but I think he hears me because he lets go of me.

"Come."

"That's kind of what I was hoping for the first time you offered."

"Don't make me regret taking you out, Hadley."

I frown and walk past him to the front door. When he

doesn't follow, I turn to face him, and he's standing across the room. "I'm parked in the back."

"Oh? I'm surprised your fancy-ass doesn't have a driver."

"He's off for the evening." He holds out his hand to me, and I reluctantly walk over to him and take it again.

He leads me out of the library through a darkened back entrance. He turns to lock the door and sets an alarm before he takes my hand again and leads me to a sleek dark graphite BMW.

"This is yours?"

"She's my girl," he says modestly.

"She's beautiful. What is it?"

"She's the latest i8," he says as he opens the door, which swings upward instead of out.

Yup. Fancy-ass motherfucker.

Seated, I look up at him again, and his eyes are roaming down my body, drinking in every inch of me like I'm his favorite amber liquor. "You look good in her."

"Just as I'm sure you'll look good in me."

He chuckles and closes the door before walking around to get in and starting *his girl* before we take off down the Magnificent Mile. A few people are milling about and turn their attention to the BMW as we drive past them.

I cross my ankles and lean my knees toward the center console, wishing I had worn a dress instead of leggings. I purse my lips when he subtly tilts his head to glance down at my movement. His eyes move back to the road, and I notice his grip on the steering wheel tighten a fraction.

"Where to?"

"I'm staying at Walton on the Park."

"Good. You're in the same direction as I am."

"I don't know whether that's a good thing or not, considering the fate of my libido."

"For now, consider it a good thing. Rules be damned."

A heady trance comes over me at that statement. There's a static in the air, and it crackles between the two of us. I glance down at how I'm seated, and I realize that my body has gravitated toward him of its own accord. This cannot be good or healthy.

We drive in silence for the last few blocks until he comes to a stop outside of Lola's building just as my phone chimes. I pull it out of my purse and glance down at a text message from Holden.

ARE YOU AWAKE?

Thank fuck. It looks like I'll be getting some dick after all.

WANT ME? I type out quickly before I open the door. "Thank you, Wade. I suppose I'll see you tomorrow."

"Until then," he says. For some reason, his body has gone from comfortable to taut in just a moment. I swear this man is a living myriad of reactions, and I've just officially met him. I shut the door and step into the high-rise building. My phone goes off again, and I slide my finger across the screen: COME OVER. OWEN IS WITH LOLA TONIGHT.

I swore to Lo that I wouldn't mess up this thing she has going on with Owen, but right now, my needs are achingly obvious, and they need to be met by more than just my purple vibrator. ON MY WAY.

I head up to our floor and stop at the third door down instead of going to the double doors at the end of the hallway. I knock twice and wait for what seems like forever while I try and wrap my head around going out with Wade tomorrow night. How is it possible that he's the one that owns the whiskey library? Out of all the people in the world, it would be my damn luck.

"Are you just going to stand there or *come* in?"

"Oh. Hi."

I hadn't even realized that Holden had opened the door. I smile up at him and take a few steps inside before he brings his arms around my waist from behind. "You look like you've seen a ghost."

"In a way, I did, but it's nothing." I lean my back to his front as my body relaxes in his arms. He's the exact opposite of Wade in looks and personality, but I'm beyond attracted to him. Holden just has this carefree spirit about him that draws me in like a damn metal object to his magnet.

"Are you okay?" He seems sincere, but I wouldn't even know how to explain what just happened.

"I'm fine now," I say as I turn around and face him. He's wearing a gray shirt and black sweatpants. I lower my hands and move them up underneath his shirt, touching his skin for the first time. My fingers run over the ridges of his abs and up to his pecs.

His sharp inhale of breath makes me glance up at him. "Are you sure about this?"

"I am."

His lips slide across mine to my jaw as he lifts me into his arms, making me wrap my legs around him as he strides to-wards his bedroom. His lips lock with mine in a hard embrace as he nudges the door open with his foot and we move into his room. He lays me down on the bed before we both remove our shirts. I toss mine to the side, and when I look back up, his body is moving over mine. He covers me with his perfectly sculpted chest as he pulls the cups of my bra down. My nipples peak from his proximity and the sudden cold air hitting them. His mouth comes down on one of them while he pulls on the other with his finger. My body quivers and thanks me for the incredible feeling.

God, what I wouldn't give to ride a dick every day of my life. A connection-free enjoyment where two bodies meld into one for a few moments before satisfaction takes over, and he takes my breath away with an orgasm that I've been craving for a week. It's nothing more than a few inches of penetration and response once it's all said and done.

Holden satisfies every ache I have running through my body

before he pulls out of me and I suddenly miss the full feeling.

After we settle our needs in the bedroom, I head back to Lo's place, feeling sated yet more anxious than I can ever remember.

Freshly fucked, no thanks to Wade, I get into bed and drift to sleep as I dream about an ocean turning to ice as a wild blizzard takes over what once was a sun-kissed sea. Wade's eyes fill my dreams. In those eyes, I see a potential to destroy anything in his path in the most beautiful way.

Six

Wade

ONE THING THAT I refuse to do is break my rules, ones that I have lived by religiously for years to keep myself on the straight and narrow. However, last night I did just that. Willingly.

I stride across the marble floor of my office, deciding that I might as well break another rule today, considering I've bent them out of formation already. I walk into the reception area to my office and to Adriana, who glances up at me, disbelief marring her face as I walk up to her desk.

"I need my phone, Adriana."

She looks stunned, which she should. I have never left in the middle of a meeting, nor have I gotten my phone back from her before the day's end, but this intense need to speak to Hadley is weighing too heavily on me, and I need to put a stop to it immediately. I need to feel the static energy that I felt last night with her again. *Now.*

"Yes, sir," she says as she fishes my phone out of a locked compartment in her desk. "Is everything all right?"

"Yes, everything is fine."

I turn my back to her and return to my office while I pull up my call log. I pause on the threshold of the dark wooden door when my recent calls appear. Whiskey and Rye graces the top of the list and I smirk. I detest nicknames, especially when they are listed as phone contacts, but for some reason, this doesn't bother me as much as it should.

I click on the contact and type out a message, well aware of Adriana's eyes locked on my back as well as the three sets of eyes staring at me from the conference table in my office.

WHISKEY AND RYE, HUH? WHAT AM I IN YOUR PHONE? AGED SCOTCH?

I place the phone into my suit jacket and take a seat at the head of the conference table again. As I do, my phone vibrates, calling my attention back to it.

WHAT? YOU DON'T LIKE IT? YOU CAN'T TELL ME THAT YOU DON'T ENJOY RYE WHISKEY EVERY ONCE IN A WHILE. AND NO, IT'S NOT *AGED SCOTCH*. I THINK YOU'RE HOLDING YOURSELF UP TO TOO HIGH OF A STANDARD.

I glance up at the men in front of me who are still staring in disbelief. I raise my eyebrows, and one of them clears his throat before he starts speaking about the acquisition of the Australian properties that is coming up in a few short weeks again.

I type out a quick response: TELL ME WHAT IT IS, HADLEY.

GENTLEMAN JACK.

I can't help but crack a smile at her reply. I'm no longer invested in the conversation that's happening in front of me at the table, but rather in the one on my screen.

A RATHER INEXPENSIVE WHISKEY, YET SOMEHOW MOUTHWATERING ALL THE SAME. IT REMINDS ME OF LEATHER, TOBACCO, VANILLA, AND CO-COA. ARE YOU CALLING ME CHEAP?

I can imagine her smile as she reads that. A moment later another text message comes through: NOT AT ALL. I'M CALLING YOU RICH AND PRETTY.

I actually laugh at her reply. The men in front of me grow silent for a moment, and I look back up at them. "Continue."

They nod as I send my last text to her: PRETTY IS NOT THE WORD I WOULD USE, ESPECIALLY WHEN IT COMES TO YOU. GORGEOUS IS MORE LIKE IT. I'LL PICK YOU UP AT EIGHT. BE READY.

I turn my phone off and pocket it so I can attempt to concentrate on this damn meeting, but my mind decides to wander back to Whiskey and Rye. Whiskey just got that much sweeter to me.

The day passes slowly—too slowly, but when I check my watch again, it's seven-forty. I grab my phone and turn it back on to text Jacobs before heading into the bathroom hidden behind the hard paneled walls of my office.

After I change and freshen up for the evening, I head downstairs to find Jacobs standing in front of my Magellan gray 750i BMW. He swings the door open for me, "Good evening, Mr. Brass."

"Evening. I trust that you have the address of the apartment high-rise that I sent to you earlier."

"Yes, sir."

"Very well," I say as he shuts the door and I settle into the cream-colored leather seats before he pulls into the Chicago traffic.

A few minutes later we've arrived at Hadley's building. I grab my phone and send her a quick text: IF YOU'RE NOT DOWN HERE WITHIN TWO MINUTES, I WON'T LAY A HAND ON YOU.

I wait for a response that doesn't come before stepping out of the car and shutting the door behind me. I lean against the car and wait.

When I look up from my phone again, she's walking out of the glass doors toward me. I pull in a deep breath of air when she steps under a streetlight. The light from above cascades down on her, making her platinum hair look angelic around her flawless features. Her hair isn't straight this evening as it's been every other time I've seen her. Tonight it falls in loose curls over her shoulders.

"You have no choice but to touch me now," she says as she

steps toward me.

I feel my eyes hood with need as they deliberately roam down her slight curves, which are hugged by a cropped white lace top and a long skirt with two particularly high slits on each of her thighs. She's fucking gorgeous. I adjust myself in my slacks before I take the last few steps to get to her.

"I don't see how I would be able to restrain myself with your wearing this."

She purses her lips as I slide my hand around her exposed midriff. She jolts from my touch and the current that ran intensely between us last night is back and eagerly humming. A thick layer of sexual tension moves between us as she looks up at me through her lashes.

"I'd prefer if you didn't stop touching me tonight."

The confidence she instills in me makes me stand up straighter as I pull her to me. I move her curls behind her ear as I lean down to place my lips on her cheek. My lips stray from her cheek to find her ear, whispering, "You're breathtaking."

Her body jolts once again under my touch, and my cock stirs at her involuntary response.

"Thank you, Wade."

"Let's go. I'm not sharing you this evening," I say as two men walk out of the building and watch Hadley interact with me for a few seconds more than what might be deemed appropriate.

She nods and I open the door for her to slide into the backseat. Once we're settled, Jacobs takes off, heading north of the city.

"So you weren't kidding about having a driver."

"Not one bit. This is Colin Jacobs."

"It's nice to meet you, Colin."

He glances in the rearview mirror and gives her a tight smile. "Likewise, miss."

She looks back at me as a stray curl falls onto her face.

"What are we doing on this forbidden date? Fucking?"

"No, Hadley. We're headed up north to Belmont Harbor."

"A harbor? Are you going to try and make me swoon on the docks or drown me in the water?"

I move my hand to rest on her exposed thigh and shake my head. "No. I'll be swooning over you while you work on your sea legs."

"What!" She turns to face me, with terror marring her features.

"I have a yacht, and we'll be dining on it this evening."

"Holy crap. You seriously don't hold back, do you?"

"Not if I'm after something that I believe I want," I say firmly as we turn off of North Lake Shore Drive and into Belmont Harbor. Jacobs stops at the third dock from the end of the harbor, and I don't wait for him to get out of the car. I open the door and get out before offering my hand to Hadley.

"Wade, this is more like fifth-date material, not first. I mean . . . not that I've ever even made it to the second date before, but this is excessive."

"You agreed to one date. I need to take full advantage of it while I have the opportunity to do so."

"There we go again with your taking advantage of me. You're going to make me wet."

I stop and take her and her dirty mouth in. "I've never met a woman with balls of steel like you have."

"They're lady balls, Wade, but I don't mind thinking about your balls. Mmm, the way they would hit my clit while you take me from behind does something to my panties."

There it is.

Once I've gotten it down, my cock stirs again and hardens. This woman is determined to be fucked on every possible surface, and my body does not understand why I'm refusing her. *I do, though, because there's something in her eyes when she says* things like this that looks as if it's compulsory or part of a routine. She obviously craves sex, but who doesn't? Yet, I've never met a woman so blunt in her offers and approach before. I've had my fair share of women—more than I'm willing to admit—but none of them have been as mouthy as she is.

"Hadley, I won't be fucking you this evening. I'd like to get to know you." As much as it pains me to say this, I feel as if it's the right thing to do, to take it slower with her than I ever have with any woman before.

Her shoulders seem to relax, and though I would assume she'd put up a fight, her body tells me otherwise—that is until she opens that pretty little mouth of hers. "You have got to be kidding me."

"Listen closely, Whiskey and Rye." I pull her flush against me just as we step foot onto the dock and move one of my hands through her curls to the back of her neck, forcing her to look up at me while my other hand rests at the small of her back.

"I don't date women in Chicago. I don't date in general. I fuck, and when I fuck women, that's the last I see of them because I don't want a thing more from them. This, though . . ." I move my hand to gesture between us. ". . . There is something more than just sex hanging in the air between us, and I know that you can feel it as well. You might tell me that all you want from me is a good lay, but your body says otherwise."

Her lips part as she draws in a shallow breath. "I . . ."

"No. I will not allow this to be negotiated as if it's some sort of exchange for sex. This evening, you owe me your company during dinner and your thoughts. Not your body."

"I don't have a say, do I?"

The static hum between us grows louder as if it's waiting to shock one of us.

"You don't, but I'll oblige you for a second, considering your body won't take no for an answer," I say, and she looks down at her body. She's pressed herself against me entirely without even thinking about it. Her feet are nestled between mine, and her hands are resting against my chest.

When she looks up at me again, I shift my hand from the back of her neck to the side where I run my finger along her pale jaw. Her eyes move to mine slowly as I bring my lips toward hers. She's perfectly still under my touch, despite the urgency I sense within her, but I refuse to let her rush this.

Her body starts to tremble as I take in her very essence. I lower my lips to touch hers for the first time. The electric current that was in the air surrounding us passes through our lips as she kisses me back. Her lips part without my having to ask for permission and I take the opportunity to explore more of her. I dip my tongue inside of her mouth, and she doesn't stop me or force me to take more. I'm possessing her completely as our lips lock and our tongues travel together.

Her hands move off of my chest, and she brings both arms up to encircle my neck, pressing her chest to mine. With this one kiss, I can feel my world crack open as she leans into me . . . before we both break away from each other. She looks up into my eyes and captures her bottom lip between her teeth before one of her hands comes to touch her lips as if she's shocked by the intimacy of the kiss.

"Would you like for that to happen again?" I ask her as she tries to regulate her breathing.

"I think so."

"Good, now come." I pause as I take her hand in mine, speaking again before she can. "And do not turn that into anything sexual."

She looks stunned as she lets me intertwine my fingers with hers. She nods and walks quietly with me down the quay with yachts flanking us on either side. She remains quiet until we reach the end of the berth and we come to a stop in front of my yacht.

"You own this thing? It's enormous." She looks up and takes in its pure brilliance and majestic features. "When you said yacht . . . I thought you meant something like *row, row, row your boat*. Not this . . . vessel."

I chuckle and dig my hands into the pockets of my slacks, angling my head to the entrance. "Climb aboard. I do own her, along with two more on this quay."

She peers down at the gap between the gangway and the yacht before looking back at me. "You're not going to make me walk the plank or something, are you?"

"Not for a second." I step over the gap effortlessly and offer her my hand. "Come."

She opens her mouth to respond with a witty retort, but closes her lips when she sees the expression on my face, daring her to say more.

Wisely, she keeps silent as she takes my hand, and I help her across the gap, pulling her hard enough for her to crash into my chest. I automatically ring my arms around her as she begs me for my lips without a word.

I give them to her, pleasing her when I slide my tongue against hers before pulling away.

"Aren't you supposed to kiss me at the end of the date? Like in all of those other fairy-tale dates?"

"This is not a fairy tale, Hadley. This is real."

I watch as tension dissipates from her body, causing the features on her face to somehow become softer. In this silent moment, I take the opportunity to study those turquoise eyes of hers, which are swimming with something unnamed . . . what? It's some kind of emotion, but it's hidden in the depths of them. Fear, maybe. Possibly, but of what, I'm unsure.

I lead her up a flight of exterior steps to the second deck where the crew waits for us. "Hadley, this is our crew for the evening. If you need anything, please feel free to ask them."

"Thank you."

"Mr. Brass, the captain is ready to depart, and your table on the upper deck is prepared."

"Good," I say before taking Hadley's hand and leading her inside. She gasps when she sees the contemporary, yet warm and inviting design of the vessel. I chuckle at each of her reactions until I lead her up two more flights of stairs to the top deck.

"This is where we're dining?" she asks as she looks around at the burning tiki torches placed on the deck and the tropical fruit spread out on the table.

"It is unless you'd prefer to go elsewhere."

"This is . . . impeccable."

The yacht starts to move, and she grabs hold of my forearm as I'm pulling out the chair for her at our table for two.

"Sorry, I—"

I cut her off before she can finish her sentence. "You have nothing to apologize for."

She lets go of my arm once she takes a seat and her eyes scan the upper deck. There's something so sexy and vulnerable about her. I decide to make it my mission to find out what causes her reckless behavior and what put that fear behind her eyes.

I take a seat just as a cheese plate is brought out by a male waiter who then proceeds to ogle my date. I make a mental note to remove him from my crew. Regardless if this is the only date I'll get with her or if it's the start of possibly more, I won't let him desire something that is completely out of his reach. It's this thought that makes me realize that I've already marked her as my own in my head, but I believe that she's the furthest thing from being mine at this point in time.

I turn toward the waiter and wait patiently for him to remove his eyes from her long enough to look at me. When he does, he meets my glare and cowers underneath it. Bastard.

"Bring us two WhistlePig ryes, neat, when you return."

"Yes, sir."

"And one more thing. If you look at her once more this evening, I will have you removed from this vessel in the same second. Do you understand?"

His eyes stay planted on mine, but mine stray to Hadley whose cheeks are glowing with a soft pink blush before I look back up at him.

"Yes, sir," he says before disappearing back into the yacht's interior.

Hadley's eyes haven't left mine and she's sporting a winning smile. "Jealous much?"

"More than ever. I don't appreciate my staff enjoying a view that was made for me."

She reaches for the cheese knife and cuts off a piece of one of the blocks. "You're rather territorial and confident in yourself, Mr. Brass. I wouldn't like to work directly with you. I mean, Lawson was bad enough."

"You have worked beneath me, and I couldn't give a shit what authority Lawson thinks he holds because he does not have it. Enough about someone who sleeps with his staff. This evening is about you."

She blanches and I know at that moment that he's had his way with her. A flash of envy warms my body, catching me off-guard. I'm territorial over something that's not mine. My bitterness is an indication that she has gotten into my head in a few short days.

"I think that's a good idea. So what is it that you do exactly?"

"I'm an entrepreneur of sorts. I've built my company from the ground up with the help of one of my C-levels, who is also a silent partner in the company. I own a number of properties across the globe, all of which fall under Brass Global."

"Huh, well I suppose that makes sense considering the lap

of luxury that you live in."

"Does it bother you?"

"I'm not sure yet. I've been in the orbit of it before, but I'm not one to experience it on such a direct level. I suppose we'll have to wait and see."

"I'll take that as an implication that you wouldn't mind my taking you out again."

She glances away from me when the waiter appears with our tumblers. She takes hers and lifts it to her lush lips, taking a drink before placing it down in front of her. My eyes do not move from her mouth, and she knows it.

"That would depend on how the rest of the date goes."

"I'll take that over being let down. Now tell me . . ." I take a drink and watch her, unable to take my eyes off her beauty. "Why did you corrupt my phone with your outlandish nickname?"

A small laugh rises from her before she answers and fuck, I want to hear that sound again. I want to swallow it as I take her mouth with mine again. *Who the fuck is this woman?*

"Well, it's not all a nickname. My last name is Rye, so I figured it would work well with you."

"Rye, huh? I'll be damned."

She moves her hair to the side, but her curls move back into place a moment later. "Mmm-hmm, now you tell me something. Why did you break your rules for me?"

"It was a risk-or-regret situation. What would you have chosen?"

The grin she gives me is not one that I've seen before. She looks content at this moment as if no one has taken a risk on her before and for some reason that truly bothers me.

"If given the choice, I would have taken the risk."

"Precisely."

A few moments of silence pass between us as we both absorb the truth of our taking a risk on each other. I feel the yacht hit a larger wave that rocks the vessel harder than normal for this kind of weather. I lift my chin and look out into the darkness at Chicago's skyline in the distance.

"Come with me."

This time, she gets up and places her napkin on her seat without an argument. I'm surprised that I didn't have to ask her twice. I walk with her to the bow on the upper deck and stand next to her with one hand in my pocket and the other turning the whiskey tumbler between my fingers.

"Glance to your left. Chicago is showing off for you this evening."

She looks in the direction of the Chicago skyline, which is lit up in all of its grandeur. "Oh," she gasps and reaches for my pocketed hand. I slip it out and move my arm around her waist to pull her side against mine. She doesn't resist my advances, and she takes her own risk too, by resting her head against my bicep.

A clearing of a throat interrupts us. I glance over my shoulder, ready to maul the motherfucker who just ruined this for her.

"My apologies for the interruption, Mr. Brass. However, the storm that was forecast to hit the city in two hours has sped up tremendously, and we are right on the edge of it now. I would advise you to make your way to the vessel's interior immediately."

"Thank you," I say dismissively, and he leaves without another word.

Hadley's body stiffens in my hold. "Are we going to be okay? I mean, we're so far away from the city."

"We're farther out than I would like to be during a storm of this magnitude, but my captain is well trained and capable of handling her in the rougher waters."

She scrunches up her face at my words as the first few drops of water hit us. "Uhm, I think we better head inside if that's what he asked then."

"I agree."

I take her hand and walk her back to the table where I place my tumbler down and grab my suit jacket just as the skies open up above with a crack of thunder. Large chaotic drops hit us as the gusts of wind carry them around, extinguishing the torches with harsh hisses.

She squeals and steps closer to me, but we're soaked within seconds. Platinum blonde tendrils cling to her cheeks, and I couldn't give a fuck about the weather at the moment she looks up at me with want—or is it need—in her eyes? A need for me to keep her safe. I drop my jacket onto the deck and bring my hand up to her face to move the wet tendrils from her cheek. A shiver runs through her petite body when I cup her cheek. Her eyes are locked on mine as she leans up on her toes. I lower my mouth, a breath away from her red-stained lips.

"I'll keep you safe."

"I know," she says before she closes the distance between us and her lips touch mine.

I move my hand to the back of her head, twisting my fingers into her wet hair as she pushes her chest up to me and locks her arms around my neck, getting as close to me as possible.

Seven

Hadley

I THINK THERE is a flaw in my genetic code. How did I go from wanting to jump this man's bones to wanting him to just touch me to calm my soul?

I'm surrounded by his warm arms while he kisses the life out of me in the middle of this downpour. His tongue is massaging mine as one of his hands moves down from my shoulder to the small of my back, applying pressure to secure me to his body. I break away to remind myself to breathe before I pass out from the lack of oxygen.

Rain falls steadily down on us; the drops are starting to hit with a heavier sting as the few intimate seconds of watching each other tick by. A drop falls on my bottom lip, and I lick it off with my tongue just as his lips crash against mine again. His tongue prods at the seam of my mouth, begging me for entrance. When I finally give it to him, he takes full advantage. His hand moves out of my hair and down my back to my ass. I expect him to cop a feel, but instead, he lifts me with both of his arms.

"Wrap your legs around me," he says as he breaks away from the kiss for a split second.

I've never been more thankful for the slits in my maxi-skirt than I am now as I do what he asks. When he's comfortable with holding onto me, he starts to make his way across the deck just as a bolt of lightning lights up the skies.

Holy shit, this storm is going to be intense, and we're stuck out here, somewhere on Lake Michigan.

He's made it halfway across the deck when he stops and removes his lips from mine. "Focus on me, Rye."

How did he know I was starting to panic? Some male testosterone instinct?

"Okay, Whiskey."

His soft, yet firm lips find mine again, and I lose myself to his touch and osculation of his tongue once more. I've never been kissed like this before. As if I actually mean something more than just a place to get a dick wet. If I had to guess, I'd say that he's savoring this moment just as much as I am.

I exhale contently against his lips as he pushes a door open. The raindrops suddenly stop hitting my overly sensitized skin. Instead of the water, a brush of cold air circles my body and I start to quiver in his arms. He walks down a flight of stairs without putting me down as he speaks against my lips. "You're cold."

"A little," I say with a smile. My teeth start to chatter, and he kisses me once more as he walks down a hallway that I haven't seen before. He sets me down on my feet when he comes to a stop outside of a stateroom door.

I use this opportunity to take in the sight of him. His white button-down is plastered against his chest, showing off his rather impressive body. A moan unintentionally escapes my lips as he swings the double doors open.

"Like what you see?" he asks without a hint of cockiness in his voice. He's genuinely curious about my opinion of his physique.

I purse my lips. "Yes."

The smile that I receive in reaction would soak my panties if they weren't already wet.

"I'm glad. Come in and let's get you warmed up," he says as he leads me through the doors. "This is the master, and it's where

I stay when I take an overnight trip," he says as he disappears through another door. I glance around the room that's encased in dark wood walls, varnished to a high gloss. There is a row of windows that wrap around the room in a half circle, which are now covered with storm shutters. His bed sits against the only flat wall next to the double doors we came through, and there's a seating area on the other side of the room. It's such a warm and inviting space. I'm surprised it's not decorated in all whites with straight lines and an overuse of odd shaped objects . . . it's just . . . normal. Pricey and elegant, yet normal. He comes back into the large bedroom with a pair of sweatpants and a shirt.

"You can wear these since your clothes are soaked through, but I think that you should take a shower to warm up first. I would hate to be the reason you catch a cold or possibly something worse."

He sets the clothes on his bed before walking through another door. I slip my shoes off in his bedroom before following behind him. When I get to the bathroom, he's already removed his shirt, and I stare at his bare muscular back that, to my surprise, is covered with an intricate black and gray tattoo. When he reaches into the shower to turn it on, I use the brief movement to study it; the tattoo hugs his shoulders and moves down across his back as if it's going to disappear underneath the hem of his boxers, but it stops right at it. The tattoo is of a detailed forest. I've not seen so much detail in a single tattoo before: it's stunning. It's dark, wild, and sexy as hell. I'm transfixed watching his muscles move underneath his marked skin when he turns around and freezes, bringing my attention back to him instead of his body. His eyes pause at my breasts, and I glance down, wondering what the hell has caught his attention as much as his tattoo caught mine.

My nipples are hard from the cold, but they harden even further from his gaze. My lacy white crop top has left absolutely nothing to the imagination since I didn't bother with a bra today.

"Jesus," he says under his breath before breathing hard through his nose.

I close the distance between us and press my chest against his before I lift up on my toes to kiss him again. His lips are addictive, and if it's all that he's willing to give me tonight, then I'll take it.

His arms weave around my waist again as his lips work against mine before I feel his smile against mine. I slowly open my eyes and gaze up at him as if I'm in his trance.

"I broke my rules for you, Hadley. Please, don't make me do it again."

"Breaking them worked in your favor, though, didn't it?" I try to make a point, which I doubt he'll go for.

"You're right, it did, but if I fuck you right now, then you won't come back to me."

I pause because he's got me pinned. He's exactly right, regardless of what I try to convince myself of—so much so that I'm at a loss for words. He takes my silence as my acknowledgment of his statement because he lets go of me and presses his lips to the top of my head before walking out of the bathroom and shutting the door behind him.

Twenty minutes later, I emerge from the bathroom. We've hit some rough water, and I'm feeling rather queasy. Wade knocks on the door before cracking it open and allowing himself in. He takes in the view of me in his clothing before frowning, "You're too pale. Are you okay?"

I shrug as I finish rolling his sweatpants around my waist to ensure that they don't fall off and take a seat on the cream-colored couch. "Not entirely. I'm feeling ill."

He quickly strides over to me, and it's now that I notice that he's showered and dressed in dry clothing. "Is it from the rough water?"

I nod. "I think so."

"I'm sorry," he says as he walks back to the double doors where he turns the lights off in the bedroom so we're nestled in pure darkness. I jump when I feel the couch dip next to me, not expecting him to join me.

"It's me. Try and relax, okay?"

"I'm trying," I say weakly as he pulls me onto his lap. I rest my head against his hard chest and take in a deep breath. His cologne, body wash, and his natural scent fill my lungs before I breathe out in a loud exhale.

"You smell good."

Did I just say that out loud?

He chuckles as he adjusts me on his lap, getting comfortable in the dark. "You smell like me. I'm not sure if I like it or not. I prefer your floral and fruity fragrance rather than my cologne on you."

"Mmm," is all I manage to say. If I speak again, I'll be sick, and that is the very last thing I want him to see. He runs his fingers through the wet tendrils of my hair as I shut my eyes, hoping for some relief from this storm. I can hear the wind whipping around the mass of the yacht, and I think that it's only making things worse. Silence looms over us for a few minutes before he speaks again.

"We're on our way back, and I don't think that we're too far out. Just close your eyes and think about something else."

I nod and nuzzle into his chest, breathing him in again before smiling to myself. He's actually making me feel a little odd tonight. I'm not someone who can easily set aside my past. Instead, I find it easy to hide from, but tonight I feel as if he has woken me up for the first time in my life . . . as if his kiss has somehow stolen the breath from my broken soul and breathed in something new and exciting . . . something so appealing that it may coax me out of my hiding spot.

"Tell me what you like to do in your free time, Rye."

I think for a minute because really there's not much to me other than sex, yoga, and whiskey. Oh, and romance novels—*ah, the irony.*

"I'm, uhm, usually busy doing yoga or reading."

"Or fucking?"

How does he read me so well? I'm not a goddamn open book. It's almost terrifying.

"Yes. Mostly that."

"Why, if you don't mind my asking?"

I shrug and stay quiet. I've just met this man. I can't tell him that I use it to keep myself alive and the nightmares of my past at bay. No one but Lola knows those details about me. I swore at an early age that I would keep my struggles to myself because in general people don't fucking care. I won't be able to speak of my insecurities to anyone until I heal the wounds of my past, but for that to happen, I have to bleed out and again experience the pain that's holding me back.

It's something that I've thought about hundreds of times, but I cannot bring myself to experience such things again. Never again. We are all addicted to someone or something that can numb the pain and sex is it for me. The control that sex has over me consumes every inch of me: my heart, soul, mind, and body. Particularly my body. When I don't get my fill, I'm immersed in a frantic nightmare of fear and a barrage of memories devours me.

"I'll take your silence as a refusal to answer."

The yacht rocks back and forth, and he tilts my chin up. "That motion is the yacht docking. Let me get you onto solid ground."

"Please," I say as I'm about to shift off of his lap, but he stands effortlessly with me in his arms. He takes the stairs down, where he places me on my feet, and a crewmember meets us on the dock, handing Wade an umbrella as the storm rages down on us again.

"Thank you," he says as we walk back down the dock to the waiting BMW. He opens the door and ushers me in. I slide over and rest my head back against the headrest, closing my eyes as I will the seasickness to fade.

I don't remember the majority of the ride back to Lola's apartment, but I remember bolting out of his car the second it came to a stop and up to the apartment before I got sick in front of him. I don't think that I even said goodbye to him. God, I'm horrible at this dating shit.

When I wake up, I'm lying under the cool sheets of my bed in the pitch dark. I no longer feel like the bed is rocking back and forth, and my skin isn't clammy anymore. I sit up and reach for my phone on the nightstand, seeing a text from Wade waiting for me: I APOLOGIZE FOR GETTING YOU SICK. PLEASE LET ME KNOW IF YOU NEED ANYTHING. I'LL SEND WHATEVER IT IS RIGHT OVER. I ENJOYED THIS EVENING, HADLEY.

A genuine smile forms on my face as I reply to him: I'M OKAY. I'M SORRY FOR RUNNING OUT ON YOU EARLIER. THANK YOU FOR TAKING ME ON MY FIRST DATE, WHISKEY.

I look at the time and frown to myself when I see that it's after four in the morning. Maybe it's a good thing, though, because I want him to reply to me more than anything, and that's simply not healthy.

I lie in the shadows, willing myself to fall asleep again to stop the thought of his lips on mine when there's a knock on my bedroom door. It cracks open before I have a chance to answer and a tall, lean man walks in. Holden.

"Hads? Are you awake?"

"I am now."

"I didn't mean to wake you up, I just wanted to check on you. How are you feeling? Lola texted me and told me that you were sick."

I sit up and run a hand through my curls. "Hey stud. I'm okay now. Just a little weak from being sick so much."

He sits next to me on the bed and runs his fingers down my cheek. "What the hell happened tonight?"

"I was on a yacht when that storm came through."

"A yacht? One of the sightseeing ones? Or were you with that guy I saw you leave with?"

I look at him and decide to go with honesty. "I don't know when you saw me, but I was out with someone, yes."

"Mmm. I'm glad you got sick of him," he says with a cocky smile.

"Don't be an ass, Hold." I roll my eyes and rest my head back on the pillow.

"I'm not, but I rather enjoy sneaking over here in the middle of the night, and I'm not ready for that to change. You feel too damn good on me."

I giggle and move onto his lap. He feels entirely different from Wade, and for some reason, when he wraps his arms around me I wish that it was Wade's arms instead of his tattooed ones. *What is going on in my head?*

"You're absurd, you know that?"

"Or maybe you're just too enticing," he says as he trails kisses down my neck. I lean back, giving him easier access as his hand moves to the apex of my thighs.

"Let me eat this beautiful pussy and show you what you were missing while you were out with another man."

My eyes go wide as I watch him move me back to the bed, and he settles between my legs. It's now that I realize that I'm still in Wade's clothing.

Betrayal.

The word courses through my body as if it's the purest form of sins, but I'm not *with* Wade. Then why does this feel so . . . wrong?

"Don't deny me this pussy, Hads."

I purse my lips when my phone starts to ring. I look down at Holden and then at my phone on the pillow next to me with Gentleman Jack flashing on the screen.

Damn it!

I reach for my phone, unable to let it go to voicemail because I'm selfish and I want to hear his voice. With a swipe of my finger, I answer. "Hi, Whiskey."

Holden raises his eyebrows at me and frowns but doesn't stop trying to get Wade's sweatpants off of me.

"How are you doing, Rye?" His voice is rougher with sleep, and my body reacts to the sound of it. The seduction in his voice kisses my skin with goose bumps, masking any fear I had of him moments ago.

"I'm holding up." *Pun intended.*

"Did you want me to bring you something to eat? There's an excellent French bakery around the corner, and it's open around the clock."

Maybe Gentleman Jack is the perfect contact name for him after all. Anticipation and hope surround me at the thought of seeing him again tonight. I squirm on the bed, thinking of this incomprehensible emotion he instills in me.

"That's incredibly sweet of you, but I wouldn't want you to go out of your way. Hey, what are you doing up anyway?"

Holden gets my sweats off, and I watch his eyes light up when he sees that I don't have any underwear on. I realize that he has mistaken my excitement over Wade's phone call as excitement for his tongue on my pink flesh. His mouth finds my sex a moment later, and he starts to caress my clitoris.

"I had just fallen asleep when you texted me back. I couldn't get my eyes to open enough to read your message, so I figured that I'd call you instead. And I don't mind going to the bakery, Rye."

I wonder if his eyes are still shut while he speaks; the simple thought makes me smile. When did I become so enamored with this man?

My body responds to Holden's tongue when I go to reply. "Ahhh . . . I . . ."

"Hadley?" he asks as I try to quiet my moans. Holden sure as hell knows how to make a woman writhe underneath his lips, and as much as I usually enjoy it, I just want to push him off of me right now. One side of my brain argues back with the logical side, telling me it's exactly what I've wanted all evening—what Wade refuses to give me.

"I'm here, sorry."

"I'm going to walk over and pick up something for you to eat before I come over. What is your apartment number?"

"No," I say in a moan, and he doesn't reply for a bit too long. I know that my breathing has changed as I try and fight off my orgasm . . . I sigh as my pending climax makes itself very well known to each extremity of my body.

"Rye. You're with someone." It's not a question, but a statement.

"What?" I moan out, and I know that he knows what's currently taking place in my bedroom.

Shit.

"The next time I call, and you're about to come, don't answer the phone. The only time I want to hear you come is when it's because of me. Goodbye, Hadley."

"Wade, please. Wait . . . I . . ." My orgasm rips through me when I can no longer fight it off for another second.

"At least, you yelled my name out while you came."

"Wade . . ."

"Goodbye, Rye."

He hangs up, and I feel like my heart just hit the lowest place in my empty stomach, making me ache in pain instead of melting into the pleasure that Holden just bestowed upon me. I tell myself to ignore the guilty feeling because I don't owe either of these men a single damn thing, but that doesn't help ease the guilt about Wade.

"You always taste so good and having some asshole on the phone made me want to get you off sooner. Did you enjoy that?"

Did I?

Physically, yes. Mentally . . . no. Not one bit.

I plaster on my sham of a mask and smile up at him. "I did, but I think I need some rest."

"I don't doubt that. I'll see you later, babe." Holden leans in and kisses me sweetly, but it's not the lips that I want against mine. My body yearns for Wade's lips instead.

If I close my eyes, I can feel his lips on mine, and it sends me into a sensual state of intoxication. I imagine our breath mingling as he locks his lips on mine. I push the thoughts aside for a moment before my body reacts.

Holden leaves and I sit up, hugging my pillow to my chest. Why do I feel nauseous again all of a sudden? The ache in my chest pisses me off, but I can't seem to put a stop to it. I can't decide whether I want to smack Wade for making me face my emotions or kiss him senseless. I know that what I do isn't healthy for me, but it gets me through the day and calms my demons. Until now. Now, they are dancing around a goddamn fire pit, chanting Wade's name.

Guilt washes over me in waves. A sinking feeling overcomes me, and I'm horrified that Wade won't want to see me again. I grab my phone and dial his number without even thinking about it, feeling as if I need to fix this. The phone stops ringing, and I glance at the screen, waiting for him to say something.

"Wade?"

"Hadley."

I let out a breath, thankful that he at least answered my call. "I'm sorry."

"You're not, but what can I expect after denying you?"

"I didn't do it to spite you, Wade. It's just something that I need."

"You do not need to explain anything to me. Why are you calling? Is he still there? Is he fucking you right now?"

I'm unsure if his voice is masked in anger or disgust, but it hits me in the gut like a wrecking ball. "No. I asked him to leave."

He goes quiet for a moment, causing my heart to sink even further into the dry, empty pit of my stomach. That heavy weight that I swore to myself that I would never wear seems to be blanketing my most protected organ.

"Will you take me to that bakery?"

"You're sick, Hadley, and I'd rather not see you after another man has made you glow."

"Please?"

"No. You were right to get your sexual needs met by someone else because I won't take advantage of whatever it is that you are hiding from. It's glaringly apparent to me that you are using sex as a coping mechanism, but when I take you, it won't be to merely satisfy a physical need. It will be because you won't be able to stay away from me, and you'll beg me for the physical connection, to experience more of what the static is between us. Fuck whomever you want. I'm the one that will make you swoon."

"I'm not someone who is interested in more than sex, Wade."

"You are. I saw it this evening when the storm hit. I'll fight to get to know you because I know that there is more to the current that surrounds us than the physical act of sex."

The line grows quiet when I don't respond to him. How has he essentially figured me out in one evening? He doesn't feel like a stranger anymore either. It's as if I've known this man for years.

"Sleep well, Rye."

"Goodbye," I say because I'm dumbfounded. I don't understand how I made it so easy for him to see right through me.

Do I loathe the thought of love? No.

Do I loathe the thought of my being in love? Without question.

I know that I'm frightened to let anyone in and that it's hindered me in more ways than one in my life, but it's shaped who I am. I'm content with my life. Why would I shed light on my hiding place when there is no need to? I know that once I show my cards, there will be no going back to my dark and safe, albeit claustrophobic, hiding spot.

It's what he wants, though. Why do I want to be with him when he's forcing me out of my safe zone?

Eight

Wade

NOT ONLY AM I competing with an addiction to rid Hadley of some sort of history, but now there is also another man—if not multiple men—involved. How do I allow myself to go after a woman who is going to let me lure her in, but then use that energy on another man in the same night? Is it something that I will be able to handle time and time again? I don't know the answer to that.

Is she worth it, though? Without a doubt.

I hardly know the woman, but I'm drawn to her like a madman. This attraction bullshit is going to ruin me, and I'm going to dive willingly into the rough sea to try and save her from herself. To save her for me.

It's been a solid week since I've seen her and I can still taste her lips on mine. I know that she's been into Blended three times since our date because I've asked Isla to inform me of when she's there. Aside from the phone call we had when some asshole had just left her room, I have not spoken to her.

If I want her as much as I believe that I do, then I need to man the fuck up and find out what is holding her back. Yes, it was just one date, but I'm willing to make an effort and figure out if there is more behind her mask.

I've left my office early—yet another rule I've broken for her—to head into Blended. Isla just called the office to let me know that Hadley is there on her own. Isla has been the manager of Blended since before we opened the doors to it, and she's been a friend of mine since college. She's someone I have learned to trust in this world of scheming and lying assholes.

I walk in through the front door and scan my preferred spot for a gorgeous and damaged platinum blonde. When I see her, my entire body reacts and fights itself at once. I want to run to her and sweep her into my arms before kissing the life out of her while the other half of me wants to retreat. She's sitting in a nook at the back of the venue with her knees drawn up and a book resting against her thighs. She's lost in the words, and I can see the sentiment roll over her face; it's the only time she allows the slightest bit of her emotion to show, and I do not think that she realizes it.

Isla greets me as I walk behind the bar and stretch my arms up to grab a bottle of Dalmore 62 Single Highland Malt Scotch Matheson. It's the only 62 of the Dalmore that I own, but I'm not concerned.

"So are you going to tell me why you have a thing up your ass for this woman? She kind of reminds me of a twenty-five-cent whore, regardless of how put-together she appears to be."

I glance at her once I've gotten the bottle and exhale. "I would tell you if I knew the answer to that, but Isla?"

"Mmm-hmm?"

"Don't judge the book by its cover."

"Waylon," she says, using my first name, "I've known you for years, and I've never seen you pay this much attention to a woman before. I mean, I've never met her before seeing her in here. Why her?"

I shake my head, trying to rattle an answer free, but nothing comes willingly. "I don't know, but I can't stay away."

"I have a bad feeling about this."

"As do I, but it's like running into a hurricane. The rare

beauty of it captivates me, and I can't stop myself from going to it."

"You're so screwed, you ass."

"We'll see about that, won't we?"

"Two hundred bucks says that it lasts less than a week before she jumps another man's dick. You should see how many men approach her in here, and I swear that she's given out her phone number more times than not."

I look over at Hadley and fish out my wallet from my pocket. I take out two crisp one-hundred-dollar bills and set them on the bar counter in front of Isla. "Then it looks like you've already won."

A puzzled look crosses her face. "What? She's already fucked someone else, and you've just started to try and win her over?"

"I don't know the details, but I know she's been with another man since I took her on the date."

She pockets the two bills and shrugs. "I'll need to make another wager against her then if it's going to be that easy."

"Easy is not what this is going to be. Behave yourself around her."

"Whatever you say, brass balls."

"And fuck off with that nickname."

She gives me the finger before handing me two tumblers. I walk across the venue, past a few members who greet me, until I'm standing in front of her.

"Rye."

Her head pops up, and a radiant smile graces her face. "Hi."

"Is anyone sitting here?" I nod toward the empty section of the nook's bench.

"Yes. You are," she says as I hand her an empty tumbler. She puts her book aside and sits up before taking the other tumbler. I pour the amber liquid into each glass and set the bottle aside before taking the seat beside her.

"It's Dalmore 62. Let me know what you think. I haven't had this one before."

She nods and breathes in the limited vintage. She sighs before taking a sip and closing her eyes. "This is incredible. You didn't have to share this with me. Thank you."

"You're most welcome. What are you reading today?" I take a drink and savor it.

"It's just another romance novel. I know, you don't have to say it."

"Say what?"

"That it's senseless that I read romance novels when I don't believe in the notion."

"As much as it shouldn't make sense, I believe that it does. I think that you'd be capable of more than sex if you allowed yourself to feel more than just a heady orgasm."

"You wouldn't understand," she says as she twirls the tumbler, watching the liquid inside of it swirl around and around.

"Try me."

"Can we please not do this now? I feel like I've just been put in an interrogation room with a stranger."

"We'll do it when you're ready then."

"I thought that you wanted nothing to do with me after what I did."

"You were wrong. I've been consumed with Brass Global, and I haven't had much free time for anything other than sleeping." That's one hell of a lie. I wasn't sure what my final decision was until I walked into the library and saw her again.

Her face lights up at my untruthful confession, and she leans against my body, "So what's next?"

"I need to know where we stand before we can move anywhere. I've told you that I won't be fucking you until you're ready. Will you be sleeping with another man or men in the meantime?"

"Would that end whatever this is?" She gestures between us with her hand, and as much as it kills me, I give her my answer.

"No, because I understand that you think that you need it more than you need the air in your lungs, but I won't push myself further than I am able to."

"I think you just earned yourself another date."

"I have?"

"Mmm-hmm," she says as she leans into me, angling her chin up as I angle mine down to press my lips against hers, tasting the Dalmore on her tongue.

"I have one rule," I say against her soft red lips.

"What is it?"

"That you won't fuck another man when I know about it."

"I swear it," she says as she stands up and moves between my legs, wrapping her arms around my neck.

I ring my arms around her waist as she nips my bottom lip before taking what she needs from me at this moment, what I'll allow her to take.

Our lips are locked together as I graze the visible skin between her shirt and her jeans with my fingertips. What the hell have I just agreed to with this woman? She pulls away and fishes her phone out of her pocket when it goes off. I use her distraction to look up at Isla.

She's watching. She's always been overly concerned about the women who come into my life. In the last few years she's been a record on repeat telling me that I need to find someone here in Chicago, but by the look on her face now, I know that she meant anyone but the woman standing between my legs.

A shake of her head verifies my thoughts. I give her the

finger, and she laughs across the room. She knows that she will get to say *I told you so* sooner or later. I do not doubt it. Not when it comes to Hadley Rye.

Nine

Hadley

I'VE BEEN BACK at the apartment for over an hour after sharing a drink with Wade. I'm sitting cross-legged on the couch with the television on, but my thoughts are pre-occupied with him and his reaction to who I am. He didn't fight it when I said I needed what he wouldn't give me. He didn't even flinch when I said that there would be other men.

But will there be?

I mean, Holden is handsome, and he knows how to fuck, but is it worth using him for sex when he might want more from me as well? I don't know the answer to that. I might need to put him on hiatus for a while, at least until I figure out what I want with Wade, but I sure as hell won't be telling Wade that. He doesn't need to know that he's already gotten to me in a way no man has before. Not even Lawson.

I hear the front door open, and Lola walks into the living room a few seconds later. "Hey doll," I say as I set my whiskey down on the coffee table.

Whiskey. Shit. I can't even drink my favorite liquor without thinking about him. Where is all of this coming from? I've never let my guard down to anyone and here I am inviting this gorgeous stranger into my life.

"Had-Lo," she shrieks as she sets her purse down and kicks off her heels before falling back onto the couch next to me in dramatic flair.

"Did you have a rough day?"

"Nope, I just wanted to be theatrical." She laughs and pokes me in the side. "Did you hear from the company that you had that phone interview with?"

"Yes! I got the position, and I'm so relieved."

I had the interview this morning before I went to Blended in the afternoon. They offered me the position on the spot, and I'm thrilled. With a new job under my belt and the possibility of Wade, I feel giddy and lightheaded.

"And what exactly will you be doing?"

"You have to swear that you won't judge me because of this, okay?"

"Scout's honor." She holds up her middle finger toward me and I crack up.

"I'm serious, Lo," I say with a laugh.

"Blow me."

"I mean . . . not that I need the practice, but I'll need to figure out how to make it believable over the phone."

"Uh, what?" she readjusts herself on the couch so her legs are tucked underneath her and she's facing toward me.

"You're looking at Low-Sound's new phone-sex operator."

"Shut the fuck up." She waits for me to play my imaginary drumset on my joke, "Are you kidding me?"

"Nope. It's something that I love to do, and I'll be getting paid."

"You're going to feel like a paid whore, Hadley."

"I might like it," I shoot back at her and she shakes her head, apparently disapproving.

"Fine. I won't argue with your happiness, but I will make the first phone call once you're all set up. I need my girl-on-girl fantasy met before I die."

"As if." I toss a throw pillow at her, and we both keel over in laughter.

"You love me, Hads. Don't deny that you wouldn't give it a go."

"With you? Nope. There's not enough money in the world, but I have with another woman, and I have to say . . . I prefer the dick."

She gasps and speaks through her fingers that are now covering her mouth. "I could so live vicariously through you for the remainder of my life."

"I don't think that it would be too exciting," I say honestly.

"Are you kidding me? You were out with some guy, and then you came home . . . then literally came when Holden showed up."

"You know about that?"

"Duh. Who the hell do you think let the stinker into the apartment?"

"Fuck you," I say with a smile so she knows that I'm not entirely serious.

"I love you too." She giggles and sits up. "But seriously, you need to tell me about the man that you went out with."

I groan and sink into the couch, wishing that it would swallow me whole. "What about him?"

I dare a glance at her, and she's glaring at me with her amber eyes. "Seriously? Do I need to drag all of the information out of you?"

"I honestly don't know what to offer up, Lo. He's just, I don't know, different. Demanding. Serious. Attractive as all hell."

"It sounds like my little Hadley has a crush." She claps excitedly.

"A crush? What are we? Thirteen?"

"Oh my God, you do like him, you bitch."

I turn away from her and glance out of the windows. Like him? As in more than sex? As in . . . I like him even though we haven't fucked? This cannot be happening. I'm about to willingly step over the edge of the rabbit hole and plummet to my heart's death. Queen of hearts, my ass.

"Earth to Hadley," she says as she leans over and waves her hand in front of my face just as my phone goes off with a text message from Gentlemen Jack. She snags it from my lap and holds it up, reading his words out loud: "I NEED TO SEE YOU TO-NIGHT, RYE."

"Holy demanding, Hads. What does he look like? Do you have a picture of him? What's his name?"

"Holy shit, Lo. Have you heard of privacy?" I grab my phone back, and my heart does this tiny offbeat ache when I see his words scrolled across my screen. I quickly type back a message to him before I answer any of Lo's grilling questions: WHY, WHISKEY, ARE YOU THAT NEEDY OR DO YOU JUST MISS ME ALREADY?

His reply is almost instant as if he was waiting for me: YOU'RE NOT MINE TO MISS.

I grimace when I read over it. Why does that leave me wounded? I exhale, resigned, and type out my response: LET ME KNOW WHEN AND WHERE. I'LL SEE YOU LATER.

He doesn't respond right away, and I set my phone down in my lap again.

"Well . . . ?" Lo asks.

"Fine, but I'm only giving up what I want to and nothing more."

"I'm not asking for your anal virginity. I'm asking about a man who has you intrigued."

I roll my eyes at her. "His name is Waylon Brass, but he goes by Wade on a personal level."

I swear that her jaw drops open like she's about to swallow a girthy cock. "Excuse me?" she squeaks.

"Uhm, Wade. That's his name and no, I don't have any pictures of him."

"My God, you're a lucky bitch. Are you serious? Do you know who he is?"

"What?"

"He's only Chicago's most eligible bachelor. All of the women would give their ovaries over to have him in bed with them. He's the owner of Brass Global. The man won't date anyone, though . . . until now," she says as she raises a perfectly shaped brow at me.

"We're not dating, Lola."

She scoffs. "Yes. Yes, you are, and don't you dare deny it. He could be good for you." She grabs my phone and types in *Waylon Brass* into Google Images. In a second the screen is bursting with images of him. I take my phone back and click on the first picture. He's wearing a navy suit with a white button-down and no tie. The collar of his shirt is undone, and my heart palpitates.

"That man is dapper as fuck," she states matter-of-factly.

This man is unquestionably gorgeous. There's no doubt about it, and my attraction to him is obviously not something I can hide, considering I'm almost hyperventilating at his picture, just thinking about his lips.

"You're blushing," Lo yelps and throws her arms around my neck in a hug.

"I am not." I touch my cheeks, and they are warmer than normal. *Damn it.*

"Hads, you really like him."

"I don't know anything about him, Lola. How can I like him?"

"An instant attraction, that's how. You may not want to give up your whorish ways, but no one comes into our lives by accident, and we seem to attract what we're ready for, what we want."

"I mean, I know I'm physically attracted to him, but that might be it."

"Nope. I believe that there's more. Why don't you give him a chance?"

I lean away from her suffocating hug and shake my head. "I have, and I am, but I feel as if he's seen inside my soul with just a glance at me—it's as if he can see straight through me."

"And? I don't see the problem with that."

I pull up my knees and hug them, resting my head on top as I look over at her. "Me either. That's the issue."

My phone vibrates, and I swear my heart physically slams against my chest. I pick it up and swipe my finger across the screen: I COULDN'T WAIT. WHAT'S YOUR APARTMENT NUMBER?

"Holy shit."

"What happened?" Lola asks as all of the color drains from my face.

"He's here."

"What? Here? Like in the building here?"

"Mmm-hmm. He wants to come up."

"Well, what are you waiting for? I'll just say hi and vanish. I just want to see him in person. I never have before, and I've heard that his pictures don't do him any justice."

"You're ridiculous."

I send a short reply to him: 1324. I don't want him to know just how much his wanting to be with me has affected me. I mean, I just saw him some two hours ago, and I'm desperate to see him again.

I watch as Lo jumps up and runs over to her purse, pulling out her lipstick and applying it at the hallway mirror before fluffing her hair out.

Uh, hello? He's mine.

Mine?

Before I'm able to finish the thought, there's a knock on the door, and Lola rushes into the foyer to answer it. I sit completely still, straining to hear their conversation.

"'Evening, and my apologies. I must have the wrong apartment," he says darkly. I swear I hear the slightest bit of annoyance in his voice as if I've lied to him about what apartment I'm in.

"It's Waylon Brass, right?"

There's a short pause before he answers. "It is, but I think I have the wrong place. My apologies."

I get up and walk faster than necessary to the foyer before my mind can stop me. My body pulls me toward him of its own accord, and for right now, I'm not going to fight it. I don't want him to leave. I don't want him to think that I lied to him just because Lo answered the damn door.

"Wade?" I say as I walk up next to Lo just as he's turning away from the front door.

He halts and turns back to the foyer entrance. An entirely different emotion from the one he was wearing two seconds ago passes over his face when he sees me. He beams at me and holds out his hand, asking me to go to him without a word.

Once again, I don't think about it. My body simply reacts to him as I place my hand in his, and he pulls me to his body, flush against his chest.

"I thought that you gave me the slip."

I shake my head and glance over at Lo, who is standing there waiting for a cock in her mouth again. "No, this is my roommate, Lola. Lola, this is Wade."

He reaches one of his hands out, but leaves the other at the small of my back, holding me to him.

"It's nice to meet you, Lola."

"You too. Why don't you both come in? I was just about to leave."

He looks into my eyes as if he's asking me if I want him in my place. I nod and step out of his grip before walking back into the apartment with him on my heels.

"Wait," Lo says, "how did you get past the doorman?"

I turn to look at him and he's got a knowing smirk on his face. "I own the building."

Of course he does.

She nods and shuts the door. "Well, that I didn't know. Let me just grab my things and I'll be going. Hads, I'll be down the hall with Owen and Holden. Text me if you need anything, okay?" she says as the three of us walk into the living room, and she picks up her purse.

"Will do, thanks," I reply while looking up at Wade. I'm dying to feel his lips against mine again. He looks down at me from Lo, and takes in a deep breath. As if he's just found something prized.

Lola clears her throat, sings out, "Bye," and she's gone, the front door closing softly behind her.

My eyes still haven't left his as his hand comes up and moves a fallen curl from my bun behind my ear. I freeze before glancing down at my attire.

My blonde curls are up in the messiest of buns, I'm in my Whiskey & Yoga T-shirt, his sweatpants from our date, and heather gray socks. I scrubbed my makeup off once I got back to the apartment in order to apply a facial mask, which, thank God, I took off before Lo arrived at home. I'm the definition of chaos, yet he's looking at me like the way he is, making me feel beautiful and wanted.

"Hi," I say softly.

His arms tighten around me as he leans down and takes my lips with his. His kiss is pure, raw, and it physically connects us more than any sexual act has with the dozens of men before him.

He riles up my insides and my stomach burns with the sudden onslaught of fireworks. I can feel the static rise up my spine, electrifying my entire body as our lips move slowly together. His tongue slides against mine in this deep, slow kiss. An involuntary moan escapes me, and I couldn't care less. He makes it difficult to think or remember to breathe.

He renders me defenseless.

One of his hands moves up my tingling spine to the back of my head, holding me to his lips as if he thinks that I'm going to make a run for it, but I don't think that I would be able to leave these lips of his.

His grin breaks our lips apart and possibly cracks the safeguard around my heart.

"That was a greeting that I could get used to," he says as he looks down at me.

"I know," I reply without thinking. I bite my lip at my slip-up and push my body against his, feeling his apparent need for me hit my lower belly.

"I needed to see you."

"So you said. Why did you come here, though?"

"I just got back from the office, and I couldn't stay away. That's all I'm willing to give up."

"So you did miss me," I say with a sly smile and kiss his cheek before taking his hand and leading him to the couch.

We both get seated before he pulls me against his side. "Possibly, but as I said earlier . . . I can't miss something that's not mine."

"But you did," I say as I look up at his features. His bone structure is perfectly symmetrical. His dark hair is tousled with finesse, and his arched brows are just as dark as his lashes. My eyes move to his angular jaw and really, his looks should be illegal. The softness in his eyes does something to me at the apex of my thighs when I notice that he's inspecting me as I am him.

"I did," he murmurs before adding, "you look gorgeous like this. Just you."

Suddenly I feel self-conscious and frown. "If I'd had more time, I would have at least put on mascara and lip-gloss."

"No, this is my favorite look on you, Hadley . . . or Hads . . . as your roommate called you."

My cheeks burn from him calling me Hads; not many people have, and he just broke the mold on every man for me. I know in my heart of hearts that I won't recover from him because he's going to break me without my knowing it. He wants it. I can see how thirsty he is to have the truth. The queen of hearts may have just doused my heart with red—he's going to make me bleed out.

"You can call me that."

"And you can keep my sweatpants. They look a hell of a lot better on you than they ever did on me."

My smile falls when he reminds me that I'm wearing his clothing.

His chuckle rumbles through his chest. "I think you missed me as well."

"I . . ." Did I? Was this an unconscious way in which I was telling myself that I wanted to be with him? How odd.

He decides to let it slide. "Was I interrupting anything?"

"Hmm? Oh, no. I was just going to lounge around tonight. If you decided to show up twenty minutes earlier, you would have seen me covered in a facial mask. A green one at that, and you would think I was hideous."

He laughs again and adjusts me so that I'm straddling his lap. I automatically grind my hips into his, feeling his need for me rub against the thickness of his pants.

He lets out a harsh breath and crashes his lips into mine, kissing me with apparent need. It's verging on violent, but it's hot as hell. I take a deep breath of driftwood, whiskey, and spice. He smells incredible and addictive and of pure masculinity.

He shifts to lay me on my back on the couch and climbs on top of me, never taking his lips off of mine as he does. "I could do this for hours."

"Me too," I say breathlessly just as his tongue steals another breath of mine away. My body molds to his as his hands roam down my curves, touching me as if I'm breakable. He doesn't grope or slap or pinch; he just touches me. His hands never wander to my ass or my breasts or even the apex of my thighs. A man has never treated me like glass before, and it shocks me a bit. Like the electricity that was running up my spine has splintered off and bolts of it hit my skin with every touch he lays on me. I will my thoughts away and focus on his touches and his lips.

I'm completely lost in him when I hear Lola. "Oh sh—I'm so sorry," she says with a gasp.

Wade looks up at her but doesn't bother getting off of me; it's as if he's telling me that he's not done yet. I wonder what we must look like: him dressed to the nines in a designer suit and me in sweats.

"I uhm, I figured I could grab a bottle of wine since it's been over an hour. I didn't expect you two to still be here."

It's been over an hour? I've been kissing him for that long? My God, it feels like I just got his first kiss. I push myself up from underneath him and touch my lips, feeling just how swollen and tender they are. When I look at him, he's already watching me with needy eyes.

His lips are red and inflamed from me and triumph soars through my body.

"It's okay, Lo," I say as I cup his cheek, not looking away from him for a second.

"All right, well, did you want to join us for a late dinner?"

"No, we'll order in," Wade says without glancing up at her. I'm reveling in his eyes, and I don't plan on moving anytime soon.

"No problem. There are a bunch of take-out menus in the kitchen's junk drawer. Enjoy," she says proudly before leaving the apartment.

His lips find mine again, but this time his kiss is chaste. "I should feed you and then get going. It's past ten."

"I'm not in the mood for pizza or Chinese."

"What are you in the mood for then?"

"You," I say honestly.

His smile lights up the darkened room, and I swear he just burnt a hole in my heart's defense.

"I know the feeling," he says as he pushes his hard cock against me.

"But you won't give it to me."

"No, I won't because I won't lose you over a fucking orgasm."

I still and blanch. Lose me?

"You know what I mean." He adds, "I should get going before this becomes too much to abstain from."

"Oh."

I feel like that armor that he was slowly chipping away at just re-erected itself; the walls become impenetrable and more weather resistant than before.

He gets up and offers me a hand, but I refuse it and stand up on my own. I've gone from swooning to upset in a matter of two seconds. I wasn't asking him to fuck me or deliver an orgasm; I just wanted to be around him. Jesus. I might be a skank, but for some reason, I don't feel the need to be one around him. And he just insisted that I was one. *Asshole.*

He moves toward me, and I hold out a hand to halt him. "You should go," I say as I pull his sweatpants down and step out of them, leaving me in white lace boyshorts. I lean over and pick up his sweatpants before shoving them into his arms and retreating to my bedroom.

The asshole hurt me. He actually *upset* me. I fight back the unwanted tears, and I shut my bedroom door and get into bed in the dark, not giving a crap whether I see him again.

Lie.

I bury myself underneath my cool comforter and hold onto it as if I'll drift away if I let go. The bed dips and my stomach sinks even further.

"Hadley."

"I said go, Wade."

He shifts and stands. It's silent for a minute or two until the bed dips on the other side and the comforter lifts. His arms come around me and pull me into his hold. I keep my eyes shut because I don't want to see him. I don't want to see what he thinks of me.

I might know who I am, but for some reason seeing it in his eyes kills everything inside of me.

He brings me closer and wraps me securely in his arms. I bring my arms up and push away from him, but when my hands touch his bare chest, I still.

"I'm not going anywhere. Talk to me. What happened?"

I remain quiet and despite my earlier attempt at pushing him away, I curl up into his arms and rest my cheek against his chest. I hear him breathe in deeply as he places a kiss on the top of my head.

The war waging inside of me settles down as I shut my eyes, feeling safe even though I'm mad at him . . . myself . . . the world. I didn't mean to, but I fall asleep in his arms into a dreamless sleep.

Ten

Wade

IT'S TWO IN the morning, and I'm still in Hadley's bed. She's been asleep in my arms, murmuring things, since just past ten in the evening.

I should leave. I need to leave, but I cannot bring myself to let her go. No woman should be this beautiful while she sleeps, but she defies everything that a woman should be. I remove the headband from her hair and watch her curls fall around her face and onto my chest.

I move my hand across her face to slide the curls behind her ear and lean in to place a kiss on her lips. She's addicting, and I know that I'm a fucking goner when she sighs contently and nuzzles into me.

I know that I wounded her earlier, but I'm still trying to figure out what I said that made her want to give me up so effortlessly. She just took my sweats off and dismissed me. I couldn't leave knowing that I was the reason for the scowl on her face. She shifts and moves her hand around my torso in her sleep. We're intertwined and for once, it doesn't bother me to have a woman need me.

It's one of the reasons for my rules. As much as sex is a part of our human nature as well as nurturing, I'm not attracted to a needy woman. My mother raised me on her own and never once needed a man to take control or tell her how to live her life. Today, women come to me looking for just that: a man who will ultimately consume and control them and their needs. Some men may relish having a woman solely rely on them, but to me it's a turn-off. However, having Hadley need me right now is something that I'm all right with. For her I've broken almost every rule I've kept for the past ten years, and I don't regret doing it—yet.

Her bare leg moves between the two of mine, and I pull her lower body closer. She stirs and her eyes flutter open. "Hi," she murmurs.

"I didn't mean to wake you, my apologies."

"Are you leaving?" she asks as her body clings to me, begging for me to stay.

"Would you like me to?"

She doesn't respond, and I think that she's fallen back asleep, but then she nuzzles me and speaks again. "No. I'm comfortable."

I chuckle and pull the comforter up higher on her. "Then I'll stay."

"But I thought that you needed to go," she says through a yawn.

"I did, but I would not give this up for anything."

She smiles up at me before lowering her head and closing her eyes again. "'Night, Whiskey."

"Goodnight, Rye."

I'm startled awake. My throat is too dry, and I have a slight headache. I'm unaware of what day or time it is. It takes me a few seconds to realize where I am at first. Hadley. I'm at her place. I look down at her in my arms, and I don't think that either of us has moved since I fell asleep. I look over her comforter at the alarm clock. It's past four in the morning, and I'm very much aware of how content it makes me feel with the knowledge that I have a few more hours with her in my arms before I go back to the fast-paced real world.

There's a knock on her bedroom door before it opens. My back is to it, so I assume that it's her roommate. I'm about to let her know that I'm still here when a male voice interrupts the silence of the room.

"Hads? I knocked twice, but I figured I'd just let myself in."

Hadley doesn't shift or even wake at the sound of his voice. Who the fuck is this? I turn to face the darkness, trying to figure out where the hell this son of a bitch is in her bedroom.

He must hit the bench at the end of the bed because he curses. "Jesus, babe, we need to get rid of this shit before I break my leg. Are you awake?"

"Who the fuck are you?" My voice booms in the quiet room, vibrating with power and command, anger splitting every ounce of quiet reprieve that we were in moments before.

"What the fuck is going on?" he says to himself.

I reach over and turn on the light on her nightstand. It takes me a few tries, but when I finally get it on, there's a fucking hipster-looking punk at the end of the bed.

"Get the fuck out," I demand.

"Who the hell are you and why are you with my girl?"

His girl? Fuck that.

Hadley sits up and gasps, "Holden, get out."

"Hads, who the hell is this asshole?" He gestures toward me.

"That doesn't matter, Holden. You need to leave. You can't just come into my apartment unannounced, expecting to get your dick sucked."

"You've never complained before," he says as his eyes roam over her and then move to me, sizing me up.

"Leave, Hold."

"Fuck this," he says. "Is this the fucker that you were on the phone with when I ate your pussy?"

My entire body goes rigid. This motherfucker has had her?

I throw the comforter off of the bed and charge toward him. My hand comes around his neck, and I shove him against the wall as he tries to land a punch on my jaw.

In that frozen second, I see my mistake as his other hand, apparently his dominant one, comes up and hooks my jaw, greeting me with daggers to my face. My head swings to the other side, but I don't relent or give up my grip on his neck. My other hand comes up, and I bring his head forward and then slam it back against the wall, leaving an indent in the drywall behind him.

"Stop," Hadley's voice breaks me from the brawl, and I step back from the fucker who is gripping the back of his bloodied head.

I look over my shoulder at her as a sudden gush of pain hits me in the jaw again, in the same spot as the last. I snap my head to face him and lick the corner of my lip, which is now stained with blood. I charge at him and slam my head into his forehead, not giving a fuck about who he is. He doesn't see the movement coming, and his head knocks back from my impact. He stumbles backward and hits her dresser.

She runs up to me and puts both of her hands on my chest. "Wade, stop, please," she begs and the shadows don't dissolve. The darkness takes over my thoughts.

"You motherfucker," the shitbag says as the bedroom door opens and Lola stands in the doorframe.

"What is going on?" she cries out and looks from Hadley to me and then to the shitbag leaning against the dresser.

"Lola, get Holden out of here, please," Hadley says as she looks up at me, pleading with me for something. What, I don't fucking know. It only ignites my rage, and I want to go after him again. I want to damage him for touching her. I'm about to lunge forward when she pushes on my chest. My eyes dart down to hers, and it's now that I feel her hands burning into my chest. I'm achingly aware of her presence, and I remind myself of who I am, instead of this agile beast that took over.

"Fuck this," I say and move away from her, grabbing my shit and striding out of her bedroom. She comes hauling ass around the corner when I swing the apartment door open to walk out.

"Wade, please, don't leave."

I turn, hostility on my face. I'm fucking fuming, and I cannot be with her while I can barely contain myself. I'll hurt her because that's exactly what tonight just did to me. It fucking destroyed me.

I shake my head and step out, slamming the door behind me as I stride down the hallway. I get to the elevator and punch the down button more times than necessary before the doors open. Once I'm inside, I dress quickly before pacing back and forth in the small space, smashing my fist into one of the oversized mirrors. It cracks underneath the pressure of my fist just as the doors open, and I glide out. Out of the building, down the stairs, and out of her fucking life.

You win, Isla.

Isla is over, and I'm once again thankful for her friendship. I called her while I was walking the three blocks to my place from Hadley's. I went off on her and told her about everything that happened, and to my surprise, she didn't tell me off for waking her up, and she hasn't muttered a thing about *I told you so.*

"I can't believe that he just came into her apartment. Does that mean that he has a key?"

"I have no goddamn clue."

My phone vibrates again with a text message from Hadley. I look down at it: I'm so sorry, Wade. Please, just call me?

I toss the device across the couch as Isla applies the icepack to my jaw again, making me flinch.

"He got you good, Brass."

"Fuck him and to hell with her."

"Don't say that, you ass. I saw the way you looked at her at Blended today, and I know that you won't give up on her that easily. Plus, you owe me another two hundred."

"It's in my wallet, and it will be the last."

"No, it won't, and I'll grab it before I go."

I scoff and recoil as she presses the icepack too hard against my jaw.

"You know, I've never seen you so riled up about a woman before."

"And?"

"And . . . I don't think that you should give up on her that easily. You knew what you were getting into with her, and you decided to go ahead with it anyway."

When I don't respond, she pushes the matter further. "She obviously cares for you, because she went after you when you walked out of her bedroom, instead of staying in there with him. He's probably just a dick she can ride."

"I want to be the goddamn dick that she rides, the only one she climbs on."

She laughs and runs a hand through my hair. "Listen to you, getting all possessive over her."

I shake my head and lean back against the cold leather couch. "She's not worth it."

"I think that you're lying to yourself again. When was the last time you broke your rules and went after a woman like this? Huh?"

"Never."

"And that is exactly why you shouldn't give up on her."

"You don't understand what I see. She's hiding something, and it's what is holding her back from life. It's the same thing that is holding her back from me."

"Make her realize that and bring her out of the darkness, Brass."

"Easier said than done."

She rolls her eyes and walks into my kitchen. She comes back with a tumbler of amber liquid and a beer for herself; she's the only reason why there is beer in that damn fridge. I don't even open it; my staff is in charge of what comes into the penthouse.

"Don't you have a vital meeting about Australia in the morning?"

"Yes, I do."

"Then you should get some sleep. And by the way, I'm coming with you in your fancy jet next week. I'd like to experience life down under again."

"I've already told you that you are invited."

"This is me taking you up on that offer," she says with a smile before drinking from the bottle. "I'm crashing in the guest room until noon, and don't you dare wake me up again. You'll be in biting distance this time, and we wouldn't want to risk your appendage."

I shake my head and stand up, holding the icepack to my jaw. "I'll see you later. Stay as long as you want." I head up the stairs in my duplex penthouse to my master bedroom, where I strip down and crash on my bed.

I pick up my phone and decide to grow a pair by texting her back: GOODNIGHT, HADLEY.

She responds soon afterward: I'D RATHER BE SLEEPING IN YOUR ARMS AGAIN THAN IN THIS BED ALONE.

I'm surprised that shitbag didn't stay: WHERE'S THE OTHER GUY?

DOES IT MATTER? HE'S NOT HERE. YOU'RE THE ONE THAT I WANT TO BE CURLED UP WITH, NOT HIM.

Now she wants to be normal and not insist on sex and dirty deeds? Her fucking decisions are giving me whiplash.

GOODNIGHT.

I've been inundated by myriad issues with the Australian property acquisition since I stepped foot into the office this morning. Adriana has kept herself on her feet with bringing me exactly what I need, when I need it.

I remind myself that I need to give this woman a raise before I leave for Australia.

"Mr. Brass, I took the liberty of clearing your schedule for lunch. I believe that today is going to be a late one," she says, and she types away at her laptop on the other side of my desk.

"Very well. Arrange for delivery. It will give me time to read through the remainder of the Australian files."

"Yes, sir."

My phone goes off, and I glance down at it. Adriana hasn't kept it in her desk since I broke my rule the first time with Hadley. It's a text message from Isla: BRASS, SHE'S HERE AGAIN. CAN I KICK HER TO THE CURB OR ARE YOU GOING TO GIVE HER ANOTHER CHANCE? SHE WALKED IN AND ASKED ABOUT YOU.

I sigh, resigned, and reply to her: I HAVEN'T DECIDED. HAVE HER FILL OUT THE MEMBERSHIP FORMS AND GET HER SETTLED. HER DRINKS ARE ON ME.

YOU'RE TURNING INTO A SOFTY. WHAT HAPPENED TO THOSE BRASS BALLS?

I raise my eyebrows and chuckle: EXACTLY WHERE THEY SHOULD BE—ALONGSIDE MY COCK.

She sends me a picture of herself flicking me off. She's undeniably beautiful, she always has been, but she's more of a sister to me than anything else. We got together at a college party in our senior year when we were too drunk to function, and it hasn't happened since. Sure the sex was great, but our friendship outweighed the sexual attraction.

"Mr. Brass?" Adriana asks softly.

"Yes?" I look up at her, and she hands me another file.

"I've just emailed you the itinerary for Australia next

week. Here are the specifics regarding your flight and hotel arrangements."

"Thank you. Please ensure that Isla Madden has been added to all of the functions that I will be attending."

"Of course." She nods and gets up, leaving my office in silence.

Eleven

Hadley

"ARE YOU GOING to tell me what exactly went down last night? I don't think that I've seen Holden that mad before."

"Yeah, well, you need to stop letting him in. He shouldn't have free range over me."

"Okay, I apologize for that, but I had no idea that Waylon Brass was asleep in your bed. I didn't know that it was that serious."

"I don't know what it is, Lo," I tell her honestly as I sip on my whiskey. When I told Lo that I needed a drink, she decided to tag along even though all she can drink here is water.

"I get it. I mean, this thing with Owen and me has gotten pretty serious fast, so I get that it's difficult to grasp onto what a relationship or fling or whatever this is means."

"I don't think that he's going to want much to do with me after last night."

"I think that you're drunk." She giggles and scoots closer to me on the couch.

"I wish I was. Maybe I'll make it my goal for today."

"You're insane, you know that? Don't go getting drunk over a man who is probably not worth your time in gold condoms. I'm sure he's been with another woman since you two haven't made yourselves exclusive."

"That's the thing, even though we haven't, I don't think that he has."

She sighs and reaches into her tote where she pulls out a magazine. "Have you seen this? I think that you might have some competition since this came out this morning. I saw it on my way to grab Owen and myself some coffee."

"What is it?" I ask as I reach for it. My eyes widen at the image on *GQ*'s cover. Impeccably dressed in suit and tie, Wade stares back at me with the title *Man of the Year* written above his name. "Holy shit."

"That's what I thought. He's fucking gorgeous, Hads, and it says in his spread that he's single. I think that you should read it. He seems to be rather dedicated to his work as well as a charity that he heads. He kind of made me swoon in my panties."

"Lola," I scold her as I flip through the pages to find his article, "you're not getting this back; I hope you know that."

"I figured, so I bought the rest of them that were on the stand, and probably saved eight women's panties from death via drowning."

I groan and take another drink of my whiskey. "To me, he's just . . . Wade. He's not this celebrity billionaire that the media makes him out to be."

"Sweetheart, the man basically owns and runs Chicago, as well as Las Vegas."

"I get that, but I don't understand why they make such a big deal about him. He's not an actor or anything."

"So? Have you seen him? He's absolutely gorgeous and worth every drop of ink that went into printing these magazines."

I flip through another page of photographs of him before I settle on one of him looking away from the camera and out at the lake. I run my finger over his jawline and sigh. "He makes me feel wanted."

"I'd say that you are. Especially by him."

"You think so?"

"By the way he messed up Holden last night, I know so. If Holden didn't know any better, I'm sure that he'd sue him, but I don't think that he wants to mess things up with you."

"You and I both know that I'm not interested in pursuing anything with Hold."

"I might, but I doubt that he does." She pats my knee and stands up. "I need to get to the boutique and open up. One of my girls called out sick."

"All right." I stand up and give her a hug before she grabs her things and walks out of Blended.

My mind goes to Wade and how last night must have looked to him. I sigh and throw my head back before placing the magazine into my purse and moving across the room to a quieter spot where I pull out the current novel that I'm reading to occupy my mind.

This shit feeling has made itself comfortable inside of me as I sit in his whiskey library alone after Lo left for work. I thought that coming here would soothe me in a way, but it's only made the unease grow stronger. The emotion nestles itself in for the long haul, and I'm confident that I won't be able to shake it, at least until I speak to him.

To add to the pressure on my heart, Isla keeps glancing over at me with her phone in her hand, and I swear, if she does it again I'm going to march over to her and demand for her to tell me what her issue is. She beats me to the punch, though, when she walks up to me, holding an application to the library.

"Hey Hadley. Mr. Brass is insistent that you fill out these forms," she says and hands them to me.

"Hi, okay. I can do it now."

Something about her stance makes me think that she's somehow got more to say to me than to hand over an application. I'm sure that he wasn't the reason she brought it to me, but what do I know?

"Great. Just bring it up to the bar when you're done, okay?"

"You've got it," I say, wanting her to leave me alone for the rest of the day. I just want to sit here and wallow in my self-pity after last night.

"And one more thing," she adds, *and there it is*, "I know that it's not my place to say this, but I'm going to regardless. Wade is one hell of a man, and if he's too much for you to handle, then you need to let him go. He's not someone who will fuck around with you, or go out of his way to let you know what he's feeling. With that being said, it was sure fucking obvious as to how he felt last night with a swollen and bruised jaw. He deserves better than you, and why he's stooping down to your level baffles me."

My mouth drops open in bewilderment. I'm usually the woman who takes people by the balls and swings them around a bit, but she just shoved my lady balls up into my throat. I force a swallow before I try out my voice.

"H-how the hell do you know about any of this?"

"Wade and I go back to our college years. He's pretty much my best friend, and if you fuck with him again, I swear that I will roofie your drink and watch some asshole drag you out of this place by your nipples. Getting a call from him at four-thirty in the morning never happens."

I swear, if she wasn't threatening me, I think I would actually get along with her assertive, bitchy self.

"He called you?"

"Uh, yeah. Who the hell else tended to his fucked-up jaw since you were too busy with the other guy?"

I pause because I want to launch myself at her like Wade did to Holden last night. "I didn't give aid to anyone." I shift in my seat and brush a stray curl off of my face.

"Sure you didn't. Bring me that application when you're done filling it out."

I look down at the form and don't respond to her as she walks away. My mind goes into overdrive trying to figure out if there is something romantic going on between them, but if there were, why would she know about me?

She wouldn't, I tell myself.

An anticipation to see him boils deep in my belly, the build-up of it will be too much to handle pretty soon. The knowledge that he was with another woman last night adds to the buzzing uneasiness that I feel. I never compete with another woman for any man, but for some reason, I'm more than willing to for Waylon Brass.

I dig a pen out of my purse and proceed to fill in the membership forms. My mind is still reeling with what Isla said and how pissed off she was. I dare a glance at her, and she's watching me while she's on the phone with someone. Wade maybe? I don't know, but I think we're too much alike in a way. She's not afraid to take charge and wrestle a bull by its balls, which pretty much describes me as well. An argument between the two of us could be catastrophic.

I finish filling out my information and set the application down on the coffee table before me and take a drink of the whiskey I ordered when I first arrived.

Despite my unease, I lean back against the leather seat and shut my eyes, remembering last night. I've never slept that soundly before, not since my mother took her own life. The numerous flashbacks to last night make me tense up. He was beyond irate, and Holden just egged him on. I seriously need to speak to Holden about his behavior, but even more importantly, I wish Wade would at the very least call me back so I can apologize to him.

I have no idea when or how I became attached to the thought of having him, but it's engraved itself into the breast-plate covering my heart. I would do anything to give last night a redo. I'd make sure that my door was locked and that Holden knew to stay away, but in reality, I know it would never happen. I told Wade that it was what I was going to do, regardless of what I had just talked myself into earlier that day. He doesn't know that I've decided to give him a chance—sans another man's dick.

He won't know that I'm going to actually try to stop using the physical act of sex as a coping mechanism for depression. My anxiety rears its ugly head at the thought of my setting aside my sexual habits while I figure out what's different between Wade and me. I use deep breathing in an attempt to ease it, but it does not seem to help.

I'll have to figure out something else to numb the pain and memories while the guilt and shame of my past creep back into my heart. It's going to be like breaking an addiction: I'll be off-balance, but the withdrawal from something physical for something emotional might be worth the cost. Not everyone agrees that sexual addiction is an actual diagnosed addiction, but I can vouch for it. I've gone to extremes for sex, none of which I am proud of, but it was what I thought I needed to heal—until now. Now it's almost obvious that I've been sprinting down the wrong path for all of these years.

It's time to find my dopamine high somewhere else, and I think I know exactly where I can get it naturally. Only time will tell, though. I'm deciding to fight for myself for the first time in my life, and it's all because I met Waylon Brass—the one man who refuses to give me what I want, what I need.

A glass of whiskey later, and I've moved to the couch next to the fireplace with my paperback. I hadn't realized that I had fallen asleep until I'm jolted off of the couch. I force my eyes open and glance at the arms surrounding me. I begin to panic, but relax into them when I hear his dark voice.

"How long has she been asleep? Is she drunk?"

"Nope, at least I don't think so. She just had two tumblers.

She's just been lights-out for over an hour. I figured I should let you know, though. I wasn't sure if she was sick or whatever. Maybe just desperate for your attention."

"Thank you, Isla. I owe you for this shit."

"Oh, you have no idea, buddy. I'm banking on that Australian trip."

I keep my eyes shut as they speak, trying to stay awake, but I end up drifting off in his arms as I feel his body move.

When I open my eyes again, I'm surrounded by darkness. It's pitch black in here, and I cannot figure out where I am for the life of me. A door to the unknown room cracks open and a stream of light illuminates a neutral-colored bedroom. I sit up and push my hair off of my face before realizing that I'm in a bed.

"You're awake."

"Wade?"

"Yes. You know, you shouldn't go around falling asleep in public places. Some asshole could take you home with him without your realizing it."

"Where am I?"

"We're at my place. I wanted you out of the public eye, and I didn't think going back to your apartment would be a good idea because if I see him again, *I will slaughter him.*"

I push the plush bedding down my body and realize that I'm not even wearing my outfit from earlier. I frown and look up at him as he crosses the room to stand next to the bed.

"You changed me?"

"Yes. I didn't for the first couple of hours, but I figured that I should eventually, seeing as you'll be staying the night."

I swing my legs off of the bed and drink him in—in all of his deliciousness. He's wearing a dark suit, his jaw has a large bruise on the left-hand side, and his stubble has grown in heavier than I've seen on him before.

"I don't need to stay the night, but thank you. I don't know why I fell asleep either. I've been exhausted these last few days."

"You are staying the night, seeing as it's one in the morning. There won't be any arguments about it." I watch his jaw move as he speaks and my panties reap the effects of it.

"Are you serious?" I search around for my phone but come up empty-handed. I turn toward his body, and I can feel the vague rumblings of the static making its presence known.

"Yes. Did you eat before you drank those two tumblers?"

"No, not really. I haven't been able to stomach too much in the last few days."

The lines in his forehead deepen as he sits down next to me. "Then you should not have been drinking. Especially on your own."

"I know, I just . . ." I stop myself before showing my hand of cards. "I was hoping that you would be there today. I'm so sorry about last night. I had no idea that he would come in or . . ."

"Stop," he says as he cups my cheek with one of his large hands. "I know that his coming there wasn't something that you knew about. The shock on your face told me that, but as I said before, I understand that he's going to give you what I won't. Him or others."

"He's not." My stomach twists. I'm not sure if it's from his words or if I'm just not feeling well. "Where's the bathroom?" Waves of nausea add to my misery instantly. I clutch my mouth and get up quickly.

His eyes widen as he takes my hand and leads me from the bedroom and into the bathroom attached to it. "Are you ill?"

I rush to the toilet, unable to get the words out before I purge whatever is left of the whiskey I had consumed earlier today.

I hold my hand out to stop him when he approaches, but he comes toward me anyway, taking my hair into his hands and holding it out of my face. "I'm not leaving. Now, try and relax."

Another bout of it comes over me, and I squeeze my knees as my body eradicates itself of whatever it can. A heaving lurch rips through me, and I start to quiver.

"I'm sorry," I choke out.

"Shh," he offers and lets go of my hair when he thinks it's safe. He leaves my side, but he's back in a short amount of time with a warm, wet washcloth. "Use this, Rye, and I'll get you to bed."

I wipe my face off with the cloth and then my mouth, hoping that he has an extra toothbrush lying around. The second I go to stand his arms come around me, and he helps me up, moving my hair out of my face. I look up at him, and he has a small private smile on his face as he inspects me.

"Do you need a doctor?"

"I don't know. I don't think so."

"I want you in my bed instead of this one. Come, and I'll get you some cold water as well."

I nod as he laces his fingers with mine and leads me through the bedroom door out into a too-wide hallway and down it until we come to a closed door. He pushes it open, and I'm suddenly engulfed in his scent. It surrounds me entirely as we cross his bedroom to the bathroom attached to it. It's dark in here, so I'm not able to see much, but it feels warm and inviting.

Without speaking, he fishes out a new toothbrush and hands it to me. "Freshen up and I'll get you something to drink."

"Thank you," I murmur, feeling thoroughly embarrassed.

He places a kiss to my temple before disappearing. I stare at my reflection in the mirror; I'm too pale, even for me, and ashen-faced. A heat wave of mortification scorches my blood as cold sweat breaks out over my skin. I glance around the lavish fancy-ass bathroom until my eyes find a vast glass-encased shower.

I make quick work of brushing my teeth, scrubbing my

tongue until it feels raw and clean before I strip out of his shirt and my bra and panties. I walk on unsteady legs to the shower and somehow figure out how to turn it on. When I step underneath the spray, the icy water hits my body from multiple showerheads. I know that if this is a fever, I need to crush it and fast. I just hope that this works. I'm going to be having horrifying flashbacks of getting sick in front of him for weeks to come.

Feeling faint, I sink down against the shower wall until I'm seated on the floor as the water washes over me, cooling my overheated body. I pull my legs up against me and rest my head against my knees as I exhale.

I'm unaware that he's stepped into the shower until his strong arms come around me and pull me to my feet. "Jesus, baby, it's fucking freezing," he says as he pulls me against his clothed chest.

If this fever wasn't melting my insides already, then I think his term of endearment would have. I lay my cheek against him and shut my eyes, forcing my body to relax at this moment.

"How are you still so warm? This water is glacial."

I shrug and wrap my arms around his torso, not wanting to be anywhere else but in his arms right now. My mind wanders to the tattoo scarring his back, and I smile to myself. There may be a streak of recklessness in him that he's not ready to show. He's keeping his cards close to his chest, and I'm desperate to cheat and take a peek at what he's holding. Does he hold the king to my queen?

"Let me wash you." It's a statement and not a question, one that doesn't need a reply.

He pulls his body away from mine and takes off his suit jacket that I'm sure is completely ruined now. It slaps heavily on the shower floor before he unbuttons his collared shirt as well. The white cotton fabric clings to him, and it reminds me of kissing him in the rain on our date.

I reach my hand out to the shower wall to steady myself. Apparently getting turned on and sick at the same time is not a good combination for me because I'm feeling weak again.

He reaches out to a pump attached to the wall before running his fingers through my hair. I moan at the contact of his fingers as he massages my scalp. I close my eyes and stay still, enjoying his hands on me. I'm not ashamed that I'm standing naked in front of this man, and I'm not even pissed that he hasn't dared a glance down at me.

Once he's done rinsing my hair out for the second time, he runs his bare hands over my chest. My eyes flutter open as I watch him spread suds over my breasts. His eyes are watching his hands move methodically against my skin as he does, and it's the most intimate thing that I have ever experienced. His brow is furrowed in concentration and his stance changes slightly.

His hands move lower, covering my stomach, hips, and back in suds before he kneels down in front of me and starts at my thighs, running down my legs to my feet before he looks up at me. "Are you okay?"

"Fine," I say before I run my hand through his dark, wet hair, loving how silky it feels now that it's wet.

He must decide on something because his hands stop against my skin, and he looks up at me. "I'm going to wash you. Do you trust that I won't take advantage of you?"

The word hits me in my gut for the first time, but I nod and take a step, widening my stance for him. He soaps up his hands and runs them up my inner thighs before touching me intimately without a loofah or a washcloth. It's just his skin against mine. I don't shut my eyes as he washes the apex of my thighs. Instead, I watch his hands move as they send jolts of pleasure through my body and I cannot help but lean into his touch when he cups me. Before I can get used to his touch, though, he removes his hands from me and spins me around slowly to wash the backs of my legs, but pauses when he notices the three microdermal piercings that grace my lower back. They are centered on my lower spine and in a straight line, stopping at the curve of my back. He continues up to my ass; he doesn't linger or prod, he just washes me, cleansing me of this fever.

"All done," he says in a dark, raspy voice before standing and moving me under the spray. He turns the heat of the water up to lukewarm instead of ice as he rinses me off slowly. He takes his time as if it's the one and only time he'll see me naked in front of him.

Once he's done, and all of the suds from my body are long gone, he reaches behind me and turns off the showerheads. I look up at him as drops of water fall from his hair, his lip, and chin to his sculpted chest. This man is gorgeous. Every muscle on his torso is well defined and visible. He's the kind of man that will stop anyone in his or her tracks, regardless of sexual preference. He might be a private person, but he's not ashamed to show me just what he has underneath his clothing. His self-confidence is palpable.

He takes my hand and leads me out of the shower where he pulls a fluffy black towel from a rack on the wall, wrapping me in it before he undoes his belt buckle. I hadn't even realized that he was still half dressed because I was too preoccupied with his skin burning mine while he was touching me.

His fingers work to undo his pants, and he pushes them down his legs while his eyes never leave mine. He removes his unbuttoned shirt, and it hits the floor. I dare a glance down at his bare legs, which are shaped perfectly, just like every other part of his body. His legs are strong and bold. He kicks his pants aside and hooks his fingers into his white boxer briefs. They outline his cock flawlessly, and I can see every inch of him through the wet material. He doesn't hesitate to push the briefs down and kick them to the side as well. Every man will pale in comparison to him from now on. He's natural perfection. I flush every shade of pink as I openly gape at him.

He's standing entirely naked in front of me with his cock pointing in my direction as if it's leading the way. He reaches for another towel and wraps it around his waist, hindering my view of his glorious cock before running a hand through his hair. I watch him carefully as his tongue darts out to collect a drop of water on his top lip.

"Come," he says as he offers me his hand. I take it without a word as he leads me back into his bedroom. The two lights on either side of his bed are now on. They must be set to dim, and I am able to actually see around his room this time. It's done in neutral colors with white sheets on his bed and a gray blanket folded down. There are floor to ceiling gray curtains, which are drawn, cloaking the room from the city. A large marble fireplace sits across from his bed with a coffee-colored couch and ottoman in front of it. Above the fireplace is a large flat-screen television, which is currently off. It's a simple space, but gorgeous nonetheless.

He leads me to the side of his bed and pulls back the sheets. "You need to rest," he says as I sit down and take the glass of water he picks up from the nightstand and two deep blue pills.

"You don't have to do this, Wade. I can call Lola to come and get me."

"No. I want you here if you're ill. I don't trust anyone with you," he says with a gentleness that wasn't there before.

"You don't?" I ask as I take a sip of the fresh water after placing the medication he gave me on my tongue, the ice clinking against the glass the only sound in the room for a moment.

"No," he says forcefully as I watch his sharp jaw and angular cheekbones flex. I'm not sure if it's the fever or if I'm truly seeing just how beautiful this man is for the first time. I knew he was attractive, but he goes far beyond the average person.

"Why?"

"Look at you," he says as he glances down my body, "you're vulnerable, attractive, and if someone realizes how truly unique and remarkable you are, then he'll try to take your heart from me."

I stop with the glass to my lips, my eyes meeting his seaside blues in question. "Who will?"

"Every single man out there." He cups my cheek and leans down to place his lips against mine. They move softly as if he's going to chip the thin, fragile layer of glass that I've quickly become.

He breaks away far too soon for my liking, but compensates for it by placing a kiss on my temple. "Lie back."

I do as I'm told and get comfortable in his bed. *His bed*. The only man's bed that I have slept in before was Lawson's. I push the thought from my head and get comfortable. Once he pulls the comforter over me, he walks to his bedroom door as if he's going to leave.

"You're going?" I ask wearily.

"Do you want me to?"

"Not for a second." The honesty in my voice is easily heard, and it surprises even me.

His smile lights up the room as he walks to the opposite side of the bed and climbs in, tossing the towel off of himself once he's under the covers. Dare I do the same thing?

He turns the light off on the side of his bed, and I follow suit, turning off the one on my side before I feel brave enough to pull the towel off of my body and toss it onto the floor beside me.

We lie in silence for minutes before one of us decides that we are comfortable with moving. I shift and reach for him, realizing that he won't push himself on me, especially since we're both naked. I extend my hand out to graze his chest, running my fingers over his pecs and down his abdominal muscles. He turns toward me, taking my hand in his.

"Wade?"

"What is it, Rye?"

"Why did you say that someone will take my heart from you?"

He takes a few minutes to answer, but when he does, I can hear the truth and conviction of it. "Because it belongs to me. If I'm being honest . . . the thought of losing something that I don't truly have terrifies the fuck out of me."

Remember that armor that was in place? The one that added another layer of protection to my heart? Well, it just completely shattered and fell to pieces at his words.

"I'm not going anywhere," I offer him, hoping that he knows that I'm giving this thing between us a chance.

He lets out a steady breath before reaching for me and pulling me into his arms. Our bare bodies unite and truly touch each other's for the first time. I'm hyper-aware of every point where we touch. My spine tingles and sends bolts to those spots, making sure I'm well aware of where he is.

"You may not be going anywhere, but that doesn't mean that there aren't other men trying to pull you out of my grip."

My hand finds his face, and I run my finger over his lips. "I don't think that there's a man strong enough."

I feel him breathe in deeply at my words. "The knowledge that I share you with others kills me, Hadley. Just the thought of it sends a blunt and rusted knife through my skin."

It's now or never, I tell myself, especially since we're already having this conversation. I yawn and nestle into his chest. I can feel the medication start to work its magic, and I'm beyond grateful for it. "You don't share me, Whiskey. After our date . . . after that phone call . . . I realized that I wanted to try."

He tilts my chin up, attempting to find my eyes in the dark

room. "Try?"

"Mmm-hmm," I say sleepily. "I'm going to try and be with you. Just you."

"Jesus . . ." his voice is a praise as he tugs me closer to his naked body. I can feel his cock stir between us, but I'm half asleep, and I wouldn't do him any justice right now if he wants me. His lips find mine in the darkness and his kiss is tender, searching for the truth as his tongue slides against mine. He must find it because he stops kissing me and pulls my head against his chest where I close my eyes and stop fighting off the medication as it lulls me to sleep.

Twelve

Wade

IF SHE ACTUALLY meant what she said to me before the medication took her from me, then I'm not letting her out of my goddamn sight.

She's still asleep by the time I've showered and gotten dressed. Fuck, I don't want to leave her alone, but I cannot miss this final meeting with the CEOs of the Australian companies and properties that I will be taking over. I've had three of them specifically flown out to add a few addendums to their contracts before I make my trip down under to visit and secure each property individually.

As far as the properties go, the majority of them will be turned into offices, shelters, homes, and clinics for Mothers of Brass. I cannot risk losing them because I am unable to leave Hadley alone. I pick up my phone from my nightstand while I watch her. This sudden possessiveness has dug its claws down my spine and locked around me completely.

I NEED A FAVOR. I send the text before moving around to Hadley. My fingers brush her hair out of her face and I press my lips to her temple.

Thirty minutes later, Isla is standing at the foot of my bed with me, watching Hadley.

"I'm still having a difficult time trying to figure out why you actually let a woman sleep in your bed."

"She's not just any woman, Isla. Please, just do this for me today. I know that you don't have to be at Blended until later this evening."

"Listen, just because you are technically my boss does not mean that you can creep on my schedule or interrupt it for that matter."

I smirk and rest my hand on her shoulder. "You should start making a list of what you want to see while we're in Australia. I'm sure that I can make it up to you."

"Fuck you and your bank account."

"You have, and I don't believe my bank account has anything to do with our friendship."

"It doesn't, and you know that. Fine. I'll hang out here for the day, but I'm drinking your whiskey."

"Go for it," I say and walk over to Hadley's side. Isla walks out of the room before I have to ask her to. I kiss Hadley's temple to say goodbye, but she stirs, and her deep turquoise eyes flutter open and closed again.

"Rye, wake up for me for a minute?" I ask, and her eyes flutter open once again.

"Hi, Whiskey," she says with a small raspy voice.

"How are you feeling?"

She stretches out on my bed. The sheets slip below her breasts, and I dare a glance at her perfectly pale white skin. She seems to notice, and her nipples harden under my gaze. "I'm okay. I'm tired, though, and my throat is sore," she says as she takes inventory of her body.

"I'll get Isla to bring you something for your throat once you're dressed."

"Isla?"

I sit down next to her and cup her cheek. "Yes. I've asked her to stay here today while you're ill. I have a couple of meetings that I cannot miss, and I wanted you with someone that I trust implicitly."

"Oh," she murmurs and pushes herself to sit up.

"God, you are beautiful." The words unwantedly spill from my mouth. She cannot know how she affects every inch of my body yet. Not when I haven't had her.

A warm blush kisses her cheeks as she leans into me. I take her lips, not giving a fuck if I get ill because of kissing her. I'd rather risk my health than not kiss her at this moment.

I feel her smile cross her lips before I pull away and hand her phone to her. "Text me today when you're awake. I need to know that you're all right."

"I will."

"Good. Feel free to grab anything from my closet to wear. I'll see you later, Rye."

"Bye, Whiskey."

I haven't been able to check my phone all morning, and it's burning a hole in my desk as I finish up this meeting. I've heard it vibrate more than once, and as tempting as her texts are, I cannot risk losing these properties.

It starts to vibrate again as I'm going over the last contract for the day. Instead of a short vibration it keeps going, making itself known to the man across from me. He glances down at my desk before looking back up at me, and I'm waiting for him to say something, but he keeps his words to himself. Smart man.

I ignore it and finish up this damn meeting. By the end of it, my phone has gone off another three times. I'm sure it made me look fucking pathetic to the man in front of me, the man whose business I am purchasing, a small clinic, for the charity I am setting up in Sydney, Australia.

I walk back into my office once I've seen him out and I notice that Adriana is not at her desk. I glance at my watch, and it's almost one in the afternoon.

I walk meaningfully to my desk and pull open the top drawer where I have my phone charging. There is a couple of missed calls from my mother and one from Isla. I chuckle to myself when I pull up the one text from Hadley.

Hi, Whiskey.

I type out a reply to her: How are you feeling, Rye?

It takes her a few minutes to reply and when she does I'm finalizing my Australian itinerary.

I'm hanging in there. I think that it's just a cold, but your bed is keeping me warm.

I glance at the document in front of me before making an instant decision. I call her instead of texting her back because I need to hear her voice instead of reading it. She answers on the fourth ring. "Hi."

"Rye. I need you to answer two questions for me, all right?"

"Uh, sure."

"The first one is in regard to us. Did you mean what you said last night? That I don't have to share you with another man?"

"Uhm, yes."

I turn my head away from the phone and let out a breath of air. "Good, so then I can call you mine, correct?"

"Yours?" I hear the hesitation in her voice, but I keep pushing her regardless.

"Yes. You're *my* girl. Do you agree to that?"

"You're asking me this over the phone?"

"Not entirely. I'm simply clarifying."

She giggles and I cannot wipe the smile off of my smug face. "Okay. Well, I hope that it's clear now."

"It is. Now for my second question, Rye."

"Hit me with it," she says. I can imagine she's smiling.

"What are you doing in three days? And the week that follows it?"

"I guess I'll just be getting into the swing of my new job.

Why?"

When the fuck did she get a job? I ignore my controlling ego and take a seat at my desk.

"Do you have a passport?"

"I do. What's going on?"

"Cancel anything you have planned for the next ten days. You're coming with me."

"Oh? And where, pray tell, are you dragging me to? A sex dungeon?"

"Sydney, Australia."

"What?" she squeals loudly into the phone, causing me to pull it away from my ear.

"I'll pay for anything that you need to get there, and we'll fly out on Friday."

She doesn't say anything for a few seconds before I hear her clear her throat. "Okay."

"Okay? I was expecting a fight about how little you know me."

"I told you that I would try, Wade."

The excitement that I hear in her voice is something that I haven't heard before, and the knowledge that I put that there lights me on fire.

"Thank you. I have to go, and I'd like to see you later if you go home."

"Goodbye, Whiskey."

———————————

Seventy-two hours pass in the blink of an eye.

We've just boarded my private jet and Isla seems pissed as fuck at me. I've been all too consumed with Brass Global and spending my evenings talking to Hadley to remember to call Isla and inform her that Hadley would be joining us on this trip.

Isla takes a seat in one of the leather chairs and Hadley takes the one next to me. "Brass, when did this become your big idea?"

I glare at her, daring her to do this in front of Rye. "Big idea?"

"Yeah, bringing some woman you know next to nothing about on an overseas trip. These trips were supposed to be *our* thing."

Hadley shifts uncomfortably in her seat, and I reach for her hand. I don't need Isla's bullshit right now. "Listen up, Madden. It was my fault for not telling you about her coming, but she's with me, and you are well aware of that."

"Mmm-hmm," is all I get in return from Isla.

"It's okay, Wade," Hadley offers, carefully speaking without emotion lacing her words.

"The fuck it is," I boom, anger rolling off of me in waves. "Isla. Quit your shit and accept it. Pull the dildo out of your ass and enjoy the goddamn trip." The muscles in my neck strain as I fight the spat of words that I'd like to shove down her throat.

"Fine, but you owe me . . . again."

"All right," I say and reach for Hadley's hand again, intertwining my fingers with hers. She's looking out the window in an attempt to separate herself from my and Isla's argument. Rage consumes my body knowing that Rye is now uncomfortable being here with us. It's easy to tell: the subtle way that she angles her body away from me, and the fact that the corners of her lips are downcast.

I've been patient with Isla giving me shit regarding Rye, but enough is enough of this hot and cold behavior. I will not stand for it any longer. This onslaught of fury reminds me just how much I need Isla to support my decision to be with a woman. If I'm going to fight my battles, then she needs to be my goddamn cheerleader. The tension is palpable in the cabin; suffocating might be a better way to describe it.

Thirteen

Hadley

THE JET IS stunning, designed in dark wood paneling and white leather seats with maroon accents around the interior. Everything feels extravagant when I'm around Wade as if this air of luxury follows him around constantly.

This is not *normal*.

I went from wanting sex with a normal dick to being on a private jet without sex. I won't say that I haven't brought on my own orgasm more than twice a day since I said that I would be exclusive with him, but he still hasn't touched me—not since his hands roamed all over me in the shower.

I'm desperate for it, though. Anxious to fuck. I want to drown out the pain and stress of my past with sinking down on a dick and riding the hell out of it. It's the only thing that works for me to get away from the demons in my head.

To say that I crave the man sitting next to me is an understatement because it's much more than that: it's a physical and mental need that I have to have met now that I'm *his*. He should be simplifying my life and my needs with being a constant, but he's like water, slipping through my fingers.

I haven't slept in the same bed with him since I had that cold because of how busy he's been. I'm not looking for love: it's inconvenient, consuming, and pointless. I've only agreed to be his in the sense of fucking him and only him because I don't think that I'll be able to take another cock without thinking about what he would feel like.

Deep down, though, I know that I'm lying to myself, but I allow myself to believe my own lies for now.

I look over at him after looking out of the window. I tried to distance myself after Isla made those comments about my interrupting their trip. I really don't have a problem with her, but I think she might hinder any sexual activities that could occur on this trip.

I just want his hands on my body and his lips roaming over my burning skin. I sneak a glance at Isla, and she's passed out for the moment. I unbuckle my seatbelt and stand up before straddling his lap. His eyes open, sleep filling them, but I can see the blizzard that he tries to hide from me. I can see his hard, cold need for me in those ocean-blue eyes. He's my *vitamin sea*. I need him to maintain my health: my emotional, mental, and physical wellbeing.

"Rye," he says with a raspy voice. It's the sexiest sound.

"Shh."

I run my hands over the back of his hair as his hands drift to my hips, settling me against him. Once he's content with my position, he splays a hand at the small of my back to keep me in place as his cock hardens against my pussy.

My heart flutters and I'm completely unprepared when he thrusts his hips up to meet mine. He torments me with his lips brushing against my neck and across my shoulder. He makes his way back up to my jaw, which sends tingles of desire through my core until his lips finally find mine. Lust blooms in the place of desire as I circle my arms around his neck and deepen the kiss against his hungry mouth. His mouth is warm, and the caress of his tongue against mine is far more wanton than what he's shown me before.

This kiss. It's a promise to me that he'll soon be burying

himself in me, claiming me.

Warmth radiates between my legs as his rigid cock presses against my clit again. I stare at his seaside eyes the moment our lips part. Those perfectly soft lips of his have stolen my words and have coaxed a shiver to run down the length of my spine.

His hands move over my back, and I shut my eyes in preparation for another kiss filled with euphoric bliss. He captures my lips again, and pure, raw elation washes over me. He tastes like crisp fall air, spice, and whiskey. His hand moves up and clasps gently into the back of my hair, holding my lips to his.

The confidence that he bestows upon me is one of the few reasons why I'm trying this for him. I open my mouth against his firm lips, and his tongue takes full advantage of the move. The kiss changes from rough and hard to a soothing one. One that is slow, inexorable.

The kiss lingers between us for a few moments until he shifts sideways to look at me. He runs his thumb over my lower lip, making me squirm on his lap.

"Do you have any idea how much you turn me on? Ever since the first time I saw you in the elevator in Vegas, I haven't been able to think of anything but burying my face between these thighs of yours and eating you until you lose control again and again. You're intoxicating, Rye."

The current between us burns me as he moves his hands to my thighs.

"I know the feeling, Whiskey."

"I'll be making you mine on this trip. Truly mine when I take what I've wanted to take over three weeks ago."

I start to quiver in his lap just thinking about him penetrating me and sending me to a much-needed vaginal orgasm. I don't know if my emotions are capable of handling what will happen between us afterward, but I cannot deny myself.

"You need to understand that I won't fuck you just for

pleasure. I'm going to fuck you to build this relationship and keep our souls content. I want it to be adventurous and a hit to your addiction that you won't be able to get over. This won't just be for fun; it will be to show you just how I feel about you." His eyes never stray from mine as he tells me this.

"That sounds . . . intriguing."

"I'm sure it does. Aside from my taking what belongs to me on this trip, I want you to accompany me to a few social events that I will need to attend."

I glance over at Isla and frown. "I thought that she would be going with you."

"I'd prefer to have my girlfriend on my arm, but if you'd rather not attend, then I can take her."

Girlfriend? I decide not to question him, but I let the word soak in while I get lost in his gaze.

"Oh. No, I want to go, but won't she be upset?"

"No, she prefers the beach and bikinis to my high-society functions."

"If she doesn't want to go, then I would really like to attend something with your fancy-ass."

He chuckles and kisses me innocently before lifting me off of his lap and standing. "Good. Can I get you a whiskey?"

"Please. A rye if you have it."

"Mmm, I've got all the Rye I need right here, baby," he says, and he wraps his arms around my waist and presses his lips to mine again.

Isla clears her throat, and I quickly stop kissing him and glance over at her. I'm sure that I am the deepest shade of crimson. A sure-fire thing. I have no doubt about it, considering my cheeks feel like I'm burning under her gaze.

"I'll take a rye too, please, Brass."

"I think I'll hog all of the Rye," he says playfully while he lowers his hand to my ass.

Why the hell am I blushing like it's going to wreck me? Holy shit. This man does something to me, and I'm not sure if it's even natural.

Wade lets me go before walking across the cabin to pour three tumblers of whiskey and handing one to each of us.

"Hey Hadley?" she says as she takes a drink. "I want to apologize for being a bitch earlier. I'm just not used to having to share my best friend is all."

I'm almost positive that my face has gone from a deep blush to a pale ghost white. "Uhm, it's okay. Thank you for apologizing."

"Sure thing. If I'm going to be stuck with your cute ass for the week, then I might as well get used to you now."

I half-smile as Wade brings his arm around my waist. "I suppose that we are."

He kisses the back of my head, and I relax into his touch, leaning a little closer to him, wondering what comes next in this relationship.

She smiles at the two of us. "You know . . . as much as I'm a bitch and I will probably continue to fight this relationship you two have . . . you do kind of look good together."

He spins me around in his arms and locks them around me as I look up at him. He seems content and relaxed. "Come," he says as he leads me to the back of the plane. "We need to adjust our bodies to the different time zone."

"Oh?"

"Yes. We need to sleep in order to do so."

"I'm not really someone who can sleep on a plane. Where are we going?"

"To the bedroom. Isla, are you good with the pull-out in here?"

"I sure am. 'Night, you two."

"'Night," he says to her, and I notice that his speech is

different around her. He's not the billionaire and fancy-ass when he's around Isla, and it makes me smile, knowing that there is something more behind his CEO façade. Sure, I've seen bits of it, but I don't think that he has completely turned off his demanding CEO role around me as of yet.

We walk into the bedroom at the back of the jet, and it's a lot more spacious than I thought it would be. I sit down at the end of the bed and watch as he undresses and hands me the shirt he was just wearing.

I take it willingly and see it as my cue to undress as well. I do so and fold my clothes, placing them on the side table before slipping his shirt on, not caring to button it up as I get under the sheets. He's already in the bed and reaches for the light switch once I get settled.

"Tell me something that no one else knows about you."

"Right now?"

"I don't see why not," he says as he reaches for my hand under the sheets.

"Uhm . . . my . . . uh, my mother killed herself when I was ten," I say softly, "but I don't think that counts, considering Lola knows."

"It does, yet doesn't. You owe me another then."

His arms come around me as he shifts to my side of the bed.

"Okay. I've never been outside of the United States before."

"I think I'm going to enjoy being your first, Hadley."

"For some reason, I really don't doubt that for one second."

He basically attacks me and rolls me onto my back as his body moves over mine. He seems to know that once he kisses my neck, I will crumple underneath him because it's the first thing that his lips touch when he brings them down to my skin. One of his hands slides down to my waist as his lips move up and along my jaw.

His fingers trail down the side of my ribcage, and I'm

suddenly ecstatic that I didn't button up his shirt. I can hardly bear it as he caresses me, slowly and gently. He's been making me wait for what seems like an eternity before he'll touch me. He's the only one that will be able to quench the thirst he has instilled throughout my body.

"You taste so good, Hads."

"Wade . . . please."

"Mmm. You know that I'll put you first, and that's what I'm going to do. I know you need me, but I'm not willing to strip you down bare yet. Not sexually anyway. When I have you away from the States I will, because you won't have anywhere to run but back to me."

"I wouldn't run, Wade. You have to know that."

"You can prove it to me when I finally sink into you."

I moan at the thought of him inside of me and shift underneath him, looking for some kind of pressure to relieve the ache between my legs.

"I know, gorgeous. Resisting you has been the hardest thing I've done. You're a temptress and one with my name written on your skin."

"Please, just . . ." I plead with him, needing to feel more than what my heart is expelling, which is turning out to be more than I am able to handle.

"You haven't begged me for anything in a while, Rye. Why? Is it because you're accepting the fact that I won't give it to you unless you give me what I want from you?"

My body reacts to his movements as his fingers burn my skin, riling me up even more than I already am. "What do you want?"

"I want to break you."

I go still at his words. He didn't even hesitate to say them. "What do you mean?"

"It's obvious that the only way I will be able to hold onto

you is by breaking you first, and I think I'm more than halfway there. You're so quiet lately, and you've kept that dirty mouth that I like so much in check. But as much as I like it, I need to break this sexual addiction you seem to have before it screws us both over."

"How did you figure me out?"

"It takes one to know one, to see another struggle with the same invisible illness, Hadley."

His words pull me from his spell, making my body still underneath his touch. His surprise admission has me startled. I can hear the truth behind his words.

"I didn't know," I confess.

"I know you didn't, which is why I'm telling you. I've fought through it body, mind, and soul. The addiction shows no mercy to anyone, and it becomes everything you breathe for and more. It changes you into someone that you no longer recognize and without its control, you easily fall into what you're trying to hide from."

"Is that why you won't give me what I want? Because you think it's consuming me?"

"It is consuming you." His pelvis presses into mine, and my body automatically reacts to his, pushing up to meet him. "I fought my battles with help from multiple specialists and testing, but I'd rather not subject you to that when I believe I know what you need."

"But from the signals you gave me, you were ready to fuck me in Las Vegas."

"I was. I cave in to the addiction from time to time, and when I do, I make sure that it will not affect my life as you are allowing yours to."

"You don't know that."

"I fucked around to find the love that I saw but never received from anyone but my mother. I fucked up my life with an addiction wearing my skin until I was unrecognizable. My addiction wasn't to porn or masturbation, but to the actual act of sex. I took what I wanted to try and prove that there was more to the act of sex than a physical high. I used it for something to protect my feelings as well, but it was something I used to find my place. To find exactly where I fit into this world by fitting into as many pussies as I could—each of which I neglected and didn't pay any real interest to. I was devoid of emotion and the capability to love. The sexual bonds were enough for me for years, but now I will never be satisfied with just the physical act of sex."

"I think I do something similar," I admit before I am able to stop myself.

He nods and kisses my lips once. "I think that what you are hiding sits deeper than mine ever did, which is why I refuse to trust someone else with you."

"Why me, though?"

"Because I knew from the second I saw you that I had to have you." He shakes his head and rests his forehead down against mine. I catch the quick and quiet breath that he takes. "You look shocked."

"I think I am. I don't understand why you'd pursue me, even if you could. My coming to Chicago was just fate."

He chews over my words without saying anything, but the smoldering look that he's giving me sends a wild vibration down my spine. I lean up and bite his nipple without any warning.

He quirks his eyebrow and glares at me. I shrug innocently before laughter escapes my lips. "You're going to get hell for that," he says as his hands move to my ribs. The feeling of being wanted and the warmth of his hands on my body might make me lose my mind one day soon.

All of a sudden his fingers are digging into my sides before he starts tickling my ribcage.

"Holy shit," I squeak as I try to move out from his grip, but he kneels up and locks me between his legs so I'm unable to escape. "Wade!" I shriek out.

"Not so feisty and mouthy now, are we?" he taunts as he continues his assault on my body, making me writhe underneath him.

I place my hands on his chest and push up, trying to buck him off of me, but he's too strong for me to budge. "Damn it," I cry out.

His throaty chuckle fills the room, and it's a sound that I know I won't tire of. A small smile plays on his lips as he leans down to whisper in my ear, "I know that you think every man out there is the same. That they all just want one thing from a woman, but I'm going to prove to both you and myself that I can and do want more."

His fingers still when he finishes speaking those words, but before I can respond to him, he starts to speak again. "I'm going to show you that you are worth more than a piece to fuck. I'm going to make you see that you are someone's first choice, and when you finally break through the haze of addiction, I will have found you."

"Wade . . ." his name comes off of my lips as a praise. "You're so sure of yourself when it comes to me."

"I know what I want, Hads, and it's you."

Goose bumps break out over my skin at his words. "You sort of make me want to be something better. Someone worthy of you."

"That's where you're wrong. You already are. I'm just going to be the one to show you."

He tilts his head to the side and watches me closely for my reaction.

"As much as I want to believe that, I can't."

"Which part? The fact that you are already worth having me and so much more or that I will be the one to show you?"

"Both," I tell him honestly as I reach up and cup my hand over his cheek. He leans into my touch, and my body does this weird jig inside as if it's in its happy place.

"I'll make you see it, baby. Just give me time."

The endearment hits me in the heart, and this time, there's nothing stopping it from piercing through the organ. My armor is no longer protecting me, and I believe he knows it. He's going to push me until I can't stand the number of knives he's throwing at me.

For those who believe in the notion of love, they see it as a bright red heart, thumping away eagerly, but when I imagine it, I see it differently. I see knives, daggers, bullets, and arrows piercing it from all angles. But of course, I don't believe in it . . . so I choose not to see it at all.

I lie to myself. *Again.*

"Most men who call me baby say thank you for the fuck and leave." My eyebrows furrow at the thought of how many of those there have been.

"Trust me?" he asks me softly before turning his lips to my palm and placing a kiss there.

"I'm trying to."

He nods and lowers himself over me, speaking against my lips without kissing me. "That's all I'm asking for."

He shifts his body off of mine, and I instantly miss the weight of him and his heat. The warmth of his lips caresses my neck as he fits my body to his. I shut my eyes and will my racing heart to follow the sound of his breaths in order to calm myself down. He might not notice that his words have me on the verge of a panic attack, but I just went from zero to one hundred in a second. I will not cry. I will not break down in front of this man.

I will myself to realize that this fear is just an illusion and soon I'll be free from it. My depression and panic attacks are not and never will be signs of weakness. They are proof that I fight to remain strong, whether it is through sex or fighting away the painful memories. As I lie here, I feel like my skin is turning inside out and that I am being consumed whole.

"Rye. You're shaking." His voice breaks through my inner monologue of reminding myself to keep breathing.

"I'm sorry," I say with a shaky voice.

"What triggered it?"

How does he always know that there is something wrong?

"I just . . ." I take in a ragged breath, trying to stop myself from hyperventilating. "I can't breathe."

He shifts his large body so that he's eye level with me. I can just make out the shadows of his face as he cups my cheeks with both of his hands. "Do you have any anxiety medication in your purse?"

I nod as my chest starts to ache and dizziness ensues.

"Are you able to take it now?"

I nod, realizing that I forgot to take it this morning while I was packing. Intense tingling starts at the tips of my fingers and begins to crawl up my wrists, taunting me.

"I'm going to grab your purse," he says simply. He's telling me his movements before he makes them, and I'm grateful because anything could make this worse. Any sudden or hectic movement could cause me to plummet deeper into the attack.

He lifts his body from the bed and strides across the room and out into the cabin. He's back with my purse within a minute, and he walks to the side of the bed that I'm lying on.

"I need you to sit up for me, gorgeous."

Slowly, I push my body up with my arms, feeling the pressure of thousands of needles in them as I do. He opens my purse and hands it to me. I point to the inner pocket and watch him unzip it and remove a clear orange prescription bottle. He uncaps it and spills the pills onto his palm before keeping one and returning the rest of them into the plastic container.

"Here," he says and gets up again before walking to a small refrigerator that I hadn't noticed before, retrieving a bottle of water.

"Thank you," I manage to say as he uncaps the bottle and holds it out for me to take my anxiety medication.

With shaking hands, I slide the pill into my mouth before raising the bottle of water, which he doesn't let go of. Instead, he assists me with it as I bring it to my lips and swallow enough to get the pill down and into my system.

Once I nod to him, he sets it aside and sits down on the bed next to me, offering me his hand to help me sit up. "Put your arms above your head and breathe for me."

I'm finding it hard to comprehend that he's actually helping me. The other times that this has happened around men, they disappear. I take his hand and pull myself up, my chest rising and falling in rapid succession. He intertwines his fingers with both my hands before raising our arms into the air, above our heads. I watch his breathing and try to match mine to it.

The big black hole opens up and threatens to suck me into it. I know that once I'm in its grasp, I won't be able to climb out for a few days because depression will sink in and I will spend my nights crying myself to sleep, each time hitting harder than the one before.

"Hadley." His voice demands my attention and my eyes dart to his, fear lancing through my body. "Stay with me. Don't become the victim of your mind."

Chaos. Danger. Threats. Panic. Frustration. It all hits me at once, and I just want to curl up into his arms and force the world to take a step back and allow me to breathe. I need him to let me escape, but I know that he won't allow me to cave into my mind where it's not safe. I squeeze my eyes shut, desperate for relief. Anxiety overwhelms me completely until I feel his lips on mine. His kiss is slow, gentle, yet deep. I open my lips to his and force myself to stop thinking about anything other than the feeling of them moving with mine.

Endorphins make their way through my body as my mind is redirected and refocusing on him instead. My heart accelerates and then slows down, causing me to pull away from him.

"I can't, just . . ."

"I'm sorry. I thought that it would help." I can hear the worry in his voice as I lie back down on the bed and tug on his hand.

"Just hold me and don't let go."

He lies down next to me and pulls me into his body so our fronts are touching. With my head tucked under his chin, I turn my head sideways to listen to his heartbeat.

It takes me another hour before I'm able to regulate my breathing again and stop the tingling that had taken over my fingers. I let out a steady breath, loud enough for him to hear. He shifts and peers down at me. "Hadley?"

"I'm fine. I'm sorry about that."

I tilt my chin upward so we're breathing in and out together as his lips are only a whisper away from mine. He strokes my bottom lip with his fingers and gives me a sly smile before closing the distance between us and taking my mouth in an all-consuming kiss. He kisses me like it's the last thing that he will do, as if there is no time left.

He must feel the tension melt away from my body because his mouth parts with mine and I cling to him. "Don't ever apologize for needing me. Is that understood?"

I smile to myself, feeling as if he just brought me back from someplace dark and raw to somewhere pure. "Yes."

"Good. Get some rest before I kiss you for the remainder of

this flight."

"I wouldn't mind that, you know?"

"I figured as much."

He drowns me in his lips again as that blizzard stirs behind his eyes until he closes them to kiss me lifeless.

Fourteen

Wade

WE LANDED IN Sydney about two and a half hours ago, and we've just walked into the Sydney suite at the Park Hyatt Hotel. Isla has gone to her own suite, which is not far from Hadley's and mine, but it's enough distance between us—it might be needed.

The plane ride here was everything but what I expected it to be. She didn't argue when I told her that I was going to break her, or when I told her about my personal experience with this invisible illness. Given that I didn't go into too much detail about my sexual past, she understood.

What took me by the balls in a death grip was when she had her panic attack. I felt useless and incapable of helping her. She hasn't told me what brought it on, and it's not my place to ask either. I decide to wait it out and see if she offers up an answer in the coming days.

"What do you think?"

"Are you kidding me, Wade?" She spins around and almost leaps into my arms.

I catch her and move her now-straight hair out of her face as she giggles up at me.

Fuck me.

If I thought that she was beautiful before . . . She seems to have come alive after our experience on the plane. Her eyes look like they are filled with glitter instead of the turquoise color that they are. Appeal. Desirability. Seductiveness. Allure. I feel it all while I watch her. This attraction to her has not remained constant; it's been growing ever since I first laid eyes on her.

I find that my attraction to her runs deeper than her skin, eyes, breasts, and all that she has to offer physically. It goes far beyond that realm. I'm interested in the person she is. I can feel the pull toward her from my core.

I'm used to superficial bullshit laced with sex. This time, though, is different. I realize that I haven't answered her yet because she's staring at me as if I've forgotten how to speak.

"This is ours for the week."

"Do you always travel in such luxury?" she asks as she blinks up at me and she seems genuinely curious.

"I do. I don't think that I could travel any other way. Are you tired?" I move her hair off of her shoulders, showcasing her breasts for me.

"Not really. I mean, I did fall asleep while you kissed me to death, so I'm not complaining."

"You'll be jet-lagged later on. If you're up to it, though, I'd like to take you out to see some of the city."

"Of course I want to go with you." She places a quick peck on my lips before rushing over to her suitcase. "Where are we going to go? Do I have time to freshen up?"

"You do, and you'll need to wear a bikini. We'll head out to Bondi Beach for the rest of the afternoon and possibly watch the sunset. Isla has her heart set on going to the beach and then shopping, but I might leave the latter to you two and my credit card."

"Excuse me?" she stops rifling through her suitcase and looks up at me.

"Isla has a crush on Westfield; it's a mall filled with everything designer. We'll head there after the beach."

"Oh. Wait, I thought you weren't going to come."

I smirk at her word choice. "I wasn't, but I'd like to spend time with you before I have to dive headfirst into work."

"I like the sound of that," she says as she pulls out something black from her suitcase before walking gingerly to the bathroom to change.

I stand here, staring at her ass before it disappears behind the bathroom door. I glance down at my erection and shake my head at my own needs; it must take me a full two minutes to rein in my raging hard-on. I adjust myself in my jeans before I grab my swim trunks from my suitcase and strip bare in the middle of the bedroom. I cannot stop myself from thinking about the way she looks when she doesn't have a scrap of material hiding her flawless body. Burned into my head is the image of her bare in front of me in the shower. I can almost feel the softness of her skin underneath my fingers again.

My cock rears to life once again as she walks into the bedroom, and I only have one leg in my swim trunks.

"Wade, do you . . ." Her words cut off when she looks up at me, holding something at the back of her neck. I wink at her and my cock twitches when I feel her gaze on me.

I step into the other leg and pull the trunks up and over my erection. "Do I what?"

"Fuck," she mumbles.

"Yes. I do fuck. Rather hard in fact. I tend to bruise the woman I'm with, both inside and out," I tell her honestly.

"I . . . uhm . . . that's not what I meant."

"I'm sure that you have thought about it before, though."

"I mean, yes, I have, but I was going to ask you to tie me."

"Shibari? I can do that while I fuck you as well if you'd like. I hope that you're not opposed to rope burn."

She purses her lips and walks up to me before dropping her hand from the back of her neck and lowering it to circle around my shaft through my trunks. "Show me," she dares.

The thin black straps of her bikini top slip off of her shoulders, which in turn exposes her beautifully shaped breasts to me.

"You have no idea what you're getting yourself into, Rye."

"And what? You don't think that I'll be able to handle this?" she asks as she squeezes my shaft. I pulse in her grip before I bring my hand up to cup her breast and tug on the peak of her nipple.

"I believe you will be able to. With some practice at the very least."

I get down on my knees in front of her and pull down the thin material of her bikini bottom to place a chaste kiss on her pubic bone before standing again. Her chest rises in anticipation and desire for me, which only intensifies my need for her. I lean forward and slide my tongue over her left nipple before moving down to lick her line of cleavage. The sounds she makes when she moans my name are sinful coming from her lips. I release her breast from my other hand as she pumps me once before I take the other nipple into my mouth, teasing her with my tongue.

"Wade . . . oh God. Please," she cries and starts to push down my trunks to get her hand around my shaft. She manages to move her hand down the waistband of my trunks, and I realize as she grabs hold of my bare cock that it's the first time that I've allowed her to touch me and fuck if it doesn't feel right.

She gets the trunks past my ass, releasing my cock as I move to her other breast, adoring how she tastes and writhes under the pressure of my mouth. My hands find her hips where I dig my fingers into her delicate, pale skin. I lift her up, forcing her to relinquish her hold on my cock. When I lift her high enough, she wraps her legs around my waist and I walk backward to the king-sized bed that I know is there. My lips find hers out of hunger, and I devour her, tasting her need on the tip of her tongue as I'm sure she does mine. The end of the bed hits the backs of my knees. I turn around before laying her on the bed and moving her up the sheets. I maneuver my body on top of hers; I can physically feel her anticipation as I hover over her. My lips leave hers for the moment to travel down her neck to her collarbone.

"Wade," she whispers in a plea.

She reaches around her torso to undo the string of her bikini top that's still holding it onto her just as I trail my fingers down the center of her rib cage and past her belly button. I reach into her bikini bottoms to feel her for the first time since I washed her. I gingerly run my finger through her slit causing her to push her hips up, begging me for more as my fingers find her clitoris. I stroke her once and then again before moving my index finger between her lips, feeling exactly how much she fucking wants me to sink into her and pound away until she comes undone. Until I fully stake my claim on her.

"Yes . . ."

"You're soaked for me, Hads."

She doesn't speak as I sink my middle finger into her, feeling her inner walls, touching what no other man will while she's mine.

"Do you understand that you are mine?" I ask her as I tease her neck with my lips.

"I d-do," she stutters while one hand fists the sheets at her side and the other weaves into the back of my hair, pulling at the strands that she's able to lock her fingers around.

"I will not share you. Have I made myself clear? Not with anyone while you're mine. Is that understood?" I repeat myself for good measure.

"Yes, Whiskey. I . . . please."

The anticipation and need in her voice make my cock stir and harden even further, so much so, that it's on the verge of being painful.

I crook my finger up inside of her to find her sweet spot, the place that will make her pure putty in my hands. I know when I hit it because she lets out a tortured whimper. I watch her limbs tighten for me before she releases the tension that I have helped her build up.

The sound of the doorbell, followed by a sharp knock, draws my attention and I remove my finger from her while I watch the wanton expression on her face change to surprise and then shock as I move off of her.

"What are you doing?" she asks frantically as her eyes dart to mine, silently begging me for more of what I was finally giving her.

"Answering the door, Rye," I tell her as I place my middle finger into my mouth so I can taste her cream.

"But . . ."

"Get dressed. We wouldn't want Isla knowing how sexy you look when you get what you need, or when you're half-naked and spread out on my bed."

She sits up quickly and covers her breasts with her forearm while I pull my trunks back over my ass and stride out of the bedroom and across the expanse of the suite to the door. I run a hand through my hair before I swing it open—at the same time as I hear Hadley letting loose with a string of obscenities, whether to herself or toward me I don't know.

Isla greets me with a ravishing smile and throws her arms around me in a hug. "My God, Brass, I fucking love the suite you got me. And to think I was complaining about our vacation interruption on the plane—because of her, I get my own suite." She throws her head back and gives me one hell of an evil laugh before letting go of me.

"You're welcome, Isla. Do you mind helping Hads with her bikini?"

"Hads, huh? Look at you, growing a pair of balls and letting them hang a little lower."

"Fuck off." I offer her my finger while she walks across the suite and into the bedroom where I know Rye is in fucking pieces with need.

The late afternoon sun beats down on the three of us while we lounge on the white sand. We're shaded in a cabana, but I've noticed that Hadley's skin has grown the slightest shade darker. I rest my head back against the lounger and take in the view in front of me. It's not often that I let go of work and fully immerse myself in the luxury of relaxation.

Bondi Beach isn't overcrowded like it was when we first arrived. Many beach-goers have left, and it has grown quieter. Despite the heat of the day, I find myself content as I watch the waves crash against the shore, and the sound of the water has helped to soothe any residual stress that had been lingering.

I must have drifted off because I wake to Isla and Hadley laughing together as they walk toward the cabana. My eyes go to Hadley as she takes one step after the other in the white sand. She's wet. They must have gone down to the waves without my noticing. Her now-sun-kissed skin is shining with small droplets of saltwater, and I would have been fucked if Isla didn't walk past the cabana as Hadley walks up to me. My cock rises as she nears me.

"I could get used to this sight."

I can see her blush through my sunglasses. She mustn't have realized that I had woken up because she was gazing at me as well.

"I could say the same thing," she says as she takes a seat next to me on the double lounger. Instead of lying down, though, she leans over my torso and wrings her hair out over me.

The water is ice cold on my heated chest as it hits me.

"Fuck," I curse, and I leap up, knocking over the small table holding our drinks beside me. She stands up just as quickly and starts to back away from me. I grin to myself before I take a step and then another at a faster pace in her direction.

She must realize my intention because she turns and takes off down the sand and toward the ocean. The vision of her ass moving slows me down for a second before I bolt after her.

She looks over her shoulder at me and shouts, "Wade! Don't you dare!"

"Ah baby, payback is an evil bitch," I tell her as I reach my hands out for her and grab her by the hips, sweeping her off of her feet and spinning us around.

"Wade." She giggles and moves her wet hair from her face.

"You've done it now, Rye."

She starts kicking her legs as I hold onto her. We've captured the attention of a few beachgoers now, but I couldn't give a fuck as I walk into the waves with her. Her arms wrap around my neck as I hold her up, and she watches me intently.

"What are you going to—" she gets out just as I get deep enough into the water to toss her into the air and watch as she splashes into a wave a few feet in front of me while squirming.

I swim over to where she landed just as she surfaces, sputtering for breath.

"You asshole," she manages to get out as I pull her to me. Her arms move around my neck as I swipe the wet tendrils from her face.

I'm met with her radiant smile, and I chuckle. "Two can play at your game, Hads."

She locks her legs around my torso as I hold onto her. "I think that I like this side of you, Waylon Brass."

"Mmm, you haven't seen anything yet, baby."

"Oh?"

I drop to my knees in the water, taking us both down as a wave crashes above our heads. She pushes up and swims to the surface and out of my grip. I follow behind her until I break the surface. She's moving strands of hair out of her face when I lock eyes with her as she treads water. I realize that she can't stand here so I pull her close and kiss her sea-salted lips.

"You're captivating, Rye."

"You think so? I was thinking just how much of a prick you are."

"A prick?"

"Yes. All I did was cool you off," she says through a laugh and splashes me.

I run my finger over her lips before placing a kiss against them, tasting salt and everything that makes up this gorgeous woman. "I enjoyed it, and I'm enjoying having you to myself right now."

"You can hog me all you want."

"I'll take you up on that offer, be warned."

She purses her lips and runs a hand through my hair. "Deal."

"Are you hungry?" I ask to distract the both of us from plunging into more than a conversation in front of our spectators on the beach.

"A little, but I think I want another one of those Aussie Beach Blonde drinks."

"Come with me, I'll get you buzzed."

"Don't make promises that you can't keep, Wade. Specifically, ones made with your fingers. I'm desperate for you since you touched me in the suite."

"I keep my promises, Rye. You'll just have to give me the time to prove it." I run my hand down her back under the water, running my fingers over her piercings before we make our way back to the shore.

I take her hand, intertwining my fingers with hers while she adjusts her bikini with the other. I haven't been able to take my eyes off of her this afternoon. She's unquestionably the woman on the beach that has all of the men boning after her.

She's untouchable with me around, though, and I'm going

to keep it that way.

"There you assholes are," Isla greets as we walk up to the cabana, and she's holding one of those Beach Blonde drinks in each hand.

"Please tell me that one of those are for me," Hadley says, and she lets go of my hand and walks up to Isla.

"Sure as shit. I don't think that I've ever seen Wade drink anything but whiskey."

They each take a drink and moan in unison while I grab a towel and dry my hair off before wrapping it around my hips.

"Baby, did you want a towel?" I ask without thinking, and Isla's gaze shoots up to meet mine.

"Holy shit," she says as I realize my mistake. I've just called Hadley 'baby' in front of my best friend. I've never called a woman anything other than her full name before, with the exception of Hadley.

Hadley sets her drink down and walks up to me to take the towel. "Thank you."

"Uhh," Isla voices and I stare at her as I watch her confusion turn into a smile, and I'm flooded with relief that there won't be another bitter moment between the two of us.

I watch Hadley dry off and take a seat on the lounger again with her drink before I join her while Isla lies out in the sun.

"Thank you for bringing me here, Whiskey. It's undeniably stunning."

"I'm glad that you agreed to come so quickly. The thought of not seeing you for over a week wasn't something that I was willing to contemplate."

She blushes and takes a drink, trying to hide her pink cheeks from me. I pull her body closer, and she drops her leg between mine as I stretch out on the white cushions.

"Brass, why the fuck haven't you gotten on a board yet?"

I chuckle at Isla and look down at Hadley. "I'm rather

content right now."

"So I've noticed, but you can't come all the way down here and not surf."

"Wait, you surf?" Hadley peers up at me through her sunglasses.

"I do. I have for years now. Maybe I should teach you one afternoon."

"Uhh, sure, if you want to see me eat wave."

"Oh come on, Hadley," Isla cheers her on, "even I have done it. Mind you, I never actually stood up, but it was fun watching Wade get so frustrated with me."

They laugh together, and I shake my head. "I'll take you out, Hadley."

"If you really want to, I suppose, but will you have time with all of your meetings and appointments?"

"I'm not sure, but why don't we head down to the beach before the sun rises tomorrow and I'll show you how to get up on the board at the very least."

She readjusts herself so she's seated on the lounger instead of lying against me, "All right. I'll give it a go."

"Now that we have that sorted, can we please go spend Wade's money? I'm dying in this heat," Isla says.

I watch Hadley swallow the remainder of her drink before she gets up and reaches into her bag for a cover-up. As much as I don't appreciate the material hindering my view, I would not enjoy watching other men gawk at her as we make our way around Sydney. I grab my belongings after pulling a T-shirt over my head and hold my hand out to her. "You coming?"

She purses her lips and lifts her bag onto her shoulder. "I should be."

"Dear God," Isla spits out and starts to walk away from us as Hadley reaches for me. I pull her into my side as I let the cabana girl know that we're heading out and to charge my company for the expenses before we fall into step behind Isla.

I've never understood how women are able to walk around stores for hours before settling on what to buy. I think that Isla took it easy on my credit card because Hadley was with her. Isla eventually got Hadley to agree to purchase a Burberry bag and a matching purse. I'm rather pleased that Hadley isn't swept up in my lavish lifestyle as I'm sure many other women would be.

She may be the *normal* that I was in search of.

Fifteen

Hadley

I'M IN PARADISE.

I've been watching Wade out on the waves for an hour now, and I didn't think that I could be so attracted to someone else as I am to him at this moment. I watch as he rides out the largest wave that I've seen him on this morning before he picks up his board, clamping it underneath his left arm and starts to make his way out of the water toward me. I have my legs splayed out in front of me while I lean my arms out behind me, soaking up the early morning Australian sun in a white and navy strapless bikini that he picked out for me during our shopping trip last night.

This morning when we woke up to his alarm, the sun hadn't risen yet. He kissed me quickly and told me to get ready, and that we'd have breakfast before he goes into his meetings for the day. We got ready next to each other, all the while stealing glances in the mirrors.

After picking up his board at a friend's house on the way, we arrived at the beach before anyone else was here. We sat next to each other as the sun decided to wake up over the ocean, spilling vibrant colors over the sky. We didn't talk or touch each other, and I've never enjoyed just being around someone as I was with him this morning. Once the sun rose, he taught me how to get up on a surfboard on the sand before we made our way to the water.

We had plenty of laughs, all of which were at my expense until I told him that I wanted to see what he could do and he's been catching waves ever since.

I'm snapped back from this morning's memories as he comes closer to me. The roar of the waves is all I can hear until he pushes the end of the surfboard into the sand to the right of me before taking a seat beside me.

"You're incredible, Whiskey."

He runs his hand through his wet hair, trying to comb it out of his face as he beams at me, "You think so?"

"Are you kidding me? Those waves are huge. I could watch you do that for hours."

"You weren't so bad yourself. You got up rather quickly."

I laugh and nudge him with my shoulder, "I got up twice, and once you were holding my hand."

I watch him as he stretches his arms back and his legs out in front of him. He rests his arm behind my back so I take the opportunity to lean back against his shoulder as I look out at the crashing waves. He leans his head against mine, and I can feel the smile on his face.

"You're beautiful, you know that? Those few times that I fell off of the board were your fault. I caught the sight of you out of the corner of my eye and lost focus on the wave. You distract me, Rye."

I sweep sand onto his calves with my foot while he speaks, taking in his words, "Don't blame your clumsiness on me," I joke with him.

"I'm merely placing blame where it is due." He swings his right arm over my body and pulls on my left hip until he has me straddling his lap.

Placing my hands on his tanned, muscular shoulders, I look down at him. "Mmm, I'm not so sure about that," I say as I move closer to him. "Wade?"

"What is it?"

"Can we do this again before we leave the country?"

"You bet your fine ass that we can. I'd like you to get a chance to meet Liam before we leave as well. Isla and I went to college with him before he dropped out and moved down here. It was his house we went to earlier to pick up my board. I think he'd rather enjoy meeting you."

"Oh?"

"Yes, but for now, let's go get you fed."

"I was hoping that you'd take me in the waves instead," I tell him without giving up my prime spot with my pussy right above his erection.

"Did you now?"

"What? You don't want me?"

He eyes me curiously, cautiously, before answering. "I believe that you already know the answer to that. I've told you that I'll take you when you're ready and not a second sooner."

"Jesus, Wade. I'm dying since you fingered me. I'll have to get myself off."

"I'd like to watch that."

"Ugh! Of course you would," I huff and get up and off of him before grabbing his shirt and sliding it on over my bikini.

He gets up and pulls his board out of the sand and clamps it underneath his arm before offering me his hand.

I scowl at him before I concede and lace my fingers with his as we walk up to the boardwalk and to the black-tinted SUV that Jacobs has been driving us around in since we landed in Australia. He climbs out of the vehicle just as we arrive at it and he takes the board from Wade to secure it. Wade ushers me into the BMW and closes the door once he gets in, enveloping us in the air-conditioned interior.

It didn't take too long to get back to the hotel, but Wade seemed to be on edge once he opened the door to the suite. He withdrew from me and went into his CEO-asshole mode. I think that it might have to do with his acquisitions of the few properties I heard him mention to Jacobs on the ride back, but I'm unsure.

When he left, I was seated on the deck overlooking the Sydney Harbor, eating a breakfast of fresh fruit, croissants, and coffee. I watched him through the sliding glass doors as he put on his suit jacket and armed himself with his essentials before buttoning up and walking to the suite door. He didn't even bother to say goodbye, or hell, even glance back at me.

At times, I feel like I know him, and then at others, I feel like I'm sharing a suite with a complete stranger. This is one of those moments. I get up and head inside to get ready for the day by showering and getting dressed in a simple black tent dress. It's large, comfortable, and flowy. Perfect for this kind of warm weather.

I should have brought my yoga mat with me, seeing as I'll be alone for the majority of the time here or with Isla. I exhale loudly once I've dried my hair and masked my face in makeup. I decide to call Lo while I wait on Isla to get up, since it's just past nine here and she's probably still asleep. I lie down on the bed and dial Lo's number, but it sends me straight to voicemail. Oh right . . . the time difference.

I throw my head back against the pillow and pull my legs up, feeling incredibly alone in this moment. This feeling of dread and loneliness is one of the emotions that I have been protecting myself from over the years, and I've walked into it willingly with Waylon Brass.

After checking and replying to a few emails, I decide to take a chance on my new job and log onto the system with my username and passcode that Low-Sound provided for me earlier this week. I roll onto my stomach as the line beeps in my ear, informing me that someone is calling in. I hit one to accept the call.

"Hello?"

"Now don't you sound like you have a dirty cunt."

Oh. I thought I was harsh with my words, but I suppose he's paying by the minute.

"What's your name, girl?"

"Does it matter?" I retort, wanting to have control over this phone call. I know that if it gets out of hand that all I have to do is press nine, and his number will be blocked from my user ID.

"It's whatever you want, sweetheart."

I envision that it's Wade on the other end of the line, and the bedroom scenario evolves in my mind.

"Tell me what you want. Are you stroking yourself?"

I turn onto my back when he answers me with a guttural groan.

"I want you to concentrate on every wanton word that I'm going to say to you because I want you to fantasize that it's my mouth running over your cock right now. Can you do that?" I ask him with confidence in my voice. I'm not wet. Not in the slightest, and it surprises me. I'm usually able to get wet if a man says my name with want in his voice, but I have no desire toward this anonymous stranger.

As the call continues I try my damnedest to get into it with him, but I'm finding it a lot harder than it really should be. He proceeds to tell me how badly he wants to fuck me and that he needs me to humiliate him in public by beating him.

I go along with his fantasy and start yelling at him before he grunts again, and I start moaning along with him. I continue to tell him how good he feels, and how big his cock is, and when I tell him that I'm about to come, he lets out an ooaf into the phone as he yells out that he's coming on my face.

He hangs up on me before I'm able to get another word in, saving himself a few dollars. I check the time and grin to myself: thirteen minutes and a wallet full of cash. Simple.

I decide to stay online for the next fifteen minutes in which I manage to squeeze in two more phone calls, one being a couple and the other a college-aged boy who I'm sure is using his father's bank account for this call.

Sixteen

Wade

I'M BEING SHOWN into a large conference room when my phone vibrates in my jacket pocket. I pull it out and slide my finger over the screen, revealing a message from Isla: I SWEAR TO GOD THAT I DIDN'T KNOW YOU TWO WERE FUCKING, OR I WOULDN'T HAVE LET MYSELF IN.

I scowl at her message. What the fuck is she talking about? WHAT?

JESUS, GET OFF OF THE PHONE WHILE YOU'RE BURIED INSIDE OF HER. I WAS JUST APOLOGIZING, IN CASE YOU HEARD ME AT THE BEDROOM DOOR.

Hadley.

I realize now that I didn't take the time to say goodbye to her before I left and guilt swims through my veins but anger shortly replaces it when I read over Isla's messages again.

ISLA, I'M ABOUT TO WALK INTO A MEETING. I LEFT THE HOTEL OVER AN HOUR AGO.

I'm seated at the head of the conference table when her message comes through: THEN HOW . . . OH MY GOD. WADE, I'M SO SORRY.

I get up from my seat and pace the length of the room. I'm the first one in here, so I take the minute to call her. She answers on the first ring.

"Wade?"

"I cannot speak long. What the fuck is happening?"

"Well, I let myself into your suite with the keycard that you gave me. I couldn't find Hadley, so I went to the bedroom, but as I was about to knock, I heard her moaning and telling you just how good it—" she cuts herself off.

"I'm across the city, Isla. Who the fuck is with her?"

"I don't know. I left assuming that it was you."

"How long ago was this?"

"I texted you just as I left your suite."

"I'll be there in thirty minutes."

She gasps. "Wade, you can't just walk away from this meeting."

"I'll postpone it," I tell her as the first gentleman walks into the room. "Be outside of my suite in thirty minutes."

"All right," she tells me, and we hang up.

I send Jacobs a text message, telling him to bring the car around front immediately. Once I hit send, I slide my phone back into my jacket pocket before I walk up to one of the owners of the properties and excuse myself due to a personal emergency.

He agrees to postpone the meeting for an hour and a half. I ensure him that I will return as soon as possible and thank him again for making time to come in on a Saturday morning.

With that, I step out of the conference room just as another four men approach. I greet them and walk out of the office building and to where Jacobs is waiting.

The thirty minutes that it takes for me to get back to the hotel has me ready to fucking explode. I know that I haven't given her what she needs—and I won't—but I'll be fucking damned if she's fucking another man in my bed.

I won't stand for this shit, and I refuse to subject myself to this negative side of the illness again. I walk up to the suite door with rage flowing through my veins. Isla is waiting there for me.

"Brass, I'm so sorry."

I cut her off. "Did you see him leave?"

"No, I left and went back to my suite until about three

minutes ago."

I let this woman in, and I was willing to break her of an illness that hindered me for the majority of my life. This journey with her has just come to an end. I don't see the reasoning behind keeping her as mine when she cannot dedicate herself to me.

I open the suite door and stride in with purpose until I come to the closed bedroom door. Isla isn't far behind me, but I hold my hand out to halt her as I push the door open.

I take in the room, looking for Rye, but my eye catches the sheets on the bed that are now rustled and unkept. Unlike how it was before I left.

Hadley walks out of the en suite bathroom and jumps when she sees me. "Holy shit! You scared me, Whiskey."

"Where is he?" I demand as I take in her flushed complexion.

"What?"

"Don't make me repeat myself, Hadley."

She raises her brow and frowns. "Wade, what are you talking about?"

I take a step toward her, and she involuntarily takes a step back, retreating from my tangible wrath.

"Where the fuck is he, Hadley?"

"Where is who?" she yells back at me.

"The asshole that you were fucking. Don't be a fucking dumb blonde when it suits you best."

She gasps and her hand flies up to her heart, covering it, shielding it from me and my words. "I've been alone all morning. Why would you think—"

"Because I heard you when I came to see if you were ready to go explore Sydney with me," Isla interjects from the threshold of the door.

"Isla. Leave," I tell her without turning around to face her. My eyes bore into Hadley's, and she seems lost.

"I—no—you . . ." she stutters and takes a step toward me. "You shouldn't be here, Wade. What about your meeting?"

"Is he in the bathroom?" I ask her in a cold voice before I blow past her and into the bathroom. I slam doors open and closed until I'm satisfied that there is nobody in here but the two of us as she watches.

Ire builds and consumes every space inside of me without a thought of consequences. I grab hold of her hips, and she blanches. "Wade! Please. I didn't—"

"You brought some motherfucker into my bed." I watch her full eyes drain, and she squares her shoulders as if I've smacked her.

"If you let me get a fucking word in edgewise, Wade, I could explain." With each word, she raises her voice toward me, and it's pushing me to physical violence.

"I thought that the lines were drawn. That they were straight, and you understood where I stood with you." The combination of anger and hurt boils over, and I turn away from her with my hands pulling at the back of my hair.

"Wade . . . please. Just listen."

"There's nothing that you can say, Hadley. Give me ten minutes and pack your shit. I'll check you into a different room where you'll be able to swallow as many cocks as you please."

With a weak smile, I turn to see her ashen face before I spin back around and walk out of the suite. Isla catches my arm as I turn into the hallway. "Brass, I'm sorry. I know that she truly meant something to you even if I've given you shit about her."

I glance down at her, but I have to look over her head again as my eyes begin to sting, and the floor seems to crack beneath my feet. I've never experienced this aching hollowness and earth-defying gravity before.

I nod and step around her on my way to get Hadley a new room and make my way back to the office block where the most important conference of Mothers of Brass—Sydney will be held.

Seventeen

Hadley

I THOUGHT THAT I lost all of my fight before he left, but as soon as the suite door shut, I found it once again. Then why am I struggling to breathe? My hand still rests against my heart, internally begging for that shield to come back, to protect me from him.

I feel . . . fragmented. Wounded.

Each and every vulnerability that I kept safe and coded in my heart has grown roots, and I can't force the emotions to retreat back to their safe place.

Where did he go? Why didn't he let me explain?

I feel as if I'm fading in this room. I tell myself to retreat into my mind's prison and leave. The sweetness and pure spark that set my heart on fire has turned into the burning flames of hell. I force my body to take in a deep breath. The suite smells of him, though, and it burns the interior of my lungs before I grab my phone and search for the next flight out of this country. Away from him and his negative assumptions about me.

Once I find a flight that leaves in four hours, I run across the room, searching through my purse for my wallet and then my credit card. I input all of my details before booking my overpriced ticket, and I slip my feet into my new Coach flip-flops. I toss everything of mine that I am able to get my hands on into my suitcase. Once I believe that I have everything, I sit down on it and zip it up. I pull it up to stand on its wheels, and my eyes catch the Burberry shopping bag with my purchases from Wade stowed away inside. I don't want anything to do with his fancy-ass bank account, his heart, or his cock.

Lies.

I know that lying to myself will only put me at a disadvantage, but who am I kidding? I'm a woman who loathes the thought of love and relationships. I live for sex. I live for penetrating orgasms and bruised vaginal walls. But with Wade I think that I was different. He forced me to see past my sexual needs and to possibly find what has been hidden inside, what I have deprived myself of for my entire life. I connected with him on a level that was raw and beautiful, and there were moments so incredibly real that I was able to see the world in vibrant colors. Now, though, I realize that it was all a lie. I interlocked myself with him for nothing. I'll recoil to protect the pieces that now make up my shattered soul.

I refuse to let him break me in this way. He's slowly made me become the person that I never wanted to be. Bitterness rises like bile at the thought of never seeing him again, but I cast it aside.

I don't want this. I've never wanted this. This is not who I am. I subjected myself to a lifestyle that I knew would never work for me. I can feel myself withdrawing by the second because I can't feel much of the pain anymore as the depression, addiction, and anxiety supplies me with relief.

Within an hour and a half, I've made it through the Sydney airport security as I walk unseeing to the terminal and then to the correct gate. I take a seat, not paying attention to anyone or anything around me. I know that my bloodshot eyes and smeared makeup must be drawing a lot of unwanted attention, but if I'm honest, I don't give a shit. Yes, I'm wearing my fucked-up emotions on my sleeve, and no I can't control them because I don't know how to. I want to yell at everyone. I have never been so emotionally messed up in my life. It's all because of him—his screwed-up way of breaking me and his way of dismissing me from his life. His way of calling me a whore.

"Fuck you, Waylon Brass," I say as I rummage through my purse for my anxiety medication.

I'll find that sanctuary that I masked myself in for most of my life again, and I don't plan on ever coming back from it. The boarding process begins, and I wait until everyone goes through before they announce the final boarding call for Los Angeles. Only then do I stand and hand the woman my boarding pass. She scans it, and I walk past her without a word. I repeat the notion as I walk onto the plane, finding my seat toward the back of the aircraft. Somehow, I've gotten a row of seats to myself. As soon as I take my seat, the tears start to flow again. I dig my phone out of my purse before I have to push it under the seat in front of me and type out a text. He needs to know that whatever the fuck we were is no more. Whether he says it or I do. I stare at the screen for a long while before I hit send and stuff my phone into my purse before stowing it.

I GAVE YOU MY WORD. I NEVER WENT BACK ON IT. GOODBYE, WHISKEY.

I've gotten sick on the flight a total of three times in the first four hours of the fourteen-hour journey to LAX where I'll have to connect to Chicago. I've been contemplating staying in Los Angeles and starting over there, but I can't simply disappear on Lola.

The flight attendant comes by with a drink cart again and asks me if I'd like something to drink. I refuse her again, but this time she insists that I drink something because she's worried that I'll get dehydrated from being sick so much. I loathe being cared for. I let it go when Wade was mine, but now it needs to stop. I cannot stand letting someone see my weaknesses so easily.

I honestly couldn't give a fuck that I could be dehydrated, though. Maybe the physical reaction to it will put a stop to my emotional state. I ask her for a ginger ale in hopes of her leaving me alone. After I drink the soda, I shut my eyes in an attempt to keep the rest of the world at bay.

I'm woken suddenly by the plane jerking as it lands at LAX. I take in a deep calming breath and exhale loudly. It takes a while before I'm able to get off of this metal death trap and get the slightest bit of fresh air when I walk out onto the jetway. The cooler air doesn't settle my mind, body, or soul. It just reminds me of the ache that blankets me. Of my morning with Wade in the sand.

I need alcohol and sex. Maybe I'll get lucky on my next flight and get seated next to some sex god who won't be able to keep his hands off of a cheap thrill.

By the time, I find my next gate to Chicago they are calling my name, and I want to punch the fucker who keeps saying Rye.

Note to self: change your last name.

Once I'm seated next to an older man who looks hornier than hell, I pull out my phone and text Lo: Hi, doll, I'm on my way to Chicago. I'll be there in a few hours. I just didn't want to catch you and Owen naked on the couch.

I hit send and then type out a text to Holden: I need you.

I plug in my headphones and hit play on the first song that pops up. As much as I've fought the urge to check my phone for a message from him, I lose at this moment.

I'm more surprised when I realize that I don't have one from him, but rather I have a few from Isla. I scroll up and read the first one that she sent me: Listen, I don't know where the fuck you went, but Wade is a mess.

Then a second one: You're a bitch, you know that? Prepare yourself for that fucking roofie that I told you about.

Those two came approximately two hours after my flight took off. Then, her next one says that it came in four hours ago: WADE WAS JUST INVOLVED IN A BOATING ACCIDENT. I WASN'T WITH HIM. HE WAS WITH A FEW MEN FROM THE MEETING HE WAS IN. THEY HAVE AIRLIFTED HIM TO ST. VINCENT'S HOSPITAL IN SYDNEY. THIS HAPPENED ABOUT AN HOUR AGO. WHERE THE FUCK ARE YOU, YOU SELFISH BITCH?

My stomach lurches and I think that I'm going to be sick again. I scroll down again to her last message that came in two hours ago: HE WAS ASKING FOR YOU BEFORE HE WENT INTO SURGERY.

Adrenaline spikes my body as I get up and fly out of my seat to the cabin door, just as the flight attendant is about to shut it. I blatantly ignore her reprimand as I squeeze through the opening and run up the jetway, bursting through the security door and back into the terminal. I run back to the international terminal while I search for a plane that leaves for Sydney on my phone. I must be fated to be on this damn flight because there's one leaving within fifteen minutes. I haul ass through the terminals until I come to the gate that it says the flight it supposed to leave from. I rush to the counter and inform the woman my situation. She frowns and nods in understanding. She then spends too much time typing in my details before she confirms that I will, indeed, be able to board. They had a few seats available for their standby passengers.

She ushers me onto the flight, and I quickly find my seat. My knees are bobbing up and down, anxious to get off of the ground and closer to him.

"Please place your purse underneath the seat in front of you, ma'am," a flight attendant says as I fish through it to find my phone again.

Once I do, I type out a message to Lola: NEVER MIND! CHANGE OF PLANS.

Her message comes almost instantly: ALL RIGHT. LOVE YOU. BE SAFE.

I'm about to reply to Isla and text Hold again when the flight attendant stops in front of me again. "Ma'am, if I have to ask you again, I will escort you off of this plane."

What a bitch. I chuck my shit underneath the seat as we taxi down the runway, and I beg no one in particular that Wade hasn't suffered anything horrific.

Sixteen hours later, I'm exhausted, both mentally and physically. I've been away from him for over thirty-five hours, and I don't know when it was exactly that he was in the accident. When I check my phone as I get into a taxi, it's dead. I huff and toss it into the seat beside me as I give the cabbie my destination.

I swear this driver is giving me the run-around because it takes forty minutes to get to the hospital. Once we arrive, I throw some cash at him and jump out of the cab. It's now that I realize that I have no idea where my checked bag is, but I don't give a shit. I just need to see him.

I stride in through the hospital's main entrance and give the receptionist his name just as Isla walks past me, carrying a cup of coffee.

"Isla," I call out, and she turns in my direction.

She scrunches her nose at me and sighs. "You look like shit."

"Thanks. Where is he?"

She shakes her head and takes a sip of her coffee. "I'll show you."

I walk beside her, wringing my hands together as she leads me through a maze of hallways.

"Where the fuck were you, Hadley?"

"Los Angeles."

She stops walking and looks at me. "You ran?"

I shrug and motion for her to keep walking.

"You're the one that hurt him, lady, not the other way around."

"I didn't sleep with anyone, Isla."

"Don't try and bullshit me. I heard you in there. I texted him, apologizing, because I thought I had caught you two in the heat of it. As it turns out, he was about to start his meeting across town."

I let her get out what she needs to, instead of stopping and correcting her. If I'm going to explain anything to anyone, it's going to be to Wade.

She stops outside of a closed door and pushes down on the handle. It swings open to Wade who is uncharacteristically grim-faced, lying on a bed with a thin white sheet covering him.

"He's asleep right now," Isla says as I move to his side and run my hand through his unkempt hair.

"What happened?"

"I don't know all of the details of the accident, but apparently they were on one of those speedboats that companies rent out, and the captain lost control of it. One of the men on board said that Wade jumped in to help steer it clear of another vessel. When he did, though, they lost control of it again. There must have been something faulty with the steering. They piloted straight into a sea stack. There is nothing left of the boat. It shattered upon impact and Wade got the worst of it because he was up front. The captain lost his life, though, so I suppose that it could have been worse."

"Oh my God."

"I'll give you a few moments with him."

"Thank you, Isla."

She nods and walks out of the room, shutting the door quietly behind her. When I look back down at him, his eyes are open, and he's watching me.

"Wade," I say in a whisper.

"I shouldn't have treated you the way that I did. I'm sorry, Rye."

My heart splinters as he pulls me out from my internal prison, and back into the emotions of yesterday. I dash the unwanted tear away before I sniffle and cup his cheek. "No, stop. I'm so relieved that you're okay. I've been sick to my stomach thinking about all of the things that could have happened to you."

"You ran from me."

He keeps changing the subject from his current state to us, and I'm having a difficult time controlling my emotions. It's all too much for me to comprehend right now. I swallow the burning lump in my throat. "You didn't want me to stay; you were sending me to another room, Whiskey. I'm sorry I left. I just . . . I couldn't get you to listen . . . I . . ."

He places his hand on top of mine as the tears flow steadily now.

"Tell me where you went. To him?"

I shake my head, unable to speak through my gush of tears. I think I've cried more in these last two days than I have in my entire life.

"God, Rye." He reaches up to cup my cheek before moving his hand to the back of my neck, pulling me down to him until his lips press against mine, making my heart flutter. I have every intention of pulling back from him until I realize that this may be our last. The unhealthy frenzy sparks my mind as his lips heal me without a word. If I could only live in this present moment, then I would be content, but my tears falling onto his cheeks help me to detach my lips from his.

"Are you okay?" I sputter as I wipe my eyes.

"I'll be fine with time. I had a punctured lung, but the doctor performed surgery soon after I was admitted. They recently took me off of the breathing tube."

"Anything else?" I ask as I inspect his body, which I can't fully see because of the sheet covering him.

"A couple of broken ribs, which will heal with time as well.

I'll be okay, Hads."

"You swear it?" I sniffle and run my hand through his hair again.

He nods and gives me a weak smile. "Where did you go?"

"I was on my way back to Chicago. I got Isla's message when I landed in LAX."

"You shouldn't have run. I understand that you need what you need, and I blame myself for not giving it to you when you asked me for it."

I shake my head as the tears turn into a river pouring down my cheeks. "I-I didn't sleep with anyone."

He doesn't say anything to me as he watches me fight my fears. "I got this job as a, uhm, as a phone-sex operator a few days before we left Chicago. I was so furious with you for rejecting me earlier, and I didn't have anything to do once you simply closed yourself off to me yesterday morning and just . . . left me."

"Hadley—"

"Please, just let me get this out," I say before he can continue. He nods and takes my hand. "I didn't know what to do once you left so I logged on for the first time and I gave it a go. That's what Isla must have heard."

I shrug and look away, feeling ashamed of myself.

"Rye."

I turn back to look at his face and see the pained expression etched across it.

His eyes are wide as he pulls me closer to him. "Fuck, baby. I'm so sorry. I fucked this up more than I care to realize. You were trying to explain, but I saw red. Can you forgive me?"

I nod as a sob rips through my lips. He reaches up and runs his thumbs underneath my eyelids.

"I took you for granted yesterday morning. I swear to you that I won't let it happen again. Please, Hadley, don't run from me."

I've not seen him so vulnerable before now, and I know that I won't be able to leave his side. Not now, and not when he's helped me surface my emotions. Not when the world around us seems to blur with the static electricity surging back and forth between us.

"I won't."

"You're beautiful, do you know that? Even when you cry."

My sob turns into a laugh, and I smile at him, my body lost in a trance to his. "I think I missed you."

"I know that I missed you. Especially since you're mine."

"I am," I tell him and lean down to kiss him gently, trying not to apply any pressure onto his body. I'm scared shitless that I'll hurt him. The current between us is explosive and sends tiny shocks to my heart, reviving it after the blinding grief that had consumed me entirely.

"Knock, knock," Isla says as she walks into the white, bleached-out hospital room. "Are you feeling any better, brass balls?"

"Fuck off," he murmurs and winks at me. "Have you found out when I am able to leave?"

"Yup, never. The nurse said that she needed to sew up your balls before she let you go. She thinks the shrinkage is due to the amount of pussy that you don't eat."

He shuts his eyes and takes in a deep breath. "Very well."

"Hadley, I was about to grab some sandwiches. Would you like one? Seeing as you two have made up."

"No, thank you, though. I'm not really hungry."

Wade clears his throat. "Grab her something to eat, Isla. I doubt that she's eaten since she left. Am I right?"

I purse my lips and look down at my hands, playing with the gold ring on my left index finger. "Not entirely."

"You got it, boss man," Isla says before picking up her purse from the chair next to his bed and walking out of the room.

Blended 171

"Are you tired?" I ask him as he shuts his eyes.

"I am, but I doubt that I'm as tired or jet-lagged as you are. You're putting your body through hell, flying back and forth."

"You don't have to worry about me, Wade."

"The fuck if I don't. I cannot stomach the thought of not sleeping with you in my arms for another night."

"Wade, I could hurt you."

"Don't deny an injured man his wishes," he says with a content smile on his face. I run my thumb over his stubble when he shuts his eyes again.

"Get some sleep, Whiskey. I won't run. You have my word."

"Mmm."

Eighteen

Wade

I HAVE NOT told her that I cannot feel anything below my waist. The accident caused some sort of spinal injury, and the doctors are unsure how it will affect the functions of my body, let alone if my current state will be permanent or not. I've been advised to treat it as if I will not recover; however, recovery is possible. Luckily, treatment was administered almost immediately after the injury occurred, and the severity of it will have the final say on my recovery. Due to my other injuries, my doctor refuses to take me into surgery again. If I am to pull off a full recovery, I will need to go through countless hours of rehabilitation in order to get my body to function correctly again.

I turn my head to look at her while she leans against the bed, fast asleep in the veil of darkness over the hospital room. I run my hand through her wild curls and curse myself for the way I treated her. The raw abandonment that took over me when I realized that she had run is something I do not plan on feeling again. When I went back to the meeting after refusing to listen to her explanation, my crowded mind pushed everything else aside but the thought of her. Once we concluded the meeting, I hardly remembered agreeing to go out on the boat with them, but I did, and it's why I'm in my current position.

When the captain lost control, my body reacted before I was able to think about the consequences of my actions. In a matter of a minute, I had put everyone's life in more danger than they were in before. Each passing second that followed was a memory of the look of agony and disappointment on her face from our earlier argument. The next thing that I remember was waking up to the smell of bleach.

I thought that I had lost her when Isla told me that none of her things were in our suite, nor in the second room I got for her. Since lying in this bed, surrounded by the sensory calm of isolation—with the exception of Isla—it made me realize what I had thrown away. She's not a woman who is plagued by vanity or who wants her own fairy tale. She's the person she's had to be to save herself.

A thudding in my chest makes me relive the deepest fear I have in losing her as I move her curls out of her face to ensure that I didn't dream her up.

She shifts and reaches for my hand. "Hi, Whiskey."

I will pay whatever medical professional I need to in order to recover from this injury to live my life to the fullest with her by my side. She lifts her head and smiles sleepily at me. "I didn't mean to drift off."

"It doesn't matter. I could watch you sleep for hours."

"That verges on the side of creepy, Wade."

"It may, but it's the truth." I'm interrupted by a knock on the door.

A moment later the doctor who performed surgery on me walks into the dark room and flips on the light switch.

"Good evening, Mr. Brass," he says in an Aussie accent.

"Dr. Heath," I greet him. "This is my girlfriend, Hadley Rye."

"Good evening, Miss Rye. If you will both excuse my intrusion, I needed to come by and check on your long list of injuries. Your nurse seems to be impressed with your recovery thus far."

"Very well," I tell him, knowing full well that he's going to shed light on my paralysis.

"I'll start with your lungs and work my way down."

He gets to work as a nurse joins us. She takes my vitals while my girl stays by my side. I won't let her move. I have her hand locked in mine, and I refuse to let her go.

"Your lung seems to be healing well thus far," he says, and he moves the sheet off of my lower body, revealing my legs. He presses against my ribs, and I flinch each time that he does it.

"As I said before, the two ribs that were injured will take a minimum of six weeks to heal. I'll keep my nurses administering drugs to make it easier to take deep breaths."

I nod in acknowledgment.

I glance up at Hadley, who is watching Dr. Heath intently as he moves the sheet off of my feet. He walks to the end of the bed and lifts up my left foot. I watch him press his thumb against the sole of my foot.

"Mr. Brass? Are you able to feel that?"

I shut my eyes for a brief moment before opening them and stare into Hadley's eyes. She looks frightened and grief-stricken.

"No," I tell him honestly.

Hadley's hand flies up to her mouth in an attempt to hold back a sob that escapes her lips regardless. I squeeze her hand in apology. This is not how I wanted her to find out.

"Don't go," I ask her quietly as the doctor moves his hands up my calf.

"What about now, Mr. Brass?"

"No. Nothing."

"All right. Try flexing your ankle for me."

I attempt to force the movement, but nothing comes of it. I cannot even figure out where the movement should start.

"Wade?" she asks as she wipes a tear away.

"Swear to me that you'll stay, Hadley."

The doctor looks up at us and clears his throat. "I'll be out of your way in a few minutes, Mr. Brass. Please stay with me."

He sets my left leg down and then starts with my right, going over the same routine he has done multiple times since he first met me.

"Dr. Heath?"

"Yes, Miss Rye?"

"Oh, just Hadley, please. Would you mind if I asked you some questions of my own?"

My eyebrows shoot up, surprised that she's still holding onto my hand, let alone that she wants more information regarding my paralysis.

"Of course, Hadley. What would you like to know?"

"Will he ever be able to recover from this? I mean . . ."

The doctor smiles and sets my right leg down on the bed. "It really depends. I have had many patients suffer through multiple surgeries with no results while others have made a full recovery. To be frank, I'm not certain as to his condition yet because I have not been able to operate on him while his lung recovers."

"Oh."

"Luckily for Mr. Brass, I do not believe that the nerve was directly injured in the accident, which would have caused a spinal cord injury. I'd like to believe that the paralysis that he is experiencing is caused by compression of one of the lumbar nerves. In his case, the underlying cause seems treatable, but the prospects for his recovery are the same as they are for anyone else. The likelihood of a full recovery is slim if I'm unable to perform surgery soon."

"Oh my God," she says under her breath and squeezes my hand.

"Nothing is impossible. Keep that in mind."

"Thank you, Dr. Heath," she says as they shake hands before he notes a few things on a device and exits the room.

"Rye?"

"Yes?" she looks down at me with worry marring her face.

"You haven't answered me."

"Wade," she exhales, "I'm not going to leave you. I ran because I thought we were over and because you wouldn't give me a chance. I'm not a cold-hearted bitch, and an injury isn't going to change the way I feel toward you." Her eyes seem to widen at her own words as if she hadn't realized what she was saying.

"I'll have to be here for a while, Hadley. I understand that you'll need to fly back to Chicago. Isla needs to get back to Blended once the week is over."

"How long did they tell you that they'd keep you locked up in this place?"

"A minimum of two months. I've been trying to convince them to at least let me go back to the hotel where I'll be more comfortable."

"Would you like for me to say something?"

The thought of her going out of her way to help me settles the war zone in my head a bit.

"Not exactly. Isla contacted my lawyers, and they are working on it as we speak."

"Your lawyers? Would they have that kind of power?"

"Money has as much power as the man who accepts it."

"I suppose," she says as she looks toward the door when it opens again and Isla walks in.

"How are you holding up, brass balls?"

Hadley lets go of my hand and steps back, allowing Isla to lean over my torso and hug me. She brings her lips to my ear and whispers, "Does she know about the paraplegia?"

"She does," I tell her so that Hadley can hear me as well. Isla stands up and turns to my girl. I watch the two of them comfort each other because of my injury. My stupidity. If I hadn't taken action and steered the boat into the rocks, I would be walking out of this hospital room with Hadley tucked under my arm.

"Isla, what have my lawyers found out?"

"Oh! That's what I came here to tell you. I honestly didn't expect that you would be awake at five in the morning, but I figured I'd come anyway."

I raise my eyebrows at her as anger heats my soul. "Tell me, Madden."

"Cool those balls off, would ya? They came to an agreement with the hospital and your doctor. They will be moving you to your hotel suite at nine this morning, where you will have an around-the-clock nurse. Dr. Heath will remain your primary doctor and be on call as well as be around to check on your progress once a day until he deems you fit enough for surgery."

I lean my head back on the pillow and shut my eyes, grateful for the team I have behind Brass Global. "Very well. I'll need to arrange a web conference call when I'm back to finalize the properties in Sydney. Have Adriana arrange it. I may need you to fly her out if I'm going to be stuck in a fucking bed for two months."

"Right. I spoke to her this morning, and there have been multiple media outlets calling into the office, asking for an update on your situation. You've made international news after your accident, Brass."

"Nobody needs to know to what extent I'm injured. Have the lawyers draw up non-disclosure agreements in addition to the doctor- and patient-confidentiality agreements for all of the doctors and nurses who have worked with me during my stay here."

"Yes, boss," she says sarcastically, "so much for our vacation, huh?"

"You know where my credit card is, Madden. Don't let me hold you back."

"I didn't mean it like that, Brass. Look . . ." she sighs. "I'm sorry that came off in a negative way; I'm just as distraught as anyone else over this."

"I think I need two fingers of something spicy, clean, and going to burn," Hadley says from her seat beside me.

"I like your thinking. I'm sure that Isla can find something unique to Australia while she hits the stores."

"I sure can. Bourbon, rye, Tennessee, Canadian, Scotch, or Irish?" she asks, and it gets us all to laugh.

"Something strong," Hadley replies as I reach for her hand. She glances up at me and gives me her shy smile. It's odd how my feelings for her have intensified since she left. Everything that she says and does is of extreme interest to me. For the first time, I don't mind a woman being around me when it's not just about sex. Hadley seems to accept me for who I am and doesn't have this need to change me. Meeting her was fate and chasing her was ultimately my decision, but falling in love with her was entirely out of my control.

This love, the emotion, and the passion that I feel deeply for her have made me temporarily insane. The desire I have to be with her at all times is overwhelming and all-consuming. I refuse to let this feeling burn away, regardless of my physical state. This may have all happened rather quickly, but I refuse to fight it because my accident made me realize just how quickly life can be taken from us.

The next time I open my eyes, Hadley is running her hand through my hair in an attempt to wake me. The smile that she gives me when I blink and look up at her is ravishing. She may be wearing the same outfit that I saw her in a day ago, but her beauty doesn't go unnoticed for a minute.

"You're like my personal shot of caffeine, Rye."

The blush that kisses her cheeks is beautiful, and it's one of the reasons why I cannot seem to get my fill of her.

"You're my shot of whiskey," she says against my lips as she offers me the breath she was holding, the very one that I needed to breathe. A feeling of peace comes over me as our souls breathe life into each other's. The unpredictability of this kiss describes our relationship flawlessly. With this one kiss, I realize how every other one with every other woman meant nothing. We both seem to be communicating what neither of us is able to voice. I'm telling her the words that I haven't said.

To hell with my rules.

Dr. Heath clears his throat, and Hadley pulls away from me suddenly. I realize that he must have been in here the entire time.

"Mr. Brass, we are set to transfer you back to your suite."

"Good," I tell him without breaking eye contact with Hadley.

She purses her lips, her physical sign to me that she's contemplating what just happened between us. I thrive with the knowledge that she felt it as well, that there was more behind that kiss than the mere physical act of all the others that we've shared before it.

Four nurses walk into the room once I've signed my release papers and I've put my mother and Isla, as well as Hadley down as emergency contacts. The four of them transfer me from the uncomfortable hospital bed and into a wheelchair. They lift my feet and place them on the footrests before strapping them down. I'm assuming it's to ensure that I don't fall out of the chair rather than some sort of sexual bondage fantasy.

"Mr. Brass, my name is Madelyn Elyse, and I will be your live-in nurse," says a tall, attractive brunette, introducing herself to me. I shake her outstretched hand.

"Thank you for agreeing to do this."

"It's no problem whatsoever."

I wouldn't assume that it would be a problem considering the paycheck that she will be receiving from me on a weekly basis.

She moves behind my wheelchair and starts to push me

toward the hallway. "Rye?" I ask because I can't find her in the crowded room anymore.

"I'm right here, Whiskey," she says as Madelyn wheels me out into the hallway. I hadn't even realized that she walked out of the room. When I take in her appearance, she looks utterly exhausted and spent from the jet lag and the hell that I put her through.

"You need to rest."

"Are you insinuating that I look like complete shit, Waylon Brass?"

"I'm insinuating that you look tired. I've put you through a lot since we left the States."

"I suppose that I'll find some way to forgive your fancy-ass."

"I wouldn't give you another choice," I tell her as I'm wheeled to the rear entrance of the hospital where Jacobs is waiting. He insisted on using this door to exit because of the crowd of media and paparazzi that are camped out front.

"Mr. Brass, I'm glad to see that you are well."

"It's good to see you, Jacobs."

"Hi, Colin," Hadley says, and she goes to hug him. He hesitates at first, but then he hugs her lightly in return. Envy sprints through my veins with the knowledge that I can no longer hold her like he is right now.

He must sense my mood because he steps aside to assist the nurses who are transferring me from the chair and into the vehicle.

Once Madelyn secures me, she walks around the vehicle and climbs into the seat beside me. I scowl at her before glancing at Hadley through the window. I watch as Jacobs opens the front passenger door for her and she climbs in.

"Why are you up front, Rye?" I ask her as she's fastening her seatbelt.

"I, uhm, I didn't think that it would be appropriate to sit

between the two of you."

"Bullshit."

I turn to face Madelyn. "From here on out, you will be seated in the front with my driver instead of next to me where my girlfriend belongs. Am I understood?"

She flinches at my demand. "Yes, sir. I apologize. I was not aware."

"It's fine, Madelyn," Hadley interjects and offers her a sympathetic smile. "I'm Hadley. Thank you for volunteering to do this for him."

I raise my eyebrows at my whiskey in a teacup, daring her to overstep my authority. With an exhale, she undoes her seatbelt and climbs out of her seat before walking around to the backseat just as Madelyn gets out. I may be suffering through paralysis, but nothing will stop me from being able to touch her whenever I am able to.

Instead of sitting on the other side of the vehicle, she scoots into the middle seat and buckles up.

"Hi Whiskey," she says as she splays her hand out on my thigh. My eyes drop to where she's touching me, and I internally curse myself for not being able to feel that static electricity that hits my skin every time her body is near mine. "Is this better?"

The calm and strength that her kiss provided for me earlier are now gone. I reach for her hand and intertwine my fingers with hers. "Barely."

Her smile falls, and she looks away from me. I silently curse myself.

"I'm trying," she whispers as Jacobs heads in the direction of the hotel.

"I know, Rye. This is just . . . it's a lot to take in."

I let go of her hand and move my arm around her shoulders. She leans back against my chest and gets as close to me as the seatbelt will allow.

"I apologize."

She tilts her chin up and gives me a small smile. "Please don't. I understand that all of this is new to you. You're learning to rely on others instead of taking charge, and I can tell that it makes you uncomfortable. It's simply a minor setback that you will recover from, and it'll help you to take greater strides afterward."

"I'm a lucky son of a bitch to have you, you know that?"

Jacobs pulls into the main entrance of the hotel and Madelyn has my door open before I can hear Hadley's reply. Jacobs brings the wheelchair around as a horde of media crews jumps out of their vans.

"Stay close to me, Rye."

"I swear it."

Jacobs and Madelyn get me out of the SUV without much trouble before the first camera is on us. Hadley steps out of the vehicle and starts pushing my chair into the hotel's expansive lobby while Madelyn grabs her medical supplies from the trunk.

Rye and I head up to the elevators, and she gets us onto one before Madelyn can catch up to us. Once it starts to ascend, she leans over to the panel and presses the red emergency stop button.

"What's the matter?"

"Nothing. I just wanted a minute alone with you."

I chuckle and reach my arm out for her. She walks to me and locks my chair in place before taking a seat on my lap, "I'm not hurting you, am I?"

"Not one bit, baby."

Her smile is contagious as she rings her arms around my neck and plants her lips on mine in a frantic kiss. A kiss that she needs. One in which I can tell her that I'll recover from this bullshit without using the words. I think back to the first time I kissed her on the dock, and her lips met mine tentatively. As if she was protecting her foul and destructive soul from me, but she's neither of those words. She's come alive with me, and I believe that I'm on the verge of breaking her if I haven't already. The affection she shows me is no longer linked to sex or a need for an orgasm. It's a simple need to be with me, and the feeling is mutual.

"Don't you dare do anything so stupid again, do you hear me, Whiskey?" she states suddenly as she pulls away in the middle of our embrace.

"Are you scolding me, Miss Rye?"

"Absolutely! You were reckless, and you put your life at risk. I could have lost you completely," she sobs and buries her head in the crook of my neck.

"I know, but I survived, and you're in my arms. I couldn't ask for more."

She sniffles loudly and tightens her arms around my neck. "When I was on the plane to Los Angeles, I thought that I had lost your heart. When I was on the plane back to Sydney, I thought that I had lost mine. I thought that you were dead. I couldn't breathe with the thought of never seeing you again."

The static sizzles in the negative space between us as she weeps in my arms. "Your heart is well and secure with me as mine is with you."

She jerks her head back and stares at me. "You swear it?"

"I do. Do you not understand what I feel for you, Hadley?"

She shrugs and wipes a tear off of her cheek.

"I'm in love with you. I crave you in every form possible. Whether innocent or dirty, you're the rye to my whiskey, Hads. Everything about you to me is fucking addictive."

She places her hands on either side of my face, and the confined space that we are in ceases to exist. "Tell me again?"

"I confess that I am in love with you, Hadley Rye."

Her tears fall freely again. "There isn't a single person in this world that I want more than I do you, Wade."

As she sits on my lap, I watch the final chink in her armor give way with my words. "There's no running now, Hadley. I won't allow it."

She nods as the elevator jerks. Someone must be controlling it remotely.

"Holy shit," she squeals and jumps off of my lap as we start to ascend again.

I watch her as she calms herself down while holding a hand over her heart. The elevator door opens to a rather confused Madelyn.

"We got stuck," I tell her as Hadley unlocks the brakes and wheels me out and down the hallway to the suite doors. Madelyn uses her key card that Jacobs provided her to open the double doors for us.

"Colin told me that there was an extra room in the suite. Would you mind directing me to it so I can set up my supplies?"

"Down the hall, it's the door on your right."

"Thank you, Mr. Brass. Once you're ready, I'll set up your seat in the shower stall, and we'll get you cleaned up before bed."

"Very well."

Nineteen

Hadley

FIRST OF ALL, this Madelyn bitch better stop giving Wade *fuck-me* eyes before I murder her. Second of all, Wade just told me that he's in love with me. Hearing those words, especially from a man who I haven't slept with, was . . . freeing. I've had multiple men tell me that they are in love with me after they've had their dirty way with me, but this is entirely different. I don't have a single thing to compare it to.

As much as I don't believe in the notion of love, I can see it in the way he looks at me, and now, I can feel it. He says my name differently since the accident, and I know that I'm safe with him because I trust this man. I don't know how he dug his way into my heart, but he's taken it as his own just as I have captured his.

It terrifies me knowing that I would do anything for him. The fact that I would lay my bare heart in his hands is beyond frightening, but he knows that. He understands my soul without my having to confess my fears. It's taken me years to face my demons that live deep inside of me, but I believe that I can with his help.

"Hadley?" his voice breaks me from my thoughts as I go through the clothing hung up in his closet for an outfit for each of us to wear. I walk toward his and Madelyn's voices and find them in the bathroom. She has his shower seat set up, and he's refusing to move.

"I do not need, nor do I want your assistance in this."

"Mr. Brass, I'm only trying to do my job."

"What's going on?" I ask.

"Thank fuck," he says through his gritted teeth. "I need you to be the one to do this, Hads. I cannot—"

"Okay," I tell him before he works himself up over a shower. "Madelyn, I'll take it from here, but stay in the room in case that I need you, please."

"Of course," she says as she walks out of the bathroom and into the bedroom Wade and I shared before I left.

"You're lucky that I happen to love your stubborn ass," I say as I go to pull his shirt up and off of him, but he doesn't move.

"What?" I ask as I take in his bewildered expression once I've gotten his shirt off.

"Say it again, Hadley."

"Say what? That you're stubborn?"

He shakes his head and chuckles. "No, gorgeous. Do you even realize that you just said that you love me?"

My hands still on his chest as I gaze into his eyes. "I did?"

He nods and pulls me closer to him until I fall onto his lap.

"Risk or regret. You chose risk whether it was an unconscious decision or not."

"I'm scared to love you," I say honestly. "But I'm also terrified that you'll leave."

"I have nowhere to go." He gestures to the wheelchair that he's currently seated in.

"I like my odds right about now."

"I'm sure you do. And I hate to ask you to help me with this but I'd rather be ass-naked in front of the woman I'm with instead of another."

"You did it for me when I was ill, Wade. I don't mind."

"This isn't going to be a one-time thing, though, Hads."

"Then you're lucky to be stuck with me."

I would much rather be the one to help him in the shower than have Madelyn accidentally choke on his cock. After a few minutes of struggling and trying to figure out how to get him undressed and seated in the shower, we finally manage to get it right.

He's naked in front of me, and he's hard. Absolutely solid. His cock is just as gorgeous as I remembered it to be.

"Can you tell that, uhm, that you're hard?"

"I can. By some miracle, I didn't damage the nerves in my lower back."

I watch him as I strip out of my tent dress, bra and panties before turning the shower on. "I'm glad."

The water hits my back and his front, warming us in the glass-encased stall.

"I want you, Hadley. Now that I can't have you . . . it's killing me."

"I'll hurt you if I do anything. You'll need to get your doctor's approval before we attempt anything."

He leans forward and pulls me to him. I move between his legs and cup his face as he looks up at me. "I should have given you what you wanted while I was able to."

"You are what I want, Wade. Screw the circumstances. If you did this any other way, you know for a fact that I would have left as soon as you slept with me."

He drops his head in defeat. "Now I'm concerned that you're going to run because I no longer have the ability to."

"Just because you can't, does not mean that I can't. Between the two of us, we'll figure it out as soon as Dr. Heath says it's safe for you to do so."

He rests his head against my bare breasts and breathes in deeply. "Thank you for coming back."

"You wouldn't have been able to keep me away."

He's unbelievably vulnerable when it's just the two of us. He's terrified. I know that he is. He's petrified that he won't be able to stand or walk again. That he won't be able to surf or be in control of his world any longer.

"I need to tell you something," he says against my breasts and rests his hands on either side of my hips.

I grab the body wash and loofah and start to rub down his back, "What is it?"

"My mother, Lillian, is flying into Sydney as we speak. Isla went to collect her at the airport. I want you to be the first woman that I introduce to her."

My hand pauses as I wash over the licks of his tattoo. "I'd love to meet her. Does she know that I'm here?"

"She knows all about you, gorgeous," he says as he raises his hands to rest on my waist.

"You've spoken to her about me?"

"From time to time, yes, when I needed her advice. She was the one who pushed me to seek help for my addiction when I was younger, and I wanted to know what she did for me that helped break its hold on me. I wanted to know what I could do to break you of it."

I move the loofah up over his shoulders and down his chest as he speaks.

"Oh."

"You know, I'm more than capable of washing myself, Rye."

"Oh," I say again and hand him the loofah. "I'm sorry."

"Stop apologizing to me. Your touch soothes me. Please, continue."

He digs his strong, agile fingers into my skin, forcing me to remain in my place as I find it hard to breathe. I'm unquestioningly frightened for him. I manage to swallow the lump in my throat and continue to wash his pristine body, careful not to open any of the shallow cuts that mark his skin, or apply too much pressure to his bruises.

He helps me as I wash his legs, by holding onto the bar above us. He's essentially standing, but he's holding himself up. The muscles in his upper body flex as I help him lower himself down again. I'm sure that it's difficult to sit down when you're unable to feel half of your body.

Once we've got him rinsed off, dressed, and back in his wheelchair, I'm about to call Madelyn in to help me get him into bed. "Wait. You need to freshen up as well. I'd like to watch you shower and get ready to meet my mother."

"You should be resting, Wade."

"There's not a chance in hell."

I'm still naked when I roll my eyes toward him and step back into the shower, making quick work of it. Forty minutes have passed since we first got him into the shower, and now Madelyn is knocking on the bathroom door, "Mr. Brass, is everything all right?"

With just a towel around me, I open the door as she's about to knock again. "We're fine, thank you."

"I need to administer the next dose of his medication. He must be in pain by now."

"Oh. Okay, come on in."

She strides past me purposefully into the bathroom to where he's fallen asleep in his wheelchair. Once she has him in the room, I quickly get dressed into a pair of his sweatpants and one of his undershirts before helping her, and Colin maneuvers him into the king-sized bed.

I watch her closely when Colin leaves as she connects him up to an IV stand she has set up. I wince at the needle she puts in his skin before pushing the medication into his bloodstream through the IV.

He doesn't stir once through it all.

She puts on a blood pressure cuff on his other arm and sets

it to take his vitals every half an hour. I lean over him and adjust the pillow beneath his head until he looks comfortable.

"Sleep well, Whiskey."

"Hadley?" I hear Isla call from outside the door.

"Come on in."

I hear the door open as I pull the comforter over his body and run my hand through his hair when I'm startled by a sob.

"Oh, Waylon."

I turn around quickly and come face-to-face with a beautiful older brunette woman. She's tall and unquestionably stunning.

"I just administered several medications, so it will be at least three hours before he's able to wake up again," Madelyn says, extending her hand to Lillian. "I'm Madelyn Elyse, his in-home nurse for the next two months," she says as if she's the most important person in this room. She's honestly pathetic.

Lillian smiles at her but turns her attention toward me as Madelyn starts to speak again. "You must be Hadley, sweet girl."

"I, uhm, yes. It's nice to meet you, Mrs. Brass."

"Please, call me Lilly," she says in her English accent as she pulls me into a comforting hug.

"How are you holding up, Hads?" Isla asks as she rubs my back as I'm hugging Lillian.

I'm stunned that these women both seem to care about my well-being just as much as they care for Wade's.

"I'm okay." I release Lillian, and she walks to Wade's side.

"I'll give you three a moment. Madelyn, if you don't mind leaving them in privacy, I'd appreciate it."

She looks me dead in the eye and dares me. All right, bitch, stay if you please. I walk into the closet and pick out one of his workout sweatshirts before walking out of the bedroom. Maybe I should get Colin to get Madelyn her own room. That way, I won't have to deal with her when she's not tending to my Whiskey.

Exhaustion overtakes me as I settle down on the couch and pull his sweatshirt on. It smells like him, and I feel like I'm home. My home, though, has a heartbeat.

I'm woken by soft voices arguing. I force my eyes to open, and I realize that I'm draped around Wade on the couch. He's seated next to where I fell asleep, and he's holding onto me while I rest my head against his shoulder.

"Mr. Brass, she shouldn't be applying her weight on you."

"She weighs next to nothing. You're dismissed for the evening, Madelyn," he hisses at her.

"Waylon, respect the nurse, please," I hear Lillian's voice from across the room.

I force my eyes to open the remainder of the way and jolt upright.

Wade finds my eyes with his and his face softens. "Hi, gorgeous."

"I'm sorry, I didn't mean to pass out. When did you . . . how . . . ?"

"You've been out for hours, and when I woke without you in bed next to me, I couldn't stand it. I had Jacobs bring me out here while Madelyn was on her break. Now, she's pissed because I pulled you up against me."

I roll my eyes and kiss his cheek before I turn to face Madelyn and Lillian, who are now having a discussion across the living room.

As I watch them he moves my frizzy curls behind my neck and leans down to brush his lips against the column of my neck. "I love you," he murmurs.

A tremor runs down my spine at his words. I turn to face him and brush my lips against his. "I love you, Wade."

His eyes are locked on mine when his mother walks up to us, and I feel as if we're teenagers who just got caught making out.

"I haven't seen Waylon this happy in years, Hadley, and considering the circumstances, I'd say it's a rather large achievement. Thank you for all that you do for him."

I want to tell her that it's Wade who has changed me, who has given me a life full of emotions that I have never experienced before. Yes, I may still be on my anti-depressants and anxiety medication, but he makes me feel, I don't know, whole.

"She's one of a kind," Wade says to his mother as she leans down to hug him.

"I'm headed to bed, you two. Would you like for me to help to move you back to the bedroom, Wade? Your nurse is rather upset about finding you out here."

"Jacobs was in the kitchen the last I saw him. He'll help me."

"I'll just go and get him then."

She walks away from us and I stand up, careful not to disrupt how he's seated. I stretch out my sore limbs, but stop when I hear him chuckling.

"What?"

"You look ridiculous in my clothing. It's as if you're drowning in fabric."

I shrug and set my hands on my hips, "I'm comfortable, and they smell like you. Plus, I have no idea where my suitcase ended up with all of my flights."

"I'll have Jacobs look into it, and you can wear my shit for as long as you'd like."

Madelyn clears her throat and Wade and I both say "What?" in unison.

"Excuse me, but Colin is here to assist me in moving you back to the bedroom."

Colin Jacobs is, for lack of a better word, a machine. His arms barely fit into his suit jackets, and he's got more muscle on him than I've ever seen on a person before. If I could guess, I'd say that he's a bodybuilder, and not much older than Wade. He steps forward and helps Wade move into the wheelchair before Madelyn almost runs over my foot with it on the way back to the bedroom.

This bitch needs to go. There is no way in hell that I'm going to let her treat me like this for two months. Colin looks over at me with a look of disgust on his face. "She's one hell of a grumpy bitch."

I cannot help but burst into a fit of laughter at his words. "Colin! I didn't know that you actually spoke English."

"Yeah, yeah. What do you say we get in there before she mauls him?"

I nudge him in the arm before following behind him.

Madelyn refuses to leave after getting Wade settled in. I glance over at him from where I'm seated at his feet. The anger radiating off of him is almost palpable.

"Are you sure that there isn't anything else that I can get for you, Mr. Brass?"

"For the third time, Madelyn, no, there is not. You're dismissed."

"Yes, sir," she bows her head to him as if he's going to whip her with his dick. Jesus, this woman needs help.

I watch him shake his head in disbelief as I crawl up onto my side of the bed and reach over him, turning off the light on his nightstand as she walks to the door.

"One more thing, Mr. Brass. Dr. Heath would advise against sex this soon after the surgery," she twirls around and exits the room before either of us is able to respond.

I lean up on my elbow and watch him stare in disbelief at her. "How the fuck did I end up with this insane woman?" he mutters to me in case she is standing just outside of our bedroom door, which I wouldn't put past her.

"I have no idea, but I think that Colin might do us a favor

and get rid of the body."

We laugh together as I settle down against him. His arm comes around me, pulling me closer. I lift my leg over his and kiss his neck. "Will you tell me something?" I ask.

"What is it that you want to know?"

"Anything about you, really."

"As long as you take off this sweatshirt. I want to be able to touch you."

"Deal," I say as I sit up and pull his sweatshirt off and toss it to the end of the bed before I move back into the spot where I was lying before.

"Do you remember what I told you about myself? That I have struggled with what you are going through?"

"I do."

He sighs and lifts his shirt off of my lower back until he can touch my skin and run his fingers around the studs of my piercings.

"One of the things that I would use to kill the craving I had for it was to pay for multiple women at once, or I'd participate in group sex sessions at an underground club in Las Vegas."

My eyes widen as I stare up at the ceiling in the dark. "Sex parties?"

"Exactly."

"I've always wanted to venture into one of those, but I never found a club that I was comfortable with doing it in."

"The thrill of fucking someone and then five minutes later being sucked off by two different women is overwhelming, and it satisfied me immensely."

"I'll be damned."

"I've been countless times. Each time I've made a trip to Las Vegas, I'd find one to attend."

"Did you go when I met you over a month ago?"

"I was on my way to one when I first saw you in the

elevator."

"That feels like a century ago, Wade."

"It does, and I still have those pink lace panties."

"Oh? Did you ever get off on them?"

He chuckles and lowers his hand to my ass. "No, I wanted the real thing. I wanted you."

"I did too. I still do."

"Come here," he says when he pushes upward on my ass until he's able to lock his lips with mine. I run my hand down his chest and smile against his kiss.

"It's your turn to tell me something that I don't know about you, Rye."

"All right. Since we're on the topic of our sexual addictions, I'll tell you why I use sex as a coping mechanism. I mean, really, you were the one that brought to light just how deep in the trenches I was with it—am with it—but I've known that I've done it for years now."

He nods in understanding and waits for me to continue, deciding not to push me for answers. It's another thing that he gets about me. I won't speak if someone is forcing me to. I'll shout out what I need to when I'm comfortable instead of when I'm told what to say and when.

I clear my throat, preparing to tell this man, *my* man, what brought me to my knees at an early age. "When I was ten, my mother killed herself in a bathtub. She slit her wrists, and I sat in that water with her until I couldn't feel my toes anymore because of how cold it was."

He turns his shoulders to face me; it takes him a few tries, but he gets there.

"Go on." He must notice the worry crossing my face because he says, "I'm fine."

I nod. "Well, I was immediately placed in a foster home and two weeks after living with my new parents, the man raped me. I remember the piercing feeling and the smell of semen and sweat as if it were yesterday."

His body stiffens as he wraps me in his arms. "I'm sorry."

I shrug. "I'm not going to say that it's okay, but it's in the past, and it's what's been holding me back. Once I was switched from one house to the other, I landed in a house with Lola Marc. That's who you met at our apartment in Chicago."

"I remember."

"She's been through a lot as well. When I was placed in this new house, she was already there. It was just the two of us for a few years and during those years, our foster parents would take turns on us. Him as well as her."

I shake my head trying to rid myself of those memories, of those horrors, the demons that haunt me, day in and day out.

"How is it possible that you were put into two foster homes with adults like that?"

"Lola and I have spoken about it a lot. We figured out that we both had the same social worker on our cases. As it turns out, he was selling us to these families while using his name to foster us under. There were a few other girls that I remember seeing when I was with him, but we only found out the truth once we were nineteen. Lola saw his picture in the paper."

"Jesus."

I purse my lips as I think back to the day that I got the call from her. It intensified my need for sex to a level that I hadn't experienced before. I was dick-hopping as if my life depended on it. That's when she first sought professional help, and it's when I grew the need to help her.

"I've lived in and through a lot of dark, yet the only thing that made me feel anything was the physical act of sex—until you." I yawn and curl into his side.

"Desire. It's more than lust and aching for the rush of sex. I'm not going to let you go, Hadley."

"I wouldn't want you to." I pull the comforter up and over the both of us with his help. "Are you comfortable?" I ask quietly.

"As comfortable as I can be. Get some rest. I've got you."

"And I've got you."

"Goodnight, Rye."

"'Night, Whiskey."

Twenty

Wade

AN UNPLEASANT WARMTH wakes me from a deep sleep. I blink in the darkness as a sharp pain sears through my abdomen, surrounding me in the heat of a branding iron.

"Fuck," I hiss out as the burn intensifies. I attempt to move my legs, but I'm quickly reminded of my paralysis when I don't feel a single thing. As the pain increases, it takes with it the ability to think clearly. The penetrating burn moves from my abdomen to my ribs and then to the small of my back. I buck my shoulders back as continuous currents of debilitating agony drag through what I can feel of my body.

"Hadley. Jesus." My voice is weak, and I'm too quiet to wake her.

Sweat breaks out over my chest as I'm dragged through the throes of hell. A raw scream emits from my throat as I'm unable to bear it for another second. White spots begin to fill my vision as I feel her hand on my chest.

"Wade!" the bed shifts as a light flickers on.

"Madelyn," I hear her shout beside me as my body starts to tear me away from her, from her voice.

"Whiskey, you're okay. I'm here."

Something cool touches my face as another voice joins in the chaos, which I cannot see.

"His medication has worn off faster than it should have. I'm going to give him morphine for this."

"What's going on?"

"The pain is too much for him to bear because he's been overly active today. He's suffering."

"Please, just . . . help him," my girl cries out as I feel a warm, stinging sensation entering my arm.

"Give him a minute. The morphine will take over shortly."

Slowly, sections of my body seem to go numb as a coolness douses the fire inside of me.

"I'm so sorry, Wade," I hear her sniffle. "Please. You're okay, I'm not going to leave your side."

I try to fight the calming sensation that the medication pushes me into, but I can't open my eyes. *Goddamn it.* I need to see her. I flex my fingers and realize that she's holding my hand. I manage to squeeze her petite hand weakly; it's my only attempt to ensure her that I'm okay before I plummet into darkness.

I reluctantly wake in soft sheets as I'm shaken into reality. I debate letting sleep overcome me again until I hear her voice. "No, I'm okay, thank you, though."

"You really should eat, Hadley."

"I'm not hungry. Thank you again, Lilly."

"All right, sweetie. I'm going to go pick up some clothing for you with Isla. We'll be back shortly."

"Okay," she says, and I can hear agony lacing her words.

I think I drift off again because when I finally force my eyes open, and I'm able to turn my head to where my shot of whiskey is lying on her side facing me with her hands under her head and her eyes closed. She's stunning. Something radiates from within her, making her irresistible to me. She's unaware of how much she affects me, and waking up to the sight of her is something that I could get used to.

I reach out and run my fingers over her flawless cheek. Her

softened features scrunch as her eyes flutter open.

"Whiskey." There's a softness to her voice, a hesitation in her body movements. I can tell that she wants to touch me or jump into my arms but she doesn't reach for me.

"Rye."

"How are you feeling?"

"I'm hanging in there. I'm stiff, but whatever she gave me helped me a lot."

She sighs in relief. "You scared me last night. I've been overly concerned for hours. You wouldn't wake up, and I just . . ." She fights to hold back her emotion. "I just wanted you to open your eyes and hear you tell me that you loved me."

The corners of my lips angle upward. "You're rather emotional, Hads, and I love you."

"You do this to me, damn it," she complains as she wipes at her weeping eyes angrily. "I can't explain what I feel for you, but it's—it's like you give me something that no one else can."

"Come here, Hadley. I'll give you everything that you want."

She shakes her head and refuses to move closer to me. "Hadley," I state, "get that gorgeous ass over here. Now."

"I'll hurt you again."

"You haven't hurt me and you won't. I need to touch you."

"Madelyn said that you pushed yourself too hard yesterday, and that's why you experienced all of that pain last night."

"Fuck what she said. Hadley, if you don't move into my arms, I will send Jacobs a message and have him physically move you closer to me."

That gets a smile out of her, and she squirms closer to me.

"Whiskey?"

"Yes?"

She lies on her side and rests her head on my shoulder. "I think that you've spun me into glass."

"You've always been fragile, Rye. You just haven't seen

exactly how vulnerable you are until I made you see it."

"Possibly," she grumbles. "Oh, Dr. Heath will be here soon. Madelyn called him to inform him of the night you had. I think she may have a little crush on you."

I think this is Hadley telling me that she's jealous, but I don't push her on the subject. "It's a damn good thing that she knows that we're together then."

"I don't think that she cares."

"She's wasting her time."

We're interrupted by a knock on the door again, and I'm beginning to realize that this will be my life for the next two months. I fight the internal battle to tell whomever it is to leave, but I need to be stronger than I have been to survive this ordeal. I'll recover from this injury, and I'll do it with this dangerous and beautiful woman by my side.

It's been a week since I've been trapped in this suite. It's turning into more of a prison than a luxurious hotel. My mother walks into the room and takes a seat on the other side of the bed. "How are you faring, Waylon?"

"How much of an honest answer do you want to that?"

"Talk to me, dear."

"About what? How the top half of my body aches from being still for too long, or the fact that I can't feel a damn thing on the bottom half?"

"I understand that this must be difficult for you. It's tough watching you go through it all, but you have a strong team of professionals behind you, and you need to put your faith in them."

"Mother, have you ever known me to trust another with the outcome of my life?"

"I understand that you are finding it difficult to let others help you and give up control over your life, but you need to allow it just this once. You need to heal not only for yourself but for Hadley as well."

"You don't need to tell me twice."

"I'm not preaching to you. I just came to speak to you about her."

I shut my eyes and rub a hand down my face before opening them again. "What about her?"

"I think that she's as right for you as you are for her. After what you've told me about her and how she seems to be suffering from the same thing you went through, I understand the attraction to her. I understand the desire you must have to help her when no one else wants to."

"It has not simply been about breaking her of an addiction. I enjoy who I am when I'm around her as well as how we react to each other, whether it be emotionally or physically. I feel connected to her in ways that I never thought would be possible with anyone."

She sits up and pats my shoulder. "That's what us old folks call love, Waylon."

"I know. I've told her."

"You have?" She seems shocked, but she quickly recovers.

"I have."

"I'm glad. I think that she might be good for you, and I have enjoyed getting to know her in the few hours we spend together while you're not hogging her."

"I need her." I laugh to myself. "I bet that you never thought you'd hear me say those words about a woman."

"Nonsense. I've known that you've needed to find the right woman before you'd even attempt to make something out of a relationship with her, and now that you've found her, I couldn't be happier for you."

"Thank you, Mother."

"Of course. Now, I need to run and get some things sorted

out for Adriana. I'll be back to check on you this evening."

"I owe you for what you've been doing for Mothers of Brass this week."

"Not at all, I'm simply being a mother to my Brass, as well as the charity. Sleep well."

I nod to her as she gets up and leaves the confines of my room before I turn my head to the side and stare out the windows, and out onto the waters of Sydney Harbor.

The first month passes by agonizingly slowly and in organized chaos. I've managed to work from my prison cell with overstuffed pillows and fake backdrops, thanks to my mother. I've secured all of the properties that I made the trip out here to achieve, and I have multiple teams currently working on revamping them. My mother has been assisting Adriana with Mothers of Brass, as well as working with my lawyers and my PR mavens to keep my personal life out of the media.

I've refused to have Adriana enter into my suite, but having her a few doors down has helped with my current situation, and it has made working from a wheelchair easier.

As far as any news outlets that I do not own are concerned, I've gone dark. Adriana has been working nonstop with my PR team and lawyers to ensure my complete privacy.

Hadley hasn't left my side through all of this, and we have yet to be granted permission to fuck from Dr. Heath. To say that I'm frustrated with absolutely everything would be putting it lightly. I'm constantly surrounded by people, and it's beginning to wear on me. The only reprieve that I've found is in the evenings when it's just Hadley and me in bed.

Hads has been my constant, though, whether it be helping Madelyn or just reading one of those sappy novels that bring the emotion out of her next to me in bed.

She's currently speaking to Dr. Heath across the room from

me with regard to my surgery tomorrow morning. He believes that he will be able to stabilize my spine now that my condition is stable, and my lung is no longer a concern while administering anesthesia. The delay in my surgery will be the deciding factor of whether I walk out of that hospital room, or if I'll spend the remainder of my life on two wheels.

In order for this surgery to take place, I had to heal from my injuries, show a clean bill of health, and spend four hours a day with a physical therapist to keep my immobile muscles strong as well as to prevent blood clots. I've been lucky, in a sense, since I have not experienced spastic muscles, respiratory problems, pressure sores, or loss of bladder functions.

I hear him tell her that instead of transferring a tendon, he plans on inserting a robotic device that will reawaken the nerve and allow me to move again if it comes to it. Dr. Heath does not believe that my muscles were severed, and it may be as simple a fracture or broken bone that is pinching a nerve in the lumbar section of the spine. If that is the case, then healing from this may be easier than they have predicted.

In addition to my physical therapist, Dr. Heath has insisted on the use of an occupational therapist, a recreation therapist, and a rehabilitation psychologist. The living room area of the suite has been cleared out, and a dozen different machines for my rehabilitation were brought in approximately three weeks ago.

"Wade?" Hadley walks up to me as my physical therapist unstraps me from one of the machines that I have been working on.

"Hey, gorgeous."

"Are you ready for tomorrow?"

"More than you know."

"Dr. Heath just left, and he's more confident than he has been that it's simply a pinched nerve because of your progress in rehabilitation. He said that he hasn't seen any of his spinal

cord-injured patients show so much progress in such a short period of time. He doesn't believe that it's as severe as he thought
it was at first."

"Good to hear it."

I'm helped up by Madelyn and my physical therapist as they
transfer me to my chair. I've been able keep my muscle strength,
but I still cannot feel any sensation. It's incredibly frustrating.

Once I'm seated, I wheel myself closer to my Rye girl and
reach out for her. She squeals when I pull her down onto my lap
and wraps her arms around my neck, holding on for dear life.

"I've got you, Rye."

"And I've got you," she tells me as she presses her lips to my
neck.

"Madelyn, we'll be spending the next few hours alone.
Please do not let anyone interrupt. That includes you."

Hadley eyes me suspiciously and smacks my chest as I roll us
down the hallway, "What are you up to?"

My cock stirs underneath her at the thought of what I'm
about to do to her. "I'm going to show you just how much I've
got you."

Once I've made it into the bedroom, she reaches over and
shuts the door behind us as I wheel to the side of the bed.

We've managed to transfer me from my chair to the bed
alone a few times before this, and I think she's more confident
in doing so this evening because she doesn't hesitate to take the
reins.

A few minutes later I'm lying in bed as she walks around the
room picking up and turning off the lights.

"Leave your nightstand light on and get undressed, Hadley."

Her eyes shoot to mine in question. "What?"

"You heard me. Do it. Now."

Instead of arguing, she simply pulls off her dress before removing her panties and climbs into the bed beside me. When I

offer her my hand, she allows me to pull her toward me until I have her straddling my waist.

I want her, and I want her to feel desired, respected, and appreciated by me. By threading my fingers into the back of her hair, I pull her down to me until I'm able to take one of her nipples in my mouth. They peak instantly at the contact, and she whimpers in wonder.

"I'm going to make you come."

"But . . ."

"No. You won't fight me on this. Straddle my face, Rye."

"Wade, you don't have to do this."

"I've got you. Let me experience this. I need to taste you."

I watch as she purses her lips before moving up my body and reaching her hands out to hold onto the headboard for support. Her thighs settle on either side of my head as her pink pussy moves over my face. My hands steady her as she gets comfortable before roaming down from her hips to her ass. I turn my head to the side and nip at her inner thigh, and it elicits a cry from her.

"Come here."

I press down on her hips until she's positioned herself above my mouth. I take my time as I run my nose up her slit, breathing in the scent of her for the first time, other than from her panties. It's fucking heady. I place my lips over her clitoris and kiss her there once, before running my tongue over her lips. Her body jolts in my hands, and I grin to myself as I begin to tease her lips, and she starts grinding against my motions.

The room is thick with tension as I run my hands down her ass and down the backs of her thighs. I kiss across her outer lips before spreading her apart and warming her up with broad licks of my tongue. As my tongue circles around her clitoris, I can taste her—her skin, her warmth, and her cream. I would fuck her senseless if I had the ability to do so right now.

As much as I want to power into her and steal her thoughts away with the force of my cock, I want to make love to her even more. When I get the opportunity to, I'm going to take my time with her and adore her body. I'll find out exactly what she likes, and how I can please her.

Her hips buck as I take her clitoris between my now-wet lips and gently suck her while caressing my tongue over the tip of her clit. She moans her approval as she increases in sensitivity. I press my index finger into her and hook it against her G-spot to stimulate her from the inside as I lick up her cream.

She starts to arch her back and lets go of the headboard with one hand, lowering it into my hair and tugging, holding my mouth to her gorgeous sex. My hard cock twitches under the covers of the comforter as I pleasure her.

My tongue darts against her most sensitive spot harder as I add another finger inside of her soaking wet entrance, drumming my fingers against her.

"Oh God . . . Wade," she says my name like a prayer and I want to devour her. She tastes incredible as she squirms above my face. As I finger her, I move my wrist so I'm able to press the pad of my thumb against her back entrance. Her body twitches as I push the tip of my thumb into her.

She screams out piercingly as her body wracks against my mouth as, mindless now, she takes what she wants from me. She free falls as I look up at her and watch her come apart under my touch. I don't halt my assault on her clitoris until she starts to come down from her high.

By the time the waves start to slow, I can feel her clit pulsing in my mouth and her hand shaking in my hair when the bedroom door flies open.

"Mr. Brass? Are you—"

Madelyn.

The intrusion stops my movements, but Hadley doesn't

move from her position as I start to eat her again. She starts to rock her hips against my face once I slide my hands up to her naked ass.

"Leave," Hadley says breathlessly to our intruder.

It takes longer than it should for us to hear the door shut, and when it does, she explodes into another orgasm. I hold her against my lips as she rides it out, throwing her head back in pure reverence.

"Holy shit, Whiskey," she murmurs as she swings her leg over, freeing my face.

I smirk knowingly to myself and lick my lips, tasting her once more before she leans down and fucks my mouth with her tongue.

"You are damn good at that."

"And you're unbelievable when you come."

She giggles against my lips and reaches down for my cock, gripping me in her petite hand.

"I'd like to taste you."

"I never agreed to it, Rye."

"And?"

"If I'm going to come, it's going to be inside of this warm pussy of yours," I say as I reach down and cup the apex of her thighs.

"Oh."

There's a knock at the door, and it's now that I remember our intruder. "Yes?"

Madelyn peeks her head in the door before opening it all of the way. "I'm so sorry about earlier. I thought that something had happened when I heard a scream."

"Please do not assume that again."

"Yes, sir," she says and clears her throat. "Dr. Heath has asked me to administer your medications earlier tonight so that it does not have an impact on the anesthesia tomorrow morning."

Hadley exhales next to me and rolls over, kissing my cheek. "I'll miss you."

I know that she abhors it when the medication floods my system and takes me to another world, away from her. "I've got you."

The smile that she gives me is nothing compared to the expression that she had on her face minutes go.

"Madelyn, if you'll please give me a minute or two to change, I'd appreciate it."

I watch as Madelyn rolls her eyes at Hadley, and I know that Rye is pushing herself to her limits in dealing with her. Madelyn steps out of the room, and when the door clicks shut, Rye makes her way to the closet that now hosts her new clothing, as well as mine. When she comes back out, she's wearing one of my shirts and holding a pair of lace panties. Pink lace panties.

"I want to bury myself in you, Hadley."

Her cheeks rise up and bring color to her face as she purposefully bends over while picking up a pillow that we knocked onto the floor, showing me her pussy.

"Jesus."

She tosses the pillow at me and walks across the bedroom and into the en suite to clean up. When she emerges, Madelyn is at my side, paying too much attention to me for my liking. Her fingers flutter down my bicep and down to my wrist to where she's inserted an IV.

"You're fucking kidding me, right?" Hadley spits out in my direction. "Did my pussy in your face not satisfy you enough? Do you have to have another woman fucking swooning over you?"

I jerk my arm away from Madelyn, and she pouts her pink lips at me. "That's bullshit, Rye, and you know it is. Come here."

Madelyn is grinning like a fucking fool beside me as she prepares to insert the medication into my blood stream.

"No. I can't stand her being so close to you. I'm sick of her flirting with you and laying touches on you."

"Hadley," I warn her.

"Fuck this, Wade. I can't deal with any of it any longer."

I know that this has more to do with my surgery tomorrow and her fear of losing me to the knife, than it does Madelyn's flirtatious ways. Instead of heading to the bed and to me, she walks over to the door and slams it behind her on her way out.

I inhale a deep breath before expelling it noisily from my body.

"Madelyn. I understand this infatuation you have with me, but this shit needs to stop, or I will have Dr. Heath replace you with someone who is more capable of doing the job."

"Mr. Brass, I'm not sure what you're talking about. I've been doing what I've been instructed to do by Dr. Heath."

"Don't fucking push me. Hand me my phone."

Her brows furrow as she picks up my phone from my nightstand and hands it to me and I type out a message to Jacobs: I NEED YOU TO FIND HADLEY AND PHYSICALLY BRING HER TO ME. NOW.

"Give me the medication and go, Madelyn. If my girlfriend is still uncomfortable with you by the morning, then you will be permanently dismissed. Am I understood?"

Her face fills with shock, and she nods her head before inserting the liquid into my IV, and leaves the bedroom. As she's closing the door, I hear Hadley yelling something before the bedroom door opens again, and Jacobs delivers a squirming Hadley to my bed.

"You're an asshole, Waylon!" she complains as he sets her down and walks out of the room.

"Don't make me get him back in here," I tell her as she sits up to leave.

"Why? Huh? Do you want her? Tell me."

"You already know the answer to that. Listen to me, gorgeous." Her tear-filled eyes meet mine, and I reach out for her.

"You're concerned about tomorrow."

She tries to swallow past the lump in her throat before coming to lie down beside me. "I'm terrified."

I circle my arm around her and press my lips to her forehead. "I love you," I tell her, because I don't have the reassuring words that I should have. Tomorrow will have one of three outcomes, and only one of them is positive.

Recovery.

Permanent paralysis.

Death.

"I know. I love you too, and I'm sorry," she says as she wipes her eyes. "I just . . ."

"Don't apologize, but I need you to understand that I'm not interested in her or any other woman but you."

"Okay."

She buries her face into my chest and caresses the skin directly above my waistline—the last part of my body that I'm able to feel. A few nights ago, she was determined to find out where I was able to feel any sensation until I lost feeling completely. Ever since she's found the spot that borders on nothingness, she runs her fingers along the imaginary line.

"Tell me the first thing that you want to do once I've been given the all clear to walk?"

"What I want? You've been the one suffering, Wade. You shouldn't be asking me that question."

"But I am."

She shakes her head and kisses my bare chest while running her fingers along the imaginary line. "Lilly and I were talking about it last night when you had fallen asleep."

"What did you two come up with?"

I'm grateful that the two women in my life have been getting along famously. My mother has strict instructions on what do to if I don't make it through this surgery or any others succeeding it. I've had her sign off on a new will when my lawyers flew in to finalize the Australian contracts.

Hadley Rye is now one of the four beneficiaries in my will. The other three include Colin Jacobs, Isla Madden, and Lillian Brass. My mother is the only person aside from my lawyers who has seen the will, and if it's up to me, I intend to keep it that way for as long as possible.

When I asked my mother to be the witness to my new will, she never once objected to the addition of Hadley. She was rather pleased to know that a woman meant that much to me.

Here I am in love with a woman whom I've known for just over two months. I'm about to go into a surgery that will decide the remainder of my life, and if today is my last day, then I'll go being content because of her. I might have saved her from an addiction, but she's saved me from myself. I was on a path of self-destruction, leaning toward the addiction again in more ways than one, and she stopped me from diving in headfirst.

"Well?" I prod, wanting an answer before the medication sends me into the darkness.

"We both agreed that you needed to head to the beach and feel the waves hit your feet."

"I'd like that, Rye."

"I've got you, Whiskey."

"Good," I say as I close my eyes and feel her lips on mine just as I can no longer fight off the medication. It sweeps me into a dreamless sleep, surrounding me in nothingness. If this is what death feels like, then I hope I'll, at the very least, have the image of her stuck in my head instead of this nothingness.

Twenty-One

Hadley

DR. HEATH TOLD us that the surgery could take up to three hours. Well, it's been four, and I'm about to burst through those fucking doors and demand an answer.

Isla's flight came in late last night once Wade had fallen asleep, and Lillian went with Colin to collect her while I stayed with my man. Between the three of us women in this waiting room, one of us has been pacing at all times. Right now, it's me who's walking the length of the room, turning and walking back, as thoughts run through my head, bombarding me with the worst of possible outcomes. I think I've cut my bottom lip from the amount of pressure I've been applying to it with my teeth.

My phone goes off in my hand, causing me to jump. I glance down at the screen that is now lit up with a text message from Lola: HEY. HOW'S IT GOING? IS HE OUT YET?

I want to chuck the device across the room, but I type out my response instead: NO. THEY STILL HAVE HIM IN SURGERY. I'M GOING INSANE, LO. HOW'S HOLDEN? I ask her to distract myself. I wait for her to reply as I start to pace again. One foot in front of the other is all that I can manage right now. *Just keep moving, Hadley Rye.*

I'M SURE THAT HE'S OKAY. WADE TRULY MUST HAVE YOU WRAPPED AROUND HIS DICK, CONSIDERING THAT YOU'RE STILL PLAYING NURSE ON

THE OTHER SIDE OF THE WORLD. HOLDEN HAS BEEN ASKING ABOUT YOU A LOT. I HAVEN'T TOLD HIM THAT YOU'RE WITH WADE, BUT JUST THAT YOU'RE IN AUSTRALIA. I DON'T NEED TO BE THE ONE TO EXPERIENCE A PISSED-OFF PARKER BROTHER AGAIN.

I sigh and look up at Lillian. She's been watching me as I pace this entire time, and I think that the action is hypnotic, almost soothing to her. She half-smiles and pats the seat beside her, inviting me to join her. I send a reply to Lo before walking over to her.

I'M GLAD THAT HOLD'S OKAY. AND LO, I'VE NEVER HAD SEX WITH HIM, SO I COULDN'T BE WRAPPED AROUND HIS COCK, EVEN IF I WANTED TO BE. I haven't told her that yet, and I'm sure that right now is a little inappropriate, but I want to be seen as more than just the girl who would walk across a busy interstate to be fucked.

Her reply comes just as I take a seat next to Lilly: HOLY SHIT.

Lilly takes my hand in both of hers, supporting me when I should be the one supporting her. "Are you hanging in there, sweetie?"

"I'm trying to. All of this is still so new to me. I don't think that I've ever cared for anyone the way I care for him. It frightens me, and being here isn't helping with that."

"I'm sure that he would be saying the same things about you if the roles were reversed. Through all of my years with him, I haven't been able to experience Waylon without the fear of him falling back into his addiction. Well, until now. Until you came into his life."

"Oh no. He's the one that has been providing me with a sanctuary, not the other way around."

"You may not realize it, but you have been providing him with the same thing, Hadley. You're good for him, and I'm thrilled that he is able to see that."

I look down at my feet and let out a breath. "I love his ridiculously stubborn ass."

"I know you do, sweet girl. It's easy to see, and I know that he feels the same toward you."

"He's told you?"

"Not as directly as you just did, but yes, he has."

My eyebrows rise in shock just as Isla joins us and sits next to Lillian, patting her knee for comfort as she speaks. "Hadley, I wanted to say thank you for helping to open him up. Since he's known you, he's been able to express himself the way that he wants to rather than the way that he thinks that he needs to. Thank you for taking care of him."

A tear leaks free, and I shake my head. "Don't talk to me like that, like he's not going to make it. I can still feel him. I can feel the static that draws me to him."

"I didn't mean it in that way, Hads. I was truthfully just thanking you."

I sniffle and nod. "I understand, and I think that it's he who's opened me up."

"Maybe, but you've changed him just as much as he has you. I don't think that I've ever seen the man so content with life."

I lean my head on Lilly's shoulder and stare at the blank white wall in front of me as I let their words sink in.

"I'm contemplating a whiskey when we get out of here," Lillian says to the both of us.

We join her in a weak laugh as Isla adds, "You don't drink, Lilly."

"Dear Isla, after today I do."

We're all smiling for the first time since they rolled him back there and it's now that Dr. Heath chooses to walk into the almost-empty waiting room—the only exception being some man who has been on the phone the entire time that we've been here. The doctor pulls off his surgical cap and approaches us.

"Good day, ladies."

"Dr. Heath." Lillian stands and drags me up next to her.

"How is Waylon?"

He brushes his forehead off before speaking. "As you are well aware, the surgery took longer than we anticipated. Let's take a seat and I'll talk you through the procedure."

My immediate reaction is to yell at him and ask him how my boyfriend is doing. Did he make it? Where is he? But I contain my emotions for now and focus on what he's going to tell us.

Dr. Heath clears his throat and begins. "I made an incision in the middle of his lower back where I was able to expose the bone. After verifying the correct vertebra and upon further inspection, I confirmed that my suspicion was proved correct. Due to the accident, Waylon was suffering a pinched nerve, which caused the paraplegia. The nerve wasn't severed, but my team and I decided to reconstruct it in the case that the injury caused too much damage for it to heal. We believe that he will make a full recovery."

I sit down in the seat behind me and sag in relief, cupping my hands around my face as the tears start again. "When can we see him?" I ask through my mess of tears.

"Madelyn and my surgical nurses are tending to him as we speak. As soon as I get one more look at him, you all will be able to see him. In the meantime, though, I wanted to talk to you and Lillian about his road to recovery."

"Of course," Lilly says. We both reach for each other at the same time, and I'm not entirely sure who is holding whose hand, but I can't feel my fingers.

Dr. Heath sits down in one of the seats across from us as he begins. "After this surgery as with any other, he will experience some discomfort which we will manage with a narcotic." The three of us nod. "He will be under a few restrictions, which he needs to abide by in order to recover swiftly and wholly. He should not drive for four weeks. He should avoid sitting down for long periods of time. I suggest that he gets up and tries to walk around for as long as he is able to comfortably do so. He may not lift anything heavier than ten pounds. There needs to be no smoking and he will need to postpone any sexual activity until our follow-up appointment."

Lillian and Isla both look at me with smiles on their faces.

Dr. Heath continues as we acknowledge his list of restrictions. "He will still need help when it comes to physical activities such as showering or bathing, as well as walking. We don't plan on his wearing a brace, but if he's unable to walk at all, we'll need to consider it until his spine is strong enough after the surgery."

"You've mentioned that he'll be able to walk. Are you sure about this?" Lilly asks the question that I'm dying to know the answer to.

Dr. Heath smiles at us. "I have faith in the work that my team did. Mr. Brass spared no expense when it came down to flying in doctors who all have experience in spinal injuries and nerve reconstruction. Each of us have faith that he will pull off a full recovery within a few months."

"Holy crap," I say and throw my arms around Lilly, who is now a blubbering mess.

"I think I may need the fucking bottle of whiskey if Lilly needs a tumbler," Isla says as she pulls out a Macallan 30-Year out of her tote.

Dr. Heath chuckles and stands. "I'll go check on our patient and Madelyn will be out shortly to escort you back to his recovery room."

"Thank you," the three of us say in unison

I glance at Isla and almost throw myself at the bottle. "You sure as fuck have better brought something to drink that out of."

"Paper cups?" she says as she pulls out a small stack of paper coffee cups from her purse as well.

I giggle and move to sit next to her as she pours the mahogany liquid into three cups and hands one each to Lilly and me. "Wade would kill us if he knew that we were drinking three-thousand-dollar whiskey out of paper cups."

"Cheers to his brass balls," Isla says and holds up her cup.

"To Waylon, and a successful surgery," Lillian chimes in with a sniffle.

Instead of sipping the fragrant, rich, mahogany-colored liquid, we all down it like a cheap shot. A rich sherry aroma hits my nose while notes of clove, nutmeg, and woodsmoke coat my palate.

Lillian gasps for air after taking the shot. "That is something that I never plan on doing again, girls. I'll leave you two and Wade to your whiskey. The stuff is vile."

"It's horrific. I don't even understand why I like it. It's like sticking your face into a fire pit," Isla says as she fills up our cups again.

I lean my head on Isla's shoulder after we smile knowingly at each other. Being with her makes me feel closer to Wade. I'm unsure as to why, but it does. They seem to be cut from the same cloth, and it settles me down from the fear that I might have lost him.

Forty minutes and another two paper cups later, Madelyn walks out in her aqua-colored scrubs. "Mrs. Brass, Isla . . . Hadley," she adds my name onto the end as if it's laced with poison, "I can bring the three of you back to see him now."

All three of us stand together. I toss our cups in a trash receptacle close by before Isla comes beside me to link her arm with mine. "I lied about having eaten earlier, and I believe that you did too. We might need each other to ensure we don't walk into the wrong room or a wall."

"I may have lied as well." I squeeze her arm underneath mine as the excitement of seeing Whiskey hurtles through my body.

"Right this way," Madelyn says as we all fall into step behind her as she scans her ID card and leads us through a countless number of doors until we are led down a quiet hallway with rooms on each side. The air is stuffy, and cheap pictures are hung up on the wall in an attempt to be uplifting. Madelyn comes to a stop and stands in front of the third room down before scanning her badge, and it unlocks with a click. She pushes the heavy door open and holds it for the three of us to enter.

I let go of Isla the second I see him, and I feel like I'm experiencing *deja vu*. He's asleep and unmoving as Lilly walks up to him. Isla follows behind her, but I stay my distance as I scan over him from my spot next to the door.

He looks beyond his thirty-one years with all of the machines and wires surrounding him. The room is filled with sounds that distract me from him; I want to know what they all mean. I've started to fidget with the cuff of his sweatshirt that I've been wearing all day when I finally register my name being called.

"Hads? Are you okay?"

I turn to face the direction that the sound is coming from: Isla.

My head starts to spin as I watch Madelyn adjust the wires hooked up to him. I think that I'm going to be sick at the sight of him so vulnerable. I cup my hand over my mouth in an attempt to stop myself from being ill, but my body lurches. A trashcan meets my face just in time as Isla shrieks while holding it in place.

"Oh sweetie," I hear Lilly say at a distance.

I force my eyes shut and wipe my mouth off with a paper towel that Madelyn hands me. "You should sit down. I've got enough on my hands with watching his vitals. I'd need an extra hand if you decide to pass out on me."

I nod in compliance as Isla leads me to the single seat in the room. Before I can lower myself down to it, though, she drags both it and me closer to Wade, I sit down and curl up into a ball. I stretch my arm out and rest my hand on his as it rests on the white sheets covering the bed.

"I'm sorry," I croak.

"Oh, quit it," Isla says at the same time that Lilly says, "There's nothing to apologize for. It's a lot to take in."

I rest my head against the back of the chair and shut my eyes as I run my thumb over the top of his hand. I think back to our time on his yacht and how he took care of me. It feels as if it was years ago, but I miss it. My heart yearns for him.

"Isla, would you mind sending Colin an update on Wade and asking him to bring the three of us something to eat before you pass out on me as well?" is the last thing I hear before sleep overtakes my worried, overtired, and underfed body.

Twenty-Two

Wade

FROM WHAT I have been told, I'm alive, which has been difficult to comprehend because of the narcotics swimming through my bloodstream. I've found solace in watching Hadley sleep instead of concentrating on the ache in my lower back. There was no one besides her in the room when I woke up five minutes ago, and I'm thankful for that. It has allowed me the time to come around on my own. It's provided me with time to come to terms with just having gone through surgery instead of waking to an overcrowded room.

Slowly, I run my thumb across her palm as it lies on top of my hand. I cannot think back to the time that ultimately tied us together, but I refuse to fight what has progressed between the two of us. The door opens, stealing my moment of reprieve. I turn my head from Hadley and lock eyes with my mother. She gasps and rushes over to my side.

"Welcome back, Waylon. Isla, go fetch Madelyn or Dr. Heath and let them know that he's awake."

Before Isla responds to my mother, she joins her at the bed and leans over me, giving me an awkward hug before smacking my chest. "I'm glad that you made it, Brass."

"Fuck off," I croak out at her, but manage to wink at her.

She gives me the finger as she turns and walks out of the room to find a medical professional, returning in a minute flat with Madelyn on her heels just as my mother was explaining the results of the surgery to me.

"Good afternoon, Mr. Brass," Dr. Heath says as he follows Madelyn and Isla in. He picks up the digital device at the end of my bed, checks his watch, and then types something on it before looking back up at me. "How are you feeling?"

"I feel like I just did a line of cocaine. My back is sore, but that's about all that I'm able to feel right now, physically at least."

I look back over at Hadley, who is still asleep in the chair, and it concerns me that she hasn't woken up yet. I haven't stopped running my thumb over the palm of her petite hand, soothing the thoughts that must be running through her head right now, even in her sleep.

"Is she okay?" I ask because she's been waking up when people come into our room at the hotel, and just another voice in the room would have normally woken her up. Especially lately.

Isla giggles and speaks first. "She passed out when we were allowed back to see you. Well, she got sick first when she saw your ugly mug, but I'm sure that had something to do with the whiskey we drank on empty stomachs."

"You're going to end up killing her if you let her drink before she eats, Isla."

"I'm not her mother, Brass," she says with a smile and my mother scolds the both of us for interrupting Dr. Heath.

"Please, Doctor, continue," she says.

"Well, Mr. Brass, my team of surgeons and I reconstructed the pinched nerve, and we've supported it with hardware. We have no doubt that you will make a full recovery. I'd actually like to test out your senses now if that's all right."

"Very well."

He places the device back at the end of the bed before Madelyn removes the sheet covering my body.

"Mr. Brass, you need to understand that you will have strict restrictions when it comes to what you can and cannot do. I have provided the ladies with the information, and I will be sending you back to the suite with a packet of information that I need you to read through. The muscles around the incision area will be weak and uncomfortable for a while," he says as I feel a sharp pin-like object pressing against the bottom of my foot.

I swing my head to look at what he's doing instead of staring at Hadley. He's holding up a metal object with multiple metal pins on a wheel. He runs it down the bottom of my foot again, and my eyes widen in astonishment. "I can feel that."

My mother gasps excitedly before stepping closer to Isla and squeezing her.

"Wonderful," he says before repeating the action on my other foot and once again, I am able to feel the sensation of it. He repeats the same actions he's done over the past couple of weeks, working his hands up my calves, but this time, I can feel everything. It seems rusty, but it's definitely something.

"Good," he says to himself. "Mr. Brass, as eager as you must be to walk around, I'm going to request that you go through the regular rehabilitation process before over-exerting your body. After the nerve reconstruction, it may feel like you have a new pair of legs that you'll need to get used to. I'll have your physical therapist come by this evening, and together he and I will develop a recovery and exercise plan."

"Thank you."

"If you'll excuse me now, I need to document and finalize a few things with your records before you will be able to leave. I'll stop by later this evening before your release in the morning to your suite where Madelyn will be required to stay for another two weeks or more. I'd like for Mr. Brass to have time to sleep off the remainder of the anesthesia. Ladies, I'm going to have to close visiting hours early for him today."

I nod, and speak before the others can. "Hadley is staying

right here." I turn my attention back to her, and give them no other option but to agree with me.

I say goodbye to my mother and Isla before they leave with Madelyn and the doctor, once again leaving me alone with the woman I love—the woman who has the potential to destroy me, but I've just now come to the conclusion that she has no idea of how much power she currently wields over me.

I squeeze her hand in an attempt to wake her. The static that runs between us seems to send a live shock into my heart when her eyes flutter open. "Rye, wake up for me, gorgeous."

She stretches out in the chair as she blinks. I'm assuming that she's attempting to remember where she is. I watch the recognition sweep over her face: her body straightens and goes stiff before she moves to the edge of the seat. "You're awake," she states.

"Barely. This shit that they gave me is potent, and I think you might need a hit or two of it. You're pale."

A crease forms across her forehead at my words. "I think . . . did I pass out?"

I can't help but chuckle at her. I'm unsure if she's fully awake yet, or if she's in that odd dream-like state after waking up suddenly. "That's what my mother said."

"Wait, how are you? Where is everyone?" She seems thoroughly confused as she rubs her temple.

"They just left with Madelyn and Dr. Heath."

"You're okay? God, please be okay, I don't know if I can—"

I interrupt her before she forces herself into a panic attack. "Relax for me, Rye. I'm great."

I realize that it's going to take her a few minutes to come around to me so I throw the blanket off of my legs and pat the bed next to me. "Come."

"What about . . . ?"

"I don't give a fuck. Come," I demand and this time, she lifts herself to her feet before climbing into the small bed with me. It's a good thing that she's as petite as she is, or we would not be able to do this. She settles next to me on her side and runs her fingers down my chest and to my waistline.

Her fingers edge along the imaginary line there. "Go lower."

Her aquamarine eyes find mine as her fingers stray lower, sliding down the edge of my Adonis belt. I breathe in a sharp intake of air when I feel her touch, along with the static that always accompanies it.

"Mmm."

"What is it?"

"I can feel that."

"What!" She jumps up into a seated position and runs her hand lower until her hand is splayed on my upper thigh.

I swallow hard and tilt my head to the other side, being sure to look away from her as my breath shallows and I enjoy her touch on my bare skin as if it was the first time.

"Keep going. I can still feel you."

"Wade?" she asks as she reaches her hand into my hair. I shift my head until I'm able to see her. My shoulders stiffen when her face softens as her eyes meet mine. I'm sure that she is more than able to see the emotion rolling over my face. Her breath hitches as she runs her hand over my rough stubble. She's searching my soul through my irises.

"It feels surreal."

She purses her lips as her eyes start to water. "You're going to get through this."

"A big part of that is because of you. The thought of not being able to do the simplest of tasks with you has given me the strength to keep pushing."

"You would have made it this far with or without me."

I shake my head, disagreeing with her. I believe that I would have given it all a shot, but other than Brass Global and its subsidiaries, I have never had an emotional connection to anyone or anything in my life. I would have fought off the despair that has accompanied this experience, but instead of conquering it, I would have drowned in its murky waters.

"No. I wouldn't have. I need you to understand . . ."

She places her lips on my temple and lets out a sigh. "You don't have to prove anything to me."

"You and I have a connection, Hads. I need you to see just how much you have affected me through all of this. I need to prove to you just how deeply I feel for you."

"Here's the thing, Wade, I've already fallen in love with you. I've met the person that I'm supposed to love without having to settle for a lesser you. You don't owe me a single thing; you just need to recover."

It baffles me as to how I've been given an opportunity to change her life and watch her change mine. I don't think that she has realized just how much of an impact she's had on me, and I don't believe that I did either until I said goodbye to her before surgery. The thought that it might have been the last time I got to see her almost destroyed me.

"You are worth every single broken rule. Fuck, baby, your touch feels good on me."

She blushes and runs her hand farther down my leg. "You're going to have to pry my hands off of you, you know that, right?"

In an unguarded moment, I tell her my truth. "I'll never want to."

She clears her throat and lowers her head to mine. I raise my chin until our lips graze against each other's. "I feel like I can breathe again."

I close my eyes and rest my head back. "These narcotics are going to take me away from you."

"Go to sleep, Whiskey."

I secure my arm around her back, and rest my hand on the

curve of her ass. "Don't disappear on me."

"I've got you."

A week has passed since my surgery, and I have been able to get around with the aid of a walker and my physical therapist. I've been giving it my all in order to recover as cleanly and as quickly as possible.

To say that this experience has shaped me is an understatement. I've found myself in these last few weeks. I've found the man I was when the addiction had me by the balls. But instead of allowing myself to relapse into the addiction, I've beaten it. I've simply found myself: the man who has been at the center of my confusion for years. My suffering had provided me with this unforeseen clarity.

For years I denied that the mental illness still existed, but today I'm able to see that I was not free of it when I thought I was. I still took weekends out of my month to immerse myself in my personal world of sex. I went out of my way to find women who were clean, and I was able to pay them off to have them do exactly what I needed to be done.

For as long as I can remember, I've thrived on fucking multiple women at once and watching them tongue each other. However, the thought of sharing Hadley with anyone, even another woman, is one that splinters my soul with revulsion.

Through it all, I've realized that recovery is not for those people who need it, but rather for those who want it. It's a powerful thought that I only came to know when she entered my life.

I lost my head at a young age, and I've pushed through the tranquility that this invisible illness provided me, searching for the daylight. It was causing an internal war to rage until I was able to conquer it completely. I've found my purpose; I've found my control as well as my calm. I've found it all in Hadley. Nothing binds me now, nothing but her, and if she's my new compulsion then I'll welcome every second of it.

I shut my eyes as I think back to last night when Hadley walked out of our bedroom suite to where I was strapped to a heart monitor as I took slow, yet steady steps on a treadmill with my rehabilitation specialist beside me. She walked in front of me and into the kitchen area, and my heart gave out.

She was wearing the shortest pair of shorts that I have seen on her to date. Back home, the fall weather would have hindered my view of her ass, but seeing as we're about to start summer here in Australia, she's still wearing thin materials and small scraps of it.

Her voice brings me out of myself when she reaches for my shoulders. "Hi," she says in my ear as she wraps her arms around my neck from behind. I lean my head back, and I'm greeted with her lips just as her hands splay across my pecs.

"Mmm, good morning, Rye."

"How did you get out here?"

I managed to get out of bed this morning with Madelyn's help, but once she left the room, I wandered out onto the deck and managed, with much difficulty, to seat myself on one of the chairs facing Sydney Harbor.

"Madelyn helped me out of the bed, but I got here on my own."

"Did you now?" she says as she circles my body before taking a seat on my lap where my arms automatically ring around her waist. Before Hadley, I couldn't stand when women touched me without my permission. In doing so, they took away what little control I had over the addiction. It made me crave more, and it would cause me to go after it, to pursue the one thing that ruined my life. Yet when Hadley touches me, she provides me with resolve instead of igniting an internal battle of wills.

"The weather looked too good not to enjoy it." Her hands run up and under my shirt to that invisible line around my waist.

"Dr. Heath said that you needed to rest today and not exert yourself. Is there anything that you have wanted to do?"

"I've been meaning to get into contact with Liam."

"Oh, that's right. Are you up for heading over to his place?"

"Getting out of this hellhole is the best idea that you've ever had."

"I'll go grab your phone," she says as she squirms out of my grip and walks back through the sliding glass door to retrieve it.

Liam insisted that I bring Isla with me. I'm sure he believes that this will lead to some sort of sexual healing bullshit. We're seated on his patio, which leads down to the beach in front of us.

"Who's the girl? I hadn't realized that we had nurses that fucking hot in Australia," he comments as he takes a drink of his beer. He's been watching her closely ever since we arrived. I haven't cared to inform him of my relationship with Hadley as of yet. I should not need to justify myself for bringing a woman with me.

Isla and Hadley are walking back up from the beach in their bikinis, and I'm having a difficult time hiding my need for her in these pants.

"She's not a nurse."

"Ah, so she's one of Isla's bitches?"

"One of her bitches?"

"Yeah, man. Like back in the day when she brought them back to the dorm for us."

I chuckle as the two of them reach us. "It's nothing like that."

He drops it for now as Hadley takes a seat next to me. "You have a gorgeous home, Liam."

Isla laughs and rests her feet against the arm of my chair. "If he didn't, then I'd be shocked. His trust kicked in when he was eighteen, and he's been living the easy life ever since."

"It sounds like you need a drink, Isla."

"Possibly. Do you still have the whiskey we left the last time we were here?"

"Sure as shit. I'll show you where it is," he tells her as they both get up and head into the house.

"He seems like he can be a lot of fun," Hadley says with a smile on her face.

"He can go over the top at times," I tell her as I take off my shirt and hand it to her. As much as I enjoy the view of her semi-naked in front of me, I don't like Liam eyeing her in plain sight.

She takes it without argument and slides it over her head. "Thank you."

Liam and Isla walk out holding up two bottles of whiskey and four tumblers as Hadley pulls the fabric over her tanned skin. "It's a damn good thing that you still have that personal driver, Brass."

Isla cheers and shakes the bottles in her hands. "Hadley, we're getting buzzed up."

Jesus, Isla.

I reach over and place my hand on Hadley's knee once she readjusts herself in the seat. My eyes are on Liam as he watches my movement. I understand the attraction any man would have toward my naturally platinum blonde beauty, but I'm rather astounded when I catch something dark cross behind his eyes.

She shifts herself closer to me as Isla pours the amber liquid of a Sullivans Cove Tasmanian whiskey into four tumblers before handing them off to each of us. Liam takes the single seat on the other side of Hadley while Isla sits across from us. We all do cheers and then take a drink of the one-of-a-kind whiskey.

"Oh, this is exceptional," Hadley comments as she watches me take a drink. The doctor said no smoking, but he never mentioned a thing about alcohol, yet I won't push it.

"I'm glad that you like it," Liam says to her. "Wade and I bought it the day that it came out, and there were only two bottles ever made. I only crack out this beauty when this motherfucker is present."

She gives him a radiant smile, and I squeeze her knee as envy courses through me. I've become used to her constant attention, and having another man, albeit a good friend of mine, divert any of it away from me starts an internal war.

Isla starts to speak, but my focus is on Hadley as she looks from Liam to me with that smile still in place. She places her hand on top of mine, and I intertwine my fingers with hers, staking my claim.

"Are you okay?"

"Impeccable," I say, endeavoring to keep the sarcasm out of my voice, but I'm certain that she notices.

My eyes find Liam, and he nods his understanding. *Don't placate me, you fucker.* I know the kind of power this woman has over a man, and he's struggling with it. He wants to bend her over and take her from behind while I watch. It wouldn't be the first time, but it would never happen with Hadley; I wouldn't allow her to be touched by anyone else.

"Uh, hello? Did anyone hear what I just said?"

We all glance to Isla who is now downing the remainder of her tumbler as if it didn't cost ten thousand dollars.

"Hadley, let's hit the waves, and let these assholes catch up."

I see the indecision in her face at Isla's demand before she leans back against the cushion and pulls her sunglasses down. "I'm pretty comfortable here. I wouldn't want to get wet and ruin this plush seat."

Liam's brow perks up at her comment, and if I were able to get up and rush over to him, I'd fucking castrate him.

Isla pouts her lips, but pours herself another drink and stands to turn the music up. "I love this song," she yells out as she starts to dance.

"There are some fine-ass memories associated with this one," Liam adds.

The song sparks up a conversation about our freshman year in college together before Liam dropped out and moved down here. Hadley is consumed in the stories that the two of them are telling her about our past. Isla is in the middle of telling her about one of the nights I was black-out drunk after being paddled by my fraternity brothers.

"Hads, I swear, if I could have recorded it, I would have. I remember him just lying in the front yard of his frat house with his head under the bushes. He was completely passed out without his pants on."

I watch Hadley's face light up, and she squeezes my hand at Isla's story of one of my many drunken nights with my frat.

"How do you have the capacity to remember all of this, Isla? I'm sure that you were just as drunk that night, if not worse," Liam adds.

"I have a picture, that's how."

"Ah, sweet blackmail."

"Don't I know it." She gives me a wicked grin and holds up her tumbler to me in cheers.

I remain quiet as Liam keeps his eyes dancing up Hadley's bare legs. I grind my teeth together in an attempt not to say anything throughout our time together.

The afternoon passes, and between the four of us—and by four of us I mean mostly Isla and Liam—we have finished half a bottle of Pappy Van Winkle's Family Reserve, a 20-year-old straight bourbon whiskey with a smooth and rich profile.

Hadley is leaning back against me in the dark as I run my fingers up and down her ribcage. I think that she's got a buzz going on because she's been getting handsy with me throughout the evening. I've noticed that it's the one thing that she doesn't do in public. She doesn't mind my kissing her, but when we're around people we know, she tends to keep her hands to herself, and I'm unsure how I feel about it. She slides her hand down my torso, running her fingers along the ridges that outline each muscle. She's been doing it for about fifteen minutes now, and I've been enjoying Liam throw me glances of disbelief.

"I believe that I need to pee," she says with a giggle and sits up. "Isla, would you mind showing me to the bathroom?"

I watch as Isla stumbles to her feet and holds out her hand to my girl. "Follow me, Hads."

Hadley takes her hand as they walk inside and out of my sight.

"So you and the girl, huh?"

The right corner of my lips turns up with the knowledge that he finally fucking understands that she's mine. "Indeed. It took you a while to catch on. Keep that cock to yourself."

"Fuck off, dude. I thought that you brought her here to share. You know, like the good ole' days? Fuck, do you remember the time you and Isla banged like fucking drums when you were piss-drunk at my farewell party? I figured that the two of you would end up together . . . fuck, everyone in our freshman year was waiting for you to get down on one knee. You two were a sure thing."

"What?"

I turn around in time to see Hadley's face fall. *Fuck me.*

"Rye . . ."

"I, uhm, I just had to grab my purse." She picks up her Burberry that I bought for her and quickly makes her escape. I reach out for the cane that I've been using to get around instead of a boxed walker.

"Dude, where's the fire?"

"You just fucking lit one," I say as I struggle to get my legs to cooperate. I need to go after her. I need to know that she's okay.

Fuck, the look on her face tore me in half.

By the time I've managed to stand—without Liam's help—Isla comes back outside, humming to the song coming from the speakers.

"Where's Rye?"

"Uhm. I don't know." She shrugs and takes a drink. "She said that she had to come and get her purse, but then she never came back. So she must be lost in the house somewhere. You know how big this place is."

I blow out the anger that has made its way through my body and slip my phone out of my pocket. I pull up her number and hit dial. I wait, and wait, but it eventually goes to voicemail.

"I need to go, Isla. Please go look . . ." I stop, remember what Hadley had just heard. Isla can't be the one to find her. Not now.

My phone vibrates in my hand, and I glance down at the text message from Hadley: I JUST NEED TIME.

WHERE ARE YOU? I type out and hit send as I take slow, but calculated steps toward the house.

DOES IT MATTER?

I groan as my legs won't move me fast enough to her: YES, IT FUCKING MATTERS. WHERE ARE YOU, HADLEY?

I NEED TO BE ALONE.

NO. I NEED YOU TO BE WITH ME. I WILL WALK THIS ENTIRE HOUSE UNTIL I FIND YOU. RYE, PLEASE. ALLOW ME THE CHANCE TO EXPLAIN.

I walk into the open living room area and glance around the open-plan house for any signs of her when I hear her sniffle. The sound of it churns my soul.

"Baby?"

Silence.

The cane clicks against the tiled floors as I struggle to the center of the room.

"I texted Colin," she says.

I turn in the direction of her voice to find her standing in a doorway, her shoulders sagging with an emotion that I'm unable to place.

"Rye, baby. Come here."

She shakes her head back and forth. "I'm going to head back to the hotel. Enjoy the rest of your evening," she says to me as she walks down the hallway and toward the front door. I know that I won't be able to walk fast enough to catch her, and it only angers me more. I grunt as I take a step toward her, but when I hear the door open and close, I take a seat on the nearest couch.

"Where did she go?" Isla asks from the entrance to the patio.

I shrug and run my hand through my hair. "Call a cab. We're leaving."

"I was actually going to . . ." she stops when I glance up at her. "All right."

Hadley's leaving packed a powerful punch. I have to suppress the violent impulses coursing through me now to go after Liam. He must have seen her standing behind me, but he went for it regardless. This fucker is trying to ruin what I have with her just so he can bury his cock inside of what belongs to me. The rage doesn't subside as Isla helps me get settled in the cab and Liam nods his head toward me. "It was good seeing you two fuckers. I'll see you soon."

I pull the door shut before my mouth spews words that I will be unable to take back. I understand that he's had more than his fair share of liquor, but he still should have known better. Isla gets in beside me, and the cab takes off.

"Are you going to tell me what happened? I may be more than a little drunk, but I can still speak English."

"Rye just found out that you and I fucked."

"She w-what?" she stutters. "How?"

"Liam."

"God, he's still such a pig. We'll find her, Brass."

If Hadley is made of glass then I'm holding a handful of the broken shards, cutting and splintering my palm. The look in her eyes told me that she was essentially shattered. My head drops back on the headrest as we make our way across the city and to our hotel. My luck, though, we get stuck on an interstate behind an accident, allotting her more time to run.

Twenty-Three

Hadley

"HEY, I'M GLAD that I got ahold of you. Are you too busy to talk?"

"Nah, not for you. What's up? I've missed you around these parts."

I know that I shouldn't be talking to Holden, but I just need to be comforted, and Lola is apparently too consumed with work and her designs to answer my S.O.S text and phone call.

"It's good to know that I'm missed."

"Possibly more than you are aware of."

"I think that I'm ready to come home. What are you doing?"

I won't tell him my reason for calling or why I'm upset. I just need to talk to someone right now to distract myself and not do anything stupid like walking down to the bar and sucking off the first man that I come into contact with.

"Right now, I just got back from the gym, and I was about to head out to mail you something. Lola gave me the address where you're staying. I hope that's okay."

"Oh. Wait, don't send it. I just left that hotel. I'm thinking about flying home."

The minute I got back to the hotel, I calmly packed up all of my shit before leaving Wade a note. Am I being unreasonable and possibly childish? Maybe, but I have my reasons. I've literally given up a life back home in Chicago for him, and he has yet to open up to me as he said he has. I think that sleeping with a woman that I've been around a lot lately would be something that you would tell your girlfriend.

But why would I know this shit? It's not like I date exclusively. I fought with myself as I wrote him that simple note. We might have a lot of history now, but it's nothing compared to what he and Isla share. She's right for him according to Liam, and I don't blame him for thinking so. She pulls him out of himself, and I think that is what ultimately helped me decide to pull away tonight. There is someone better out there for him than me. I'm not it for him. I can't be because it just doesn't make sense. Regardless, Liam's comment helped me to solidify this decision.

"You are?" I hear the hope and excitement in Holden's voice. It's dirty and raw, and I know that he wants to fuck me. At least that makes one man.

"I think so. I just need to find a flight. It won't be for a day or two, but I'll give you my flight information once I have it."

"I could pick you up."

"I think I'd like that."

Holden might not be a man who brings me flowers or sets my heart on fire, but he'll give me what I want and need on a physical level.

"Miss Rye?" my name is called out, and I glance up from my seat in the lobby of a hotel closer to the airport. "I have to run, Hold. I'll text you soon, okay?"

"Sounds good, Hads. Later."

I grab my purse and walk up to the check-in desk where the clerk hands me a room key. "Sorry for the delay, but your room is now ready."

"Thank you."

I've been a passenger for over eighteen hours, and I have made no effort to contact Waylon Brass in three days.

My phone has been off since I placed a call to Holden. The only other time I turned it on was when I sent Hold my flight details. Needless to say that it froze at least three times while it played catch up to Wade's onslaught of messages. I read through some of them, but not many. I shut my eyes as I remember his words, message after message, on my screen.

—HADLEY, YOU CANNOT FUCKING DISAPPEAR IN A FOREIGN COUNTRY.

—GODDAMN IT. WHAT THE FUCK DO I HAVE TO DO TO HAVE YOU BACK?

—YOUR NOTE KILLED ME.

—I SHOULD HAVE TOLD YOU. I APOLOGIZE FOR BEING THE ASSHOLE I KNOW I AM.

Each of them came through out of order, and I detested the last one. He's not an asshole, not even close. Should he have told me? Absolutely. But is he an asshole for sleeping with her all of those years ago? No. Not in the slightest. The two of us share an illness when it comes to sex, so I understand.

I did not leave him because of those two points. I left him because I came to the realization that Isla would be a better match for him in the long run. You know, best friends falling in love and all. They just haven't seen it yet . . . but I have.

My body jolts as my final flight touches down at Chicago O'Hare. It's now that I realize that he won't be running after me because, once again, he can't. Dr. Heath won't clear him to fly for at least another three weeks.

I'm walking—not running but walking—away from the man I love because I believe that there is always going to be someone better than me for him. If I'm honest with myself, I've already gotten over the simple secret that he kept from me, but it made me realize that I'll hold him back in life. It's the hardest thing that I'll ever do to walk away from him.

I hold my head high as I stride through the airport terminal and out toward baggage claim where I'm met with Holden's open arms.

"I would like to say that you should go away more often because you're fucking sexy as hell coming back to me . . . but I'd prefer if you stayed here."

"Hi, Hold."

"What's up, beautiful?"

His arms come around me, and I speak against his shoulder. "Thank you for coming to get me. I hate the cabs in Chicago."

"It's no problem at all. Let's grab your bag and get out of this madness. This fucking airport is constantly overcrowded."

I laugh at how ridiculous he is. "I think that I missed your cocky self."

As the words leave my lips, I recall what Wade said about missing someone who doesn't belong to you. He can't miss me now, and the same thing applies vice-versa.

Holden takes my hand and leads me out of the airport while he rolls my suitcase next to him. "Does Lola know that you're coming back?"

"Nope. I'm surprising her, so you better not have mentioned it to her."

"Cool those pretty tits of yours. I haven't said a word."

An hour through Chicago traffic later, Holden helps me get my crap into my bedroom. Once I'm settled, he blatantly attacks me by pushing me back onto my bed and pinning me down.

"What are you—?"

He reaches between my legs and I shy away from him, pulling his forearm until he dislodges his hand. "I, uhm, I'm on my period."

Lie.

"Fuck," he says as he climbs off of me and strides to the door. "Text me when you're DTF."

When I'm *down to fuck*? Seriously? "Sure thing."

I roll over onto my stomach once he leaves and huff loudly, blowing a strand of my curls out of my face. I knew that sleeping with him the first time would come back to bite me. I'm surprised that he threw himself on me, though. Surely that's not the only reason that he came to collect me from the airport?

I throw my forearm over my eyes in an attempt to stop the tears that threaten to take over.

I've been back on US soil for approximately twenty-four hours while my heart is on the other side of the world. It's an odd sensation being separated from an organ that beats within you but isn't present. I sigh as I apply the last bit of mascara to my lashes before turning my head from side to side in the mirror, inspecting my handiwork. With a large amount of concealer and foundation, I've managed to cover up the dark circles under my eyes for this party that Lola has decided to throw. Apparently, it's been in the works for weeks, but I've been too preoccupied with Wade to even realize the date.

This evening, November 2nd, we'll be celebrating her twenty-seventh birthday, and I swear that she's invited the entire city of Chicago. Her apartment might be large, but with over sixty people inside, it feels cramped and stuffy. She went all out for it, though; there are two bartenders and catered food. I walk out of my bedroom and shut the door behind me as I make my way through the throngs of people to the small hors d'oeuvres station that is set up in the kitchen.

I dip a crostini into the baked crab dip and moan when the tastes explode in my mouth before I'm pulled in another direction with Lola. "Hadley, this is . . ."

I zone out. I don't even remember the guy she introduced me to before I disappeared back into my bedroom to apply some more makeup because I felt like I was being stared at. All I can remember of him is that he shared Wade's hair color. I excuse myself and make my way across the room and to one of the bars, ordering a glass of Champagne. Just the thought of whiskey makes my heart sink into my stomach. I take a long drink before I allow myself to breathe again.

"There she is," Owen says to me as he approaches. "Lola wanted me to introduce you to my buddy Ford."

"Oh, hi, it's nice to meet you," I say as I shake his hand.

"You too. Owen has told me a few things about you," Ford says in a tenor voice.

"He has?"

What the crap would Owen have to say about me other than I used to fuck his older brother?

"Hadley." I look toward Holden's voice just as he sweeps me up into a hug.

Thank God. I throw my arms around him in an embrace in an attempt to make Ford uncomfortable. It seems to work when he walks off toward the bar I just left.

"Hi, Hold."

"That guy is a fucking douche, and if you fuck him, my cock is going nowhere near that sweet pussy of yours."

My eyes bug out as he makes his statement a little louder than necessary. I get a few glances from the women around me, all of whom work with Lola. Great, I'm sure that they will be talking for the remainder of the year about the blonde who doesn't know how to keep her legs closed.

"Lo is going to slaughter you for being drunk at her birthday party, you ass."

"Nah, she's pretty fucking gone herself," he says as he nods in a direction.

"Oh yeah?" I turn to take in the room until my eyes lock on Lola, who is downing a shot.

"Yeah. Maybe she wouldn't mind if I took you for a ride while the party goes on."

"I'd rather not ruin her party, Hold. Thanks, though."

Lies. I don't particularly want to be heartbroken and sur-rounded by revelers all evening, but what other choice do I have? She's my best friend.

"Hads," she yells from her new position on the dining room table. Mother of all hell, I'm going to need a few more drinks for this.

"Come dance with me, you skank." How she is able to yell above the music, I have no idea, but I cannot deny her on her birthday. I go to the bar and ask for two shots of tequila silver and down them before making my way over to her.

"I'm not sure how safe it is up there, Lo."

"Ah fuck it. Get up here." She starts to dance, throwing her arms into the air, speaking with her body instead of verbally. Her personality is shining through as she sways her hips. She's an ex-trovert at heart, an open book that will talk anyone's ears off. It's most likely why the apartment is overcrowded tonight. Everyone loves her bubbly personality.

"Fine," I grumble and step up onto the seat before I climb onto the wooden table with her. She lunges for me, hugging me tightly. I shriek and hug her back as I look down at the people who are now staring up at us, particularly the same group of women from earlier. Great.

"I missed you so much. You're never allowed to leave me again, or I'll punch you with my tit."

I laugh with her. "I don't even know if that is possible."

"I'll figure it out," she stammers as I start to dance with her, but she suddenly stops and stares at me. "Holy shit, Hads. You are hot."

"What?" I squeak out as her eyes roll down my body.

"Your outfit. I fucking love your street style, and I'm stealing it." I have on a white, sleeveless crop top with black floral embel-lishing and black boning with a pair of high-waist white palazzo pants.

I shake my head and start to dance with her again, but I'm grateful that I don't look as jet-lagged as I feel at the moment. Two songs later, we both stumble off of the table with the help of a few outstretched hands. The men cheer once we straighten ourselves up and she throws her arms around me. I may not be as drunk as she is, but I have a steady buzz going on, and it seems to be containing my emotions quite well.

"I think that Holden might be staring," she whispers in my ear. I turn to face the direction where she's looking, and he's got himself propped up against the doorframe at the far end of the room, watching me.

"I think that you're right."

"So?" she slurs her words. "Are you going to sleep with him again? We need to get your mind off of Waylon-sexy-as-shit-Brass."

The smile that was adorning my face vanishes when she says his name. "I don't think that's going to happen. I just got back, and I still want him, Lo."

"Who? Holden?"

"No, you drunk. I still want Wade, but I understand that I needed to let him go so he'll be able to live the life that he's supposed to lead. The one that was set out for him before I so rudely interrupted."

She scrunches her face up at me as if she's having difficulty seeing or hearing me. "What are you talking about?"

"Never mind."

"I'm going to go find Owen. Go kiss Holden, okay?"

"Whatever you say, birthday girl."

I watch her as she leaves the room in search of her hipster before I lock eyes with Holden again. He takes a step toward me, but I turn around and walk back toward my bedroom. As much as I need a friend tonight, I need to be alone more.

On my way to my room I grab a bottle of whiskey from a

bar and slide through my bedroom door without being noticed and this time, I make sure to lock it—to seal me and my messy sentiments away from the world, as well as to keep any horny intruders out. The only man I want is Wade, but I've taken that away from myself.

I flop back onto my bed and kick off my heels before I unscrew the bottle and take a swig from it. The amber fluid burns my throat as it slides its way down into my system and I groan in delight. This. This is what I need to chase away the thoughts of Wade and why I left him.

Yup. I left him. *Again.*

I toss the bottle back as I take another large swig from it and I realize just how permanent this loss is. The shitty part about it all is the fact that I can't even bring myself to be upset with him because all of it is on my shoulders.

I sit up and roll over onto my stomach as I take another drink, gargling with it before I swallow and speak to my headboard. "I think I fucked this one up, buddy, but there's nothing I can do to change it. I've certainly made my bed, and now I have to lie in it."

I burst out laughing because, duh, I'm already in bed. I look at the bottle and take one last drink before I set it on my nightstand and flop back over to stare up at my ceiling as the room starts to spin in uncertain circles.

Maybe I'm a bit drunker than I thought I was.

I grab a pillow and hold onto it tightly. I'll be okay, I tell myself.

Lie.

"No more chances for you, Hadley Rye," I mumble into the darkness and shut my eyes in an attempt to stop the spinning that I'm stuck in, courtesy of the whiskey.

The first of December marks a month from the day that I landed back in the US. I would give anything to lose the pain that immerses me daily. I've fucked up, and I made a mistake, but I don't have a choice to go back and fix it.

I'll never be the woman that he needs me to be, and I know that I won't get the luxury of him looking me in the face and telling me just how much he loves me again. I don't even know if he cares why I vanished, but I need to move on and keep my life on track—although, I'm not entirely sure what track I'm currently on.

I've kept up with my job as it supplies me with income that I don't necessarily need, but it's given me something to occupy my time. I'd like to find something better and more useful to do with my life, but I'm uncertain as to what I want to do exactly. My time with Wade has helped me to realize that I've been limiting myself, and I want to break that cycle. I want to find my purpose and possibly help others with finding theirs. I sigh to myself and sit up in bed, brushing my curls out of my face before swinging my legs over the edge and getting up.

After a quick shower, I throw my hair up into a bun and get dressed in a workout outfit before tying my sneakers and grabbing my yoga mat. It's just past six in the morning so there shouldn't be too many people in the apartment building's gym.

I lock the door and walk up the few flights of stairs that take me to the gym. Once inside, I set up my mat and plug my earphones into my cell and hit play on a soothing and melancholy playlist that I have specifically set up for practicing yoga.

After stretching, I position myself on the mat and take deep breaths in and out to try and relax. I need to accept the consequences of being myself, and yoga allows me to do that for the briefest window of time.

Thirty minutes later, I'm in downward dog when I notice a few more bodies in the room than before. Someone just turned on the radio station overhead, drowning out the music in my headphones. So much for a space that I can escape to.

I can't even go to the park around the corner because of this damn snow. This weather has me considering moving to a sunnier climate. Maybe Hawaii? I sit down on my mat and pull out my headphones before stuffing them into my workout bag, and jerk my shoes back on.

As much as I would love to get away from this weather, I'm unsure if I'd have it in me to leave a place where I know Wade will come back to . . . if he's not already back. I remember Dr. Heath commenting that he wouldn't be able to fly for a minimum of three weeks after surgery. Surely he's back, but if he is, that means that I've truly lost him because he's not going to attempt to try and chase me. He'd probably tell me that he doesn't even chase his whiskey.

I get up after cooling down and make my way back downstairs where I shower and decide to go out for the day. As various places run through my head, I force out the thought of going to Blended. My going there is no longer an option, and I refuse to allow myself to wallow in a place that belongs to him.

Once I'm dressed in jeans and a T-shirt, I pull on my snow boots—a gift from Lola—and head out to find coffee and breakfast. After walking a few blocks, I decide to grab a cab and head out to Navy Pier. It's one of the Chicago landmarks that I have yet to explore. After wandering around for a while, it's just after ten in the morning when I make my way inside a bakery. I order a cappuccino and toasted bagel with cream cheese and then take a seat next to a window that overlooks the lake.

My mind must be running a hundred miles a minute because a waitress comes up to me to ask if I'd like a new cappuccino. I glance down at my coffee and bagel, neither of which I have touched since sitting down over an hour ago.

"Yes, please."

She leaves me to my thoughts once again. I get lost again

thinking about Wade and wondering how his recovery is going before she comes back with a new coffee. She glances around the room before sitting down across from me.

"I don't mean to be rude, but I have a running bet with my co-workers over there." She points them out, and my eyes meet a group of three girls who are blatantly staring at us.

"Uhm, okay?"

"I'm convinced that you are the woman who was photographed with Waylon Brass a couple of weeks ago, but they think that you look nothing like her."

"Excuse me?"

"Well, you see, there was this article in the local paper of his being in an accident while in Australia, and there was a picture taken of a woman with him that morning on the beach. You kind of remind me of her, but . . ."

"But what?"

"You don't really look as radiant as she did in the picture."

"Then I suppose that I'm not her."

She groans and throws her head back. Her friends cheer and high-five each other off to the side of the counter.

"Do you happen to know where I can grab a copy of that paper?"

"I think we might have an old copy. Let me go and check." She gets up and walks over to her friends who have a paper in their hands. She snatches it from them before returning to me and giving me the rolled-up paper. "It's all yours. Sorry for bothering you, but I really thought that it was you. Lord only knows that any woman in the city would want to be her."

"Right," I tell her as she walks away and I unroll the paper, revealing a picture of Wade and me in the water with a surfboard at my side. He has his arm around me, and my head is thrown back in laughter as his eyes burn into me. He looks like he's enamored with the me I see in the picture. I dash away a tear that falls and turn away from the girls before any of them are able to understand my emotions.

I hadn't even realized that there were people taking pictures of us that morning. I grab my phone out of my purse and do an image search for Waylon Brass in Sydney, Australia.

When the results come up, there are multiple pictures of the two of us on the beach. Some are from the day we arrived, when we went with Isla to the beach, while most of them are from our surfing adventure. I swallow hard as I come across one of us sitting in the sand. I have my head resting on his shoulder, and his head rests on mine as we glance out at the ocean. I hold my finger down on the image before an option to save it comes up, which I do.

Why hadn't Lola told me about any of this? She's overinvolved in Chicago's gossip column, and I'm sure that she's seen these. I attach the image to a text message to her: WHY DIDN'T YOU TELL ME THAT THESE EXISTED?

I take a sip of my coffee before I receive a response from her: I THOUGHT THAT YOU KNEW ABOUT THEM. THAT ONE JUST HAPPENS TO BE MY FAVORITE OF THE BUNCH. I DIDN'T WANT TO BRING THEM UP IN CASE IT UPSET YOU.

LO, SINCE I GOT BACK I HAVE NEVER BEEN *NOT* UPSET.

I take a bite of my bagel but push it aside when my stomach churns.

I KNOW THAT YOU ARE. I'M SORRY. IT'S JUST . . . YOU LOOKED SO HAPPY IN THEM.

I WAS. I type out and hit send before putting my phone away and cursing the universe for reminding me exactly what I chose to walk away from. I signal to the girl that gave me the paper to come over.

She does, and I gesture for her to take a seat.

"Is everything all right? Listen, I'm sorry. Please, just don't call my manager over."

I shake my head. "No, I wasn't planning on it. How much did you just lose to your co-workers?"

She blows out a breath and leans back against the seat. "Fifty bucks each."

"Ouch."

"I was certain that it was you."

I give her a small smile and reach into my purse, and pull my wallet out, producing three fifty-dollar bills that I caused her to lose.

"What's this?"

I hand the paper back to her and stand, pointing down at the image. "That's me," I say and then walk out while she gapes openly at me.

I take slow steps to the end of the pier, past the flags waving in the wind until I reach the railing. I lean against it and stare out onto the lake, allowing it to be the only thing to see me cry.

By the time I've arrived back at the apartment, the sun has set and I'm freezing cold. I could not even manage to warm up while I took a cab from Navy Pier.

I unlock the door and step inside where I'm greeted by Owen and Lo. "Hey stranger."

"Hi," I offer up without looking up from my feet as I walk into my bedroom and shut the door behind me. I hear Lola say something to Owen, but I ignore it and go into the bathroom and start running the water for a bath.

When I'm settled into the hot water, and surrounded by bubbles, Lo lets herself in and takes a seat on the lip of the tub. "Will you talk to me?"

I set my phone down on my towel and sigh when she glances at my screen, which is filled with the image of Wade and myself sitting on the sand.

"You miss him, don't you?"

I remain quiet. I don't feel like talking about him with her because she's just going to tell me how bad I fucked everything up and that I need to move on to Holden.

"Hads. I hadn't realized how much of an effect all of this has had on you."

"Yup."

"I'm sorry. I should have asked you about it when you first got back. I figured that you were just bummed that you didn't get to sleep with him."

"It's fine. I don't need the babysitting."

"Would you stop it? Listen, I've been a horrible friend for letting this just slip by, and when you walked in just now, it was the first time that I got to see exactly how broken you are."

Broken, huh? Oh, the irony.

"How can I help?"

"You could find a way for me to erase these feelings."

"I'm not sure how to do that, but how about we try and forget about him tonight and have a girls' night in? Just the two of us. It's time to move on and forget the pain that comes along with the memory of him. You are an incredible person, and you need to find that inside of yourself again."

"It hurts when you think about how important someone used to be to you, and it's my own fault for the pain that I'm in, which is why I'm happily suffering."

"Can I make the motion that you suffer alongside me, Jack, and Jim Beam?"

I sigh reluctantly before nodding to her. "I'm not leaving this apartment. Especially if people are going to ask me if I'm the woman that he was with."

"Wait, what?"

"It's how I found out about the pictures. I had no idea that we were being followed around. He was my escape, and I was unable to see past him."

"Nosy bitches. I'm sorry on their behalf. Now quit moping in the tub and get dressed into something cozy so we can curl up with a movie and a bottle of liquor each."

Once I'm dried off and dressed, I make my way out into the living room where Lo has candles burning, a joint on the table, two bottles of liquor out, and several shot glasses.

"Where did you get that from?" I gesture toward the joint.

"Owen. He said it's a gift from him and Holden to try and lift your spirits."

"I think that I'll stick with the liquor. Thanks, though."

I plop down next to her and pull the blanket off of the back of the couch before getting comfortable.

"What movie do you want to watch?"

"I don't care."

"All right," she says as she puts on *Friends* from her Netflix account instead of a movie. "Season one, episode one. We're in for some laughs."

"If you say so."

By the time we've hit episode three, I'm hammered, and the group on the screen keeps talking about some dating language. It's now that I grab the bottle and drink straight out of it. Screw the shot glasses.

Twenty-Four

Wade

SIX WEEKS, TWO days, thirteen hours, and a couple of seconds. It's my count.

The count that gradually grows by the second since I last saw her.

Within those seconds, minutes, hours, and days, I have fought to get my life back. The desperation in my actions hasn't gone unnoticed by my doctors, and I've been told to take it slower more times than I care to count. My recovery has taken three weeks longer than the doctor initially assumed, and because of this delay I have not been able to fly, let alone do much more than focus on my recovery from surgery. I've put off all thoughts about her because each time I think about her, it hinders my ability to progress. She's gone, and I've accepted it.

Madelyn was relieved of her duties by yours truly two weeks after Hadley left me. She put up a fight with Jacobs once I told him that I had dismissed her, and she refused to leave. She had to be physically removed from the hotel, and my lawyers are insisting on a restraining order, but since I'm flying back to the States, I couldn't give a fuck. I do not now, nor ever, have time to waste on women like her.

Isla went back to Chicago two days after I lost sight of Hadley, which I refused to speak to her about. She's flown back once since then, but I need her in Chicago to maintain Blended.

My mother and Adriana left earlier this morning. The two of them are flying ahead of me to set up my life in Chicago. I've arranged for some equipment to be delivered as well as a new re-habilitation specialist. Dr. Heath has transferred the documents outlining my medical history to a new doctor in Chicago, who I will be meeting a few days after I fly back.

I've been able to walk without the cane or get up without any help for the last two weeks, but I've still been told to take it easy. If I overexert myself, I will be doing myself a disservice and the reconstructed nerve may fail me before I've given it the ade-quate amount of time to heal. Or so I'm told.

I've been looking forward to being alone for weeks since she left and tonight will be the first time that no one but I will be in this suite—the one place that reminds me of just how strong Hadley is and how she unselfishly put her life on hold to stay at my side.

I remember the night Isla and I got back to the hotel. She helped me to the suite before I dismissed her. It's when I found Hadley's note to me lying on a pillow of our bed. I've kept the note on me since it stole my soul with its black ink.

I pull out the small sheet of notepad paper that all hotels provide. It's crumpled up from the number of times that I've folded and unfolded it.

Wade,

You stole the doubt that I harbored about myself. Thank you for saving me from my own path of destruction, but I believe that by saving me, I've led you down your own. Be brave and find your way back.

Goodbye,

Rye.

I've read those words countless times but not once have they made sense to me. Why would she assume that she's not good for me? Why would she think that I've fucked up my life by being with her when, in reality, it's just the opposite? She pulled me out of the revolving cycle that I had not realized I was captured in.

I'll find her. I've got to, and when I do, I'll look her in the face and tell her that we both made a mistake. I will get on my knees if I need to in order to win her back because I'm a fool for letting her go so easily, even though I didn't have much of a choice.

I'm holding out hope that I mean enough to her that she'll reach out and pull me back into her life, but those chances dissipate with each passing second.

My packing and plane ride were thoroughly uneventful. Due to having my private jet, I did not have to suffer through the layover, but we stopped to refuel at LAX.

I've been in the penthouse for a couple of hours now. The thought of her being a mere three blocks away has done something to my head—it's messed with me in the most sinister of ways. The possibility that she may not be in Chicago anymore is a thought that I choose not to acknowledge. I'm not made out of steel, but she has had me bent out of shape for months now.

I decide to take a walk through the streets of Chicago, to stretch out my legs after sitting still for the flight home. I grab my tailored navy coat and head down the elevator to the lobby of the Waldorf Astoria Chicago Residence. When I purchased the hotel some years back, I ensured that the empty penthouse was converted into my personal residence.

As I walk toward the entrance, I'm greeted by name, and I nod to the front desk women as well as the bellhops as I cover my hands in leather gloves, preparing myself for the chill of Chicago's late December weather.

"Shall I call a car for you this evening, Mr. Brass?"

"No, thank you, Thomas."

I walk down North Rush until I reach Argo Tea Café, nestled in Connors Park, and I duck inside to escape the lake-effect snow that has started to fall during my short walk. The café is empty at this hour, particularly with a blizzard on its way in. At the counter, I'm greeted by a stunning twenty-something-year-old blonde.

"Good evening, what can I get for you?" she asks me as her eyes roam from the collar of my coat and down to the Patrick Philip watch gracing my wrist.

"'Evening. I'd like the Italiano Panini and a double espresso."

She inputs my order into the screen in front of her, and I hand her my credit card, which she stares at before swiping it through the machine.

"Thank you for coming in, Mr. Brass. I'll bring your order to you when it's ready."

"Very well."

I move to the other side of the café and take a seat while I wait for my order. The café is encased in glass, giving me an unaltered view of the snow falling heavily outside.

To say that I have been a dick toward everyone who works for me, including my own mother, would be an understatement. My decisions with Brass Global have been impacted by my perplexing feelings toward the situations that I have had to deal with in the past two months. The space that separates me from the woman who holds me captive needs to shift because I no longer have the patience to wait this out or worse, live without her.

Decisively, I pull out my phone: I need to try to speak to her before I am fully able to let her go. If she does not want to be with me any longer, then I won't force her, but I need the closure. I need to say goodbye. It may just be a word, but it's one that will put the permanent space between us.

I bring the phone to my ear as it begins to ring, and instead of being sent to voicemail, her voice comes across the line.

"Hi, Wade."

"You answered."

She's quiet before she speaks again. "I think I've had too many Baileys and hot chocolates. It's freezing back here. We're supposed to be hit by a blizzard, and I'm so not ready for this Chicago wintry bullshit."

She sounds happy and a bit buzzed. Content, though. My smile is unwanted, but hearing that she's okay is, I tell myself, what I needed to know.

"I know. I'm back."

The line is quiet for a moment before she speaks away from the phone, but I can still hear her tell someone to hold on. "Sorry about that. How are you? When did you get back?"

"I've been better." My order is brought to me, and I thank the waitress before I continue speaking into the phone. "I arrived back at my penthouse a few hours ago."

"And you're feeling all right after the flight? Are you still using the cane? I thought that you would have been back weeks ago."

"Yes, I'm all right. I'm stiff, but I was told to expect that. I haven't used the cane in two weeks, and there were some complications in regard to my recovery."

"Oh," she says quietly before speaking to someone again. "I know, okay, just wait a minute, Holden."

Holden? A male's voice comes across the line. "Damn babe, you do bite."

I clear my throat and suppress the physical ache in my chest. "You're busy, Hadley. I'll let you go."

"Wade, wait," she says as she squeals loudly. "Quit it," she yells with a laugh.

I pull the phone away from my ear and hit the red end button before setting it down next to my sandwich.

She's content, I tell myself. That's why you called. It was more of a need to know that she was living her life, rather than

to find my own peace. In the last four months, I've been physically, mentally, and emotionally fragmented. I've survived it all, and
I will get through this ache as well. Possibly.

My phone starts to vibrate as I take a bite, but I choose to ignore it. The thought of her finding happiness with another man
is like a knife in my chest. I choose not to let it consume me. I decide that I need to live my life and immerse myself into a life of
work without sex, this time being successful in separating myself
from the addiction.

"Is there anything else I can get for you, Mr. Brass?" the
blonde asks me.

"I don't suppose that you sell whiskey here, do you?"

"No, but there is a whiskey library not too far from here. I've
been there a few times, and it's a great place. You should check it
out before the storm gets too ugly."

I smirk to myself: it's gratifying to know that a personal
project has been a hit in the city. "It's pretty bad right now. You
should not be open."

"The owner just called and told me to close up."

"I won't be much longer."

"Don't worry about it. I might hit up the whiskey library
afterward if you'd like to join me. I can show you where it's
located."

I think on it for a few seconds and decide that I might as well
pay Isla a visit and ensure that she closes up the library and heads
home before this storm gets out of hand.

"I'll call for a driver."

"Okay, sure. I'll just finish up. I'm Reagan, by the way."

I reach my hand out to shake hers. "Waylon."

She hasn't stopped talking about herself since we got into my
BMW with Jacobs. He throws me a glance in the rearview mirror, evidently unhappy with my decision to be with another

woman. I choose to ignore him and try to tune her out as she tells me about her sorority. Fuck, is she old enough to drink?

Jacobs pulls up to Blended, and I get out, leaving Jacobs to help her out of the vehicle.

"Isn't it gorgeous?" she asks me excitedly as if she's waiting for my approval. I nod and open the door for her. She walks in ahead of me as a librarian walks by.

"Mr. Brass, I hadn't realized that you were back. I'll let Isla know that you are here," she says and walks into the back where Isla's office is located.

"Wait, you've been here before?" Reagan asks.

I'm about to answer her when Isla comes barreling toward me. She slams her body into mine, and I reach my hand out to lean against the bar top for support. "Wade! Oh, shit, I'm sorry."

She pulls back before hugging me again. I return my best friend's hug and place a kiss on the top of her head.

Reagan comes to stand next to me and puts her hand on my arm. I stiffen. Isla's eyes fall to her and then rise to meet mine again. "What the fuck is this?" she asks as she points to the poor girl with her thumb.

"Isla, this is Reagan. Reagan, this is Isla."

"It's nice to meet you," she beams as Isla is giving her a look of repulsion.

Jesus.

"We'd like to order something," Reagan says to Isla, and I watch as Isla's eyes bug out.

"What? A glass of water?"

"Uhm, no. We'd like two whiskeys."

"Yup, your little ass needs to go."

"Excuse me?"

"Do you even know who Waylon Brass is?"

"Him," she says as she looks up at me with innocent eyes.

"No shit. He's also the owner of Blended."

"He is? You are?" she asks me, and I nod down to her. She's nothing like Hadley, and her fake platinum blonde hair does not do anything for me.

"Get her a drink, Isla. I'd like to speak to you in private."

"Wait, I thought we came here together."

"He's taken, little girl. Run back to your frat boys."

"Fuck you," Reagan spits out, and I step toward Isla.

"Reagan, I believe it would be in your best interest to leave. Jacobs is still outside; he'll take you home."

She rolls her eyes at me and walks out of Blended while she shoots daggers at Isla with her eyes.

"What the fuck, Brass? Who was that? You've been back for a total of six hours, and you're already fucking a new piece?"

"You know that I'm not. I was grabbing a bite to eat where she works, and she was telling me that she was coming here afterward. I offered her a ride."

"Good because I still think that you should save that ring for Hadley."

"That's what I came here to talk to you about."

"Yeah? And?"

"I'm going to need to return it. Would you mind doing it for me?"

She's silent for a few seconds before she takes my hand and leads me to an available couch. "What's going on? You were hell-bent on getting her back, Wade. You've had that ring since before Liam opened his big mouth."

I pull my coat off and set it on the top of the couch before slowly resting my back against the cushion.

"I spoke with her earlier. She seems content, and she was with another man. I kept her locked up, and she now despises me for it. I won't pressure her into anything or even ask her for more. For a future."

"Brass, you're being too hard on yourself."

"No. I'm being honest with myself for the first time. I have to accept this reality and keep moving on. Brass Global and subsidiaries cannot go another day without its CEO, and that is where I plan on spending my time."

"If it's any consolation, Brass, I love you."

I chuckle and tug on her earlobe. "You know that I feel the same about you. Come now. Shut down the library and get home before the roads get too bad to drive."

"Yes, boss," she says as she jumps up and starts to collect the empty tumblers from the room with the other two librarians. I watch them clean up before pulling my phone out and replying to a few work emails.

Isla dismisses the other two employees before the weather turns too bad for them to head home. I get up and walk to the back and into Isla's office to use her laptop, seeing as I cannot answer these fucking emails on my phone fast enough.

My mind strays to the ring that I bought while I was confined to the suite in Australia. I was certain that I wanted to be with her for as far as I could see into the future. I got into contact with a jeweler, and they had the ring made to my specifications. When Isla flew out to Sydney, she went to pick it up and when she brought it to me she was stunned and elated all at once. I had no plans to get down on one knee for a while, possibly a couple of months, but when I figured out that there wouldn't be another woman other than her, I had already made up my mind.

Thirty minutes have passed when Isla returns. "All set?" I ask.

"Sure am. I could do with your fireplace and your whiskey stash. The weather app on my phone says that we're in for the long haul."

"You're welcome to come over. I'd prefer it, seeing as your place is farther away. I'll let Jacobs know that we're ready."

The door chimes and Isla sighs before she gets up. "I must have forgotten to lock that shit. Hold on."

I watch her back as she retreats from the office. "Hey guys, we've closed up shop due to the weather . . . Oh hey."

I don't hear anyone reply. "No, he's not here."

Silence.

"Yes, I know. He sent Jacobs to drive me home. Have you seen the roads, Hads? It's hell out there. You should head back home."

I stand at the mention of her name, intending to go to her, but then I hear a familiar male's voice. "We'll find an open bar, babe. Let's go; I'm sure I'll see him later."

I stop as I'm about to walk out of the office and into the main room of Blended.

"Bye, Isla. Will you tell him that I stopped by? He didn't answer my call earlier today."

"I'm not so sure that's a good idea. You need to let him heal, especially since you've let your lady balls drop and decided to bring a man into *his* safe place."

"What? No. This is Lawson Stafford. He works under Wade."

"Sure he does."

"Uhm, all right."

I walk back to the desk and pick up my phone, searching through my emails until I find the one that I'm looking for: Adriana's reminder that I have a meeting with Lawson Stafford in regard to the hotels expansion in the morning.

Isla walks in and gives me a false smile. "Ready?"

"Lawson Stafford?"

"You heard," she states.

"Yes. What did they want?"

"I think that they just came in for a drink. I'm unsure, though. I'm going to grab a bottle before we leave."

"You may as well grab one for me as well."

"Deal."

Twenty-Five

Hadley

LAWSON STAFFORD FIGURED out that I was in Chicago. It must have been when human resources called me about my new mailing address for my W2 that would need to be sent out in January.

Holden was over when he arrived on my doorstep earlier yesterday morning and I argued with Stafford about his reason for being in Chicago. He told me that he had a meeting with the owner of Brass Global and that he missed my pussy.

How nice.

On top of Lawson dropping by yesterday, Wade called me earlier this evening, and right after that, yup, you guessed it, Lawson was at my doorstep again once Holden left. I wanted to go somewhere that I knew that I would be safe, so I decided on Blended in hopes that possibly that is where he'd called me from earlier.

I remember him thanking someone so I assumed that he was out, but I must have been wrong, and now I'm stuck in the bar next door with Lawson who's trying to figure out how to get me naked.

I pull my phone out and decide to text Wade: WHAT ARE YOU DOING?

His reply takes a lot longer than I'm used to, and I'm about to give up on receiving one when my phone vibrates in my hand.

HOLED UP IN THE PENTHOUSE WITH ISLA. YOU?

Oh. Are they a *thing* now? I frown as Lawson orders me another tumbler of cheap whiskey. I've managed to drink two-thirds of the first one, and I'm feeling rather queasy. I won't have the strength to keep him away from me, and by the looks of it, he's already pushing me too far. I'm out of my comfort zone, and I don't know how to get rid of him.

I WENT BY BLENDED HOPING YOU'D BE THERE.

YES, ISLA INFORMED ME OF THE MAN YOU BROUGHT IN.

I sigh and slouch in the booth; he's being too formal with me. It's as if he's drawn back into himself and he's once again uncomfortable with showing me his true self. I know that it's my fault, but it still stings. Today is the first time that we've actually spoken to each other in two months, and it's not off to a great start.

IT'S LAWSON STAFFORD, WADE. HE SOMEHOW GOT HOLD OF MY PERSONAL ADDRESS HERE IN CHICAGO AND TRACKED ME DOWN TO MY DOORSTEP. I type out as Lawson gets distracted by the attractive bartender refilling his glass. I'm thankful for her flirtatious behavior as it has provided me with a few moments to text him back.

ARE YOU SAFE?

Am I? I look back up from my phone to Lawson staring at me. He reaches for my thigh and squeezes me there to the point of bruising.

No. I manage to respond as he leans over and nuzzles the crook of my neck.

WHERE ARE YOU? I'LL SEND JACOBS. I swallow hard as Lawson's lips meet my skin, and his hand that was bruising my thigh has now moved up to the apex of my thighs.

Why won't he come for me?

Because you left him, I remind myself.

THE BAR NEXT TO BLENDED.

The second that I hit send, Lawson snatches the phone from my fingers and tosses it into my purse as he continues his assault on my neck with his lips.

"Lawson, please stop."

"What? Why? Did you find a new cock to toy with?"

"No. I simply don't want you," I say as I push my elbow against his side to try and get him off of me.

He pulls back and grabs my jaw in one of his hands, forcing my eyes to meet his. I can feel the power that he has in his fingers as they dig into my skin. "What the fuck did you just say?"

"Nothing. I-I need to get home," I stutter, unable to get the words out the way I want to get them out.

"I'll let you go back once you've swallowed my cock. How does that sound?"

He pushes me up against the wall that the booth sits against. I'm trapped and completely at his will now. My hands start to shake as intuition tells me that I'm in more trouble than I thought was possible with him.

"I'm not interested in anything like that. Please, just . . ."

He squeezes his fingers between my top and bottom jaw, forcing my mouth to open for him. I watch him remove something from his wallet with his available hand before placing it in my mouth and clamping my jaw shut.

"Swallow like a good girl would."

I don't know what he just gave me, but I know that it will ruin me. I can feel the small pill start to dissolve as it sits on the top of my tongue, threatening me with its almost undetectable bitter taste.

"What is this?" I manage to avoid swallowing it, but it's now when I try to push him off of me that I realize that there must have been something more than whiskey in my tumbler. My body refuses to cooperate with what I want it to do, and I'm fighting to deal with side effects of his first attempt of taking me away from reality.

The force of his hand increases and I whimper from the pain. "A little sedative to take the edge off." He tilts my head back and slaps my cheek hard enough to be heard over the sound of the music in the bar. My eyes snap toward the bartender who quickly looks away from me as she counts out a stack of cash.

A tear falls from my eye as I realize that he's going to use me as he pleases. I should welcome the distraction that the pill will provide, but I know that Colin will be here soon. I need to hold on until then.

"You can either swallow that shit, or I can hold you like this until it dissolves on your tongue."

That's what he does because I refuse to allow myself to become a victim.

It takes ten minutes from the time he placed it in my mouth until I'm unable to feel it resting on my tongue any longer. He applies more pressure in the right place again to check if the pill is still on my tongue, and when he lets me go, I know that it has finally dissolved.

"You'll forget your own name soon enough, Hadley, and then you'll be wanting to scream mine out from pleasure."

"What?" I ask as he shoves my drink in my face.

"This should speed it up."

He still has me pressed into the corner with his body and what other option do I have? I take a small sip and make a face at the foul taste of the cheap house whiskey.

I've made it through half of my drink when I can no longer keep my head up. It falls back against the booth, giving my neck a much-needed reprieve. My very last thought is of Wade, and how I wish he thought I was worth it to save, but it's been over thirty minutes, and I know that he's not coming.

Twenty-Six

Wade

THE FUCKING ROADS are a mess, and getting back to Blended has taken more than twice the average amount of time as usual. By the time that Jacobs pulls up to the front, Isla is bouncing her knees in the back.

I turn to face her from the front seat. "Stay here."

Jacobs and I get out of the SUV and walk through the thick snow to the bar next to the whiskey library. I push the door open and walk in. A dank, musky odor fills my senses as I search the almost-empty place for her, but I can't find her. I walk up to the bar and turn around once more from this new angle with Jacobs next to me in search of her.

"Mr. Brass," Jacobs says as he walks to an empty booth. I watch him bend over and retrieve Hadley's Burberry purse from underneath the table.

Anger heats my body as my voice booms out above the music. "Where the fuck is the woman who was sitting here?" I say out to the room and indicate the booth on my right.

A few faces glance in my direction before going back to their drinks. The bartender clears her throat, and I swing my head to glance at her. She nods toward the back of the bar, and I surge forward to where the bathrooms are located. I push open the door to the single stall of the women's bathroom, but it's empty.

I glance at Jacobs, who is now standing in front of the men's bathroom door. I reach for it, but it's locked. I jiggle the handle once more to see if it will click free, but it doesn't. Jacobs sets down Hadley's purse and walks over to the bar to pick up a solid wooden barstool before coming back to the bathroom.

"Take a step back, Mr. Brass."

I do as he says as he picks up the stool and rams the object into the old bathroom door. It splinters under the pressure, and I hear a stream of curse words come from inside. The second that Jacobs steps back, I reach through the hole in the splintered door and unlock the door handle before twisting it open and pushing the door in.

Lawson Stafford has Hadley draped over the sink with her arms flailing helplessly at her side as he pulls out of her from behind. Jacobs reacts before I have the option to. He slams Lawson into the tiled wall of the bathroom where he lands a fist to his jugular as I reach for Hadley, who is slipping from her poised position against the white porcelain sink.

"Fuck," I say to myself, and I pull her up close to the front of my body. Her head falls lifelessly against my chest as I struggle to move her curls off of her face. Once I manage to get a good look at her, I see that her eyes are open, but she's not present.

"Goddamn it. Jacobs, kill that motherfucker," I order through a hiss.

I watch as Jacobs snaps the asshole's nose in a grotesque way before he blacks out from the beating Jacobs gave him. Jacobs tortures the fucker some more before he sags down against the bathroom wall, leaving streaks of red-tinged blood on the tile.

Jacobs washes his hands, cleaning the blood off in the sink that Hadley was bent over mere moments ago, before he walks up to me and takes his coat off to cover Hadley's half-naked body. I hand her off to him because I won't be able to carry her out of here without further injuring myself.

As I go to leave, Lawson groans, and I turn, glancing down

at the fucker. "You're fucking ruined, you piece of shit."

He brings his hand up to his mouth in an attempt to wipe some of the blood off his mouth. "For that used-up bitch? What do you care?" He laughs to himself and looks me dead in the eyes as he chuckles. "I'm sure she enjoyed it. Anyway, she's mine—the bitch promised to marry me."

It takes every ounce of energy that I have to fight my own body from reacting to his words and launching myself at him. "Shut your goddamn mouth—she's not yours."

He groans, but instead of being in agony, he seems to be enjoying this moment of confrontation that I'm allowing him. "She liked it. You should ask her about it later. If you gave me another five minutes . . ." He spits out blood, maybe a tooth or two, onto the grimy tiled floor. " . . . What's it to you, anyway?"

The ferocity that my body is holding on to right now will rip me open if I don't leave soon. "You've signed your own death warrant, Stafford. You won't ever see the light of day again," I say through a snarl.

He laughs again and tries to speak, but gets choked up on his own blood.

I slam the door shut and turn to Jacobs, who has my life in his arms. I walk out in front of him, grabbing her purse on the way out.

"Call the police and report a rape. Give them my name— Waylon Brass," I say bitterly as I walk toward the door and push it open for Jacobs to walk through it with her.

Isla must see us coming because she jumps out of the SUV and gasps. "Holy shit! Is she all right?"

"Call a doctor and have him come to the penthouse," I command as I take a seat in the back of the SUV. Jacobs places her on my lap and in my arms before shutting the door. Isla has her phone up to her ear before she jumps into the passenger seat and we start our journey back to the Waldorf Astoria.

I take off my jacket and drape it over her legs before cradling her to my chest. "Fuck, Rye, I'm sorry I wasn't fast enough." Her eyes are now closed as she leans against my chest. I bring my fingers to her neck, relieved when I feel a faint, but steady pulse there.

I push her curls back and hold her close as Jacobs struggles to get us back to my residence in the blizzard. The amount of snow that has fallen in this short span of time is taking its toll on the city.

It takes us over an hour to get back, and when we do, I demand that Jacobs park before we head up to the penthouse. I refuse to let any more people than absolutely necessary see her in this state.

Jacobs and Isla get out of the vehicle first before he comes around and swings my door open, taking her from my hold before I get out and follow both of them to the elevator.

"The in-house physician is here. I called ahead to let your personal doorman know to expect him. He said that he's waiting outside your door."

"Very well. Thank you, Isla."

I don't take my eyes off of her as Jacobs stands next to me in the elevator.

"She's going to be okay," Isla offers to me.

"I don't know. This may be too much for her to handle." She might be able to recover from this physically, but with the knowledge of her history, I'm unsure if she'll be able to fight the need to give in to her addiction again if she hasn't already done so."

The elevator doors slide open, and we're met with a doctor and his medical bag standing in front of my door. "What happened?" he asks as he takes in Hadley's appearance.

I unlock the door and hold it open for everyone to enter.

"Take her to my bedroom, Jacobs."

"Yes, sir."

I follow them up the stairs, but each step takes me longer than the one before it. I must be overexerting myself this evening. By the time I've made it to my bedroom, Jacobs has her on the bed, and he's walking out of the room as the doctor starts to unbutton the jacket we secured around her petite frame.

"I'll be in the living room if you need me, Mr. Brass."

"Thank you," I tell him and walk up to stand next to Isla.

"What happened to her?" the doctor repeats.

I take in a lungful of air before answering him. "I'm not entirely sure. I found her in the bathroom almost unconscious while being raped."

"Good God. In that case, I'll need to do a sexual-assault forensic exam." He walks over to his medical bag and pulls out multiple materials, along with envelopes and containers.

"This may take me a while."

"I'm not leaving her."

"May I ask what your relation is to her?"

"She's . . ."

"She's his girlfriend," Isla answers for me while I stumble over my words.

He nods his approval as he starts to work on her, checking her from head to toe, but focusing on the vaginal exam before setting up an IV drip. Isla has gone downstairs to let the doctor's RN attendant up into the suite; he called her in shortly after Isla contacted him. I stay standing in the same spot as he covers her up with my blankets.

"It appears that she's been drugged. I'll have my nurse run her blood samples to our lab as soon as possible, but if I had to guess, I would assume that she's taken or been given a potent sedative."

"How long does it usually stay in the system?"

"The usual dose of one milligram has a tendency to last up to eight hours, but if she's ingested a higher dose, it could possibly double the amount of time. If I had to give you a reliable number, I would give her a minimum of twelve hours to come around, and when she does, she may experience confusion, amnesia, and disorientation."

"Was she injured when he took advantage of her?"

"There is scarring from older injuries but I do see some fresh bruising from this event, which would appear to support an allegation of rape."

Bile rises in the back of my throat at his words. This beautiful woman has been hurt and taken advantage of for her entire life, and the one time that I had a chance to do something about it, I failed her.

Isla walks into the bedroom with an elderly woman who goes straight to the doctor's side as he packs away his equipment into his medical bag. He hands her the two vials of blood that he took from Hadley a few minutes ago, and she leaves under his instructions.

"Mr. Brass, I will be in contact with you as soon as I receive the results from my lab. I will be by in the morning to check on her. If anything happens in the meantime, I ask that you dial the number that your friend used earlier to reach me."

I shake his hand. "Thank you for coming."

"Of course."

Isla shows him out, and she closes my bedroom door when she leaves. I walk to the side of my bed and kneel down beside Rye.

"Hey gorgeous. You're going to be okay. I've got you."

Eight hours have passed and she hasn't moved a muscle.

Jacobs pulled a seat up to the bed, which allowed me to remain at her side. I've had to get up and do a few exercises in the room, but I haven't left her side other than to shower.

I've become uncomfortable with sitting down for all of these hours so I get up and lie down on the other side of the bed and under the covers with her. I pull her body against mine, careful not to snag her IV line as I do. I position her in the way that she used to sleep with me, her head in the crook of my arms, with each part of her body touching mine. She's dressed in one of my shirts that she used to wear all of the time, the one that I considered hers since she first wore it.

I place a kiss on her temple and breathe her in. "I've missed you, Rye. I have no right to miss you because you no longer belong to me, but I couldn't give a shit. You still carry my heart around with you, whether you are aware of it or not."

I don't close my eyes in fear that I will fall asleep. I want to be here and present when she wakes up. I've turned off all of the lights in the room with the exception of the one on the nightstand beside her, which is currently set to dim.

I search her features for a sign that she's there, that she'll be all right. I move her curls behind her back and frown at the bruises that have slowly but surely been making their appearance on her silky skin. I need to know where else he hurt her, what else he stole that belonged to me.

I place my lips against the large bruise on her jaw before running the pad of my thumb over her mouth.

"I should have left the penthouse sooner. I should have come after you when you left me in Sydney. I should have grown those brass balls and told you about Isla." I tell her my regrets as I move the covers off of her body to inspect her for myself. I notice more bruises marring the skin on her thigh. I push my shirt up until I'm able to see her hips. There's a long line that runs across her waist. He must have bruised her there while she kept hitting herself against the sink in front of her. I turn her body slightly to see the bruises, which are shaped in the form of his hands on her hips.

I shut my eyes as I pull the shirt back down her body and

settle her into her favorite sleeping position again before I allow myself to breathe. If it were up to me, Lawson Stafford would already be buried six feet below. I move her hair from her face and place my hand at the small of her back to keep her against my body.

"I love you," I say close to her ear. "I'll never be able to stop,"

The ache that I've managed to keep at bay through my recovery resurfaces and I close my eyes as I'm immersed in the pain—the pain of knowing that she doesn't want much more to do with me.

I'm jolted awake by a hand on my shoulder. "Wade? The doctor is back to check on her," Isla says.

I blink through my sleep and release her from my hold before sitting up and getting out from under the covers.

"Are you okay?"

I refuse to answer her because she knows my truths. She knows exactly how ready I was to take on Rye forever before she left me. Isla understands what I've been struggling with and how I've had to deal with it in order to keep living.

"I'll let him in. Put a shirt on."

I nod and walk into my closet to change. When I return to my bedroom, buttoning up my shirt, the doctor is taking her blood pressure.

"Her vitals are back to normal," he says as he checks his watch, "and it's been twelve and a half hours. I'm hopeful that she'll wake while I'm here. I might stay until she does."

"Very well."

There's a knock on the door, and Jacobs walks in. "Excuse my intrusion, Mr. Brass, but your rehabilitation specialist is here and waiting for you downstairs."

"Good. Isla, would you mind staying with her while I get this session over with?"

"You didn't have to ask. Go before Olga marches her ass up here to kick you into shape."

"Fuck off," I tell her and grab my sneakers from the closet before making my way downstairs to greet my new specialist.

I struggle through the first thirty minutes, and she doesn't seem too thrilled with my physical history over the last twenty-four hours. I don't apologize. It has nothing to do with her.

Isla comes down forty-five minutes into the session. "Brass? She's awake."

I start to unstrap the monitors, and I'm met with a glare. "I'm cutting today short. I will see you earlier tomorrow morning."

If I could sprint up the stairs I would, but instead, I take them slowly with Isla by my side. "You need your rest, Brass. She needs you to be rested."

"She won't want to be around me once she's given the okay to go home."

"I doubt that. Pull your head out of your ass, will ya? This may very well be your last shot with her. Don't waste it by sitting in the corner and pouting like the pussy that you've become."

All true.

We enter my bedroom, and her head moves to the side lazily to see who has come into the room. I walk to the end of the bed and take in the sight of her. The daylight that is streaming through the open curtains shows me exactly how bruised up she is. Aside from the marks that I found on her last night, her lips seem to be an odd shade, and she has dark bags underneath her eyes.

Through all of it, though, she's still the most gorgeous woman I have ever seen. The only woman I have ever loved. The only woman that I would lay my life on the line for.

"Hadley." I walk to the side of the bed, and she reaches her hand up for me. I take her one hand in the both of mine and bring it to my lips.

"What happened?" she asks in a faint voice.

I make eye contact with the doctor. "Why don't we let the kind doctor explain?"

I let go of her hand to move across the room, but there's panic on her face the second I take a step back from her.

"Please—" she chokes out.

"I'm not leaving, Rye." I take a seat in the chair that Jacobs provided and allow the doctor to explain what I walked in on and what has happened since. How her body has reacted to the drugs, as well as how she'll need to stay in bed for the remainder of the day.

"Where is he?" she asks me, her eyes locking with mine.

I uncross my leg and remove my hand that was covering my mouth before speaking. "He's in police custody. You have nothing to worry about, Rye. I won't let him hurt you again."

"You've got me?" she asks me hesitantly.

I search her eyes, waiting to see a glimpse of indecision at the words she just said, but when I find nothing but hurt and truth in them, I tell her exactly how I feel in the short phrase. "I've got you."

"What about Isla? I thought that the two of you would have been something by now."

She's not making sense, but I answer her question. "There has never been more than friendship between Isla and myself."

"All right." She swallows slowly before she sits up and winces, then moves her hand to her hip. "Can I take a shower?"

The doctor answers, "Yes. My nurse will be up shortly to assist you. I'd prefer if you weren't alone for the next twenty-four to forty-eight hours."

"All right. I was . . . uhm . . . Wade?"

"What is it?"

"I want . . . would you mind?"

"I'll stay with her. We've had enough nurses around us these past few months to last a lifetime."

"All right. You have my number if you two need anything. I'll be back to check on you in a day," he says as he disconnects her IV, removing it from her arm.

"Thank you," she says to him, but her eyes don't leave mine as he packs up his things once again and leaves with Isla.

I get up and walk across the room to shut the door when she speaks, and I'm startled by the panic in her voice. "Please, Wade, don't go."

I close the door before turning to look at her. "I'm not going anywhere."

She pushes herself up farther until she's got her legs off the side of the bed. She stands and my shirt falls into place over her bruised, skin. She's hesitant as she steps toward me. "Thank you."

"For what?"

"For coming to get me. I don't remember much of anything. I just remember praying for someone to stop whatever he had planned."

I move toward her as she does me, but we stop a breath apart from each other. "I didn't get there soon enough."

"You still came. After how I left you, I thought that you wouldn't . . ."

"Never assume that. Now tell me, what is the last thing that you remember?"

She keeps her distance as she tries to remember the last thing. "I remember texting you, and then he forced something into my mouth, which took a while to dissolve." She scrunches her brow in thought. "I think he fed me some drinks, but that's all that I can recall, until, well, until waking up a few minutes ago."

"There's nothing else?"

"No. I don't even remember him taking me to the bathroom or how he got me semi-undressed. I just . . . there's nothing. It's all so overwhelming."

"You don't remember what else he may have done to you?"

She shakes her head and folds her arms over her chest as if she's trying to protect herself. "I mean, I'm angry for being so vulnerable, and I think I'm still in shock that he did all of this to me, but I only have myself to blame for it. I shouldn't have been out with him alone."

I start to reach for her hand, but I stop and pull away. "None of this is your fault. It was beyond your control, and you should not now nor ever feel as if you allowed it to happen."

She shrugs and sighs heavily before dropping her arms. "I'll get through it, just as I have before. I may be bruised, bleeding, and sore, but at least I don't have the distinct memories that I have from my past encounters with men like him."

"Don't allow his fuck-up to mess with your head. The doctor said that I got to you before any serious damage was done, as well as before he was able to climax in his rape. I wanted to reassure you that he was wearing a condom."

"Oh. Well, that's something, I guess. I'm not exactly sure where to go from here. It feels like I'm starting over again, as if I've been pushed over a ledge and been told to free fall on my own again."

I step toward her and pull her body against mine. "I've got you."

She wraps her arms around my neck and clings onto me like she did the first time I took her out. "I've missed you," she whispers against my chest. It's barely audible, but I hear her.

I press my lips to the top of her head and breathe her in. "I've missed you, Rye. You won't have to go through any of this alone."

She sighs into my chest and looks up at me with tears in her eyes. "What happens next?"

"First, I get you cleaned up and help you forget, and then you're stuck with me by your side for at least two days. After that, if you decide that you'd rather leave again, then you leave."

She shakes her head up at me and leans up on her toes to place her lips against mine. I can feel my heart strike against my chest as our lips move together, but I pull back when I realize what is going on.

"Hadley. You need to stop."

"Stop what?" she asks as I lead her to the shower.

"I won't be your coping mechanism."

"Excuse me?"

"After last night. I won't be a replacement for the pain."

"Wade. You're not. I . . ."

"No. I am. I'll call Lola and have her come and collect you."

Fuck me if that didn't kill me—the realization of it.

"Brass?" Isla calls out as I step from the bathroom and away from the woman I love.

"Isla. Do me a favor?"

"Uh, do I want to know?"

"I just need you to stay in there while she showers."

"Why? Is your cock going to explode if you see her naked?"

"No. I need to call her roommate to come and collect her."

"Why? I thought you wanted to be with her."

"You know that more than anyone, Isla, but I won't allow myself to be an addiction to her. I've spoken to you in regard to her illness, and she just pushed herself onto me."

"How do you know that it was the illness and not that she just wants to be with you? You haven't seen her in weeks. Hell, it's more like two months."

"I don't know, and that's why I need to walk away."

"Wade, don't do that to yourself."

"I'm not. I'm doing it for her," I tell her as I walk out of my bedroom and downstairs to the spot where I left her purse when we came in last night.

I made sure not to be there when she was done cleaning up. After I called Lola from her phone and informed her of the situation, she said that she and Holden would be over shortly. The knowledge that she's with another man right now, one that she might successfully seduce, has left me empty.

I'm now seated at my desk at Brass Global for the first time in months as I try to distract myself from the events of the last day. I've contacted human resources to let them know that I want to terminate Lawson Stafford's employment effective immediately. I've also spoken to the police about pressing charges against the bastard. In addition, I've made certain that Adriana will receive her raise. It's one hell of a salary, and she will soon be getting an email regarding it.

My mother came by for lunch in my office earlier as well. She was beaming when she saw me back at my desk and in a place where I belong. She's asked me about Christmas, and what my plans are, but I don't have the energy to think about it. It's a couple of days away, and the furthest thing from my mind. I told her that I'd join her at her home, though.

She asked about Hadley, but I chose not to speak of her. Those stories are for her to tell others as they do not belong to me. They might scar my memory, but they have permanently scarred her body. Her heart. After my mother left, Isla called to inform me that the doctor had gotten back to me with the results of Hadley's blood tests. She had ingested a large amount of Rohypnol. Anger is still pumping through my blood with the knowledge of what he did to her, and what more he was planning to do if I'd decided not to go to her.

I'm having a difficult time dealing with this, unsure of how she must be feeling. I push the thought aside, and manage to bring myself back to the present.

I've been watching the sun slowly set over a white Chicago. The snow has let up now, but it's predicted that we'll get hit once again this evening. I stand and move to the glass that separates me from the *normal* down below.

I reach for the phone that usually sits in my pocket when I realize that I've given it to Adriana to keep once again in an attempt to get my life back on the track that it once was.

There's a knock on my door before it swings open and I turn to see who interrupted the solemn moment. "Mr. Brass?" Adriana walks in with two officers behind her. "These gentlemen would like a word with you in regard to Lawson Stafford."

"Very well. Hold all of my calls."

"Yes, sir. You also have another visitor who does not have an appointment to see you afterward," she says as she closes my office door. I turn to the men and gesture to the two chairs in front of my desk

"Good evening, gentlemen. Please, have a seat."

By the time my personal interrogation is over, and the investigators have enough information to file charges against Stafford, I'm satisfied. His trial date will be expedited and bail will in all likelihood be denied. Following the trial and his certain conviction, he will be sent to prison for up to ten years. I had my lawyers on the call at one point to have them remove him from Brass Global entirely as well as to change Stafford's Casino and Resort's name to Brass Casino and Resort. There will be a press release going out about it tomorrow morning, and I cannot wait for this fucker to get what he deserves. By the time they leave, it's past ten in the evening, and a new blizzard has overtaken the city. The only thing that I am able to see through my windows is the cascade of snowflakes as they hide the city behind a dense blanket of white.

The thought of returning home and having to sleep in a bed

that smells of Hadley guts me, so I choose to stay at Brass Global for the evening. I push open the door, deciding to collect my phone from Adriana's desk, when I'm greeted with the silhouette of a woman standing across the now-dark room. The reflected lights from the city light her up from behind, and I'm fixated on her.

It's only now that I remember Adriana saying that I had a guest waiting for me once I finished with the officers.

She turns when she hears my footsteps against the flooring as I take a hesitant step toward her. *Hadley.* I raise my eyebrows in disbelief. "To what do I owe this pleasure?"

"Hi, Whiskey." She walks toward me before stopping few feet away, keeping a safe distance.

"How long have you been here?"

"Uh, I arrived just as the police officers did."

"You should get home. The storm won't let up until the morning, and I believe that you're not supposed to be alone."

She shifts her position and pushes a curl out of her face. "I'd rather be stuck in the same place as you, Wade."

"Hadley, I told you that I refuse to be a coping mechanism. You've been through more than your fair share of pain, but I cannot be a simple moment of relief for you."

"I don't want you to be. I, uhm, I think I automatically went there this morning, and if you hadn't stopped me, then I would have slipped up. But you did stop me, and in that moment I realized that I still mean something to you, or you could have just gone with it. You didn't just want me for what I was offering."

She looks up at me before continuing. "You want more from me."

"You've always meant more to me than a physical act, and you still do."

"I know, but it made me realize that maybe I may still mean something to you after being so foolish." She pauses for a moment and glances down at her feet, and then back up at me. "Wade?"

"What is it?"

She takes a hesitant step toward me again and then glances down at her feet once more when she says, "I do miss you. I made a mistake in leaving, and I regret it immensely."

Her confession derails me. I've known that she'll always mean something to me, but I never thought that she would regret leaving me or that she would still want to be with me. She's had two months to get over me and move on, but by the look of it, she's done neither.

"Come here," I instruct her.

No matter how much effort I put into it, I cannot stay away from her. There's always been something different about her, and I deserve to have her—I want her. She also deserves the happiness that came of our relationship.

She doesn't move when I ask her to come to me, so I take the steps that separate us and tilt her chin up until she's looking into my eyes. "I've missed you, Hadley. You have to know that."

She purses her lips at my confession and slowly reaches out to rest her hand on my chest. I watch her closely as her body language changes from closed off and petrified to open and clean by setting aside the hurt and betrayal and her beaten soul.

"I need you. Some days I just need you more than others, and today is one of those days."

There's something beautiful about her needing me. She's always been self-assured and guarded, but her telling me that she needs me is her way of letting me in. I reach for her hand, and she allows me to intertwine my fingers with hers as I pull her toward me. "Do you want me?"

She's made herself susceptible, showing me her strength, courage, and dignity. She may not realize exactly how sensitive she is, but it provides me with many more reasons to treasure and love her deeply.

"No, Whiskey, it's more than a want. I feel empty without you. I don't know how I have been living without you. Nobody sees or knows just how much you affect my life. You uncovered the real me, and I don't want to experience this me without you any longer. I can't bear it."

The reality is that I've felt very similar feelings. I've fought with myself to come up with different excuses for the void, but once you've met the strongest person you know and that person heals you without your knowledge, it's difficult to ignore. She's the purest form of love that I will ever experience.

"Let me fill that emptiness inside you, Rye." I take her lips, stealing her breath while her defenses are down. I feel her break underneath my lips as she kisses me back with more self-assurance than I have seen in her before.

She breaks away from our kiss to speak. "I shouldn't have left you when you needed me."

"Shh, Rye. All that matters right now is that you are in my arms. It's where you belong."

Her tears start to flow as she leans her head against my chest, allowing her emotions from the last two months to take over. I risk injury as I lift her in my arms and carry her toward a single wingback seat in my office, closing the door behind me as I do. I take a seat with her in my lap and pull her body as close to mine as humanly possible.

"I'm sor-ry," she stutters through her tears.

"You need to understand that I refuse to let you run again. This is it, Hadley. You're mine, and I won't share you with another."

"You're the only one that I belong to—belong with. I'm in love with you, Waylon Brass. I haven't stopped because I can't. I don't know how to live without you anymore."

"I know. I love you, Rye." My chest aches with her spoken

words. I don't need anything but her tonight, and I need to show her exactly what she means to me. I need to give her a reason to stay.

Twenty-Seven

Hadley

WE HAVEN'T SAID much to each other since our confession of love a few moments ago. He makes the notion of love believable, as well as something that I want to be involved in. Yes, it comes with those sticky residual emotions, but I don't mind them when he has his arms locked around me. Blended might be his safe place, but he's mine.

The past two months have been filled with mistakes and regrets. I don't think that I have ever hated myself so much before. I ran away from the one thing, the one person, who made my life worth living. I've had a lot of time to think over the reasons as to why I ran from him, but none of it makes any sense now. All of the reasons why I told myself that I needed to leave seem trivial today. None of them even matter anymore because when I'm with him, he makes me forget about the negativity that has consumed my life. I ran from the love, comfort, and security that he unselfishly provided me, but now I want it back—all of it and more.

I feel him nuzzle me as I watch the confetti-sized snowflakes fall from his windows in the sky. His grip on me hasn't loosened for a second, and I think that he believes that I will leave as soon as I'm given the option to again, but I won't.

"Thank you," he says softly into my ear.

Goose bumps break out over my skin as his breath caresses

it. He makes me feel alive. "For what?"

"For coming back to me."

"I wouldn't have been able to stay away even if I tried, which I did."

"I'll make it worth your while, Rye."

"You already have." I twist in his arms to face him, and it's now that I notice how exhausted he looks. Behind it all, though, he looks content, unlike the brooding billionaire that I saw earlier this evening.

"Us, Hadley, is something that I believe in, and I'll stand by you through the hard times as you have for me. I'll sacrifice myself and compromise anything that I need to so I can be with you. You rescued me, and discovered different parts to me that I didn't know were there, and you gave me everything that I needed. I want all of that back. Please, tell me that you'll give me this last chance."

My love for him wasn't anything instant; it's been a gradual uphill that I hadn't noticed until I started to run in the opposite direction and down the steep slope. I slide my hand through his hair before loosening his tie and undoing the top button on his shirt. "I want to be, without question, everything that you've ever wanted in a woman."

"Here's the thing, though. You are exceedingly greater than any of my previous expectations."

I can't help but smile and press my lips against his sculpted jaw, his stubble teasing my bruised lips. When our lips part and I undo the knot in his tie, he simply stares down at me, never once looking up or at anything else in the room, as he watches my fingers move against the silky material. He makes me feel treasured.

"You're staring," I say softly as I pull his tie off from around his neck and drape it over the arm of the chair.

"You're too beautiful not to, and I haven't seen you in months, so you need to allow me this opportunity to take you in."

"I'm covered in bruises, Wade. I—" My mind takes me back to the bar's bathroom where I was able to hear grunts, but my body wouldn't allow me the luxury of pushing through the sedative's powers.

"Hadley. Be present and stay with me."

"I'm sorry," I say, trying to come back from the recent memories. We fall back into a comfortable silence as we watch the snow falling. He's shown me ways to love that I didn't know existed, and he's made sure that I've been able to overcome my past. For a moment, I lost faith in what I had with him as well as how he felt about me, but I won't let that happen again.

Staying away from him has been the hardest thing I've ever had to do, and it has required strength, courage, and faith in myself that I wasn't aware I harbored. He's helped me to change the direction of my life when everything was falling apart faster than I could fix it, and he did not even have to be present. Now that I feel as if that time is over, I cannot imagine living another second without him at my side. I need this man. I need him more than I've ever needed anyone.

I clear my throat to speak. "How's your back?"

He shifts me on his lap until I'm looking up into his seaside eyes again. "I have my moments. When I overwork my body, it aches, or a pain shoots up through my spine, but I'm able to walk again, which gives me nothing to complain about."

"I was concerned about you."

"As I was about you."

Silence settles over us again for a few minutes before he speaks again. "Answer me this one question, Rye."

"All right."

"Apart from what you went through last night, have you been with another man?" His jaw is tense, and I can tell that this is weighing heavily on him even though we've just agreed to be with each other again.

"No," I tell him honestly, "you're the only one that I've wanted to be with, both sexually and in general."

He shuts his eyes as if my reassurance vanquishes his deepest demons. "Lola brought that Holden guy to collect you from my residence earlier today."

"I was just as shocked as I'm sure you must have been. Hold and I are friends, and that's where the line is drawn."

"Are you certain?"

"Yes, Waylon Brass. I want to be with you. What about that don't you understand?" I smack his chest, and he captures my wrist in his hand.

"I needed you to be positive."

"I've already told you that I am." I kiss his jaw in an attempt to dull the riled-up emotions he's trying to rid himself of. I move my lips up to his, kissing him intently.

We don't talk. We just act, finding solace in one another.

His lips have hardly left mine since I told him that I was certain that I wanted to be with him, regardless of how swollen mine are. It's because of him that I made mistakes, that I'm vulnerable. He makes me feel worthwhile and valuable.

My lips have gone numb from his assault as they try to recover from Lawson's bruises, but I choose to ignore the slight discomfort because Wade is all that I want. He's what I need.

"I think that we're stuck here tonight," I tell him as we take a second apart to breathe.

"Possibly, but I'm sure that we'll be able to make something work."

"If I remember correctly, Dr. Heath said that you shouldn't be seated for too long, and you've probably been in your office all day."

"You're right." He pats my ass for me to stand and I do. I

watch as he gets up slowly, obviously in pain. "We can make it to the hotel a block away."

"Are you sure?"

"Yes. I need to lie down and rest my back," he says as he takes my hand and leads me to the coat rack in his office. I watch him pull out a small black medical bag, which he unzips and takes two pills out of a white container before returning it to his closet. He walks over to the wet bar in the corner and takes the medication with a bottle of water before returning to me. He pulls out a coat and drapes it around my shoulders and then takes one out for himself, pulling it up his arms and then buttoning it. Our fingers lace together as we leave his office and head out into the winter storm.

Thirty minutes later, I'm shivering and watching him pull his shirt off. He got us a room at the Ritz-Carlton, which is only a block down from his building and a few more from Blended. He catches me staring when he looks up to undo the button on his slacks. I watch as he steps out of them until he's wearing nothing but his boxer briefs. I let out an unsteady breath as I take his jacket off and hang it up in the closet before coming to stand in front of him and pulling my leather jacket and crop sweater off before undoing my black skinny jeans and sliding them down my legs. He takes a step toward me and offers me his white button-down without a word.

I take it and drape it over my shoulders before pushing my arms into the sleeves. It's warm from the heat of his body and it wraps me in his scent, something that I've missed terribly. He's standing in front of me as he watches me first undress and then don his shirt. I move to the bed once I have it on and pull the sheets back before climbing under the soft white comforter to warm up.

"Are you comfortable?" he asks me as I settle in and adjust the pillow, turning to look at him as he lies down beside me. He reaches over and takes my hand.

"I am." I pull the covers over our joint hands to keep the heat under the comforter. "Please don't let me go."

"Not even in my dreams, Rye." He leans over and pulls me into his side of the bed, embracing me in his warmth. I curl up against him and sigh contentedly when I feel his skin on mine. I'm back home, the home whose heart beats for me.

"'Night, Whiskey."

"Goodnight, Rye."

His breathing shallows out almost immediately, and I'm unable to contain the smile on my face as I lay a kiss against his bare chest before snuggling a little closer. I'd never have expected to be in a relationship, let alone with Chicago's most eligible bachelor. Yet here I am with him again in the dark.

In the middle of my addiction-driven prison, life plopped me into a fairytale and gave me an opportunity to explore what it meant to be with someone, what it meant to fall in love and be unable to let go of the sentiment.

He's quickly become my unexpected love—love that isn't practical. I doubt that it ever will be. He's been the light to pull me out of my darkness without having to take me to another place as his seaside eyes wash away my pain. He's engraved himself into my heart and lightened my bruises and scars. I don't think that I'll be able to turn and walk away from him again.

An hour or two passes before I'm able to put my demons to rest for the night and shut my eyes as I drift to sleep effortlessly for the first time in months.

I stir when I feel his lips trailing up the column of my neck, his warm breath waking me from a deep sleep. My eyes flutter open as he brings his lips to meet mine. A sleepy smile is on his face as I awaken but I feel as if I've only slept for an hour.

"Hi," I say as I stretch out underneath him, parts of my body still stiff from being used in the utmost vile way the night before. I choose to ignore it and allow myself to get lost in Wade's touch.

"You're gorgeous. Do you know that?"

I can't help the blush that makes its way onto my cheeks. "Thank you. Do you have to go to work?" I ask with a yawn as he moves to hover over me.

"Not when I have my girl in bed with me, and not when it's barely four in the morning."

"Oh," I say, slightly confused as he brushes his lips along the line of my jaw and toward my ear.

"Take a chance with me."

I draw in a breath when his teeth nip at my earlobe before he makes his way down my neck, placing light bites as he goes and then caressing the same skin with his lips with an apologetic kiss.

"Wade," I moan while trying to fill my lungs with a sufficient amount of oxygen so I'm able to speak, but nothing more comes out as his static touch burns me.

His hands trail down my body, meticulously undoing each button on his shirt before pushing the comforter off of us.

"I woke up thinking that you weren't next to me . . . that you ran from me again. I cannot fathom that happening again, so I'm going to give you what you need, what we both want. I need you to understand exactly how much you mean to me. I love you, Hadley. Now let me show you."

I gasp as he pulls the cups of my bra down, which in turn pushes up my breasts, displaying my now peaked nipples perfectly for him. He gently places his lips on my collarbone as he kisses from one side and then to the other before lowering his mouth to my nipple. He takes my peak between his lips before surrounding me with the warmth of his mouth. He starts to suck me gently before he applies pressure from his teeth and tugs. I squirm underneath him and wail in pleasure.

"Whiskey."

"You taste unbelievable, Rye, and I'm going to show you exactly how a man in love makes his girlfriend fall apart."

"Please," I whimper as he takes my other nipple into his mouth and proceeds to do the exact same thing as he did with the other.

"We'll go slowly, baby. I'm going to see you like this for the first time, and I'm going to savor every second of it."

I nod and reach around my body to free myself from the constrictions of my bra and his shirt. He helps me get out of it and tosses it over the edge of the bed as he cups each one in his large hands.

"We're doing this?" My voice trembles with desire as I ask him the question.

"We are, but before I do anything more, I need to know if you're all right."

"Of course I'm all right, Wade."

"I don't want to hurt you, not after what he put you through. If it's too soon, then please know that I'll understand. I want to erase what he did, but only if you're willing to replace it with the love that I have to offer you."

"You won't hurt me. I may be bruised, but I'm not broken. I want this. I want this with you, Whiskey. It's always been you."

"You swear it?"

"I do."

He pauses as he watches my face for any indication that I might be lying to him. When he's satisfied with my honest answer, his lips skim over the visible bruises on my body before taking my mouth tenderly.

This man cares for me too much, and I'm able to tell with each touch that he lays on me. I sigh longingly, and run my hands down his bare chest, down to the ridges that make up his abs as he caresses me in return. He's put me first as he always has, and regardless of the last twenty-four hours, there's nothing more that I want than this from him. I come from a life of hurt, abuse, and sorrow. I've used sex to cover it all up and stow it away, but he's helped me to overcome that crutch. He's helped me see that there's more to life than what I've been living, and I know, without a doubt, that finally being intimate with him tonight will in no way hinder the progress that I've made with ridding myself of a coping mechanism. Waylon Brass is not a hit of my addiction: he's been the cure, the road map leading me to a life that I've always longed for. It's because of him that I've unknotted my tangled life. With this man, I am free.

He presses his body into mine, and it's now that I am able to feel his hard cock pressing into my lower stomach. I've seen his cock a handful of times before, and it's striking. He may have the best-looking cock that I've ever seen, and that's saying a lot.

My fingers find the band of his boxer briefs as he trails kisses all over my abdomen, making my skin come alive with a blizzard of sensations under his touch. He leans back and gazes at me with those seaside eyes that have once more turned into a snowstorm, matching the one taking over Chicago at the moment.

He glances over my bare skin, sending goose bumps running down my spine, which is currently laced with static. He makes me feel dangerous and gorgeous all with one look.

"Lift your hips for me."

I do as I'm told and lift my hips up so he's able to tug and pull my nude panties down to my thighs. Once he has them off of me, he reaches up and puts them on his pillow before ducking his head between my legs and sliding his tongue up and over my slit.

"Oh," I cry out without shame.

His tongue runs over my wet opening as he spreads my legs wider apart. I adjust myself to watch him go down on me, leaning up on my elbows but throwing my head back in ardor as he flicks his tongue back and forth over my clitoris. My hips buck up, searching for his mouth as he continues to torture me. My orgasm comes from nowhere, surprising me when it takes over and sends me soaring. His hands push down on my hips so he is able to keep his mouth locked on my pussy as I wriggle with the static currently vibing through me.

Nervous energy circulates throughout my body as he kisses up my center until his lips land on mine. My breath is coming fast as I kiss him, tasting myself on his glistening lips. No man has ever made me orgasm that quickly before and my body shivers underneath his.

"I could eat you for the remainder of my life to watch you come like that each time."

I purposely bite down on his lip as I reach for his boxer briefs again and yank them lower, over his ass and farther down. He gets up to take them off and as he stands at the side of the bed, I sit up and criss-cross my legs, showcasing myself to him as I take in the sight of him naked in front of me. He's magnificent, so much so that I want to wrap my mouth around his head before letting him slide in and out of my throat.

"Hadley." His voice is throaty and mixed with desire.

"I'm ready, Whiskey. Swear to me that you won't end up back in the hospital because of what you're about to make me feel."

"No, baby," he says as he closes the distance between himself and the bed. "I got the all clear from Dr. Heath before I left."

I sigh and get up on my knees, throwing my arms around his neck and smashing my mouth to his. "I love you and I want you; I want this from you."

"Mmm," he hums against my open mouth. "I have one issue."

"What is it?"

"I've told you before that I don't fuck women in my city due to the extremes that I've gone to before, and to stop myself from falling prey to the habit, I refuse to carry a condom around with me."

I stare at him, kind of shocked at what he just admitted to me. He actually did struggle, possibly more than I'm aware of.

"If you don't fucking have one, then I'm going to go mad, and I will walk into the blizzard naked until I find one because we're not leaving here until I make love to and then fuck what belongs to me."

God, I love that he said that he's going to fuck me as well. I kiss him once before getting off of the bed and going to the chair that my purse is set on. When I bend over and reach into my Burberry, my heart sinks until his arms come around me.

"What is it?"

I scrounge around in my purse and huff out, "I must have left them in my old purse when I transferred everything over."

"Are you fucking with me?"

I shake my head and turn around in his arms, my eyes watering up at the thought of not going all the way with him tonight. We both need this to seal our relationship and to heal our unclosed wounds.

He takes in a deep breath through his nose before placing his lips on mine and speaking. "Do you trust me?"

"Implicitly."

"I'm clean," he tells me.

"I am too. I got tested after . . ." I don't finish my sentence because I don't want to bring up the other night at the bar.

"Are you on the pill?"

"I had an implant inserted two years ago."

His lips find mine again, and he smiles before lifting me up and carrying me back to the bed. He sets me down, and I push all of the comforters and blankets off of the bed. The only thing that I want to feel is him.

"I've never gone bare before."

"I wish that I could say the same thing."

"Don't think about it, Rye."

I lie back on the bed as he moves his body over mine, the tip of his cock pressing against my thigh.

"Slow at first, and then I'm going to give it to you."

I nod, wanting the same thing as him, if not more.

He reaches between us and takes his cock into his hand. I watch him pump himself twice before he positions his head at my entrance, but instead of pushing in, he circles my clitoris with his erection, and I moan loudly, wanting more, so much more.

He leans down and takes my lips as he lines himself up. He doesn't rush this moment or slam it in as most men would, but he slowly sinks his length into me, and he doesn't stop until he's fully seated inside of me.

"Wade—"

He hisses through his teeth as he buries his face in the crook of my neck. I can't help but love his reaction to me and my need is to fill every single want that he has.

"You belong to me now, Hads. Just me. Always me."

I sink my teeth into his muscular shoulder as he starts to move in and out of me at a slow pace, both of us losing ourselves in the penetrating hunger and adoration.

The tightness in my chest has nothing to do with the physical exertion and everything to do with having fallen completely in love with this man.

"Yours," I moan out as he slowly but continually hits my sweet spot. His skin against mine creates a kind of friction that I've not yet felt before, and I want more of it.

More of him.

More of us.

Twenty-Eight

Wade

THERE IS NO barrier between us as I slide myself in and out of her at an even, ball-twisting pace. I'm struggling with the urge to pull her to the edge of the bed, where I can leverage my feet and fuck her until she's speechless.

"Wade . . ." she cries as her breath catches in her throat. "I . . . as much as I love this . . . I want . . . I need you to fuck me."

This woman is going to destroy me.

"Thank fuck," I say as I pull out of her and tug her body to the side of the bed where she leans up on her elbows to watch me re-enter her perfectly creamed-up sex.

I slide in gently and pull out once before I start to increase the force of my thrusts.

"Holy shit," she yells out as I rock into her repeatedly. I wrap my hand around a handful of her hair and hold her in place as I drill my cock into her slick tightness. She squeezes my cock, and I groan in pleasure. I pause long enough to flip her over, which gets her to slide her legs off of the bed and hold onto the edge of it. She stands before me with her ass pressing against my cock, begging me for more. I grab hold of her hair again and tilt her head to the side until I'm able to see the expression on her face as I sink into her once again.

"Wade," she whimpers softly as her voice trembles.

Her pussy clenches around me again, and I can tell that she's a breath away so I move my hand from her hip and circle my thumb around her sweet spot, applying pressure to where she needs it the most as I watch her ass bounce with each thrust into her. The room is filled with our heavy breathing and the slapping of skin.

"Yes—"

"I've got you," I say as I lean forward and whisper in her ear. Her entire body stiffens underneath mine as she succumbs to her orgasm as a quick breath leaves her lips. I watch her slight frame shake with wave after wave; her mouth is open in a wordless cry as I continue to slam into her until I find my release.

A guttural growl leaves me as my balls tighten, and black spots begin to fill my vision, and I spill into her bare pussy, filling her up, finally doing what I've needed to do for months. She takes me, drinks me in as she whimpers.

I still behind her as I lock her almost-limp body in my arms, ensuring that she doesn't fall to the ground as our bodies attempt to come down from their highs.

"Wade," she says under her breath after a few moments when neither of us dares to move, fearing that this might be a wet dream.

"Hads."

I slowly pull my still-hard length out of her, and she pushes herself up before turning to face me. I pull her closer by placing my hand on the small of her back. The smile that she gives me breaks into my soul as she wraps both of her arms around my neck.

"That was worth every single torturous second that I needed you."

I grin and nuzzle into her hair. "I agree. Will you allow me to clean you up?"

Her eyes meet mine as she purses her lips before nodding in agreement. We walk to the bathroom, hand in hand, before I lift her up onto the ledge of the raised bathtub.

"Whiskey, you need to stop lifting me up. If you hurt your-self again, the chances of your healing and being able to do that to me again are exceedingly slim."

I pause at her words before taking her lips. "I'll stop . . . for now."

I start the warm water and grab a washcloth from the top of the pile placed at the side of the bath. I wet it and then kneel down between her legs and slowly, starting at her ankle, I run the warm cloth up her skin. Our combined orgasms have left a trail that reaches just above her knee, and I grin to myself.

"You're even more attractive when you're dirty."

Her giggle causes me to look up at her, and she sends a hundred and one feelings through my system at once. She's my ultimate fantasy, and I'm kneeling between her pale white and bruised legs. I glance up at her swollen pink pussy between her thighs once I've cleaned her off and lay a kiss on her there before standing up and offering her my hand. "Come."

I lead her back to bed and pull her against me. I'm unbeliev-ably worn out after the first round. I'm unsure if it was her or if my surgery has affected my ability to keep going, but I know that after an hour's worth of sleep, she better be ready to go again.

Less than an hour later, I wake up to a stiff back after my night with Hadley. I fling my arm out from underneath the comforter to turn off the six o'clock alarm. Hadley groans from her posi-tion beside me. I peel my eyes open and glance down to see her, but she has the comforter completely covering her. I chuckle and grab my phone, unlocking it and bring up the camera. I sit up and squeeze her hip.

"Good morning, gorgeous," I tell her close to her ear and lean back. She shifts and groans again before pulling the comfort-er halfway down her face as I position myself over her. When she sees the phone in my hand, she grabs the white comforter and pulls it up over her eyes.

I take the picture and toss my phone over to her side of the bed before I lean down and kiss her neck. "I need to get ready for work."

"No, you need to stay in bed with me," she says as she throws the comforter off of her top half, exposing her bare breasts to me.

"You're making it difficult not to."

"Good," she says as I climb off of the bed and place my lips to her temple.

"I'll order room service before I shower."

"Coffee," she mumbles.

I chuckle and pick up the phone in the room and order a variety of things for breakfast before heading into the bathroom to shower once I've texted Jacobs.

Forty-five minutes later, I walk out of the bathroom to a sleeping Hadley, a clean suit from Jacobs, and breakfast laid out on the coffee table.

Once I'm dressed, I walk to the side of the bed and pull the comforter from her head so I'm able to see her. "Are you cold?" I ask as I skim my lips across hers.

She stirs and stretches out on the bed before wrapping her arms around my neck and smiling up at me. "A little. You look good." Her eyes close again, and I kiss her once more.

"I need to get to the office and meet with my lawyers. Stay as long as you need to."

"Thank you," she mumbles and lets go of me before turning over and pulling the comforter up over her face again.

I grab my phone and leave quietly while she falls asleep again, and I make my way out to meet Jacobs.

At noon, my phone vibrates, but instead of waiting for my

meeting to be through, I slide it out of my pocket and open the image that Hadley just sent me. Once it opens I clear my throat and adjust my now-hard cock in my slacks. She's taken a picture of herself in front of a full-length mirror in the hotel, completely naked.

I MISS YOU is written underneath it before another picture of her comes through. When I open it this time, I'm more prepared to find her in a similar position in front of the mirror, but this time, she has the phone over her shoulder and the image is of her naked back and perfectly shaped ass.

YOU'RE DISTRACTING ME FROM A RATHER IMPORTANT MEETING, RYE. YOU'RE BEAUTIFUL.

My cock twitches as I think about bending her over and taking her from behind again while she rests her palms against the cool mirror.

IT'S A HEALTHY DISTRACTION, THOUGH.

I chuckle as I type out my response to her: THAT IT IS. I attach the image that I took of her this morning and hit send.

WHAT! WHEN DID YOU TAKE THAT?

The group in front of me keeps glancing over in my direction as I respond to her: THIS MORNING WHEN YOU WERE HALF ASLEEP.

FINE. YOU CAN KEEP IT, BUT I'M GOING TO NEED SOMETHING DIRTY FROM YOU IN RETURN.

"Mr. Brass, if you'll excuse my saying so, this project needs your approval before we are able to move ahead with it."

I snap my head in the direction of the woman who spoke. "I'm well aware of my obligations. This meeting is adjourned, and you no longer have my approval for your revamp."

I stand and button my suit jacket as she rises to her feet to challenge me, but Adriana steps in once I've texted her and lets everyone know that she will be emailing them the minutes before the end of the day. I stride out of the conference room and down the hallway to my office.

You're going to get me in trouble, gorgeous.

I take a seat at my desk and email Adriana to have my lunch delivered when my phone starts to ring. I look down at the caller ID before answering.

"Isla."

"Hey, Brass. I'm sorry that I couldn't make your meeting this morning. I overslept."

"You should consider yourself lucky that you're more than an employee of Brass Global to me."

"Possibly. I wanted to find out how you were doing after the incident with Hadley. Are you still going to come by Blended tonight for the members' Christmas Invitational?"

"Possibly. Hadley came by the office last night and . . ." I pause, thinking about sinking into her sweetness.

"And," she prompts.

"We're together again."

"Finally, Brass. You two have been giving me whiplash."

"I won't apologize."

"I never expected that you would. Let me know if you are coming tonight."

"Of course. I need to respond to a few urgent emails. I'll speak to you later."

"Okay, bye, Waylon."

I hit the end call button and read Hadley's text message: Don't complain. I love you, Waylon Brass.

My chest tightens as I read it over once more before replying to her: As I you.

Twenty-Nine

Hadley

I HAD AN appointment with the same doctor that tended to me after Wade found me in the bar that afternoon. He said that he was pleased with how I recovered from the sedative and to follow up with my personal physician. Apparently, Jacobs was instructed to stay by my side today because he's been driving me around and waiting patiently for me, instead of going back to Wade.

"Colin, you really don't need to follow me around all day. The doctor just cleared me."

"I'm following orders, Miss Rye."

I frown and get into the back of the BMW and fish out my phone to see an awaiting text from Wade: I'M TAKING YOU OUT TO-NIGHT. BE READY BY EIGHT.

Squirming in the seat on the way back to my apartment, I wonder what he might have in mind this time around. When we arrive, I thank Colin and head inside.

"Lo? Are you home?"

She pops her head around the corner of the kitchen wall. "Hey, where have you been? We were supposed to grab lunch."

"Oh shit. I'm so sorry, I completely forgot."

"It's not a big deal. I was just concerned. You're okay, right?" She glances at me before going back to unloading the dishwasher and I take a seat at the kitchen island.

"I'm perfect."

"Oh?" She seems surprised by my choice of words. "Well, good. Where did you disappear to last night by the way? Holden and I were worried, but you wouldn't answer our calls."

"I went to see Wade."

"And?"

I can't help the smile that stretches across on my face. "I think that we're going to be okay."

She tilts her head to the side, her gaze rolling down the top half of my body. "You finally fucked him, didn't you?"

I chew my lip, contemplating whether to tell her or not. "I mean . . ."

"You so did," she squeals and runs around the island to throw her arms around me. "What does it mean? Are you just going to fuck him or are you two like an actual couple? It wasn't too soon for you after what happened with that douche, was it?"

When she's done rambling, she grabs a bottle of cabernet sauvignon and pours two glasses of wine and hands one to me.

"We're together, Lo. As in, he's mine. And no, it wasn't too soon. For me, it made me realize that regardless of my past and what I've been through, I'm still worth more than what Lawson and those men made me out to be. He cherished me last night, and I won't ever forget it."

She holds up her glass to me and beams. "To my best friend and her gorgeous billionaire stud."

I laugh with her and reach for my glass before clinking it with hers. "To my *boyfriend*."

My phone goes off, and I reach for it, but Lo snags it off of the counter before I can, and she reads a text out loud: "I'LL BE INTRODUCING YOU TO SOME OF CHICAGO'S BEST AND BRIGHTEST THIS EVENING. IF YOU NEED SOMETHING TO WEAR, I'LL SEND JACOBS WITH THE CAR AND MY CARD. I LOVE YOU."

"Oh no, he doesn't," she stabs and holds her index finger up to me. "I have the perfect outfit for you to wear."

I'm almost shocked that she didn't mention anything about the last part of the message. Surely she knows how I've felt about being in love over the years.

"Would you quit stealing my phone when he texts?" I lean over the island and take it back from her, then read over his message before I reply: APPARENTLY, LOLA HAS SOMETHING THAT SHE WANTS ME TO WEAR. IS IT FORMAL?

He must be waiting for my response with his phone in hand because his response is immediate: SEMI-FORMAL. I'LL BE BY ONCE I'M DONE AT THE OFFICE. I NEED TO BE INSIDE OF YOU BEFORE THIS EVENING.

Blood rushes through my body at the thought of getting naked with him again. I CAN'T WAIT. I reply and hit send just as Lola comes back into the kitchen, holding up a snow-white evening gown with long sleeves and an open back. I gasp and toss my phone onto the island as I hop off of the stool.

"You'll let me wear this?"

"Are you kidding me? Of course, I will. Especially if it's a function that Waylon Brass himself is hosting."

I throw my arms around her and squeeze her before holding up the dress to my frame. "Do you think that it will fit?"

"I'm sure it will, and if it doesn't, then I'll do some alterations on it. Go try it on with those black pumps you own."

After I've tried it on with my heels, Lola takes it to make a few adjustments so it will sit snugly around me as I finish up my hair and makeup.

I'm seated in front of the vanity in a matching pair of white lace underwear with a pair of sheer nude stockings on when there's a knock on my door. "I'm not dressed. Give me a second."

The door opens and I swing my head around as I add a bobby pin to my updo. My eyes find Wade dressed in black slacks, a white button-down shirt, and a black textured vest with a black jacket hanging over his arm. My eyes scroll down his body as his run up mine.

"Fuck, Hadley."

I stand for him as his eyes wander down my body. His steps toward me are deliberately slow. "Hi, Whiskey," I offer him as I straighten my stockings on my thighs.

"You're breathtaking." He places his jacket on the bench at the end of my bed before he reaches me and rings his arms around my bare waist.

"You don't clean up too bad yourself. Would you mind doing me a favor?"

He clears his throat as Lola enters the room. "Hi, you two. Hads, we need to get you dressed."

"We do? What time is it?"

"It's eight-fifteen," Wade says. "Something came up at the office, and I wasn't able to leave when I wanted to."

I look up at him and trace his lips with my index finger before pressing mine to his. "It's okay."

Lola lays the dress on my bed after steaming it. "I'll let him help you," she says, winking at me, and leaves us alone in my bedroom.

"Other than the dress, what did you want me to help you with?"

"Well, the dress is backless, which means that I'll need to go braless. Would you mind taking it off?"

His eyebrows shoot up as I turn my back to him. His warm fingers graze my back gently before reaching the clasp. With hasty movements, he undoes it and pulls the straps down my shoulders before placing his lips where the right strap used to be. "How am I supposed to concentrate this evening knowing that you don't have much on underneath the dress?"

"You're not. Where are we going by the way?"

"I'm taking you to Blended's first annual Christmas Invitational for the members."

I turn in his arms and place my lips against the column of his neck. "So it's a date?"

I feel the rumble against my lips before I hear it. "You could call it that." His hands come up to my breasts, pinching my nipples before he adds, "Let me get that dress on you before I lay you out on the floor and fuck you senseless."

I pull back to look at him, pursing my lips in thought. "You know, I wouldn't mind missing dinner."

"I wouldn't either, but I believe Isla would, considering she's arranged all of it."

I watch him take a step away from me with a grin on his face. I pick up the white dress as I step toward him, and he helps me into it.

"I never thought that I would enjoy dressing a woman. I've fantasized about undressing you many times, but I can see the appeal in this as well," he says smoothly as he guides the fabric down my torso and then legs. He takes my hand as I step into my heels and then he takes a few steps back to look. "You're never taking that off."

"Do you like it?" I ask as I turn from side to side so I'm able to fully see myself in the mirror. After Lo's alterations, the dress hugs every inch of my body.

"I do. I'll need to personally thank the designer."

"Go ahead, she's right in the living room."

"Lola made this?"

He bends down to pick up his jacket while watching me.

"That's what I was told." I grab my merlot-colored lip stain and toss it into my clutch along with my ID and cell phone before I follow him out of my bedroom. By the time I've shut the door, he's speaking to Lola.

"I didn't know that you were a designer. I'm rather impressed with what you have dressed Hadley in this evening."

I watch as a blush sweeps over her features. "It's just

something that I had lying around, and it looks stunning on her."

"It does. I'd be interested in seeing some more of your designs."

"You're kidding me, right?"

"Not one bit. Put together a portfolio and I'll have my secretary get in contact with you."

She shakes his offered hand and agrees to have it ready by the end of next week.

"Wade?"

He turns to face me and his features shift from interest in what Lola is saying to wanton desire when he sees me again. He doesn't say anything else to either of us as he makes his way toward me, tugging me by my hand until I hit his chest. "I'm going to show you off to every single person in Chicago this evening. Let's go," he says as he circles his arm around my waist.

"Bye, Lo," I call over my shoulder as he leads me to the foyer. He has me out of the apartment door and down the hallway as the Parker brothers walk out of their place together. Both of them stop a few feet away from us as we wait for the elevator, staring unabashedly as Wade runs his fingers up and down my ribcage.

"You look good, Hadley," Owen offers up, which causes Wade to turn and face them.

"Thank you. Lo is home if you were wondering."

"Yeah, Hold and I are going to grab some dinner before I head over."

I lift my head in Holden's direction, and he's wearing an expression that I've never seen on him before: wary and manic wrapped into one look. I realize that his eyes are on Wade's and not on mine. The elevator opens, though, saving me for the briefest of moments before it closes and the four of us stand there in silence once again.

"Where are you off to?" Owen breaks the awkward tension

radiating off of each of us.

I glance up at Wade as he starts to speak. "My company is putting on its Christmas socials this evening. We'll start at one location and make our way around to a handful of my properties before the evening is up."

"I thought that we were going to Blended?"

"We are; that's the first stop this evening. I prefer to host them all in one night instead of having to attend each and every one of them on different evenings," he tells me as he draws me in closer to his side.

"That sounds like more than one date, Waylon Brass."

"That it does."

His smile shatters my deepest fears as he leans down to take my lips. I think I blush as he kisses me until the doors of the elevator open and Holden clears his throat. My eyes pop open as I remember where we are. This handsome man not only makes me forget how to breathe, but he has this thing that he does where he steals me away from the rest of the world.

My eyes haven't left Wade's as he winks at me before leading me out of the elevator and into the lobby. I smile over my shoulder at the Parker brothers in a goodbye, but Owen seems to be pale while Holden looks as if he's about to detonate.

Regret swims through my body. I truly didn't mean for that to happen, but Whiskey just has a way of getting what he wants with me. He makes me lose my mind at the most unfortunate of times.

"Come," Wade commands as he leads me out of the building and down to where Jacobs is waiting. He keeps ahold of my hand as I take my seat in the BMW. Once I'm seated, he leans into me and takes my mouth with his in a more sensual kiss than the one in front of the Parker brothers.

"I could stare at you all evening. I do not blame Holden for wanting you."

I shrug and pull him back down to me by his lapels. "It's a good thing that I'm committed to a rather domineering gentleman, then, huh?"

"It is."

He moves around to the other side of the vehicle and gets in. His fingers intertwine with mine as Jacobs turns onto the street and heads toward the Magnificent Mile where Blended is located.

It doesn't take too long to arrive at the library and when we enter I'm taken aback. Blended has been transformed into something breathtaking. White Christmas decorations are gracing the library with large round tables where I'm assuming that dinner will be served. It's obviously decorated by a professional because nothing seems to be overdone or out of place.

Once we are able to walk farther into the room, we're greeted by the stares of people I've never seen before. Isla sees us and claps excitedly before coming to join the people who have surrounded us to greet him.

"Hads, holy shit. I'm not known for being speechless, but Brass better keep you on his arm this evening because in the few steps I took to get to you, I lost count of how many men were talking about you."

"Hi, Isla, it's good to see you again . . . and I think you might be exaggerating."

Wade's arm tightens around me. "She's not. Good evening, Isla."

"It's about time you showed your ugly mug. The members have been asking for you, and I'm never wrong."

I step out of Wade's arm to hug her briefly before I'm pulled back into my comfort zone.

"Jesus, Brass. Deprived much?"

"Incredibly," he says to her while his eyes are locked on mine.

"On that note, you two enjoy your evening and let me

know if you need me to save you from any other parties tonight. Dinner should be served in thirty minutes."

"Thank you," he says before I'm pressed up against him and he's looking down at me like I'm the only person in the room. He leans down and places his lips against my cheek. "I love you, Rye."

Heat runs down my back at his words, and I lace our fingers together. "I love you, Whiskey." I feel instead of see the smile on his face before he pulls back and shakes an older man's hand before introducing me as his girlfriend.

Every hand that I shake and every person that he introduces me to seems to be stunned that he has a woman other than Isla on his arm. I'm on my second tumbler of whiskey for the night, which has allowed me to loosen up a little bit, and I'm enjoying myself as we sit down for dinner.

I'm seated between Isla and Wade at the table that is now filled with men in designer suits. I heard Wade asking Isla to switch tables earlier, and I'm sure that it has something to do with the number of men here. We're served a dinner of Beef Wellington with a variety of sides. I take a bite and almost moan as the flavors travel across my taste buds.

"Where are you two going next, Brass?"

"We'll be attending the Christmas party for Mothers of Brass. We host two a year at each location, one for the staff and the other for the women and children."

"Mothers of Brass? I'm not sure as to what's involved with it," I say as I take a drink from my tumbler.

Isla smiles as if I'm being let in on some huge secret. "It's his favorite facet of Brass Global . . . other than Blended, of course."

I watch him as he sets his whiskey down and turns to face me. "I founded Mothers of Brass eight years ago. It's a charitable organization that helps women in domestic-abuse situations as well as single mothers to get on their feet again once they are free of their situations. It offers a variety of services, all of which are free, to the women and their children. It's the reason we went to Sydney, actually. I had acquired all of those properties to set up the first safe house in Australia."

"That's unbelievable, Wade. I had no idea that you did all of this."

He just shrugs and Isla jumps in. "He doesn't tend to advertise it."

I lean in and place a chaste kiss on his lips. "You're incredible, you know."

His lips turn up in the corner. "Barely, baby. It's something that I carry close to my heart since my father was killed a few days after my birth and my mother was left to fend for herself."

"I had no idea."

We both seem to reach for each other at the same time and intertwine our fingers together. "Your mother is an exceptionally strong woman, and she should be proud of the mark that you are leaving in this world."

"You'll need to tell her that, which brings up another topic that I needed to mention to you."

We're interrupted then by a hand on his shoulder. When he turns to see who touched him, he seems uncomfortable until Jacobs speaks. "We should be leaving, Mr. Brass."

"Very well. Are you ready, Hadley?"

He rises and tugs on my hand as I stand up, straightening my dress and picking up my clutch. "I am."

After thanking Isla and saying our goodbyes to a few people around the room, we leave and head just north of the Magnificent Mile. When we arrive, Wade helps me out of the vehicle, and I glance up at the high-rise in front of us.

"This is Mothers of Brass? It looks like a hotel."

"It is, and we treat it as such. It's easier for the women and their children to feel at home, and it holds up its cover that way.

It's very seldom that we get men in here who are married to one of the clients. The entire place is staffed by women, which adds a comfort level to those who need Mothers of Brass."

We walk into the building, and he's right: it seems to be a hotel. It's not overly glamorous, but it's still gorgeous inside.

"Good evening, Mr. Brass," a few women chime in as he leads me through the lobby and down to a ballroom, which is immaculately decorated. I realize that this party, unlike Blended's, will be filled with women instead of men. My fingers tighten around his hand as the women all stand and start to applaud when they see him.

He gives a few nods of appreciation before he places a kiss on my cheek. "I have to thank them all for being here. Don't move."

"All right."

He lets go of my hand and walks to the front of the room where a microphone stand has been set up.

"Hadley? Oh, sweetie, I thought that was you. You look unequivocally radiant." I turn around, and I'm greeted with Lillian pulling me into her arms.

"Lilly, I had no idea that you would be here. It's so good to see you."

"Of course, I would be here. Who else do you think runs Mothers of Brass when my son is too preoccupied with his empire?"

"I had no idea that he did all of this until a few minutes ago."

"He's a good man."

I look up when he starts to speak. "He is," I say quietly as I drink him in. He's positioned himself in front of the microphone and has one hand in his pocket while the other moves as he speaks.

"Good evening, ladies."

I swear I hear the entire room swoon as his voice is amplified by the speakers surrounding us.

"First and foremost, I wanted to thank you all for coming. It's my pleasure to host the eighth annual Christmas party here at Mothers of Brass. For those of you who have been with us for the last eight years, I could not be more grateful. I know that it wasn't easy at times, but we seem to have found our rhythm. I greatly appreciate the efforts that are put into growing and making Mothers of Brass—Chicago the largest women's-only organization in the nation. The vision that I had for this charity has been met because of each and every one of you and the many projects encompassing the different aspects of the organization. Thank you all sincerely for being true professionals. Please, enjoy this evening and Merry Christmas."

He nods once when the women stand and applaud him again before he locks his eyes with mine and starts toward me.

"He's quite the charmer, isn't he?"

I purse my lips as he gives me a panty-dropping smile from a few feet away. "He is that."

"Now tell me, sweetie, are the two of you back together? He was moping around in Australia for months without you."

He reaches me then and takes my lips without saying a word to his mother or me.

"I suppose that answers my question, now doesn't it?"

My cheeks warm when he pulls away from me and rings his arm around my waist before he asks her, "What question?"

"I was just asking Hadley if the two of you were back together."

"Are we, Rye?" he says with a cocky grin on his handsome face.

"More than ever," I tell her honestly as my eyes are locked on his.

"Thank goodness. I was getting sick of not seeing the two of you together. The entire air seems to shift around each of you when you're around each other. Now, is this who you were going to bring over for Christmas?"

"Mother, I hadn't asked her yet." He turns to face me. "It's what I was going to ask you at Blended. Would you like to spend Christmas with us?"

"Wade, I'd love to."

Lillian hugs each of us before kissing Wade on the cheek. "You two have just made my night. I'll see you both in two days. If you'll excuse me, I'd like to ensure that my ladies are enjoying themselves this evening."

"Thank you, Lilly, have a good evening."

"Goodbye, Mother."

I turn back to Wade as a few other women approach us, but his attention is only on me as he searches my eyes. "What is it?"

"It's a bold move, you know, inviting me to join you for Christmas. It makes us . . ." I gesture between the two of us. " . . . rather serious."

"I don't need a holiday to know that. The time away from you only intensified what I feel toward you. I want you close, Rye. All of the time."

I step into his arms as the current buzzes between us, rendering me speechless. Instead of speaking the words that I'm thinking, I tell him when our lips meet. My unspoken words spill against his mouth, leaving me bereft.

"Come. We need to get to two more before I can have you to myself."

I sigh against his lips before he pulls away from me and greets the women who have been waiting off to the side to get a word in while he melted me into a puddle of nothing.

Two hours later, we're leaving the fourth and hopefully the last party of the evening. I'm exhausted after meeting so many people. I'm not sure how he does this. I've loved watching him interact with the people who work underneath him; he treats all of them with the same reverence that he receives. A yawn escapes me as we sit in the dark interior of his BMW.

"You're tired."

"I am," I say as I lean back on the headrest and turn to face him.

"I can take you back to your place if you'd like."

I shake my head. "No, I want to be with you tonight."

If there weren't a console between us, I would already be in his arms and in my safe place. I need to insist that Colin drive the SUV more often.

"It's a damn good thing that I don't mind a naked Hadley in my bed then."

I give him a tired smile as Jacobs pulls up to the Waldorf. "Take me to bed, Mr. Brass."

"It'd be my pleasure, Rye."

Colin opens my door but is quickly met with Wade taking my hand. "Thank you for accompanying us this evening, Jacobs. Head home for the remainder of the week."

"Thank you, sir. Merry Christmas to you both."

"To you as well."

I give Colin a brief hug and wish him a Merry Christmas before I'm pulled back into Wade's grasp and we're headed inside and out of Chicago's frigid winter.

"Good evening, Mr. Brass," rings out through the lobby before we are greeted by his personal doorman. "Mr. Brass," he nods his greeting before acknowledging me, "Miss Rye."

"Good evening, Thomas."

"Will you be expecting anyone else this evening, sir?"

"No. Go home for the night and alert the front desk that you are leaving."

The gentleman seems surprised by this but doesn't argue. "Thank you, sir. Have a good evening."

"You as well."

We step into the elevator, and he wraps his arms around me from behind as the doors close and we start to ascend. Once we've entered into his penthouse, I slip my aching feet from my heels and massage the bottom of my soles.

He's taken his jacket off and hung it in the hall closet before he joins me on the couch. His arm locks around me, and he moves a stray strand of hair that has escaped my updo out of my face. "We may both be beginners at this relationship game, but I'm going to show you just how much I long to have you by my side."

"I'm not going to go anywhere." I place my lips on his chest where the top buttons of his collar are undone.

His hands move into my hair, and he starts to remove each pin that is holding up my curls while he looks into my eyes until he has them all out. His fingers run through my hair, causing a soft moan to escape my lips as he does so.

"Let me get you to bed."

"Okay, but you have to help me out of this dress first."

"Come."

He leads me upstairs to the master bedroom and closes the door behind us. We're veiled in the darkness of the room with only ambient light reflected from the city below. I flinch slightly when I feel his hands move around my waist.

"I don't want to be with you to simply pass the time," he says against my ear.

"You're not. You've already used that time to find me, as well as yourself."

"I have never wanted more than sex in a relationship, but with you, it's different."

I turn in his arms and cup his jaw in my hands. I'm just able to make out the lines of his body from the city lights. "You know that I feel the same way."

"Then marry me."

I go still in the darkness as his thumb skims the bare skin of my back. "Wade—"

"You've helped me wage war on myself, and through it all, you've been the light. The one that I've been searching for without even knowing it. You, Hadley Rye, are the most precious thing to me, and if you do me this honor, I will ensure that I am everything you need. I will never go against what we are, and I will love you until I take my last breath. I've lived in a world without you, and the thought of going through that again tears my soul into pieces."

He places a kiss on my lips before sinking down onto one knee in front of me in the dark. An audible gasp escapes me as he reaches for my left hand, and if it weren't for the reflected light, I would not be able to see him holding up a ring.

"Rye, will you do me the honor of becoming my wife?"

"I . . . holy shit," the words that I want to say refuse to leave my mouth as I struggle with the emotions swimming through my body.

"Don't make me wait, baby. I know this is sudden, but—"

"Yes!" I squeal and lean down to throw myself at him, which causes us both to land on the floor laughing.

"Yes?" he asks as one of his arms pulls my body down onto his.

"Yes."

In just that one word. That one breath. I'm locked in.

His lips find mine as he pulls me even closer to him, closing the space between us. "I love you."

I bite his bottom lip and pull his shirt from his slacks until I'm able to run my fingers along a line that no longer exists on his waist. "I love you."

He reaches for my left hand and slowly slides the cool metal around my finger before placing his lips on it. As much as I want to see it in the light, I want him more. I need to be as close to him as I can possibly get.

"I need you," I tell him as he pushes the sleeve of my dress off of my shoulder and then farther down my arm.

"Then it's a good thing that you just promised me forever."

I blush as his words warm me from the inside out. I don't think that I have ever been so content in a moment before. This man has truly broken down each and every wall, shield, and piece of armor that I once used to guard my heart. Now, he's the one protecting it with his own life. He's shown me what it is to love and exactly how deep that love can run. My heart is more than a mere organ that's sole purpose is to pump life through my body. It now aches for him and only him.

He moves us to the bed while we're still surrounded by darkness as he makes love to me, showing instead of telling me exactly what he feels for me. I do the same in return as we take it slower than we did the night before. It feels different being with him as if I've found the perfect match for both my body and soul.

He's my person.

My favorite brand of whiskey.

Thirty

Wade

"I THOUGHT THAT you were tired, gorgeous."

"I was," she says as the sun starts to rise over Chicago. I glance down at her, and her eyes are focused on her left hand and the ring that I placed on it a few hours go.

Last night when Isla saw us together, she gave me the ring box that I'd asked her to return to the designer. She didn't say anything else, but she gave me a look of understanding and support. I've known since my accident that Hadley was it for me, but I wasn't sure if it would ever get much further until a couple of hours ago when she promised to spend the remainder of her life with me at her side.

I take her left hand and intertwine our fingers together. "What are you thinking about?"

"I was wondering just how long you've had this ring. I've never seen anything like it before."

"Good. She did a good job then."

"Who did?"

"The woman who designed the ring."

She shifts and tilts her head up to face me. "You had this made for me? When?"

"If I told you when I had it made, you might run for the hills."

I watch her maneuver herself until she's straddling my

waist, completely naked. "Tell me, please?"

I nod, tortured by her carnal supplication. "Two weeks after my accident."

"Two weeks? Wade . . . you've held onto this since then? How did you know . . . I mean, we were so new . . . I mean, we pretty much still are and of course there's the fact that everyone will only assume . . ."

I cut off her rambling by sitting up and moving my lips against hers. "I knew that there would not be a single woman who would be able to compare to you. I knew because of what I feel when I'm in your presence or not. I gave the ring to Isla to return, but the stubborn woman did no such thing. Before we left Blended this evening, she handed me the box. I should have known better than to trust her with the simplest of tasks."

The smile she gives me competes with the sunrise behind her. "You're sure about this? You didn't have much time to think it over if you just got it back."

"Stop speaking, Hadley."

She starts to argue but quickly closes her lips.

"I've known that you were meant to be with me since the accident and none of that changed during our time apart. If anything, it intensified my feelings toward you. Each day, I believe that I've finally figured out what love is, what it feels like and what it makes me feel when I'm around you. Yet, the next day, the love I feel for you grows again, and a new meaning of the word love comes to mind."

"Wade," she chokes out before burying her face in my chest.

I lie back against the pillows, pulling her body down with mine. I may be stronger after my accident, but I won't be able to hold the both of us up for extended periods of time as I used to be able to do.

"Shh."

She shifts off of my chest and lies on her side between my

arm and torso. Her head rests on my shoulder while she admires her engagement ring. I watch her carefully as her eyes begin to flutter shut.

I'm woken by the unremitting ringing of my phone. Hadley grumbles in my arms, and she sits up and reaches for it before placing it on my chest and then once again getting comfortable in her position.

I clear my throat and slide my finger across the screen without opening my eyes. "What is it?"

"That certainly is not the best way to greet your mother, Waylon."

"It is when I'm asleep."

She sighs. "I do not want nor need any further details. Now tell me, did you know that Liam was arriving today? He showed up on my doorstep twenty minutes ago. Anyway, I gave him your address, and he left a little while ago."

"Liam?" I try to clear my head of sleep as I register what she's telling me.

"Yes, Liam."

"I had no idea that he was flying in. I haven't spoken to him since Hadley left me."

"Well, it's about time the two of you worked your grievances out."

"Very well. I'll see you in the morning, Mother."

"Good. I think that you'll enjoy my gift this year."

I force my eyes to open and look down at Hadley's left hand on my chest, and grin. "I think that I have outdone you this year."

"We'll see about that. Enjoy your day and Christmas Eve."

"You too. Goodbye, Mother."

As if on cue, my phone starts to ring again, causing Hadley to moan. I chuckle as I answer and kiss her temple before getting out of bed and pulling the comforter over her.

"Yes?"

"Good afternoon, Mr. Brass," Thomas says. "I have a gentleman by the name of Liam Jensen here to see you."

"Let him up. Thank you." I set my phone down on my nightstand and walk into my closet to get dressed and then make my way downstairs just as there's a knock on the front door.

I pull it open and give the asshole a halfhearted smile. "To what do I owe this pleasure, Jensen?"

"I was in the neighborhood . . ."

"Good one. Come in."

"I hope that I'm not interrupting anything," he says as he glances at his watch, "it's not like you to be home at noon."

"It's Christmas Eve. Where else would I be?"

"In Vegas getting your dick sucked."

"Fuck off."

He chuckles as I toss him a beer. "On a serious note, I wanted to apologize about messing shit up with that girl you brought to my place. Isla said that you were pretty serious about her."

I don't answer him. Instead, I decide to let him grovel.

"Fuck, she knew how to get me hard by just being. I'm glad that one of us got some of her before she disappeared from existence."

I raise my eyebrow as he describes his lust for my fiancée. I start to walk out of the kitchen area and into the living room where we're less likely to wake Hadley up if he downs a few more beers. An hour of useless conversation passes, and I haven't mentioned her to him. I'd rather not stir up the tension that is already between us, one that has never been there before.

"All right, dude, I gotta take a leak." He gets up and stretches before walking out of the living room and to the bathroom.

"I'll call for lunch."

"Pizza. I could do with a good Chicago deep." There's a pause before he continues. "Holy fuck," I hear him say under his breath. I can still see him, and he's stalled in front of the side kitchen entrance instead of walking farther down the hallway to the bathroom.

"What is it?" I ask as I rise and walk over to him.

My eyes widen when I see what he's gazing at: an incredibly naked Hadley bent over the kitchen island as she fills a glass with orange juice, her pristine ass and piercings giving him a show.

"Whiskey?" she calls out.

I stride into the kitchen and wrap my arms around her from behind. She lets out a sigh and leans her head back against my chest as she stares out the windows.

"Rye, I've got company."

"What?" she murmurs and tries to turn around in my hold, but I don't allow her to.

"As much as I'm enjoying seeing you naked in my kitchen right now, I'd prefer it if Liam didn't get to see my fiancée like this."

Her hand covers her mouth as her other arm goes to cover her bare breasts. "I'm sorry," she whispers.

"I've got you," I tell her before calling out over my shoulder, "get the fuck out of the kitchen, Liam." I throw a glance at him to watch him retreat before I let go of her and turn her around to face me. The only thing that she has on is her engagement ring, and fuck, I want to keep it that way.

"Don't apologize. I'd appreciate if you did this again when I am able to do something about it," I tell her as I cup her bare ass cheeks.

She leans forward and bites on my lower lip. "I make no promises."

"Oh baby, you will when you say *I do*."

She blushes and kisses my jaw before stepping out of my hold to go upstairs, but I don't trust that Liam is out of sight. I grab hold of her wrist before removing my shirt and handing it to her.

"Put this on and stay."

"What?"

"I want you in my shirt—only my shirt—while we entertain our guest."

"Our guest?"

I help her into my shirt and lean in to nip at the base of her neck. "Yes. You may as well move in if you plan on spending the remainder of your life with me."

Her eyes light up at my suggestion, and she nods in agreement with a genuine smile, and the warm glow surrounding her seems to intensify.

"Come."

She allows me to take her hand and lead her out to the living room where Liam is seated on the edge of one of the couches with his hands steepled in front of his lips. He looks up when he hears us and stands. "Listen," he says and blows out a breath, "I had no idea that you were still with her."

"Hi, Liam," Hadley greets him and gives him a small smile.

His eyes remain locked on mine in a silent apology until he speaks. "It's good to see you again, Hadley. I should get going."

"To where?" I ask because I know that he doesn't speak to his family anymore.

"I don't know, dude. I'll get a room here, and I'll call Isla."

"You should stay here, Liam. Wade has a guest room, and you've flown so far."

His eyes shoot up to mine. "I think that's a good idea," I tell them as I lead Hadley to the couch. I take a seat, and as she's about to sit down I pull her onto my lap, and she gives me one hell of a smile. She's stunning when she wakes up, a beautiful mess.

"Are you sure?" he asks as he takes a seat again.

"Yes."

Hadley readjusts herself so her legs and feet are resting on the seat beside me and she wraps her arms around my neck. "Wade didn't tell me that you were coming back to the States."

He takes a long drink of his beer, surely thinking about what he said with regard to her earlier. "I'm referring to it as a Christmas gift from myself to him."

She laughs and kisses my jaw. "You two are ridiculous."

"Possibly. I'm glad to see that you guys are back together."

"Are you now?" I ask, my voice spilling over with cynicism.

He clears his throat and sets his beer down. "I am, and I apologize for my earlier comment."

Hadley scowls as she shifts on my lap, rubbing her ass against my cock. This woman is going to unman me in the most humiliating way. She runs her hand through my hair and rests her head on my shoulder.

"Apology accepted."

He nods once before he speaks. "I'll call Lou Malnati's and get a pie. Do you want anything in particular?"

"Get what you want. It's been years since you've had a slice of heaven. What about you, Rye?"

"I'm good with anything. I'll just go shower really quick, though."

"I'll be joining you," I tell her as she gets up and off of my lap, her long legs calling my attention. "Go get started. I'll be right up."

I watch her as she heads upstairs. I'm drawn to her at all times. If I had to choose between walking again or having her in my life, it'd be her. Each and every time.

"I don't mean to pry, Brass, but was that a ring I saw on her finger?" Liam's voice interrupts my thoughts once she's out of sight.

I run my hand down my shirtless torso and stand up. I stretch one and then the other arm before shaking them out. "It was . . . it is."

"Fuck. It's really serious then. Congratulations, man."

"More than I'm able to explain, and thank you. Now, call in our lunch and make yourself at home. Thomas, my doorman, will pick it up if you call down to him."

"Great. Thank you."

"You're welcome," I say back to him as I take the stairs two at a time, knowing that I'll be feeling it later, but I cannot get to her fast enough.

When I walk into the bedroom, I lock the door behind me and step out of my sweatpants before stepping into the bathroom. She has music playing on her phone while she washes her blonde locks. I step in behind her and move my fingers into her hair. She turns around and sighs as I start to massage her scalp.

"That feels good," she says softly as she closes her eyes; when she opens them again, I'm rinsing her hair out under the spray.

"How'd you sleep?"

"Really well, until you left, I think. I missed you—even in my sleep."

"I'm glad the craving goes both ways, Rye."

She leans up on her tiptoes to kiss me as I step under the water with her. "Are you going to tell your mother today?"

"I think that we both should. We can tell her tomorrow morning."

"I still can't believe that this is happening, Wade. Surely people will think that it's all too soon."

"I don't give a fuck what anyone else thinks, but you. You are the only woman who I want to spend every second with, and you are the one that is going to be with me, no one else."

"You're my favorite person, you know? You are kind of my person, Wade."

"Kind of?"

A smile splits across her lips. "You are."

"Always, baby."

By the time Hads and I make it back downstairs after I've fucked her senseless, Liam is passed out on the couch with a beer in hand. "Should we wake him?" she asks.

"No. He's more than likely had a long day," I tell her as I take a bite of a slice of Chicago's best pie.

She takes a seat at the kitchen counter and starts to eat as well.

"Oh, did you have any plans for Christmas Eve?"

"I did . . . I do."

"Well?" she asks as she gets up to grab us each a bottle of water.

"I plan on spending it with my fiancée."

When she sits back down, she rests her head on my shoulder and holds up her left hand. "I like that idea."

"I could invite Isla over to help us deal with our guest."

"If you'd like. Does she know?"

"Know what?" She turns her head and bites down on my shoulder. "Ah, fuck, baby. I can do kink if you'd like, but I need to regain my energy first."

She giggles and looks up at me. "We'll discuss that later, Whiskey. Does she know that you proposed last night?"

"No. The only person who knows is asleep on the couch. He saw your ring and he asked me about it."

"I didn't think that he'd be so observant."

"With you, Rye, anyone would be."

She raises her brows at me but remains quiet. She understands the hold that she is able to put on most men because she's used it multiple times in the past.

"Do we need to stop by your apartment for anything before tomorrow?"

"Oh, yes," she says before she takes a drink of water. "I need to grab an outfit or two."

"Or I could send men over to grab everything of yours."

She pauses for a moment to think and finish chewing on the bite she took. "Are you sure?"

I tug her into my arms and kiss her cheekbones. "What did I tell you earlier?"

"I know, it's just . . . it's a lot. I mean . . . not my stuff, but us. I don't want to ruin it all."

"You would not be able to even if you tried. I'm sure that Lola will understand."

She gasps and her eyes go wide. "Oh my God, Lo. How do I tell her? No, I need to go over there before we start moving my things."

"We'll go once you're done eating."

"I'm done," she says, and she stands up suddenly. "I don't think that I can stomach another bite until I tell her that I'm moving in with you. That I'm moving in with my fiancé," she says excitedly before murmuring, "Holy shit," underneath her breath.

"Come. I'll drive us over."

"Shouldn't we tell Liam?"

"No."

I take her hand and grab my keys on the way out to the foyer, stopping by the hallway closet to grab our jackets before we ride down the elevator to the lobby where I have my car brought up by the valet.

The drive is short, but I can tell that she's anxious. I park in the lot before running around the car, opening the door for her, and taking her hand.

"It's icy. Don't slip in those heels." She's wearing my shirt, my sweat pants, my jacket, and her heels, and if we weren't so fucking cold outside, I'd fuck her right here on the hood of my vehicle.

She holds onto my arms with a death grip as we walk to the entrance of her building and once we're inside, she doesn't let go.

"You're nervous."

She purses her lips as we ride up the elevator but remains quiet until we get to her door. She pauses as she's about to unlock it and turns to me. "This is happening."

"It is."

"It feels surreal. I never thought that I would be, well, that'd I'd be hopelessly in love."

I chuckle and lean down to place a chaste kiss on her lips before she unlocks the door, and we walk in together.

"Hads? Is that you?" Lola walks around the corner and smiles brightly when she sees the two of us.

"Hi, Lo."

"I didn't think that you would be coming back tonight. I'm having some people over for Christmas Eve dinner. Would you two like to join us?"

Hadley looks up at me, perplexed about what to do.

"We'd like that." I say.

"Great. Holden and Owen are in the living room with a few other women from my boutique. Dinner will be ready in about an hour. Can I grab you a whiskey, Wade?"

"Open the Macallan that I bought last week, Lo, and I'm going to get changed. Would you mind pouring me some as well, please?"

"Sure thing."

"Thank you."

I take in Hadley's stance. She's shrinking into me with her hands stuffed into the pockets of my coat. I squeeze her hip through the fabric and lead her to her bedroom, closing the door behind us.

"Rye."

"Yes?" she answers as she strips out of my clothing and folds each piece before placing it on her bed. My eyes are trained on her piercings as she crosses the bedroom to her closet.

"You don't have to tell them if you're not ready."

"What? Why wouldn't I tell them?" She turns to look back at me as I take a seat on the bench at the end of her bed. "Wade?"

"I understand if you think this is all happening too soon."

She kicks off her heels and walks back over to me, completely naked. "Whiskey, it's not too soon. Like you said, no one else matters, and I know that this is right. It's good for us."

My hands move to her waist as she leans down to place her lips against mine. "All right."

"Quit it. I love you, Waylon. Nothing that anyone says is going to change that."

I feel the corners of my lips arch upward. "Good to hear it. Now, get dressed before we make others fall asleep before I'm done with you."

"Oh," she purses her lips and wiggles her hips in front of me. "I could go all day with you."

"I'll be able to soon. I'll need to up my hours of rehabilitation once the holidays are over."

"You're senseless."

"Possibly."

She steps out of my hold and starts to get dressed across the room from me. "You should call Liam and tell him to come over. We wouldn't want to leave him at *our* place alone on Christmas Eve."

"No, we wouldn't." I take my phone out of my pocket and dial his number while my eyes never leave her.

"Brass," his voice comes over the phone.

"Liam, listen. Hadley and I are at her place, and we'll be having dinner here with a few of her friends. You've been invited to join us."

"Fuck. I hadn't even realized that you guys left. Yeah, I'll be over; just send me her address. You assholes didn't even wake me."

After picking out and putting on her gray underwear, she sits down next to me and pulls a pair of gray thigh-high socks up and over her knees. I watch her fingers move up along her pale legs, transfixed on the movement.

"I assumed that you'd need your sleep after the flight."

"Yeah, you're right. I'll be over in a few."

"Good. Just let yourself in when you get here, and we'll let the doorman know to expect you as well."

"Sounds good."

I hang up with him as she stands up and runs her fingers along my jaw before returning to her closet where she picks out an oversized black sweater and pulls it over her head. The sweater covers her entirely; it's more of a dress on her, but I don't like knowing that other men will be seeing her like this. "Okay, are you ready for this?"

"That's all that you're wearing?"

I watch her frown and look down at her outfit. "You don't like it?"

"I do, which makes me confident that other men will enjoy it as well."

"Whiskey . . ."

"Allow me to be jealous of other men lusting after my fiancée, Hadley."

She frowns at me before a small laugh escapes her and she's standing in front of me. "All right. So I won't change. I kind of like it when you get all assertive and possessive."

I take her hand and place it on the length of my cock under my jeans. "I'll be buried inside of you before the night's end, and I'll show you exactly how assertive I can be."

"I'll be looking forward to it."

I smack her ass once before standing and then grunt when a surge of pain runs up my body from my lower spine. "Fuck. We might have to put that off for a day or two."

"Are you okay?" Worry crosses her face as she reaches for me.

"I'm okay. I'll just need Liam to bring over my medications. I may have overdone it in the shower when I lifted you up."

She smacks my chest before moving against my body and holding onto me. "I told you not to do that."

"I think that we both enjoyed it too much for me to stop."

"Maybe, but not if it will cause you to be in pain."

"Agreed." I take my phone out of my pocket and send Hadley's address to Liam, as well as instructions on what medication to bring over for me.

She places a kiss on the underside of my chin before lacing her fingers with mine and dragging me to her bedroom door. We walk out into the living room together where more people than I expected are gathered.

"Lo likes to throw parties, just so you know."

"I can tell."

"There you guys are. Your drinks are in the kitchen," Lo says from across the room.

"Thank you. I have a guest staying over for the holidays; I hope that you don't mind that I invited him this evening."

"Not at all. The more people, the better."

I nod as Hadley comes back to me with two tumblers in her hand. "It's just a 10-year, but I enjoy it."

"It's great, baby, thank you," I tell her and Lola squeals besides us.

"God, I love you two together," she gushes as she is joined by the man who shared the elevator with Hadley and me last night.

I offer him my hand, and he takes it with a nod. "Waylon

Brass."

"So I've heard. Owen Parker." We shake and he smiles down at Rye. "It's good to see you constantly smiling, Hadley."

She blushes and rests her head against my bicep. "I blame him."

"I see."

"Okay, assholes, quit playing nice, and let's have some fun, okay?" Lola says as she walks into the midst of the people gathered in her living room.

"I'll introduce you around if you'd like," Owen offers, but Hadley shakes her head.

"I don't think I trust the ratio of two good-looking men in a room filled with women. I'm not letting this one out of my sight."

"As you wish," he says as he turns, but he stops when Hadley starts to twirl one of her curls around her finger. "That's new. Is Lola aware?"

"What?" she asks.

"Your ring. I'm assuming by the size and location that it means more than just a piece of jewelry."

She looks up at me and beams. "It's much more than just a ring, Owen." She says the words proudly, and it makes me want to ravage her this minute.

He nods without saying another word and walks off. I run a finger down her neck and smile at her. "That makes two people who know," I tell her.

She takes a drink and leads me into the group of guests. She's glowing as she introduces herself and me to those surrounding us.

"As in *the* Waylon Brass?" a woman asks me.

"The only one," Hads answers.

"It's so nice to meet you. I just started working for Mothers of Brass last week, and I was unable to go to the Christmas party last night."

"Welcome. I trust that you are enjoying it thus far."

"Immensely," she says as she looks down at my left hand and then over to Hadley.

I watch as Hadley splays her left hand over my chest, staking her claim on me, not that it's needed. I ring an arm around her and place my lips at the top of her head.

"It was nice meeting you," the woman says before she walks off.

"I have to say that I'm rather enjoying this possessive side of you, Rye."

"I'm sure that you do, so don't complain."

"I won't, but I need to sit down right now," I tell her as the same pain as before runs its way up my spine.

She takes my hand and leads me to a single chair. I take a seat, feeling ten times my age as she perches on the armrest beside me. "We can go back if you need to sleep, Whiskey."

"No. Let me sit here for a while."

Apprehension crosses her features again while she takes inventory of my body. "I love you."

"As I you." I get up as Lola approaches us.

"Is it true?"

"What?" Hadley asks as she looks up at her oldest friend.

"Owen just told me that you . . ." She gasps when she reaches for Rye's left hand. "Holy fucking shit."

I watch as Hadley lights up from the inside. "I was going to tell you . . ."

"Shut up and let me see it! Are you serious? You're engaged?"

"I'm serious. We're serious."

Lola throws her arms around Hadley, and they hug for a moment before Lola hugs me in turn. I don't necessarily approve of her touching me, but I won't make her uncomfortable. She grabs Hadley's hand to get a closer look at the ring I placed on her finger last night.

"It's beautiful."

"I know. I love it so much."

I watch the two of them go back and forth for a while until Lola retreats from us to announce that dinner will be served buffet style, and it's now that Liam walks into the room.

"I'm looking for Waylon Brass," I hear him say to Lola, and she gestures toward Hadley and me.

He walks the length of the room until he's standing in front of us. "'Evening."

He's tanked.

"Hi, Liam, did you sleep enough earlier?"

He raises his eyebrows and smirks. "Barely, but I'll manage."

"It seems like you've had one or two too many beers," I say as I pull my fiancée down onto my lap.

"Probably five more than what's good for me."

"I can smell it on you."

Hadley places her hand on my chest; I'm sure that she can sense my unease. After the last time he ran her off, I don't trust him around her while he's drunk.

"Should I strip then?" he slurs and starts to undo the button on his jeans.

"Liam," Hadley complains, and he stops his hands before doing up the button again.

"If the lady doesn't want to see what I'm packing, then I'll keep it wrapped . . . for now."

"I'll fucking kill you," I tell him under my breath.

Hadley turns to face me and cups my jaw in her hands. "Whiskey," she says as she presses her lips to mine, pushing her tongue past my lips and into my mouth. She drapes her hands over my shoulder and then moves them until they are locked around my neck. She deepens the kiss and grinds her ass into my cock.

"Jesus, you two, it's like watching a porno," a female voice says, and I break away from her for a second to see who spoke—Lola, and standing next to her is Holden.

"You have a room, Hadley. Use it," Holden says, and she turns to look at him.

"What is your problem?"

He goes to speak but stops himself when she brushes a few strands of curls out of her face.

"You're going to fucking marry this douche?"

"Holden," Lola says and tugs on his arm.

Hadley's gaze finds mine and instead of the glow I saw in her before we left, there's despondency behind her eyes. "Wade?" she says softly, "I'd like to go."

"Hads, don't be like that," Lola says.

"No, Lo. It's Christmas Eve, and I've just made the single most important decision in my life last night. I don't need any of it to be spoiled because people are unable to keep their mouths shut."

"I'm sorry, Hads. I know how happy you are."

I watch Holden walk away, and Hadley stands up from my lap. "I shouldn't need to explain myself to people who I thought were my friends."

"Baby," I get up and pull her into my arms, feeling her heart beat faster.

"Wade, please, take me back home."

"Hadley, you are home," Lola says.

"I won't do this tonight."

I take her hand and lead her to her bedroom, away from the stares. She takes a seat on her bed and puts her head in her hands while I go to her closet and pull out a large bag to transport some of her clothes in.

I pull some sweaters, jeans, and pairs of underwear out of her closet and set the bag next to her on the bed before kneeling down in front of her and placing my hands on her knees.

"Is there anything else that you'd like me to pack for you, Rye?"

She shakes her head in answer and lowers her hands from her face, revealing the tears that she was hiding.

"God, Rye. Come here."

I get up and take her into my arms, maneuvering her onto my lap where I am able to hold her against my chest. "Talk to me."

"It's nothing."

"It's much more than nothing, Hadley."

"I just . . . I thought that they'd be happy for me."

"Listen to me," I tell her and run my thumb over her lip. "Lola is delighted. Holden is less than delighted due to the fact that you're officially mine and he's jealous. I would have reacted the exact same way that he did if you decided to be with him."

"But—"

"I understand that it's difficult, but it must be for him as well, seeing as he seems to be hung up on you."

"I don't love him."

"I never said that you did. Just that I understand why he reacted the way that he did. Now. If you'd like to leave, then we'll go, but it's Christmas Eve, and I'm sure they would like to spend it with you."

She sighs and leans her head against my shoulder. "I'm sorry. I overreacted. I'm just . . . you mess with my emotions."

"Don't complain."

"I'm not, Whiskey."

After she's settled down and taken a few deep breaths, she lifts her head and gazes up at me before she locks her lips with mine. "Take me home?"

She keeps calling my place home, and it does something to me—it stirs my insides and makes me want to protect her even more. As if an animal instinct kicks in, and takes over me, I need to keep her safe and blissful.

"Come."

She gets off of my lap and walks into the bathroom. I follow her in with her bag and hold it open for her as she places multiple objects and bags inside before she turns to the mirror. I watch her wash her face with a warm washcloth before she sets it aside and lets out a breath.

"Okay, I'm ready to leave."

I hold out my hand to her, and she takes it before I lead her out of her bedroom and to the foyer where we're met by Liam and Lola.

Thirty-One

Hadley

THEY BOTH STEP forward as we approach.

"Are we leaving?" Liam asks as Lola steps forward to hug me.

"Don't go. Had-Lo needs to celebrate Christmas and your engagement."

I give her a halfhearted smile and hold her at arm's length. "Fine, but I'm not going to deal with Hold being a dick toward me."

"Owen is speaking to him right now, and I'm sure pouring some amount of craft beer down his throat."

I laugh and throw my arms around her again. "There's something else that I need to tell you."

"Well? Spit it out. Are you already married?"

I shake my head at her. "No, I wouldn't get married without you by my side."

"All right, so what is it?"

"I'm moving in with him."

Liam and Wade both walk out of the foyer, leaving Lo and me alone.

"You know," she says, "I'm not even surprised. Not by any of it. I've never seen you like this before, and I've known you for more than half of my life. He's good for you, Hads, and I think that you're making the right decision. Being engaged kind of sets a lot of things in motion and moving in with him is one of them.

You have my support for both, and you need to know that."

Lola Marc isn't normally the person to give out little speeches like the one she just did, and in doing so, I know that she's being truthful. Regardless of my past and my obvious bent for self-destruction, she has always been my constant . . . for other than sex, that is.

"Thank you."

"Can we drink now because we need to celebrate?"

"I think we need to break out more than just the whiskey," I tell her as she leads me into the living room where people are mingling and eating, and my handsome-as-fuck fiancé is leaning his shoulder against the wooden frame of the patio door. He straightens himself when he sees me and gives me that special grin that I've noticed he reserves only for me.

I'm drawn to him, my craving, so I squeeze Lola once more before walking across the room to get to him.

"Is everything tolerable?"

"For now," I tell him and place my hands against his chest to kiss him. When we pull back from the briefest of kisses, he gives me his tumbler of whiskey and leans against the frame again. "Are you in pain?"

"I've taken my medication that Liam brought, so I won't be drinking for the rest of the evening. Why don't you enjoy yourself?"

"Enjoy myself?"

"Have a drink or two. However, I want you to eat first."

I purse my lips and lean up to place a kiss at his jaw. "I love you."

"As I love you."

Liam clears his throat, which draws our attention to him. "I'm fucking starving. Can we eat?"

Wade shakes his head, and the three of us walk to the buffet set up in the kitchen, which is now filled with people. The same group of women who were running their mouths about me at Lola's birthday party have their eyes locked on Wade and me. I roll my eyes at the thought of them as we move forward in the buffet line.

"Wade?"

"Yes?" He says as he squeezes my hip.

"Go grab us a place to sit down and I'll bring our dinner over. I don't think that you should be standing for much longer."

"I'm fine."

I turn toward him as Liam grabs us some plates. "Please?"

"Rye, don't push it. I said that I'm all right."

"I'd prefer to have my groom standing at the end of the aisle when I walk toward him," I tell him truthfully and run my hands down his chest.

He seems to think it over for a moment before he nods and walks out of the kitchen.

"You're good for the fucker, you know that?" Liam says as he hands me two plates.

"He's good for me, too."

"I can tell," he says as he helps me plate some of the food. "He seems to be content when he's around you instead of the asshole that I know he can be."

"He's far from it, Liam."

"I don't think that you realize just how much of an impact you have on him. He would keep to himself, and when he didn't, he could be brutal toward those who work underneath him."

"How do you know this?" I ask as I pick up some silverware.

"I've been seeing Adriana off and on ever since he hired her."

"You have? But you live in Australia."

"Nothing gets past you, does it?"

We walk out of the kitchen and toward the dining room. "Oh, hush." Liam might be a jerk, but I believe that he's got a soft spot inside of him somewhere.

"She flies back and forth as do I when we're able to get away from work, but we keep that to ourselves."

"Well, does she know that you're here?"

"Not yet. I was planning on surprising her tomorrow morning."

"I'm sure that she'll love to see you. I've only met her once or twice, but I really liked her."

We find Wade, and I take a seat beside him. "Rye."

"Hi, Whiskey, did you miss me?"

"More than you know."

He places his hand on my knee and squeezes once before we each start to eat. I turn to him. "We should invite Adriana to join us for Christmas tomorrow."

"Adriana?"

"Mmm-hmm, since Liam here has quite the romance going on with her."

I watch his eyebrows raise, and I realize that he didn't know. Liam's gaze moves from mine to Wade's as if he's waiting for a reaction.

"You're with Adriana?"

They exchange a few looks back and forth between them before Liam answers him. "On occasion."

Wade stays quiet instead of responding to Liam's truth. Both of them seem to grow tense until Lola joins us. "Hi, fuckers."

"Jesus, this one has a mouth on her as well," Liam says, and it seems to break the tension for now. These two men are going to make me go gray. Wade smiles and intertwines his fingers with mine.

"I'm sure you enjoy it, Liam," Lola says confidently.

"Possibly, but you might get more joy out of it than you care to admit." Liam responds.

I'm taken by surprise that Lo is flirting with Liam while Owen is in the other room. I down the remainder of Wade's whiskey. He glances at me before getting up and disappearing without a word. I turn my attention back to Liam and Lola as they start to laugh at something said between them.

The three of us get lost in conversation, and when Owen and a few others join us, we're joking about something Liam did on his last trip to Fiji. This man has been to places that I only wish I had the guts to travel to.

I look around the room, now filled with people, most of whom I remember from Lola's birthday party, but I cannot find the one person I'm looking for. I stand from my seat, feeling the tequila that Lola has fed me as it runs through my veins.

I make my way out of the room, but he's not in the living room or in the kitchen. I try the patio doors, but they're locked. I purse my lips as I walk from one side of the apartment to the other, looking for him.

"Whiskey?"

I open my bedroom door and step inside, shutting it behind me when I flip on the light switch. He's sprawled out on my bed, on top of the covers with his eyes closed and his breathing is shallow. I turn off the blinding light before it wakes him.

I walk up to him and kick off my shoes before I climb onto the bed next to him. He's so still, even when I move to his side and curl up against him. It's only when I move his arm around my waist that he stirs.

"Hadley."

"Hi, Whiskey."

His eyes close again, and I hear him swallow before his fingers grip onto the top of my thigh. "I'm sorry," he says in a raspy voice.

"No, don't apologize. What's wrong? Are you in pain?"

"Quite a bit," he says as he pulls my black sweater up until he's able to caress the bare skin underneath the lining of my panties.

"I should call your doctor."

He moves his head on the pillow to face me and closes his eyes. "No. I'll tell you if I need you to, though."

"All right. Go back to sleep. I shouldn't have woken you up."

"If you want to leave, just let me know, and don't let me keep you from enjoying your evening."

"Waylon Brass, there is no one else that I would rather be with than you."

"Very well."

His body relaxes into the mattress, but I decide to get up and pull off his Oxfords before going to my closet and grabbing my cream-colored chunky-knit blanket. I join him on the bed again and pull the comfortable material over us before settling in at his side.

I'm woken up by a repetitive thump on the door. I stir in his arms and push myself up, checking on Wade, but he's still fast asleep. I throw the blanket off of myself and get up, trying to wake myself up as I crack open my bedroom door. "Yes?"

"I'm going to head out and back to Brass's place. Are you both staying here tonight?" Liam asks.

I glance back over my shoulder at Wade before turning back and nodding my head. "I think so. He's in a bit of pain, and I don't want to wake him up."

"I'll write my number down and leave it in the kitchen for you if you need me or anything from Brass's place."

"Thank you, Liam. We'll be back in the morning."

He nods and steps away. I close the door and lock it before walking lightly back to the bed and climbing in, returning to my favorite place.

The next time I wake, there's light spilling into the bedroom through the open curtains. I turn my head to look at my fiancé who is staring up at the ceiling.

"'Morning," I mumble.

"Good morning, gorgeous." I feel a warm blush sweep across my features as he shifts his body over mine. "Merry Christmas," he adds.

"Merry Christmas, Waylon Brass."

He chuckles to himself and kisses down the column of my neck.

"What's so funny?"

"Mmm. I just thought that you'll be Mrs. Waylon Brass someday soon."

An unintentional squeal leaves my lips as he starts to dig his fingers into my sides. The fancy-ass is tickling me again. *Holy shit!* I try to nudge him off of me, but he doesn't move an inch. "Wade, s-stop."

"Not until you give me a date."

"What?" I cry out as I writhe underneath him.

"Give me the date that we'll be married."

"I-I don't mind. I just want you."

His fingers are relentless as he continues to torture me. "I need a date. Now."

"Fine," I squeal, "Ju-June twenty-third."

"No. Sooner," he says bluntly as he continues his assault.

"Sooner? Like what? January?" I snap, derision dripping from my lips.

"Perfect," he says as he stops and leans down to take my mouth.

"I was joking, Wade. That's next month."

He pushes up my sweater until he's revealed my lace-covered breasts. "I don't see the need to wait."

"What will your mother say?" I ask him as I tug on his shirt to get it off of his muscular torso.

"I'm sure she'd enjoy having her hand in arranging things."

My mind goes over how and when I'd like to be married, but I cannot think of anything. I've never been one to dream about a wedding as a young girl. The only reason I agreed when Lawson asked was because of the safety that he would provide me within my job at the resort.

"Where would we get married?"

"Anywhere in the world, anywhere that your heart desires," he says as he takes my nipple between his lips before tugging on it with his teeth. I'm assuming that he's feeling like himself again.

"Ahh," I cry out as I run my fingers through his hair. "Whiskey."

"Once I've had my way with you here, we'll go back to the penthouse and get ready before heading over to my mother's."

"Please."

He obliges me. Multiple times. I think he rather enjoys the pitch of my screams when he makes me orgasm in succession. And in the quiet moments, our souls unite and the softness of the seconds seems to be intoxicating as we climax together for an extended moment. We've become one, and we're complete-ly drunk on each other. Being able to touch him and have him touch me mends all of my wounds, both visible and not. If I fully immerse myself in him, then I often forget the troubles I've lived through as well as the past aches in my heart.

It's just after noon when we arrive at Lillian's home. She lives in the same building that hosts Mothers of Brass, in the penthouse. It's decorated all in white, with a large Christmas tree in the liv-ing room. The fire next to the tree is lit, and stockings are hang-ing across the mantel. It's not overdone or ostentatious, but it's elegant, and I can tell that it's her space.

"Merry Christmas, you four," she says as she rounds the cor-ner and steps into the living room where Adriana and Liam are standing next to us. She takes her time in greeting each one of us individually before we're ushered into the kitchen with her.

"Ladies, did you want some tea or hot chocolate?"

"They both drink whiskey, Mother."

"I know that much, Waylon. It's Christmas, and having some variety would not necessarily be a bad thing."

He chuckles and comes to stand beside me. "Fair enough. Hadley and I have some news for you if you'd like one of your gifts now."

"Right now? It cannot wait until we open the rest of them?" She walks around the island and starts to work on something.

"Now would be best," he says as he pulls me into his side.

I watch her expression change, and her head pops up from the pie crust that she's been rolling out. "You're pregnant?" she says with so much excitement in her voice that I almost wish that I were.

"No, Mother."

"Well then? Spit it out . . . either of you."

Wade glances down at me and nods as if he's telling me that he wants me to be the one to tell her. I purse my lips at his notion before I decide on what to say or do. I glance up at Lillian and hold my left hand up, showcasing my engagement ring to her.

"You're engaged?" She cries out and drops the rolling pin before leaning across the island and reaching for my hand. "Waylon! Oh goodness, this is . . . I . . . you're getting married?"

"We are," he tells her, pride laced in both of those words.

She lets go of my hand before running around the island and throwing one arm over each of us in a hug. "Congratulations, you two."

"Thank you, Mother," he says as he hugs her in return. Elation pours through me as she pulls back and grabs my hand to look at the ring, inspecting it closely this time.

"It's stunning. Someone grab the champagne that I have

chilling in the fridge. This is definitely cause to celebrate and get lost in the bottle."

She turns from me and rushes to a cabinet in the kitchen, pulling out five champagne flutes.

"Congratulations, Mr. Brass," Adriana says as Liam grabs the bottle of champagne and pops it open.

"Thank you, Adriana. Call me Waylon this evening, please."

She nods slightly before she takes my left hand to get a better look at my ring. I can only assume that I'm glowing with pride and love, all because of Waylon fancy-ass Brass. I'm high on him. High on our relationship. I squeeze my thighs together at the sudden need for him that shoots through me. I swear I can feel my clit pulse under the lace of my panties.

He seems to notice the slight movement of my body because his hand slowly slides down from the small of my back, over my ass cheeks, to the back of my thigh. He pinches me there, and I flinch before he places his hand over my piercings again and runs his finger around them.

"Here we go," Lillian says as she hands us each a flute filled with deliciously golden sparkling liquid. "Cheers to my son and my soon-to-be daughter-in-law."

"Cheers," we all chime in and clink glasses together before taking a drink. Wade sets his down and kisses my neck before letting go of me. He grabs a tumbler out of the cabinet before filling it with one of the bottles he brought with us, a Yamazaki 35. I know that it's a rare single malt, and once I've had my champagne, I'll more than likely steal a sip of his.

Lilly pulls me into the living room, and Adriana follows us. The three of us sit down, surrounded by the quiet hum of Christmas music. I stretch my toes closer to the fire to warm up some more as the conversations start to flow.

"Now, Addy," Lillian says, "I do not recall your telling me that you were dating Liam Jensen."

A blush kisses her cheeks as she takes a sip from her flute. "I wouldn't call it dating, Lilly. It's been going on for years; I just never thought it was anything serious. He's a player, even at his own game, and he'll never settle down, but I cannot deny that I enjoy being with him. I've been able to see him for who he is through all of his bachelor and drunken ways."

"Waylon was telling me that he's been drinking more than usual. The poor man. After losing his bride . . ." She stops speaking and takes a sip. "We'll talk about that another time. We have a new bride on our hands."

"Please, don't let me interrupt," I interject.

"You're not, sweetheart. It's simply a sensitive subject. Eight years' worth of his searching for the woman he lost and finally coming to the conclusion that she's not coming back must be hard to deal with. Addy, you're good for that man. Don't let him push you away."

I watch her nod and take a drink. "Would you mind my asking what happened? I had no idea that he was married."

"Oh no, dear. He never got married. It was a few days before his wedding that she disappeared in the south of Mexico to human trafficking. The poor thing, she was away with two other friends to celebrate her bachelorette party. They found her body six months ago."

I gasp before downing the remainder of my champagne. Holy shit. "I'm sorry, I had no idea."

Adriana shifts on the couch and crosses her leg over the other. "I think it's why he's been refusing the connection between us, or even more, refusing to admit that he has stronger feelings for me than just physical ones."

"I'm sure that he will snap out of it, Adriana. I can't even imagine what he must have gone through." My heart aches for her and Liam. I didn't know that I was capable of feeling so deeply for others' loss, but this organ of mine has a mind of its own these days.

"Please, call me Addy. Only my boss and mother call me Adriana."

I laugh, and I'm about to take a drink when I realize that my flute is empty. I stand and straighten out my black high-waisted pants, making sure that my black sequin blouse is still tucked in.

"You know," she says softly, "Waylon helped him a lot in his search for her. He may be daunting and all too intimidating on the outside, but he's truly a good man."

I can't help the smile on my face as I walk around the couch. "It's why I'm getting married to him."

I watch her smile change as if she's been caught just as his arm comes around my waist from behind, taking the empty flute from my hand and replacing it with a new one. I'm sure it's the one that he refuses to drink.

"Thank you, handsome."

"You're welcome, gorgeous."

I turn in his arm and kiss him with reserve before Lillian applauds and pulls me from his spell. "I won't ever tire of seeing the two of you together. I need to finish up the pie, and I'll be back. Please, everyone, make yourselves at home."

I take a seat again while Wade returns my empty flute to the kitchen and then goes to answer the door when there's a knock.

I hear Isla wish him a Merry Christmas before they both walk into the living room, and she hugs Liam and then me before sitting down next to me. "I'm sorry that I'm late, but finding a taxi on Christmas Day is virtually impossible."

"You could have driven, Isla," Wade says as he motions for her to move aside so he can be the one to sit next to me while I hog the warmth of the fire on my other side.

"And lose the opportunity to get drunk? Yeah, no thanks, Brass."

He shakes his head as he places a hand on my knee, and I

take a drink. For some reason, I've convinced myself that this particular glass tastes better because he took a sip from it. It's as if I can taste his kiss in the bubbles.

"Shut the fuck up," Isla says and reaches over Waylon before grabbing my left hand. "Brass! You actually did it."

We all laugh at how ridiculous she's being. "Congratulations, you assholes."

She still has my hand in hers before she lets go and throws her arms around his neck. I should be jealous or at least feel the smallest bit of envy roll through my body, but nothing comes of it because he's mine. Entirely.

She pulls away from him and pats his chest once before relaxing against the back of the couch again. "Today just got so much more exciting. No wonder you all have champagne."

Addy looks at Isla and then away again as if she's grown uncomfortable with her being here. I make a mental note to ask Wade about it later. I lean my head against his shoulder as Lillian comes back into the room. "All right, kids. As we wait for the appetizers in the oven, why don't we open a few gifts?"

Isla sits up and starts to pull out small gift bags from her large tote, and hands them out to everyone except Addy. I frown, and when she looks up at me, she gives me an unenthusiastic smile.

"Wait, Rye," Wade says. "Come here. I want my gift to be your first this Christmas." He rises and offers me his hand. I place my right hand in his as I finish my champagne and put the empty flute on the coffee table in front of me before I stand and he leads me out of the room and into a bedroom that I'm assuming must be for guests.

"Why are we away from everyone else?"

"This is our first Christmas together, Hadley. I want it to be memorable."

"You're too good for me, you know."

"I won't go over that again. You know how I feel about you. Now, turn around."

I purse my lips and turn my back to him. I'm about to tell him that he cannot always get his way, but before I'm able to respond, his hands move around my neck. I feel the weight of a light necklace grace my collarbone. He pulls back from me after securing it as my fingers trail across the lettering. "Thank you, Whiskey. What does it say?" I ask as I try to figure it out by touch.

"Whiskey Girl."

My eyes light up. I quickly make my way to the bathroom and gasp when I see my reflection in the mirror. He's placed a simple gold chain around my neck with the words *Whiskey Girl* on the golden pendant in scripted cursive.

"I love you," I say softly as he joins me in the bathroom.

"It's adjustable if it's not the right length."

I turn and throw myself into his arms, forgetting about his back for a moment. "It's perfect. Thank you so much."

"You're welcome, baby. I have one more gift for you."

"You don't need to do all of this, Wade. You've already given me you—that's more than I ever thought that I would have. You are all that I never thought I wanted."

"Indulge me, Hadley Rye, please."

I think on it for a moment before I nod once as I watch him pull his phone out of his pocket. "You have two choices."

"Oh?"

"Yes. The first being a choice in color: what color vehicle would you prefer?"

"What?" I ask quietly. "Whiskey, no, that's too much."

"All right. The second choice then: I'll be hiring you your own driver. I'd prefer it, given your history of men taking advantage of you."

My mouth drops open. "Both options are ridiculous. I don't need you to give me either of them."

He raises his eyebrows. "You'll soon be Mrs. Waylon Brass, and I will treat you as such. If you do not oblige me with an answer, then you will be receiving both."

"It's all too much, that's what it is. I don't need a driver."

"Then it's settled. What color would you like?"

"Wade."

"Answer me, Hadley."

This man is incredibly caring of me, yet so frustrating at times. He doesn't need to do any of this for me, but I know that he feels as if he does. I let out a sigh and step closer to him where his left arm comes around me once again.

"White."

"Thank you." I watch him type something out with his right hand before pocketing the phone in his slacks.

"No, thank you."

"Merry Christmas, gorgeous." His lips find mine, and I circle my arms around his neck as he lifts me up onto the vanity top and pushes my legs apart so he's able to stand between my thighs. His lips become more forceful as our kiss continues. I whimper against his lips as my back arches toward him, my body wanting more contact with his than what I'm currently being given.

He pulls away from me, leaving me breathless and needy. "Whiskey . . ."

"What is it?"

I close my eyes as he runs his thumb down my line of cleavage. "I need to grab your gift, and we need to get back to everyone else, or they're going to assume that your gift to me was that beautiful cock of yours."

"It still can be," he says with a leer and pushes his hips against my sex, allowing me to feel exactly how hard he is.

I splay my fingers out on his chest and push him back, but it doesn't help much since I'm already tipsy on everything that is Waylon Brass.

"What did you get me?"

"Patience, handsome."

I went out a few days ago to pick up the gift I ordered for him, and between the two of us, we picked out gifts for everyone after he fucked me all night after his proposal. He sent his doorman out to collect them, and it allowed us to sleep in for hours on Christmas Eve after being up all night.

I slide off of the vanity and take his hand, leading him back out to the living room area. All eyes turn to us as we re-enter.

"A quickie. That's a little less than what I expected from Brass for Christmas," Isla says with a laugh.

"Isla Madden," Lillian scolds her.

I ignore the banter and go to my purse where I find the box that I'm looking for in my Burberry and pull it out. I take a seat and pat the cushion next to me. He joins me without a word, and I turn to angle my body toward him. "If you don't like it, I can exchange it for another."

"It could be a fucking used condom, and he'll love it if it's from you," Liam says boldly and throws his arm around Adriana before getting comfortable. I notice Isla shift as I'm handing Wade the gift box.

I watch him unwrap the paper, and he pauses when he sees the symbol of a golden crown on the white cardboard box covering. "Hadley."

"Just open it, okay?"

He looks back down at the box in his hands and pulls out an emerald green box and opens it, revealing the new Yacht-Master watch from Rolex.

He takes it out of the box and turns it from side to side, inspecting it. He stops turning it when his eyes catch the engraving on the back of it: *Blended Love.*

His eyes find mine.

An electrical static runs up my spine before a warmth

explodes over my entire body. The look he's giving me is filled with an uncanny amount of love, adoration, and appreciation. In one simple look, this man can make me feel a thousand and one different things. His love screams louder than any demons have before. He places the watch back into the box before setting it down on the coffee table. The room is quiet except for the Christmas song playing in the background.

He surprises me by leaning forward and taking my face in his hands. "Our life together is not measured by time, but by the flashes that turn into personal moments. You were a risk, something uncertain, yet when a real connection was made, the reward of having you stole my soul. Our passage may be far from flawless, but it's you who makes breathing easier. With you, baby, I'm home."

A solitary tear runs down my cheek. He watches it before slowly wiping it away with his thumb.

"I'm ready for our future," I tell him honestly.

"As am I."

I throw my arms around him and lock my lips to his, not giving a fuck about anyone else in the room. I think I hear his mother sniffle, but I'm unsure. All I care about is how his lips move against mine. He's not only shown me how much he loves me in private, but now he has declared it in front of the people closest to him.

Liam clears his throat and Wade smiles against my mouth. "Fuck off."

His hands move down my back and underneath my ass so they are between the couch and me before he lifts me onto his lap.

"Wade," I whisper.

"It's fine."

I lean my head against his shoulder and take in a deep breath as the rest of them start to speak again. I hear wrapping paper being opened and a few gasps in surprises as the two of us stay still and close to each other and in our own world, for at least thirty minutes before he pulls back to look down at me. "Are you okay?"

"I don't think that I could be any better."

"Good. I cannot wait to spend my life with you, gorgeous."

I kiss his jaw in answer and climb off of his lap to sit next to him, but he never stops touching me, which I'm grateful for. Once we've eaten a few rounds of holiday appetizers and opened two more bottles of champagne, I'm buzzed and content in Wade's arms. It amazes me how close I've allowed myself to get to him, as well as how I've grown to trust him.

The rest of the holiday passes joyously. Lillian prepared a delicious ham, and we've stuffed our stomachs. Isla is incredibly drunk, and Lilly has taken her to the guest bedroom to sleep it off before the four of us leave for the evening. On our way out, Lillian stopped the two of us and asked when we planned on making everything official. I paused, unsure how to tell her just how soon Wade wanted to do it, but he didn't hesitate to give her a date: January twenty-ninth.

I throw my head back against the mattress as the final waves of an orgasm rage through my body. I'm exhausted from going at it every other hour or so with him today. All of my muscles are tender and deliciously sore as I stretch out.

Wade and I spend the next five days holed up in his penthouse. Today marks the last day of this year, and this evening, Wade is hosting a New Year's Eve party in the Aon Grand Ballroom on Navy Pier. Apparently, it's an annual event that everyone in Chicago wants to be invited to and most of Chicago's high society has been. There will be a total of eight hundred people in attendance. Out of the invites that went out, almost every single person *respondez, s'il vous plait* as attending. I don't blame them—I'm sure that it's going to be incredible.

"Fuck, I don't know if I'll be able to stay up this evening after fucking you like you deserve it these last couple of days."

I smirk. "You're the one that keeps coming back for more."

"You're the one that offers it up to me without hesitation."

"Are you complaining?" I ask.

He rolls onto his back and pulls me onto his lap, penetrating me again with his beautiful cock. I moan out and start to move on top of him, riding him hard.

"Is this complaining?"

"N-no."

The next thirty minutes are filled with naked desires and endurance as he gets me to orgasm again. The feeling of him spilling into me has quickly become one of my favorite things. I love hosting him between my legs and allowing my fiancé to thoroughly enjoy himself.

After our combined orgasms leak out of me, he gets up and offers me his hand. "It's past noon, Rye. You're a bad influence on me."

"You enjoyed it, Mr. Brass."

"Indeed. Now come. I need to get you cleaned up and get us settled before the party begins. We smell of sex."

"I'm sure this entire penthouse smells of sex from what we've been doing. Poor Liam, he must be hornier than usual."

We walk into the bathroom, and I turn on the shower. While I wait for the water to warm up, I grab three towels out of the closet and set them on each one of the vanities.

"Between Adriana and Isla, I think his dick is content at the moment."

I stop in the threshold of the shower and turn to him. "Wait. He's fucking both of them?"

"Apparently. I knew that he was with Isla while we were in Sydney, but I had no idea that he and Adriana have been fucking around for years."

"Do they know? The girls, I mean."

"I believe so."

I step under the spray and run my hands through my just-fucked-curls to get them wet while I contemplate what he's just told me. Once I'm done showering, I force myself to step out of the shower before I push him up against the wall and take his cock into my mouth. I don't need him to be in any more pain as he was a week ago.

Once I've dried off, he turns the shower off and steps out. My mouth waters at the sight of him walking toward me completely naked with small droplets clinging to his powerful body. He's been keeping up with his rehabilitation as well as going to the gym on the property twice a day. I bite my lip and take a step back from him. "You'll get me wet."

"I believe that you already are."

"And? What if I am?"

"I'll need to lick you clean then."

His approach is slow and torturous; he's teasing me on purpose, and I refuse to let him win this time. I turn to face myself in the mirror and pick up my hairbrush, running it through my hair before grabbing my product and spraying it over the strands, then brushing it through. When I look up at him in the mirror, he's watching me while his hand moves up and down the length of his cock.

"Care to join me?"

"Yes, but I need to get dressed before Jacobs arrives." I pause and take one last look at the glistening head of his cock. "Unless you'd rather he saw me naked?"

His hand stops moving against his hard, silky skin, silently challenging me to do it.

I raise my brows at him, returning his silent challenge.

"You win, Rye, but you're mine after the party."

"I always will be. That reminds me: are you going to announce our engagement?"

"Possibly. It depends on how comfortable I feel. There's going to be a lot of people there. I'll decide in the moment."

"Well, I'm happy with anything you decide on."

He places a kiss on the back of my head before he runs a towel through his hair and steps out of the bathroom and into the bedroom.

I sigh to myself, content with my life for what feels like the first time. All of those times I told myself that I was happy did not feel like this. The sex and dick-hopping might have actually been holding me back. I wouldn't change a thing, though, because it's what got me through a horrible time in my life, but now that I'm with Wade, I know that I won't need another man. Ever.

Once I've applied my makeup and my hair is straightened, I toss the towel into the laundry basket and walk into the bedroom. He's seated at the end of the bed, tying the laces of his Oxfords when he glances up at me. "Jesus."

"What?" I ask as I blush. I admit that I walked in here naked on purpose: I love his reactions to me. It makes me feel beautiful and wanted.

"You're going to make us late to our own party, Rye."

"It's your party, Wade, and I am in no way making us late. Just keep that cock of yours in your pants and we won't have a problem."

"It is ours. Don't argue with me."

I raise my brows before walking up to him and kissing his cheek. "I wasn't."

His knuckles graze the outer skin of my thigh as I walk away from him and toward the closet and look at the outfit that I had dry-cleaned yesterday for this evening. I won't lie: having the extra hands of the staff in the penthouse and Colin Jacobs may come in handy when I cannot break myself away from Wade.

"Whiskey?" I call out, and he steps into the closet a moment later while straightening his bowtie.

"Hey, gorgeous. Everything okay?"

I purse my lips and point to the dress in front of me. "I'm going to freeze in this dress."

He stands next to me as his eyes run down the length of the dress. "You'll need to stay inside when the fireworks take place— most people will regardless.

"Maybe."

"Rye," he says as he wraps his arms around my middle, "the majority of people will be staying in the interior for the evening because it will be too cold to go out onto the pier or the terrace. Why don't you pick out another outfit and change once the eve- ning is over and before we make our way to the hotel? That way you can wear what Lola made, and be warm after midnight."

"I think that's a good idea. Only if you'll help me change, though."

"I'll try to get away," he says as his lips caress the skin of my shoulder and then he runs his tongue along my collarbone.

"Will you pick out what I'll change into?"

He chuckles and stares at my side of the closet. He called the moving company two days after Christmas to gather my things and transfer them here. To *our* place. He points out my Burberry wool coat, black leggings, and a black knitted sweater.

"What about those?"

"I like it. You might have a sense of fashion, after all, Mr. Brass."

"I would hope so, considering I'm going to be placing Lola Marc's designs all over the world."

I squeal and turn in his arms. "What? When did you decide to do that?"

"Right this moment."

"How?"

"That dress. I want her to be the one to dress you for all of the social events we will need to attend. Does she carry a men's line?"

"Holy shit. She's going to freak out, Whiskey. I don't think that she has delved into menswear, but can I be there when you tell her?"

"Certainly. Now get dressed, Hadley. We're already late."

"I thought you said we had time to get settled first."

He smirks and moves his hands down to cup my ass. "That was hours ago, Rye."

"Fuck," I huff and swat his arms away. "Give me a few minutes to get this on."

He nods and grabs the items that he picked out for my outfit change for midnight. I walk over to the shoe section of the closet and grab my black booties for him to add to the overnight bag. He takes them and places a kiss on my lips before he walks out.

I sigh and turn to look at the gown again. Another Lola Marc original. It's a beautiful shade of blush pink. The straps are barely visible, and the v-neck plunges past my breasts. It has a few ruffles on the right thigh, but nothing is overdone. It's straightforward and elegant. Lo knows exactly what I like to wear, as well as how to correctly dress my body type. Once I'm dressed, I slip my feet into the heels that she provided and move my straightened hair behind my shoulders, pinning the sides in place and glancing at myself in the full-length mirror before I walk out of the closet.

Wade isn't in the bedroom anymore, so I grab my coat that he left on the bed and make my way downstairs to where Liam, Addy, Isla, and my fiancé are waiting. My heels click gently against the hardwood floors, announcing my arrival before I can speak. Wade turns around, and his smile falls from his face. I watch as he takes in a deep breath.

"Rye."

It's only a word. My last name, but it holds so much more than that coming from his lips. The others turn around to look at me and Addy gasps while Isla whistles. I roll my eyes at the two of them as Wade reaches me and takes my hand, speaking only to me. "You're stunning."

"Thank you." All of the world could disappear right now and I would not notice.

"All right, you assholes, let's get going. Jacobs has been waiting outside since Isla got here twenty minutes ago." Liam's arms come around my waist once he speaks, and I wonder what Wade might do.

"Touch her once more and I'll castrate you."

He lets go of me and holds his hands up in defense. "I was making sure she was wearing underwear. No bra—you're in luck."

I smack his bicep as Wade goes to lunge at him, but Isla quickly puts her hands on his chest and pushes him backward. I know that Liam is messing with him, seeing just how far he's able to push Wade when it comes to me.

"Hadley," he growls through gritted teeth, "come here."

I've never heard him growl before, and my panties reap the effects of the sexual noise as I take the few steps toward him. Isla goes to one side of Liam while Addy goes to his other and they step into the elevator before us. Wade's arms are around me as he leads me in behind them. It descends as Liam talks to the girls about having a threesome. I think that Isla might be all for it, but Addy remains quiet the entire time until we get into the limo, and I slide in next to her.

"I need a drink," she tells me.

"Are you okay?" I ask her softly as Jacobs shuts the door behind Wade.

"I'm going to have to be."

"How about we buddy up tonight when I'm not with

Wade?"

"You've got yourself a deal. Is there champagne in here?"

Wade must hear her because he pops open a bottle and hands each of us a glass before holding it up in the air. "Cheers to one hell of a year."

"Cheers," we all chime and take a drink. Addy downs her glass in one go, and I hand her mine when she puts hers down. She mouths *thank you* and takes a sip.

She remains quiet for the remainder of the drive, and I realize just how much he must mean to her if she's willing to put up with his bullshit. I lean my head against Wade. He's been watching me the entire time, and I suddenly feel tremendously fortunate to be with him.

I haven't been paying attention as we drive, and when the vehicle comes to a stop, I can tell that it's noisy outside. I glance over at Isla and her eyes light up.

The limousine's door swings open to a plethora of flashes going off as Waylon Brass steps out. I watch him straighten his tux jacket, button it, and reach his hand back into the limo, offering me his assistance. His smile is beaming, and I take his offered hand with my right as he helps me out. The flashes seem to get more intense as I take my place beside him.

"Are you okay?" he says in my ear, and I nod as the flashes seem to intensify once again.

His hand rests against my waist as we walk away from the limousine and toward the ballroom that has a white carpet stretching from the drop-off area to the double doors ahead of us. Before we walk down the stretch of it where there are no more photographers, Wade turns us around to face the swarm of blinding flashes.

With subtlety he angles me so that my left side is toward the cameras and he places his right hand in his pocket while his left-hand remains at the small of my back, covering my piercings as he always does. I straighten my left hand out, holding my clutch as the photographers yell directions at us. There's a soft murmur amongst them before someone shouts out, "Is that an engagement ring?"

I turn to look up at Wade. His smile widens as he glances down at me. He takes my lips with his and speaks against them, "now the entire world will know."

I nip at his bottom lip before he pulls back and takes my hand, leading me down the remainder of the carpet and away from the crowd. Isla, Addy, and Liam follow behind us.

"Were they invited to take pictures?" I ask curiously.

"No, baby. They show up each year. It's a mixture of media, paparazzi, and independent photographers."

"Interesting."

"Come." He offers me his hand once he steps through the set of double doors and into a vast dome-shaped ballroom. This venue has a panoramic lakefront view, and the domed ceiling adds to its timeless look of pure elegance and splendor. He tugs on my hand a bit too hard, causing me to crash into his chest. When I look up at him, instead of the venue, I know it was on purpose. This gorgeous man cannot keep his hands off of me. I run my index finger over his newly shaven jaw, but I'd rather bite him there.

"Introduce me to the rest of your world, Mr. Brass."

"It'd be my pleasure, Rye."

He intertwines his fingers with mine and leads me to the center of the ballroom. It's already filled with people that I don't recognize. I know that Lola and Owen are here somewhere. Hold might be here as well since I invited him, but I'm unsure if he'll actually show up.

Everyone is dressed up in black tie, and waiters are walking around with champagne flutes, tumblers of whiskey, and hors d'oeuvres. Wade pulls one of them aside and asks for two tumblers of the Macallan 64. My eyes shoot up to his, and he shrugs as if he's not asking for two glasses of a bottle of Scotch worth a few hundred thousand dollars. The waiter nods and leaves us before he leads me into a crowd of men, introducing me as his fiancée to a few of what he refers to as his C-level employees—the men and women who work directly under him and make Brass Global a force to be reckoned with.

I catch a few names, but one stands out: Gage Cooper. For some reason, I can't remember the others. He's about the same height as Wade, with dirty blonde hair. He's dressed in a tuxedo that looks just as tailored to his frame as Wade's does. I give him a smile, and he nods toward me.

When the waiter finds us with the two tumblers, Wade takes them and hands one to me. I breathe in the one-of-a-kind Scotch and sigh as I take a sip. The liquor explodes in my mouth, and I almost moan. Wade's eyes darken as he takes a drink from his glass before returning his hand to the small of my back.

"I see that you're forcing your whiskey on beautiful women now, Brass," Gage Cooper says as he eyes my tumbler.

"My fiancée knows what she likes, Coop. How's your little girl doing?"

I watch the two of them interact, and it seems as if Wade is much more comfortable with Gage than he is around the other C-levels that he introduced me to, all of whom seem to have wandered off.

"She's doing well. Maggie has her this evening, though, which is why I was finally able to make one of these things."

"I'm glad that you came. I have a private whiskey stock. I'll inform the waiter that you're welcome to it."

Gage nods and pats Wade on the shoulder. "Thank you. I might need a drink or two after dealing with her excuses."

I smile up at him and ask, "You have a daughter?"

"I do, but her mother is . . . well, someone who no longer

has a place in my life."

"I'm sorry to hear that. How old is she?"

"Emery turned three two months ago."

I smile at him as two other couples join us, one of them being Adriana and Liam. Gage's eyes fall on Adriana and then to her hand in Liam's. He clears his throat and offers me his hand. I let go of Wade's to shake his. "It was a pleasure meeting you, Hadley. I'll see you around."

"You as well," I call after him as he turns his back to us and takes quick strides away.

Addy smiles at me, and I walk over to her. "Hey stranger. How are you holding up?"

"I'm drunk. Frankly."

I giggle and fix her smudged lipstick. "Should I kick Liam's ass for you?"

"Sure. How high are those heels? Go ahead and stab him while you're at it," she slurs, and he looks down at the two of us.

"Planning my demise, beautiful?"

"Fuck you," she hisses at him and takes my hand. "I need to pee."

"I'll take you," I tell her and Liam nods as I take her hand and lead her off to the bathroom where I'm sure there will either be more drinking or tears.

Thirty-Two

Wade

THE BALLROOM IS filled with attendees occupying the space and providing a loud, yet comfortable vibe for the evening. Hadley has been gone for thirty minutes now, and I cannot find her. I walk up the stairs to the interior terrace level of the ballroom where I'm greeted by more people, including Lola, Owen, and of course Holden—*the motherfucker.*

"Waylon Brass," Lola says and offers her hand to me. I shake it and then Owen's—intentionally ignoring Holden.

"I'm glad to see that you were able to make it, Lola."

"I wouldn't have missed this for the world. Where's Hads? I cannot wait to see what she looks like."

I glance over my shoulder when I hear Adriana call out my name. "Mr. Brass? Your fiancée is wanting to do you!"

Jesus. I don't know Adriana outside of work, but it's becoming apparent that she may be a handful; however, I know that Liam is to blame for her behavior as of late. He's been throwing her off with having Isla on the side.

I watch as a few people turn her way before I turn back to Lola. "Excuse me for a moment." I straighten my bowtie and walk toward Adriana. A couple of my guests watch me until I reach her.

"Adriana. I'd prefer if you didn't announce that in public. Where is she?"

She giggles and stretches her arms out, welcoming me with a big hug. "She told me that she was going to go look for you downstairs."

It's now that I notice her eyes are rimmed in red and that she's obviously been crying. "Thank you. If you need to retire to one of the private rooms in the lobby, then please, help yourself."

She sighs and looks down at her feet. "I apologize, Mr. Brass."

"I understand. Go get yourself together."

"Thank you, sir," she says as she walks off, trying not to trip over her evening gown. I glance back at Lola, who is now standing next to my whiskey girl. The smile that awakens on my face is one that I've stopped attempting to hide. I cross the space between us and pull her back into my front. I lean down and speak quietly into her ear. "I'd like to get you as drunk as Miss Hugh and then fuck that beautiful mouth of yours."

She gasps loudly and laces her fingers with mine that I have splayed over her stomach. "I'd like that."

"Good. Finish your drink and I'll order you another. What would you like?"

I watch her purse her lips before turning to face me. "A Manhattan, please."

I place my lips on hers quickly, and she pouts when I pull away to speak to a waiter that I signaled over. "Another 64-Year and a Manhattan with Old Potrero."

"Yes, sir." He walks away, and I turn back to the group in front of me.

"Waylon Brass, that man has been at your beck and call all evening. Is he your personal wait staff?" Hadley asks, and it makes the others laugh along with her.

"He is." I take her hand in mine again and intertwine my fingers with hers as a couple of other people walk up to us. I introduce Hadley to a few of them before our drinks are brought to us. I hand her the Manhattan and take a drink from my tumbler.

She looks up at me and grins, mouthing, "I love you."

I wink at her before speaking. "Lola?"

Lola turns toward me, smiling brightly. "Yes?"

"On Monday morning, please call into Brass Global and arrange a time you are able to meet with Hadley and me. My secretary, Adriana Hugh, will make the appointment with you."

"Of course. Is everything okay?"

"Yes, I wanted to make you an offer that I doubt you'll refuse. I'd like to help you grow Lola Marc and put your designs all over the world." I give her a straightforward answer.

"Oh, that sounds . . . holy crap. Of course, I'll be there." Hadley and Lola exchange a look that I don't understand, but I know that it's a positive one.

I glance down at the watch that Hadley gave me for Christmas, and the face reads eleven-thirty. This evening has passed quickly while I mingled with hundreds of people. Once we ring in the New Year, the party will kick off with a live band. I tug on Hadley's hand, drawing her attention to me rather than Owen. She seems a little giddy and I realize that we haven't exactly eaten today with all the fucking we've been doing.

"You need to eat, Rye."

"Oh? I know of something that you could eat." She turns into me and places her hand on my chest. I'm sure she can feel my heart accelerate at her touch. I nod once and excuse us from the group before leading her down to the main floor and across the ballroom, to a darkened corner behind an alcove. "That Manhattan was potent, Mr. Fancy-ass."

"Fancy-ass? You've called me that more than a handful of times."

"Yup. You know, you're wealthy beyond belief, and you live a fancy life."

She's more than buzzed, and I'm rather enjoying her loose

mouth. "You'll be Mrs. Fancy-ass soon, Rye."

She squeals and launches herself at me and pushes her fingers through my hair as her lips land on mine. She whimpers against my lips as I run my hands up her legs, underneath her dress, the feeling of her skin under my palms causing my cock to jump. I push her gown up as I move my hand higher to her thighs and then her hips until I've gathered the dress around her waist. I pull my mouth from hers. "We need to behave."

Her gorgeous nipples harden with need. I kiss down the column of her neck to her collarbone and further down to her.

"Wade . . ."

"I know, Rye, but we need to get back to our guests."

She shakes her head and grunts as I kiss each side of her collarbone before pushing myself off of her.

"Please?"

"Baby, you won't be able to walk for a day if I fuck you right now. Come have a drink with me, give me that New Year's kiss, and then I'll fuck you until you are unable to breathe."

"Do you swear it?"

"You have my heart, my word, and my ring."

"Fuck," she shouts, and I glance down at her, thinking that she's hurt herself.

"What is it?"

"I just love you," she says with a laugh, and a radiant, tipsy smile.

I cannot stop my own smile. "As I do you."

My watch shows that it's fifteen minutes until midnight, and I take her hand, leading her to one of the roped-off windows in the ballroom. Once we're immersed in the crowd of people again, I grab her a glass of champagne, and we make our way to our designated spot, ensuring that we'll have the best views this evening. My mother is usually present at this event as well. However, she decided to instead stay at Mothers of Brass and assist with their small New Year's Eve celebration this year.

I wrap my arms around her from behind. "Are you okay?"

"Perfect," she says as she takes a drink and leans her head back against my chest. I kiss the back of her head, and her body sags against mine.

"Drink up, fancy-ass. I'll get you another glass for cheers before the clock hits midnight."

"Thank you," she says softly. "Wade?"

"What is it?"

"This year has been life changing, and this next year . . . it's just the start of us."

My arms tighten around her waist as she says those words. They hit me with force in the center of my chest. "Are you ready for all of it?"

She glances at me over her shoulder after she finishes the glass off. "More than ever."

"Good because I'm not going backward again. Not when it comes to us."

"I wouldn't want you to. You're my life."

The waiter comes by with two champagne flutes. I take them and hand one to her. "To my bride."

"To my groom," she counters.

I take her mouth, plunging my tongue between her lips until mine is dancing with hers. Liam clears his throat, which ignites fire in my gut. This fucker will get exactly what's coming to him.

Pulling away from my fiancée, I look over at him, pissed that he interrupted something remarkable between the two of us.

"Fuck off."

He chuckles and lays his hand on my shoulder. Isla is next to him, but Adriana is nowhere in sight. "Two minutes, dude. Are you ready for this next step?" He nods toward Hadley and smirks.

"More than you know."

"Sweet. I get to be your best man, right? A strip club and a couple of whores will do for your bachelor party."

"I mean it; fuck off."

Hadley pulls on my bowtie to undo it. I look away from Liam as he draws Isla close and instead focuses on what she's doing.

Hadley gets my bowtie off from around my neck and pushes it into my slacks front pocket, resting her hand against my shaft for a moment before removing it.

The ten-second countdown starts, and I can't keep my eyes off of the woman in front of me. She fought this high-frequency love as if it wasn't supposed to be, but she's here now, right in front of me. Engaged to me . . . promising me her future.

"Happy New Year" rings out through the vast space as the band starts the music, and the fireworks start to go off just beyond the pier. The noise should distract me, or draw my attention elsewhere, but all that I'm able to see is her. I take her mouth with mine as if I'm dying of thirst and she's the only thing that will be able to quench it. She undoes the top button of my shirt before circling her arms around my neck and pressing her entire body against mine.

She's brought tranquility to my world.

She's my reason.

My reason for existing.

She comes first. Always.

The early morning sunlight streams into our hotel room a few hours later: January first. After an hour of celebrating, the alcohol went to Hadley's head and she was struggling to stand in her heels. We stole away to our hotel while the party was in full swing. I ravaged her while she spilled over with drunken giggles, which morphed into delirious cries of pleasure. She squirms beside me, reaching for me in her sleep; once she's reassured that I'm still beside her, I reach over and grab my phone to answer a couple of emails.

I type out one in specific that I know Hadley will enjoy when I let her in on my surprise. Adriana has been helping me plan our honeymoon, and I've just confirmed all of the details. She'll get back to me on Monday, and let me know that all of the reservations have been made.

Aside from the copious amount of alcohol we consumed last night, she drunkenly assured me that she was giving up her position as a phone-sex operator. We spoke about what she wanted to do because I know that she will refuse any suggestions of her not working. She mentioned that she'd possibly like to go back to school and get a degree in psychology in order to help others in need. I told her that she'd be welcome to work with Mothers of Brass, and at my suggestion, her eyes lit up and she told me that she would love nothing more than to be involved with that venture in Brass Global.

I get out of bed and get dressed before walking out into the suite's living room to call my mother.

"Happy New Year, Waylon," she says when she answers.

"To you as well, Mother. How was your evening?"

"I thoroughly enjoyed it, and I believe that all the women did as well. Thank you for allowing me to host the first one, dear. It meant a lot to me."

"You're welcome. I'm sure that we will host it next year as well. Hadley and I would like to attend it as she's taken a liking to the charity."

"She has? Well, I'd love to have that sweet girl help out if she'd like to."

"She's rather interested in getting involved and helping the women through their troubles. I think that it's a remarkable idea."

"Will you tell her to give me a call, please?"

"I will, Mother. I think that she enjoys helping those in need, and she'll enjoy spending the time with you," I tell her as I take a seat on one of the wingbacks and place an online room service order for breakfast on an iPad in the room.

"Now tell me, Waylon, what are you doing with regard to your wedding? I haven't heard much about it other than the date the two of you chose. That's only twenty-eight days away."

"It's one of the reasons why I'm calling you. I was considering the house that your great-great-grandfather owned in Scotland. I believe you called it the Ardunan House?"

"That would be incredible. I think that it's now named the Strathblane Country House. I believe that they have very recently remodeled it as well. Let me get into contact with them right now and find out if they have an opening, and I'm confident that they will accommodate us."

"Thank you. I'll make some calls regarding flights for those we'd like to attend."

I can hear her smile on the other side of the line. "How big would you like the wedding to be?"

"I'm not entirely sure. I know that Hads has only a handful of people whom she will be inviting, so I'll be keeping it small as well. I cannot imagine that there will be more than forty people in total. Inquire about renting out the entire house, please."

"Of course, dear. I'll call you back once I am given all of the details that we'll need."

Hadley walks out into the living room and settles onto my lap wearing only leggings and a shirt with the words *Good Morning Whiskey* on it while unfolding a blanket. She pulls the cream-colored blanket over herself, and I chuckle to myself.

"Goodbye, Mother."

"Bye, Waylon."

I set my phone down and wrap my arms around Rye as she burrows deeper into my hold.

"Good morning, gorgeous."

She groans and pulls the blanket over her head.

"Breakfast should be here soon. How are you feeling?"

"Awful," she mumbles. "Was that Lilly?"

"It was. We were discussing a wedding location."

I watch as she pulls the blanket down, her hair wild as she looks up at me, "And?"

"There was an old house that belonged to my family called the Ardunan House on my mother's side. It's in Scotland."

"Scotland? We're going to get married in Scotland?"

"If you agree to it and if they are able to accommodate us, then yes, we are."

"Of course I agree to it, Wade. I've always wanted to go to Scotland."

"Start packing, gorgeous," I tell her as the doorbell rings throughout the suite. I call out for room service to enter. The waiter delivers our breakfast and disappears within a minute. I watch as Hadley leans forward to grab a croissant from the pastry tray. She tears a piece off and places it in her mouth.

"I'll need a dress first. I hope that Lola will agree to make it."

"I'm sure she will. We'll speak to her on Monday regarding it."

"Thank you." She places a kiss on my jaw before eating another piece of croissant. She remains in my lap while we finish breakfast and make our way back into the warmth of the king-sized bed for the remainder of the day.

The next twenty-four days pass effortlessly. Hadley is currently with Lola for her final wedding dress fitting while I'm on the phone with Adriana, confirming all of the stops for our honeymoon once more. We fly out to Scotland in two days. Hadley and I will be spending an evening in Edinburgh before heading just north of Glasgow where the country house is located.

She's thrilled when she comes down the stairs and bolts into my arms. I tell Adriana that I'll call her back later and slide my phone into the pocket of my jeans.

"Well?"

"I love it, and I cannot wait for you to see it."

She's glowing . . . unquestionably radiant.

"You're always beautiful, and I look forward to you in it."

"When did you get so sweet, Waylon Brass?"

"Since I tasted you, baby."

"Oh, quit it."

"Not now, not ever." I run my hand over her piercings, wishing it was my tongue instead. "I have a dinner meeting tonight. You're welcome to join me."

"A dinner meeting?" She giggles and smacks my chest. "I don't think that any man has ever called his bachelor party a dinner meeting before."

"You have now." I chuckle when she moves off of my lap, and I stand up, holding my hand to my lower back. I need to cut out some of the physical activity in my life if I plan on walking for the remainder of my life. I may still be breathing and alive, but I've been in pain this last week again.

I watch her smile fall off of her face. "Are you all right?"

"I'm great. I need to get going soon, and your girls will be over shortly. I'm sure Isla will have some entertainment for you this evening."

She shrugs. "I don't want anyone else but you, Wade. You know that. Plus, I'm sure, with Liam being back in town again, that he's going to be taking you somewhere where there is plenty of available pussy."

"Do you trust me?"

"I do." Her cheeks heat at those two words and I lay my lips on hers before Lola calls down to us. "Wade, you need to go. You'll ruin her bachelorette party."

I keep my eyes on my bride. "Think of me, Rye."

"Always."

I let go of her, and my entire body already aches to have her near again as I put distance between us. I grab my coat and open the door, but frown when I see Liam, Owen, and a few other guys from college standing next to Adriana, Isla, and my mother.

"What is this?"

Isla pushes past everyone, holding a penis-shaped balloon. "We're combining parties."

"We're what?" I hear Hadley call out and walk up to me, ducking underneath my arm. I look down at her and grin.

"Let us in, Brass," Isla demands. "We're doing a joint party since they are both rather small. You two both need to work on your people skills, and I can't be on the bride and groom's side at the same time. I might just stand between the two of you at the altar."

"The fuck you won't."

"Get over yourself, brass balls."

Hadley and I step back and watch them claim our penthouse, placing platters of food out in the living room and removing their coats. My staff comes out to help hang up their things in the hall closet before they vanish again.

"Hadley? You need to come up here to change."

Both of us look up at Lola at the top of the stairs, holding up a rather sheer set of lingerie.

"Lo!" She yells and takes the stairs two at a time to get to her. I watch them giggle, and they walk back into the master suite together.

Liam walks up to me holding a tumbler filled with amber liquid. "Here's to you, man."

"Thank you."

Music starts throughout the penthouse, and Isla adjusts the lights to dim while Owen starts opening bottles of champagne.

"Did you bring the blow-up doll, Owen?" Isla asks, and I freeze in place.

"A blow-up doll. Is that a fucking joke?"

"What did I tell you about letting those brass balls hang, huh? We're all getting drunk, having fun, and then passing out here. I hope that you and Hads don't mind sharing a bed with two others."

"Fuck off."

Her suggestion brings me back to the many times I've been in bed with multiple women, but I shrug it off and take a long drink from my tumbler.

It takes Hadley a while to come down the stairs, and Lola seems to be just as giddy as she is when they join the rest of us in the kitchen, surrounding the island while we inspect the small buffet laid out in front of us.

She's dressed in white, with deep red lipstick staining her lips. Isla hands her a glass of champagne and she smiles as she accepts the flute. She's fucking gorgeous and all mine.

"Here's to the soon-to-be Mr. and Mrs. Waylon Brass," Isla says, and everyone agrees before raising glasses and taking a drink.

Hadley sets her flute down and looks at everyone around the island. "Are we really not going out?"

"Oh, we're going out, all right. We just need to get the two of you buzzed before the party starts," Owen counters and slams back the remainder of the champagne in his glass. Hadley follows him, and I hand her the glass that was poured for me before drinking from my tumbler.

An hour of tequila shots, champagne cocktails, and Scotch later we've all piled into the stretch limousine as Jacobs takes us to a nightclub called Underground. When we arrive, I get out before helping Hadley out. There's a long line wrapping around the building, but I walk up to the bouncer and we're given entrance without my having to say a word to him.

"We have the VIP area to ourselves, Brass. I used your card," Isla says as she grabs my bicep and pulls me in what I assume is the direction of the private area. Hadley is moving her body to the music beside me as we walk to the roped-off area, unable to fight the music surging through her.

She moves fluidly, attracting the attention of more than one set of eyes.

"I may enjoy watching that ass move, but I'm not entirely pleased that all of the other men will be able to see you as well."

"Wade," she whines and laces her fingers with mine, pulling me toward the dance floor. I stop her to remove my arms from my jacket, and help her out of the coat before I let her lead me to the dance floor. I feel eyes on us as her too-tight dress hugs her in all of the right places.

"Dance with me?" she asks as we step foot onto the dance floor, her body fitting against my front.

I grin and slide my hands down to the small of her back, and start moving my hips against her, fucking her with our clothes on. "I don't want you with another man. Do you understand?"

"Yes, sir," she teases and pushes her breasts into my chest. "Oh, and I'm thinking about getting another piercing."

"That was incredibly casual. Where?"

"Where would you like to suck on one?"

I take a deep breath, realizing that she might be serious. "Anywhere, Rye."

"So . . . my future groom approves?"

"More than you know," I tell her as we move together as if we are the only ones on the dance floor.

"What about my clitoris?"

I run my right hand down her thigh, grazing her skin with my fingers. "You could do that. I was considering these nipples of yours."

She glances down and grins, then purses her lips. "You'd like that, wouldn't you, Whiskey?"

"I would. Now dance with me, gorgeous."

We spend the next thirty minutes losing ourselves to each other's sensual, erotic movements.

Isla and Liam have joined us, and I'm surprised with Adriana when she joins the two of them. I'd like to blame it on the alcohol, but I'm unsure as to how true that would be.

"I need a drink," Hadley says against my ear. I grab her hand and pull her out from the middle of the dance floor, taking her to where Owen and Lola are getting rather affectionate on the couch.

I pour her two fingers of whiskey before pouring my own and take a seat across from the couple. "We didn't mean to interrupt."

Lola blushes as Hadley gets comfortable beside me. I stretch my arm behind her, pulling her even closer.

"Shut the fuck up. If you two were left alone up here, you'd already be naked and fucking each other until you passed out."

I chuckle along with Hadley as she downs the remainder of her tumbler. Jesus. I contemplate remaining sober this evening to watch over her, but Liam pulled me aside before we got into the limousine and told me to let loose because he and Owen were not going to be drinking. They decided to watch over the women instead. I was surprised, but I might take them up on their offer. Hadley watches me as I throw the remainder of my tumbler back and lean in to take her mouth. She audibly moans against my lips, and I'm tempted to take her back to the limousine to fuck her, but I resist the urge to be inside of her for the moment.

"I want you," she confesses as she straddles my lap, grinding her hips against my cock; she receives the rise out of me that she's wanted all night. I'm fucking hard beneath her.

"Are you wearing panties?"

Her eyes lock with mine as she shakes her head back and forth. "No."

"Fuck, baby." I thrust my hips up to her once again, and she throws her head back as if I've hit her exactly where she needs to be touched.

"We're going to dance," Owen says, and I watch the two of them walk down the single flight of stairs before moving the hem of her dress up and run the back of my knuckles over her wet, sensitive skin. I can feel her body move with the bass of the music pumping around us as I slide a solitary finger inside of her. Her hips move with the thrusts of my finger. She runs both of her hands into my hair, and I have no doubt that anyone would know exactly what we are doing if they decided to glance up here.

She whimpers against my mouth as I add my thumb and start massaging her swollen clit. I nip her bottom lip before moving lower, kissing down her neck as her body trembles on top of me. She bucks her hips as her sudden orgasm takes over her. Each wave of it seems to intensify as I watch her come apart with my guidance.

I can feel a bead of pre-come leak from the head of my cock while watching her. Once she settles down, I pull my fingers out from inside of her warm channel. Her body sags against mine just as I reach for a drink napkin on the table beside us to clean her with. I gently wipe it against her skin, freeing her of her orgasm before crumpling it up and putting it into my whiskey tumbler.

"Holy shit," she grumbles against my neck and bites down, surely leaving her merlot lipstick on the white collar of my shirt. I grab her jaw, making her look at me.

"You enjoyed that, didn't you, Rye?"

"Oh God, so much. You'll need to fuck me before we leave here because I cannot stand your not being seated inside of me."

"We'll have all the time we want in Scotland."

She frowns and wiggles her hips seductively against my erection. "That may be true, but it does not resolve the situation beneath me right now."

"You're correct, but we're about to have company. Behave yourself," I tell her as Isla, Adriana, and Liam walk up the stairs. Both of the women are still dancing to the thudding music as they reach us.

"Drinks!" Adriana shouts and a waitress that I hadn't noticed before makes herself known, asking what she can bring for each of us. All three of the girls decide on a redheaded slut shot. She leaves us, and I watch Liam take a drink of a tall glass of water, which allows me to relax and pour myself another two fingers of amber liquid. Instead of sipping on the grand liquid in my glass, I throw it back when Hadley shifts her impeccable body off of me.

I haven't had much to drink since before my accident, and I'm not entirely sure how my body will handle this, but I'm grateful that the other men have decided not to drink. It gives me pause knowing that they have both Hadley's and my backs.

The shots are brought back to us, and Hadley has a sparkle in her eye as she takes the shot with the two other women.

"Come dance with us," they whine, and she looks at me.

"You know my rules."

She nods and gets up, straightening her dress as she follows the two of them down the stairs, leaving Liam and me alone.

"I can't believe that you're getting fucking married in a few days."

"You and I both, but I wouldn't change this; it's how it's supposed to be. It's what I never considered wanting or having, but here it is, and I have never been so content in life before."

"That's one hell of a way to put it."

"It is. Now tell me, what is going on with your triangle."

"Ah," he says and pauses to take a drink from his water

bottle. "Both of them know how to fuck me. They both have a fucking dirty side and are able to suck me off until I can't fucking stand."

"You cannot keep leading the both of them on."

"They are well aware of what I do with each of them. Neither of them has given me an ultimatum, so I don't see the reason to decide. I'm not getting married or settling down. I'm fucking them each until they cannot stand the feeling of my dick inside them any longer."

"Fuck." I adjust myself, thinking about giving it to Hadley tonight and pour myself another glass.

"Take it easy on the heavy shit, dude. When was the last time you actually got drunk?"

"Don't concern yourself with that shit. Just remain sober."

"I've already given you my word."

I nod and throw the drink back before looking out onto the dance floor. It takes me a moment to find them, but when I do, their bodies move seductively in sync, pressing together in places that my fucking hands should be touching on my bride.

I slam my glass down and stand, but when I do, I can feel the warmth of the alcohol slide down into my extremities. Liam gets up and follows me down to the dance floor to the women.

I ring my arms around Hadley's waist, and she starts to push them off of her body until she looks down at my hands and glances over her shoulder. "It's you."

"Always, Rye. I've got you."

"I love you," she shouts and turns in my arms, starting to move against me once again.

"As I do you," I tell her against her ear before taking her lobe between my teeth and biting down.

"Waylon Brass," Isla yells out, "are you drunk?"

I swing my head in her direction and Liam is wearing a shit-eating grin. Fucker. "I'm well on my way."

The pair laugh together before she hugs me. "I'll get us shots."

Before I'm able to protest she walks away from the four of us as Lola and Owen join us. We're all lost in our partners when Isla announces her return. I glance over in her direction, hating that I have to remove my eyes from Hadley's body. She's followed by our waitress with a tray filled with shots, two each if my vision is correct.

"Cheers, bitches," she says as she starts handing out the drinks.

"What is this?" Lola asks but doesn't wait for an answer to down the entire shot.

"Redheaded sluts," she yells as she hands out the second round. We each down the shots before returning the glasses to the tray.

I can tell that Hadley is under the spell of alcohol by the way her body is moving against mine, and how she's unable to keep her hands to herself. "Wade," she says against my neck, but somehow I hear her.

"What is it?"

"I'm needy." Her teeth sink into my shoulder through my shirt that is now slightly damp with sweat, and I fucking swear, I might be able to see through the sheer white material that covers Hadley's breasts, but I'm unsure.

"You need to be fucked."

"More than you know."

"You'll have to wait. I'm too drunk to fuck you in the right place right now."

She purses her lips and leans up on her toes. "Maybe I'll like it."

I pull back to look at her. "We'll have to wait to find out the answer to that."

"Deal."

The alcohol may be swimming through me, but I've found solace in knowing that I'll have her tied to me for life in a few short days. A rumble rips through my chest as I pull her closer against my body and we start to move against each other again, feeling more alive than I ever have before.

Isla leans over to yell, "I like seeing you drunk. You're a fucking mess and goofy as hell. I'm glad that you found your. . . ."

I couldn't hear the rest of her sentence. "My what?" I yell back at her, trying to decipher each word that she's said.

"Your . . . nope, never mind. I'll get us all some more shots."

"Yes!" Hadley yells and throws her hands up before cupping my jaw in her hands and pulling my mouth down to hers.

Fuck, she's captivating, and she knows exactly how to hold onto who I am. If I could undress her on the dance floor without any consequences, then I would, but she'll have to wait.

Isla returns with shots of whiskey with soda, but the only chaser I need is Hadley's lips.

I do not remember much after another four rounds of shots. Nor do I recall how we got back to the penthouse, but when we wake the next morning, we're both half dressed, and sorely hung over. I look at the still-drunk woman beside me. Her makeup is not as it was the night before, and her once-straight hair has turned back into curls, but I love her all the more for it.

I chuckle to myself when she groans and grips my bicep. If I wake up to her every morning for the rest of my life, I will be more than content.

The mere thought of another man waking up and seeing her like this tears me apart. It's this morning that I realize exactly what I could have lost if she had not decided to come back to me. She would be wrapped around another man today instead of me. None of the other options are tolerable.

I do not understand what brought me to her, or how life

has handed me this deck of cards, but I refuse to argue with the queen of hearts. Apparently, my love is enough, and I'll settle for that. For my cup of whiskey.

Epilogue No. 1

Hadley

HOLY SHIT. *TODAY* is the day that will start the remainder of my life. It will take me to places and make me feel what I've been putting off for my entire life. Today's meaning marks more than a signature on a simple sheet of paper or an additional ring on my left hand. It's going to be something that I'll experience and savor.

Today, January twenty-ninth, marks the unity of two hearts and souls that have been in search of each other for as long as I have been alive and breathing. I've never thought of binding my soul to another's before, but as Lillian and Lola secure my veil into place, I've never been more anxious to make this final, for this fairy tale to be more than fiction.

I glance at myself in the full-length mirror in the embroidered gown that was specifically designed for me by Lola. I turn to the side to get a better view of it, running my hands down my thighs and over the pattern crossing my skin. After one more glance at the dress, I stare out the windows of the room onto the Scottish countryside beyond, half of which is covered in snow. This country house is quaint and undeniably extraordinary. I choose my steps carefully as Lola and Lillian watch me.

"I can't believe that this is happening," I murmur.

"Hads, you are stunning. He's going to pass out when he sees you, and I bet that he would even vow to grab your ass when you're old and wrinkly."

Lillian laughs and comes up to me, hugging me gently so as not to mess up my makeup and hair. "I'm thrilled that you will be part of the Brass family within the next hour." She wipes at an unshed tear and fixes a strand of hair that has fallen out of my updo.

"I already consider you my mother, Lilly. Thank you for raising such an incredible man. You have my word that I will be what he needs."

She sniffles and hugs me again, unable to find one of a hundred words that she has on the tip of her tongue to tell me how she feels about today, about my relationship with her son.

There's a light knock on the door, letting us know that it's time to head down. I nod to Lola and Lillian, and they each kiss me once on the cheek before walking out and leaving me on my own for the next minute.

I inhale deeply before releasing. I've already decided what I want my future to be, and now I simply have to go out there and get it. I've chosen to invest in more than just a one-night stand and instead venture into something that will last forever. He's treated me differently than any man has before, taking my heart from me to shield and protect it from all elements that the world throws at it. I'm precious to him, and he makes me feel it each and every day.

Love won't give up on me and neither will I on it. He won't give up on me either; it's a feeling that sits securely within me and I refuse to fight it for one second. There's a second knock on the door, letting me know that it's my turn to exit. I take one more look at myself wrapped in this gorgeous pearl-white dress before walking to the door and pulling it open. Owen smiles down at me and offers me his hand. I take it willingly, and he silently leads me down the hallway to the staircase, both of us unsure of what to say in this emotional moment.

When it's time, he too places a kiss on my cheek before walking down the stairs and taking his seat among those whom Wade flew out to be a part of our experience. Our unity. Our love.

The song *Bloom* by the Paper Kites fills the room, cueing me in. I take the first step down the staircase and then another. With each step I take, I'm leaving my past behind me and walking into my future with an extraordinary man.

I glance up, and my eyes meet his. The smile on his face dazzles me, making my head spin as emotion rips open my insides. In the one look, he gives me the strength to continue, erasing all doubt that I've held about this day. I see my home at the end of the aisle as I take another step toward him. His body language tells me that he wants to run up to me and carry me the remainder of the way, lead me into what is yet to come, but he doesn't.

Today, nothing is stopping the savage feelings of love from surrounding me. When I reach him, he takes my hand, pulling me another two steps closer toward him when the pastor begins. I glance at him, his Scottish accent catching me off-guard for a moment.

"We are gathered together on this beautiful afternoon to share with Hadley and Waylon as they exchange their vows for a love everlasting. You may be seated."

There's a rustling as the guests take their seats and the pastor continues his speech. Wade squeezes my hands, bringing my attention back to him. He's still wearing the same smile that he was when I first looked up from the end of the aisle.

He's dressed in a tailored tuxedo, his hair styled, and I'm having a difficult time concentrating. He beguiles me, leaves me breathless and needy beyond what is natural. Before I snap back to the present moment, the pastor asks for our vows.

"Today, Hadley and Waylon have chosen to recite their own vows. Waylon . . ."

Wade clears his throat before he starts. "Rye, I vow to love you and give you my heart. You have my word that I will not walk away in the difficult times, and that I will be your home. I promise to love and respect you, but above all else, I promise to remember that no one is perfect. I vow to be with you through each step of our future. Hand in hand. Step by step. I choose you, from the best parts to the worst. In you, I have found myself and the piece that I was missing. I've got you."

An unexpected tear slides down my cheek as he says his truths to me and everyone else in the room bears witness.

"Wade," I sob quietly.

He reaches over and wipes the tear and the one preceding it away with his thumb. He runs the pad of his thumb down and over my lips. I kiss it before he removes his touch from my face and takes my hand again.

"Hadley . . ." the pastor gestures toward me.

"Whiskey, I vow to let this moment live in my heart until the day it stops beating, and through that time, I vow to remain by your side." I take in a ragged breath in an attempt to steady my shaky voice. "This marriage will take you from a single malt to a blended whiskey, a blending of different substances into one to make it uncustomarily unique. Today, I promise to love you. I vow to communicate with you instead of shutting you out. I promise to stand by you through each stage of life. I vow to be your wife, your partner, your supporter, and your blended love. I've got you."

His chest rises with the breath that he takes, showing me his emotion without allowing the world to see what he only lets me in on.

Lola and Liam step forward and each of us lets go of each other's hand and we take our rings from them. After giving each other an eternal symbol of love and commitment, the pastor says, "By the power vested in me by the Registrar General of

Scotland, I now pronounce you husband and wife. You may now kiss the bride."

A chill wracks my body as he says those words and Wade leans into me, locking his lips with mine. I think that I hear applause, but I can't be sure. All of my attention is on the unbelievable man in front of me—the one who just promised me his life, and I him. I wrap my arms around his neck as our lips move against each other's in a kiss that I will never be able to replicate. I'll simply only be able to replay it. His hands move to the small of my back, pressing his fingers into the dress until he's able to feel the studs of my piercings.

Our kiss turns from innocent to fiery, passionate, and demanding, which is when we get a couple of louder cheers from those in front of us. Wade is the one that releases my lips first. If it were left up to me, I'd allow him to take full advantage of our situation and whisk me upstairs, but Lillian has planned an incredible reception that I couldn't imagine missing.

The applause starts again as Wade takes my hand and begins to walk back up the aisle. A few people reach out to us, congratulating us on our way up the stairs where he unexpectedly sweeps me off of my feet and carries me up the second half of the staircase, ignoring my warning regarding his back, until we get to our joint room. He manages to unlock the door without setting me down first.

"Wade, we have guests waiting."

"All I need right now is you, Mrs. Brass."

I purse my lips and tighten my arms around his neck, kissing his cheek before he lays me down on the bed to ravish me for the first time as his, entirely his.

His wife.

Holy shit.

Epilogue No. 2

Wade

WE'RE A WEEK into our honeymoon, and aside from our scheduled events, food, and alcohol, we haven't left our hotel room. This last week has consisted of private tours of whiskey distilleries, and tonight, we will be having a private dinner in the midst of the Macallan distillery just outside of Inverness, and tomorrow, I'll be gifting her Blended Rye, Scotland's newest Scotch distillery.

While she does her hair across the room from me, I lie back and watch her, realizing that I'll get to do this until I take my last breath.

"What are you staring at?"

"My wife and everything that I've wanted in this world."

She turns around and stands, wearing the hotel robe as she crawls up the bed toward me. "What were you thinking?" she asks as she unties the robe, presenting me with her bare skin.

She moves her hands up the thin fabric of my shirt. "Thinking about you and a place that I've not been yet."

"Oh?"

"Yes, Rye. Come here." I wrap my arms around her top half and pull her up the remainder of the way to me until she's lying on top of me.

"I trust you," she tells me with no pretense.

Her trust in me has become an intimate act in itself,

satisfying me through and through. She no longer winces when I touch her, physically or emotionally.

Relationships are a give-and-take; each of us takes part in giving as well as taking, which somehow makes what we have grow and forms us into something more than a mere two people loving each other endlessly.

We meet hundreds of people each year, but none of them truly understands the person that you are. Instead of trying to change and mold me into an ideal partner, she accepts me and connects with me for who I am. I've walked through life struggling to find myself, to find the niche where I belong, and I've finally found it in her.

Pain changes people, leaving scars that are physically visible as well as ones that are not. Each of us has lived through lives that have made us become who we are, and through those circumstances, we've found what suits us best to find resolve in our souls.

"What comes next?" Hadley asks about our day, but I give her the purest of answers that I am able to muster up about our lives.

"Blended love and intertwined lives."

The End

Thank You

Thank you for reading this novel, and taking this journey with me while these two characters fought for love when no one took the time to fight for them as individuals. Always fight for those you love.

With love, *Sasha*